THE ZENITH'S WARRIOR

DAMEON COX

Lezen Publishing

The Zenith's Warrior

Lezen Publishing

Original Cover Concept: Kästle Olson
Map Illustrations: Kästle Olson

Manufactured in the United States of America
ISBN: 978-0-9960063-4-7

Dedicated to

Charles F. Fallon
author, screenwriter and producer.
A supporter and friend

MAPS

THE SEVEN REALMS

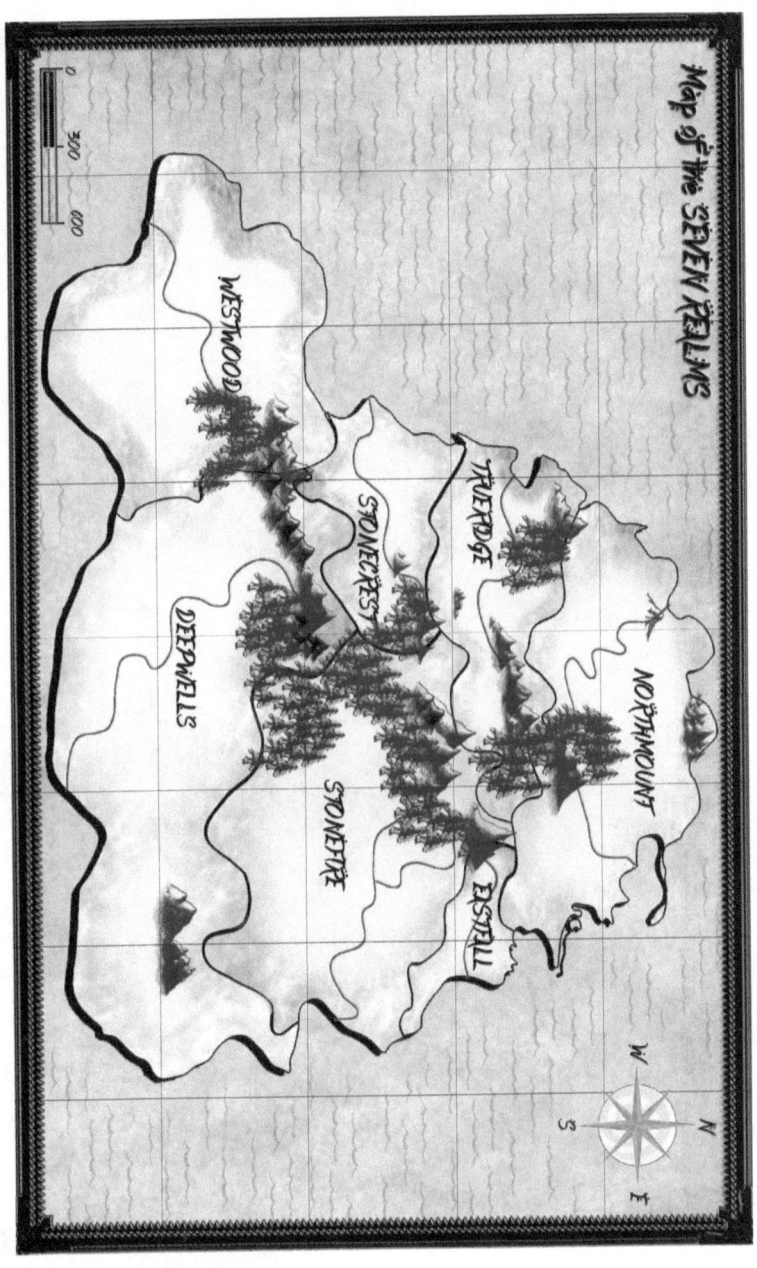

THE WESTERN KINGDOMS

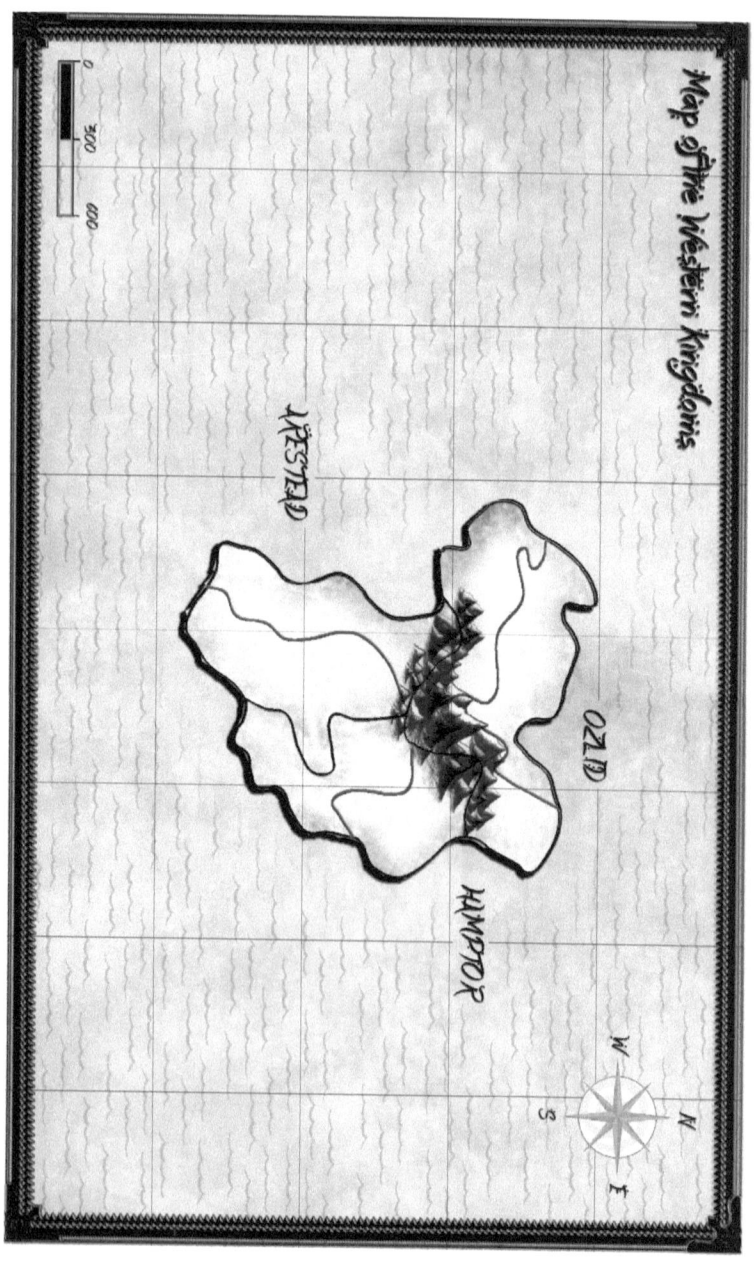

THE EASTERN KINGDOMS

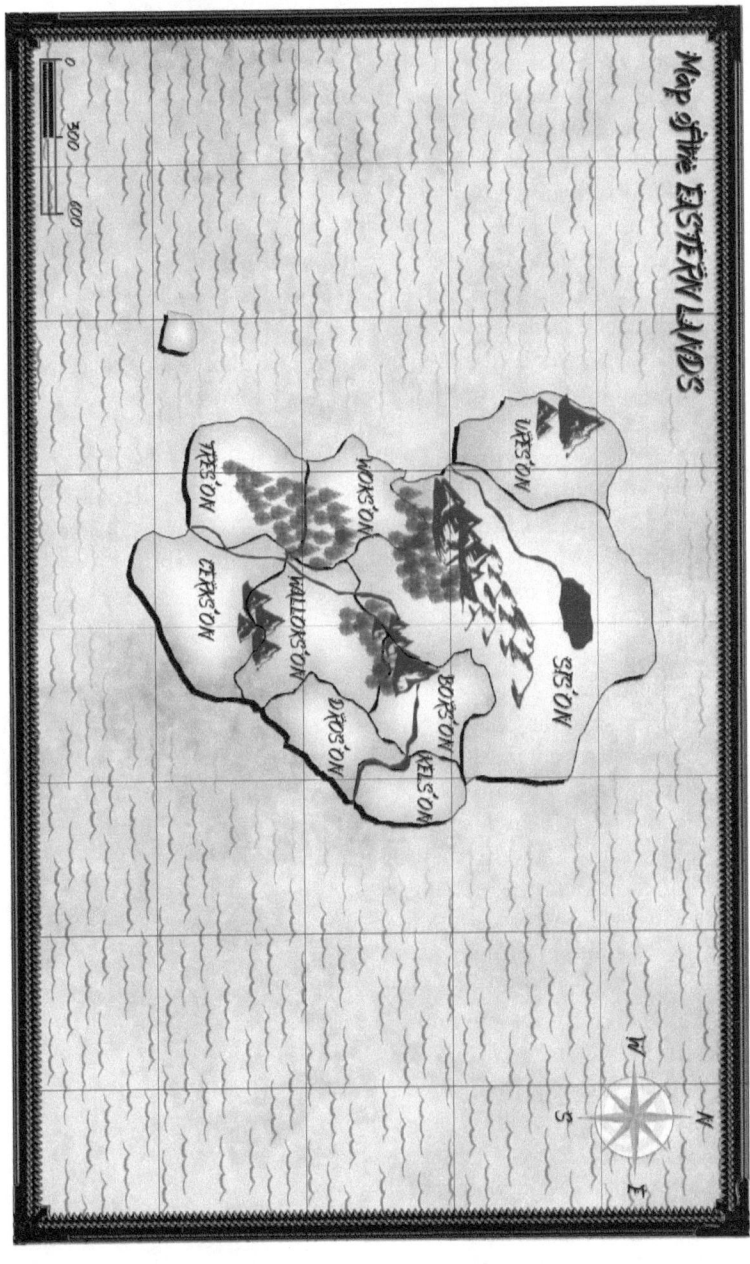

CHARACTERS AND PLACES

Barqua, Horse-master of the Clan of the Cat
Blackwind, The Zenith Lord's horse
Briggs, Ship Captain based in Hamptor
Broadric, Master at Arms
Calbris, Chief Spy at Elizabethville in Stonecrest
Ca-Ra'IL from the Noble House of the Stork, Truth-bearer
    of the Empire
Carille, Spirit Leader of the High Desert People
Cartwell Byrne, Lord of Bramble Keep, Kyle's father
Challenger, Lenzel's horse
Charlos Mattene, Member of Skimmer Andress' Pebble
Currat Duval, Spy for the Zenith Lord, from Ozlid
Daktar, Supreme Dynast of Sison
Daniel, Prelate of the Seven Realms' Religious Order
Daniell Respecton, Member of Skimmer Andress' Pebble
Darth, Captain Lord of Death
Davad Drosh, Member of Skimmer Andress' Pebble
Debgril, War Leader of Desert's Ire
Deion Russell, Lord Protector
Doris Raven, helped Zack escape from Hamptor
Dryl Fullman, Merchant
Dugwar, Bandit Chief in Stonecrest
Dusten Remming, Member of Skimmer Andress' Pebble
Ellrill, Maiden of the Cat Clan, married to Lenzel
Forrest Workman, instructor to the High Desert People
Gangedure, Plane Master and Keeper of the Gray Plane
Gangkor, Bandit Chieftain
Geoffrey Lockley, The Pinnacle, High Lord, Second in
    command of the Seven Realms
Illche, Desert Ire's Bodyguard to The Zenith Lord
Jannus Kritz, Gal from the Eastern Fortress
Jarod Greatstone, The Zenith Lord
Kaarill, Desert's Ire maiden
Kelor, The Western Kingdoms
Kelosrill, Desert's Ire Maiden
Kyle Byrne, High Lord of Stonecrest
Larrell Sontos, Member of Skimmer Andress' Pebble

CHARACTERS AND PLACES

Lenzel, Honorable Warrior, of the Cat Clan
Lorell Andress, part of Lenzel's group
Marc Greatstone, The Darkslayer, Jarod Greatstone's son
Mecqua, Warrior Commander of the Cat Clan
Michael Gaz, The Zenith's Spymaster of the Seven Realms
Mother Mavis, Head of the Seven Realms' Hospices
Pecquin, Secquin's twin, Desert Ire Maiden
Peter Byrne, Kyle's older brother
Rachel Raven, Doris Raven's young daughter
Richmon Userron, Member of Skimmer Andress' Pebble
Roberd Wells, High Lord of Deepwells
Rolo, The Zenith Lord's steward at the Spires
Roush Letern, Member of Skimmer Andress' Pebble
Rystarill, Desert's Ire maiden
Secquin, Pecquin's twin, Desert Ire Maiden
Serarelique, Another name for The Aviaries of Heaven
Shadure, Second to the Dark One
Snowflake, Currat Duval's horse
Spellbinder, Zack Stand's horse
Sorrel Billon, Member of Skimmer Andress' Pebble
Stevemon Surron, Member of Skimmer Andress' Pebble
Stonefire, the Zenith Lord's realm and Capital City
Strufford Sumtom, Gal from the Western Frotress
Syrill, Desert's Ire maiden
Ta-Cern, Noble House of the Hawk, Seeker of the Empire
Thursman Crinner, Gal Commander at River Road
Travis Grant, The Holy One
Va-A'Cil, Empress of the Aviaries of Heaven
Wathdure, second to Shadure
Wellsport, Capital of Deepwells
Welquo, Spiritual Leader of the Cat Clan
Zack Stand, Spy for the Zenith Lord.

PART I

1

SOFT panels of wormcloth shimmered in the afternoon breeze on the open pavilion. They softened the courtier's lavish and colorful dress, while mingling before the raised platinum throne with its design of multicolored feathers across the seatback fashioned from the highest quality, precious jewels. Guards formed an outer perimeter spaced every ten feet. They wore sandals made of soft leather and golden braces. Gold cuffs inset with onyx stripes denoted their rank. Their legs stood bare below the short fustanella made from the purest white linen; long and slender red, orange, and yellow feathers rose above their foreheads, held in place by an elaborately woven design in matching white linen. The pavilion guards, selected for their beautiful bodies and pleasing mores, stood at position, their certain and considerable fighting skills hardly needed in the most guarded spot in the empire.

Maidens of the Empire complemented the guards. Chosen for their beauty, knowledge, and artistic talents, they came from all levels of society. Soft pastel colors of sheer, overflowing material covering white undergarments of the same diaphanous fabric clung to them, tied with a golden belt at their waist. Their soft sandals copied the guards' in design. The courtiers may call on them for information on many areas of interest. Their sisters-in-training of lesser beauty or social status enjoyed the same opportunities for advancement in the empire. Training classes in a wide variety of subjects shored up any shortcomings, and prepared the maidens for service to the empire in their chosen fields of endeavor. Their male counterparts, the Attendants of the Empire, serve as learned and informed assistants for one or more nobles. Both groups rose in status through well-rewarded abilities.

Ta-Cern, late Captain of the Guard for the High Lord of Deepwells in the lands called Jewel, stood behind a panel of white wormcloth, waiting. His handsome face equaled any of the guards around him, and his excellent physique belied his age. He wore a platinum torque and cuffs, a fustanella of silver cloth, and sandals with silver braces; the large headdress of slender feathers from the rainbow's every color befitted his rank as Seeker of the Empire. He had not seen his empress and cousin in five years. His nerves wracked him, not from seeing the Empress, but for the emotional explosion he would cause.

Harps waxed and waned, emitting waves of melodious sound in harmony with the pounding surf a hundred yards away. The flute's shimmering crystal notes provided soft counterpoints darting among the lush notes. Suddenly, full deep chords resonated from deep-bellied string instruments played with a bow. The familiar cascading sounds, and the warm welcome he had received from family and friends, made his homecoming complete.

Courtiers moved at once to stand behind their cushions arranged in orderly rows according to rank. They dropped to their knees at a flourish of notes from the harps, and bent forward to touch their heads to the floor. Ta-Cern chuckled at the image of the empire's most noble buttocks stuck up in the air behind an elaborate sea of feather headdresses. He wondered again how his cousin kept a straight face.

Va-A'Cil, Empress of the Aviaries of Heaven, entered the pavilion while Ca-Ra'IL from the Noble House of the Stork, Truth-bearer of the Empire, followed close behind and to her left. Ca-Ra'IL wore a sarong of shimmering black wormcloth with a silver design of a magnificent eagle in flight outlined in black pearls. No other jewelry adornments graced her fingers, limbs, or neck. Her stature and movements showed no evidence of her one hundred and twelve years. Her eyes blazed with an inner fire, and her silver hair fell to a few inches above the floor. Smooth skin projected the quintessence of a woman a quarter her age.

Va-A'Cil wore a pale violet sarong of iridescent wormcloth, the color of the imperial house and only worn by her, a headdress fashioned from platinum and precious gems in the form of long slender feathers rising above her forehead. Ta-Cern once tested its weight, and decided it was the reason she did not often smile while on the throne. Platinum cuffs encrusted with sapphires encircled her wrists and a matching belt surrounded her waist. Her legendary beauty radiated from within, and outshone all the jewels in the pavilion.

Ca-Ra'IL moved forward and struck a silver triangle hanging from a leather cord, three times. The courtiers raised their heads and sought comfort on their cushions as Va-A'Cil ascended the throne. Her fourth strike on the triangle caused surprise. A Maiden of the Empire's golden voice flowed over the assemblage, "Ta-Cern, from the Noble House of the Hawk, Seeker of the Empire, comes forward to impart knowledge to the Empire."

A guard pulled the panel to the side, and Ta-Cern made his way up the center aisle while startled courtiers whispered amongst themselves; they stopped to bow when he passed by. Another sound from the triangle silenced them. Kneeling on the silver cushion before the throne, he bowed half way to the floor for exactly three seconds, and then rose upright. Ca-Ra'IL approached and knelt at Ta-Cern's left side on a black cushion. A scribe in white linen approached, bowed to the Empress, to Ca-

Ra'IL, and then to Ta-Cern before kneeling on a white cushion. He took white parchment, a glass pen, and made ready to write with black ink. Ta-Cern leaned toward Ca-Ra'IL and whispered close to her ear. Her eyes widened for a brief moment while the memory of Ta-Cern's introduction to Jarod Greatstone, Zenith Lord of the Seven Realms and the Visage of Visions to the seers of the empire, flooded and merged into her own memories. Her voice cracked when she spoke, "I have seen the true memory of Ta-Cern, from the Noble House of the Hawk, Seeker of the Empire." Her eyes moistened.

Protocol ruled the scribe would write out the message, Ta-Cern would sign and seal the document followed by Ca-Ra'IL's perusal and seal, and then Va-A'Cil would read the document and decide if it should be presented to the court. Ta-Cern leaned toward the scribe and whispered his discovery in his ear. The correct protocol flowed well except when he imparted the message to the scribe. The man fainted, spreading black ink over white robes.

Ca-Ra'IL rose and bowed to the empress who nodded once while guards attended the unconscious scribe. She turned to face the courtiers. Her stance once again firm and her voice strong, said in a crisp tonal voice, "Hear the truth! The Visage of Visions has been found!"

Pandemonium struck.

* * *

LENZEL crouched behind the green and brown foliage that constituted his cover from sharp eyes. His mind wandered over the last year's extraordinary events. He had completed warrior training. In addition, he had finished and mastered the fighting skills of Desert's Ire in three years, something few warriors ever accomplished and extremely rare for one not named a warrior; it gave him honor and status yet unrealized. His youth for such accomplishments amazed some. The strange man from Stonefire took him through much of his training in stealth, including hunting the woodlands several miles distance from the low hills marking the boundary to the High Desert People's domain. His name appropriately reflected the skills he taught, Forrest Workman. Lenzel mastered the skills easily, as if born to them. His friends, familiar to stealth in the high desert, found the woods and forests challenging.

The Seven Realms' fighting styles Forrest taught differed from those Lenzel knew, but he had adapted well. This summer would mark his seventeenth year with the High Desert People. His clan agreed to Forrest's intermittent training over the past year, again based on his accomplishments. He had met the Highest One, called the Zenith Lord by those other than the High Desert People, on two occasions in that year. Lenzel possessed certainty that he would never match the fighting skills of the Highest One and the strange priest that often sparred with him. He had never seen a priest fight, or one so large, muscular and quick. The two men's pure physical power and skills with swords left onlookers in awe. They sparred mostly without shirts, the Highest One with his sandy blond hair bound in a warrior's knot and the priest with his silvery white hair, loose and long flowing to the base of his spine. The vibrant jewels embedded in their chests, pulsing with their exercise were wondrous to see. The Highest One, perhaps two inches shorter than the priest and nearly as muscular, won the sparring battles most times. They would finish their match grinning like children with a new toy, sweat running over taut rippling muscles. They would emerge an hour later, bathed, in fresh clothes and ready for the many other duties that Lenzel knew lasted far into the night on many occasions. Their constant vigilance impressed him the most.

Alertness to a small sound of hoof against leaves snapped Lenzel out of his memories. He silently peered through his cover; a large buck and doe hesitantly approach the natural clear pool where the stream spread out over shining rocks. The buck relaxed and edged to the pool to drink and the doe joined him a moment later.

The buck never started until the arrow drove deep into his chest. The second arrow cut off the doe's shrill cry of alarm. His last task completed before consideration for warrior status elated him. The meat would feed the clan and the hides would make the leathers he needed to meld into the high desert's shadows. Neither of their hearts pulsed when Lenzel examined his kills and that gladdened him. He hated the unnecessary suffering misplaced arrows often caused. Giving thanks to Light's Source for the bounty received, he dressed out the deer, washed in the pool and went to get the horses. His peers mercilessly teased him when he had left with two packhorses. Now, he needed them as he had planned. He left the viscera for the scavengers away from the rapidly clearing pool.

He arrived at his Battle Group's camp. Reddish golden rays from dying sunlight cast coruscating reflections from quartz and glorious striations of color wrought by wind and ancient waters that disappeared millennia ago; golds, tans, reds and browns fought for attention. Welcoming cries soon brought many clansmen gathered around his pack animals. He watched his packhorses being led away for warriors to unload and groom, the hunter's partial reward for a successful hunt. His satisfaction grew with each smile he saw.

"You did well." Lenzel turned with a smile at the voice that made his heart gallop. Ellrill's smile held warmth and his blush betrayed him. "Will you walk me to my tent?" A question that needed no answer.

Round tents were arranged in two circles, one within another. Stout leather, in desert colors, formed a tent within a tent, the inner wall three inches from the outer with a fine leather mesh for escaping air. Plush rugs and mats covered the interior. Cushions covered in fur and several in wormcloth divided the area into sections with colorful wormcloth panels hanging above. A tent large enough to hold the clan stood at the middle of the circles. The encampments, often established near a box canyon, gated with ropes the size of a man's forearm, left the horses much freedom and their smells away from the tents. Lenzel knew the High Desert People got the idea from a canyon large enough to support five thousand horses located near the Spires in Stonefire, millennia ago. He could not comprehend the support people it would take to keep so large a herd, or herds, in health and separated when needs required. Nor could he understand the Spires' size and was not sure he believed the stories he had heard. Large crowds of anything were definitely not what he wanted now. His nerve peaked and he reached for Ellrill's hand. Their touch excited emotional sparks.

Too soon, sounds of running feet startled them and they withdrew a step from each other, breaking the momentary first contact. One of several boys delivering messages to the three hundred and twelve tents rushed by, slowing enough to quickly say, "Clan meeting tonight!" and ran toward his assigned area.

Ellrill shyly asked, "Sit with me tonight?" Lenzel nodded happily and left for his tent wondering about the subject of the meeting.

Sated on the finest cuts of venison—the hunter's right—Lenzel wanted to curl up on his soft furs and sleep; but one did not miss a hurriedly called clan meeting, especially a *man* of seventeen summers. Soft voices stirred around him while he fell in with others making their way to the central tent. Many lights filled the great tent and Lenzel spotted Ellrill in the first row that surrounded the raised circular dais. Ellrill waited and carefully protected the space next to her.

Lenzel did not know until that moment that one's heart could dance. He recovered nicely and soon sat beside her. Her beauty and soft brown eyes flustered his mind. Speaking came to a stop when three men and a tall woman entered and made their way onto the dais.

Lenzel started, somewhat surprised. He identified Debgril, leader of Desert's Ire, as the woman. He met her briefly when he finished his training—or as much of their training she allowed a man to receive with the Maids of Desert's Ire. Mecqua, Warrior Commander of the Cat Clan, looked everywhere except at him. Welguo, Ellrill's father and the clan's spiritual leader looked at his daughter and him sitting together. Barqua, the fourth person and Horse-master for the Cat Clan, lagged behind. Meetings with the four leaders were rare and always important. Welquo's deep, well-modulated voice sounded out over the clan. "Lenzel of the Cat Clan, step forward."

Surprise, followed by embarrassment and worry flashed through Lenzel's mind. Ellrill smiled and nudged him forward. He climbed onto the dais and looked across some smiling, some questioning faces. The four leaders stood, each facing out, in a square formation with Lenzel uncomfortably in the middle. Welquo's voice almost made him jump. "When does a man become a man? When does a man become a warrior? Tradition states that both occurrences happen on or after one of our boys reaches his eighteenth summer and has met all the training requirements given him. This tradition is the same throughout the clans for men, or women, if they choose the warrior's path. Now comes Lenzel to challenge tradition. This summer will be the boy's seventeenth summer and he, as of today, has met all the requirements to qualify as a warrior, except one— Tradition. Mecqua, Warrior Commander of the Cat Clan, how say you?"

"Welquo, Spiritual Leader of the Cat Clan, Lenzel has the training of a warrior."

"Barqua, Horse-master of the Cat Clan, how say you?"

"Lenzel rides as a warrior."

"Debgril, War Leader of Desert's Ire, how say you?"

"Welquo, Spiritual Leader of the Cat Clan, Lenzel, the warrior may ride with Desert's Ire when need's be.

Welquo remained while the other leaders left the dais and took the seats held vacant for them. He motioned Lenzel to his side. No doubt existed that all those within the tent could hear him. "Lenzel will not be named 'Warrior' tonight." Lenzel's hopes crashed, but then, he thought, *I knew nothing of this before tonight. Why should I be upset about a great honor?* He relaxed.

Welquo continued, "Lenzel will be named 'Warrior' before his eighteenth summer if a call for warriors is issued by the Highest One. A newly acclaimed warrior leaves the clan for two months. He is to use that time to reflect on his choice of becoming a named warrior and the responsibilities that come with that honor. He may upon his return, renounce himself as warrior, without shame. We will allow him to leave us for two months. He is bound to the Light's Source, as we all are bound to his clan as a warrior, bound to the Highest One as a warrior and bound to himself as a warrior in all except name. The clans will shun him if he renounces his warrior oaths once taken. Is anyone against the words of the clan's leaders?" There came a long silence, perhaps the longest moment in Lenzel's young life. "So it will be entered into the clan's history." Wild yips from Lenzel's friends and general applause from the rest of those gathered did nothing to reduce the sizeable lump caught in his throat.

His friends hoisted him onto their shoulders and carried him out while he regretfully looked at Ellrill's tranquil smiling face before others moved in front of her. They deposited him near a large fire pit where many younger men and sometimes younger women often met. Taccaw, Lenzel's trusted friend asked the obvious question. "So, Lenzel, when are you leaving?"

* * *

SHADURE, chief among the minions of the Source of the Dark, hovered unseen, observing the scene below him with great amusement.

"*You son of a pig!*" Daktar eased forward on his throne. His black eyes bore into the officer trembling before him. "You were ordered, specifically, not to enter the capital."

"Supreme Dynast...please, they made it look safe. They showed no resistance at all until we were half way to the palace. Your courier never reached me; I swear, Supreme Dynast."

Daktar taped his little finger against the golden arm of his throne. Two guards dragged a limp form face down before him and dropped it a few feet from the officer. Two arrows protruded through the dead man's chest and clanked against the marble floor. The kneeling officer shrieked and touched his head to the floor. His trembling caused his words to sound disjointed. "Supreme Dynast, I...did not do this."

Daktar's voice softened to an oily purr. "Oh, my dear general, I know that you did not loose the arrows that killed my courier. This man did!"

Guards pulled draperies aside. The general looked on his assassin and moaned in deep despair and anguish. Ropes held him up; his feet dangled at the edge of a vat containing sand to absorb his blood. Long strips of bloody skin lay atop the sand, taken from his head to his knees.

"Do you know, it is very hard to keep a man alive while flaying his genitals? My men worked hard to keep him flourishing as long as possible. I am not displeased with their efforts. He talked, oh my, how he talked."

The general cringed and then suddenly stood upright with all traces of obsequiousness gone. He pulled a knife from his tunic and made ready to throw. Four arrows pierced his chest before his arm even moved. The knife and the General's hand hit the floor at the same time.

Daktar regained his usual commanding voice. "Clean this mess up and get this vermin out of here."

He turned aside as servants rushed forward to comply. He was alone within a few minuets, looking out onto his spotless audience chamber—dead men and gore no longer in sight.

"Was it not as I said?" These words whispered in his ear proved ever so slight, but very distinct. Daktar slowly looked around and saw nothing out of the ordinary. "Do you really wish to see me?"

"Enough of these games! Who are you or are you what I suspect, my own mind and abilities?"

The laugh that filled Daktar's mind was evil and long. "Very well, as you say, enough of these games." A force moved around him and darkness entered the room, coalescing into a man's form with a cloak. The ebony face beneath the cloak's cowl showed strikingly beautiful features, masculine and virile. The aura of evil miasma surrounding it would have changed that attractiveness to ugliness in most men's eyes. Daktar was not most men.

"Now, let me speak plainly," the being started.

In an act of intimidation, Daktar slowly elevated until his feet hovered at a level with the top of his throne. Yet, the being matched his rise, slightly smiling. Fear scuttled through Daktar, repressed almost instantly, but it must have showed on his face for it did not go unnoticed.

"You wish to become the master of all the lands of this continent. A worthy undertaking, but one I fear you will not succeed in accomplishing. Well, not without help...*my* help."

Daktar tried to answer but did not find his voice. Anger flashed through him. The apparition laughed.

"You may call me Shadure. I have the power that will allow you to accomplish your goal and much, much more. You could be master of this puny land in three years with my assistance."

Daktar's anger abated a notch or two.

"You could be master of a considerably larger land and infinite riches in approximately ten years."

Shadure settled to the floor as Daktar gently floated back to his throne. Being the highest minion of the Dark's Source, he seemed content with his choice of Daktar.

"Why would you offer me help of any kind?" Daktar asked, finally locating his voice. Anger did not tinge his tone, but greed did.

"I have no need for riches and I am far more powerful than you could ever imagine. I do have an enemy I wish to destroy. One who has gold and precious jewels beyond your scope of thought. I wish to dominate everything he is and all he owns. You may rule his lands for and through me, after we bring him down."

Daktar made no effort to hide his dubiety.

"Ah, I know," Shadure said. "An undertaking of this type requires trust and I will provide the foundation of that trust by helping you first with your adventures here. There are eleven kingdoms and you have taken three. Do you really think you can conquer the remaining seven in under ten or fifteen years? You do not have the time to assimilate the people as you take their domains. Can you sustain them while constantly burdened with rebellions and skirmishes behind your lines? Supply lines will become a nightmare. I can greatly expedite your efforts and show you how to keep your lands once you have them.

"But, hear me well. I admired your handling of the traitor. Flaying a body to death is an exquisite act, but I exact a heavy price for failure and my ability for torture extends beyond anything you can imagine."

Daktar's spine chilled. He instinctively knew the words he heard were true.

"Enough of threats," the being added. "I will advise you. Only you will hear my voice. I have a gift that will make it easier for you to hear me and through it, you may call me."

A heavy gold chain appeared in the air above Daktar, then gently settled around his neck. Its pendant consisted of a dull black stone that pulled in the surrounding light. He had the distinct feeling he would never take it off while alive. He'd always been a bright fellow.

2

LENZEL left two days later with the clan's blessings. He never realized how much the clan appreciated him, and the well wishes he received brought him great joy. Ellrill and his adoptive parents had quickly deflated his swollen head. The sunny day and first warm breezes fueled his impatience. He rode Challenger, a stallion he'd captured, which nearly killed him during taming. Nevertheless, break him he did and now he held the loyalty and respect of a great horse. Always ready for a trip, Challenger cantered away from the encampment and fought to gallop. Lenzel gave him his head and they sped across the planes toward the foothills that would lead him down to the deep forests and rivers of Deepwells, which he had heard about but never seen.

He dressed in the attire he'd worn his whole life— leathers dyed to match desert colors; soft, matching leather boots; two knives sheaved in the same shade leathers that nearly disappeared against his leg; his leather belt, holding pouches that contained deadlier things than money; and a wide leather strip for a headband that also tied his red hair into a tail that trailed nearly to the saddle. His fair skin and blue eyes would convince the casual outside observer, albeit not a clansman, that he paraded in costume. Someone more observant might notice that he rode a big stallion as if it became an extension of his body with the natural grace many envied.

He followed the directions Forrest Workman gave him to the nearest town, Greenway, on the road to Wellsport. He had trained in the forests below the foothills; still, the abundance of greenery amazed him, as well as the many species of animals previously unknown to him. To practice his warrior skills of tracking and stealth, he got close enough to a stag to slap him on the hindquarter and laughed when it sprinted away. He kept small fires at night, banked and hidden from view. Few travelers journeyed in this area; he saw none until he reached a road several miles outside Greenway, and he avoided them. The night before he would enter Greenway, a thought struck him—*I am avoiding these people and they are the main reason I am here! Am I really one of these lowland people? Am I a clansman or lowlander and could I live in either place?*

False dawn held its promise of light while Lenzel broke camp located a hundred yards or so from the road in the heavy forest. Challenger became anxious. Lenzel listened closely and heard angry voices coming from the road. Trees flashed by him while he ran a few yards from the end of his cover and then, he cautiously and silently eased forward.

"I said, 'I want your money, old man!'" The man on his knees toppled to his side when the bandit slapped him hard across the face. With his other hand, he held a sword that he brandished toward his captive. The old man cringed. "I will ask one last time. I know you sold your goods and business in Greenway. I even know to whom you sold them. Now, give me the money!" Sunlight reflected off the sword when the bandit lifted it. He held a stance to strike a mortal blow.

"You might as well kill me now. I will never tell you where it is!"

"Have it your way then." The bandit twisted his sword to a death strike position when Lenzel purposely snapped a dry tree branch with his left hand. The man looked over his shoulder at the sound and clearly noted nothing out of the ordinary. After he refocused his attentions on his captive, Lenzel shook a low-lying branch to his left.

The bandit faced the line of trees. "Whoever is in the

trees, come—"

A silver arc of cold steel he never saw coming lodged in his throat and the only sounds he made after that were soft gurgles from his life's blood drenching the ground. He carried the look of total surprise into death when he fell forward.

Killing a man is not an easy thing to do and Lenzel found himself shaken. His teachings on the responsibilities of life came to him, specifically the lessons relating to when to use his deadly talents and when not to use them. He calmed himself and walked steadily toward the old man lying on his side with his hands tied behind him and a look of wonderment on his face. Neither spoke while Lenzel loosed the man's bonds and helped him sit up.

"How…how did you do that? Oh, what am I saying? Asking questions when I should be thanking you."

A wave of Lenzel's hand silenced the man while he knelt and flipped the dead bandit over. Cold, sharp steel, covered in blood, made a gushing sound like a horse's hoof pulled from mud when he removed the deadly Silver Star and carefully cleaned its gore on the grass before returning it to a pouch on his belt. He crouched before the old man and asked, "Can you stand?"

The man tried but slumped backward. Words that Lenzel took as a curse escaped the man's lips when he hauled him to his feet and supported him while they walked the short distance to the tree line. He eased him to the base of a large tree and helped him sit with the trunk for support.

"My name is Lenzel. Do you have a horse?"

"I am Dryl Fullman and I have a cart. My horse bolted when that scum pulled me off my seat, the ungrateful beast." Air caught in Lenzel's throat when he stifled a laugh.

"You stay here and rest. I will take care of the body

and then go after your wayward cart." Dryl Fullman started to object but he cut him off, "No, stay and rest."

Lenzel started for the dead bandit. A buck weighed more than the bandit did and Lenzel found little trouble after figuring out the best way to drag him. He hauled him by his feet into the trees about ten yards from where he left the old man and dumped him beside a natural hollow he'd spotted the night before. Lenzel's nose wrinkled at the bandit's stench from body and clothes. At least his bowels did not loosen, as Lenzel's lessons taught him may sometimes happen. He quickly stripped the body and rolled it into the hollow, first taking the scabbard and a purse of coins. He left the body unburied for the scavengers and also discarded the bandit's stinking clothes without care. *Do they never clean themselves?* he thought, while he cut through the trees at an angle to his small camp.

Challenger gave him an impertinent snort that indicated his irritation at his master's sudden disappearance. Slow firm strokes in all the right places soon calmed the big high-strung stallion. Lenzel saddled him and led him through the trees to where Dryl Fullman sat. The old man looked surprised at Challenger's magnificence as Lenzel tied him to a stout tree limb and stroked his neck, Challenger's most favorite spot for such attention. The horse went after the lush grass encroaching on the tree line and Lenzel went after the bandit's sword. It took a while. The hilt, still soaked in the bandit's wet blood, resisted his efforts. Animal blood had landed on Lenzel's hands many times when he'd killed for food. The bandit rated lower than an animal to him, though, and he did not want his blood on his hands.

Sunlight sparkled off the sword's tip as he pulled it out of its bloody bath and cleaned it with as much grass as possible between his fingers and the gory blade. Lenzel had trained with swords and had developed into a good swordsman as part of Forrest's teachings. Like many of the warriors, he preferred other, subtler weapons. The scabbard slid toward the hilt instead of the other way around. Lenzel did not touch the hilt with his bare hands and carried it by the scabbard to Dryl Fullman.

"Here are the bandit's sword and purse. They should be yours since you received his abuse." Then, he mounted Challenger and started tracking the cart's plain trail, catching the image of Dryl Fullman shutting his mouth from amazement before he turned away.

Screams from a frightened—rather than hurt—horse told Lenzel exactly the animal's location long before he saw it. The cart had flipped on its side, firmly stuck in a ditch along the roadside, while the horse strained to break free of its tracings. "Dumb horse! You do not have enough sense to know you cannot jump a ditch with a cart! Well, I guess you never found the opportunity before." Lenzel's mutterings calmed the creature more than his appearance did.

Challenger hung his head to finish his firstmeal while Lenzel freed the horse from his bindings and securely tied him to a nearby limb. The cart righted with little effort and once the wheels made contact where they should, it did not take much to heave it onto the road. The horse did not want any reattachment to his tracings. A calm attitude prevailed and Lenzel and his stallion soon led it and the cart to the bloody gore beside the road. Dryl Fullman stood a few yards farther toward Greenway as if he, too, did not want remembrances of the morning's events. Lenzel dropped the reins into the old man's outreached hands and dismounted.

"Young man, are you a clansman? You have the dress and actions of one, but not the physical look of one. Forgive me, if I am being disrespectful."

Lenzel's smile cut off the man's questions. "I am Lenzel of the Cat Clan. I do not know who or where my parents came from. The clan adopted me and taught me their ways." He caught the old man looking at his neck. "I will be named warrior next year. I have met all the requirements."

"Well, Lenzel, warrior-to-be." Lenzel saw the gleam in Dryl Fullman's eye and took no offense. "I am old and not in good health. The morning's events have quite done me in for the day, I fear. What say you if I stand a night at a good inn for you and good food and drink, too?"

Lenzel considered the idea a good one. He would be able to observe the townsmen under the guise of a guest rather than as an interloper. He'd heard several tales told around campfires of some men who did not like the clansmen. Who knew what he might encounter? Therefore, this proposition appealed to him.

He stood and pondered a moment longer before saying, "I cannot take a reward for your rescue—it falls under my warrior's code—but for the return of your horse and cart, I may, and will, accept."

Lenzel mounted Challenger while Dryl eased himself onto the cart's seat and guided the horse to the right side of the road leading toward Greenway.

3

TALL majestic hardwoods thinned to pines and ash. Patchwork fields resisted the first plowing of spring, leaving man and work-beast tired, even this early in the morning. Deep blue skies with a few fluffy white clouds promised good weather. Dryl Fullman hummed while he held his reluctant horse to a fast walk. Cottages became more frequent and when the road swung right, Lenzel caught sight of the first town of his life. Six streets intersected seven streets containing mostly two storey buildings. Lenzel counted five three-storey buildings and tried not to gawk. He felt the old man's eyes on him and faced him.

A smile played across the old man's face. "It is good to start with a small town like Greenway."

Lenzel returned his smile and tried not to look so amazed. The road they traveled downhill formed the middle road of the seven streets. Lenzel noticed it ran north and south. Businesses and houses rose together, tightly crammed next to each other. Other houses and cottages followed the east, west, and southern streets across the beginning of a wide valley.

Dryl Fullman watched when Lenzel caught sight of a large building off by itself. "That is a clothing factory belonging to the Zenith Lord, himself. They make the winter cloaks for the Guard. Work goes on year around and it is said the factory is well run and workers are treated fairly and well paid. It is a shame, yes indeed, a shame that more owners do not match the Zenith Lord's techniques."

The creaking wheels of the cart finally became silent in

the stable yard of the first inn Lenzel had ever visited. The old man smiled at the reactions of the young warrior while the groom stabled the horses and then led him with his saddlepacks through the rear of the inn to the common room.

Lenzel became appalled at the smell. Wisps of smoke clung to the ceiling from a poorly vented fireplace. Acrid odors from stale ale and bits of rotting meat on the floor disgusted him. Dryl Fullman chose a surprisingly clean table and benches. Lenzel sat across from his benefactor and did not like what he saw. The color had drained from the man's face, replaced by obvious pain.

"Are you hurt?"

His companion looked both pleased and surprised. He shook his head. "It will pass, shortly. I thank you for your concern." The serving maid arrived and looked over the odd pair with interest. Dryl ordered ale and a firstmeal of eggs, ham, and sweetbreads for the two of them, before continuing. "I have been ill a long time and if the truth be known, I would just as soon travel on to the Light's Source." He chuckled at Lenzel's expression. "Do not look so distressed, young warrior. I have lived too long as it is. My wife died twenty years ago. My daughter died in childbirth for a child that lived only a few days, and bandits killed my son. The Guard caught the bastards and hung them. For the last ten years, I have been alone."

He leaned forward and spoke softly after seeing his words' effects on Lenzel. "Now, do not go and feel sorry for me! I have had a full and happy life for the most part. My illness leaves a lingering pain that the healers cannot counteract without putting me out of my head with syrup of the flower and that, I do not want." Lenzel's appreciation of Dryl Fullman grew. "Sometimes, every day or so, I have these bursts of bad pain that are becoming more frequent. I will soon die."

Lenzel let the ramifications generated by the old man's

story settle before speaking. "My people say it is a good thing for people to know their place and accomplishments before death finds them. They say it takes the fear away and now I understand. Thank you for telling me your life's tale; it will allow me to begin to understand the mysteries of our existence on this plane."

Now, Dryl Fullman registered shock. "You are wise for one so young!"

Lenzel chuckled. "Wise? No, I am at the beginning of discovery and wisdom comes when the discoveries fall into place with the plan of the Light's Source."

The innkeeper brought their food and ale. Lenzel dubiously eyed the liquid, wondering how something that smelled that bad would taste. The eggs and ham smelled and looked good. The trencher and mug's cleanliness impressed him and he felt better about eating. "Have you heard about Griswell?" The innkeeper hurried on before either he or his companion could react to his question. "His brother, Deswell, just rode in; he found him dead and stripped out off the north road. I say good riddance. We would be better off if Deswell found the same end. They both resided in the Guard's prisons, more than once. Neither of the two brought any good, nor did they care who they hurt, but Deswell is the meanest. Well, I thank you for listening to me ramble on. Enjoy your firstmeal. Oh, Master Fullman, I believe you started your journey today. Will you be staying on in Greenway?"

The old man considered before he spoke. "This young man did me a great service and I am repaying him with meals and lodging for a day. I will be striking out on the morrow."

The innkeeper took in Lenzel's countenance as if he'd seen him for the first time. Puzzlement spread across his florid face. "You are not a clansman, are you? Not many come this way and some in Greenway are wary of them."

Dryl Fullman cut off any response Lenzel could make.

22

"Nonsense, you see his coloring. He is in the woods a lot and finds their dress ideal for his hunting. Besides, there are none here that have any reason to dislike clansmen."

The innkeeper clucked his tongue. "No reason is the truth of it, but several in Greenway dislike them, especially Deswell. We do not have to worry about what the brother liked, now, do we?" The innkeeper hurried off to greet a new guest.

Dryl Fullman correctly read the expression on Lenzel's face. "They are afraid of what they do not know. The ones like Griswell and Deswell use anything as an excuse to hate. Do not try to work it out; they are what they are. When I pranced around at your age, the world acted differently, or so it seemed. I think there is more meanness in men today. Perhaps, I only remember the good times of those years, as we tend to do of times past." He chuckled. "But then, you have not the years to understand my hypothesis. You will, if the Light's Source is willing, you will. Now, enough talk! Our firstmeal gets cold."

Lenzel considered Dryl Fullman's words while he ate. The food had good flavor and filled him. He took his first sip of ale and tried not to show his displeasure at the taste. He asked the serving girl for water. Her expression became hard to fathom; nevertheless, she quickly complied. The old man gave Lenzel a questioning look and chuckled when he slowly pushed the mug in his direction.

Dryl drank the second mug of ale while chatting with his guest. "I reserved us rooms with a real bed, not one of those sleeping pallets with its vermin. Have you ever slept in a bed?"

Lenzel placed his mug of water on the table and started to answer, but jerked around at the sound of the booming voice from across the common room. "Now, this here is a sad sight!" The man with the offending voice stood over six feet. Lenzel reckoned him to be the brother of the bandit he'd killed; they did, indeed, look alike. He drew up to his full height with his hands planted on his hips. Lenzel became more than a little surprised when the innkeeper stepped in front of the scowling man.

"Deswell, you know better than to come in here. Now leave!"

"Huh." Deswell snorted. "The Guard's not here this time." Deswell's raised his right fist and connected it to the underside of the innkeeper's jaw. Lenzel wondered if the punch knocked him out, or if hitting his head on the table did it. Either way, the man did not stir.

Deswell approached with willful glee showing across his face like a predator finding a kill cornered with no way to run. "You or this...what are you? You are no clansman! You do not stink; you cannot be a clansman." Deswell grasped for the thread of his lost thought. "Which one of you killed Griswell? I saw the tracks of your cart, old man."

Dryl Fullman made the mistake of rising. Deswell's fist exploded—and briefly disappeared—into his midsection. The portly man fell backwards and his cry held things more deadly than pain.

Deswell whipped around to attack Lenzel with a nefarious laugh that died when a blade slashed from his right forehead across to his left lower jaw. The knife's sharpness and Deswell's fury surely kept him from feeling the brutal cut until after Lenzel repeated it in the opposite direction. The brute bellowed in pain and increased rage that stopped when the knife slit through his windpipe. Deswell grabbed at his throat when he felt the pain of the cut and brought bloody hands to his face with full understanding of his imminent death. Lenzel completed a backward flip off the table to land beside his benefactor. Deswell's lunge for Lenzel consisted of nothing more than falling headlong onto the table with neither the grace nor the expertise of Lenzel's acrobatics. He died quietly, with only the sound of twitching muscles coming through. The serving maid, however, remained in full command of a piercing scream.

Lenzel merely pointed to her employer. The scream, muted by a clenched mouth, disappeared altogether by the time she reached the innkeeper. Lenzel knelt beside a gasping Dryl Fullman. The old man's color paled to pasty white and his face felt cool with clammy sweat. He grabbed the mug of water and dribbled drops into the man's mouth. Dryl's eyes focused on him and he started to speak, shaking off his objection.

"Tear...open...here." Lenzel found the calm voice startling. He slit open the inside seam of the old man's tunic, revealing a folded parchment. "I bequeath this to you, my young warrior. Make better use of it than I did." Lenzel pushed the vellum up his sleeve and tried to comfort the old man to no avail; Dryl Fullman was dead.

After sheathing the knife he used to cut the tunic inside his sleeve, next to the vellum, Lenzel looked up, helplessly, into the innkeeper's eyes when the man's feet stopped beside him. The innkeeper started to speak and stopped when Lenzel nodded his head. Reaching down, he pulled Lenzel to his feet, then wiped the other knife clean of blood and silently handed it to Lenzel, hilt first. He looked a little amazed, an expression that seemed to vanish a second later.

"Do not worry lad, I will see to the arrangements. Darla here saw everything. You best be on your way, soon. I do not know if Deswell has kin nearby, but you would not want to be here if they rise up out of the slime he came from." He deftly removed Dryl Fullman's purse and emptied the contents on a nearby table. "This will take care of the cremation." He pushed the remainder toward Lenzel's hand. Lenzel pulled away and shook his head. "Take it, lad. This town has taken advantage of his good nature and warm heart for years. You provided him a true service. He would want you to have it. Lenzel thought of the old man's last words and reluctantly took the silver and copper coins.

He left the inn with the innkeeper's praises, slightly dazed. One thought came with clarity: *The first time I am away from the High Desert, I kill two men.* He mounted Challenger and rode out, glad to feel and breathe clean air once more.

Lenzel camped in a secluded dell with a small stream. He quickly brought down a hare and readied it for the fire with well-practiced precision. He opened the vellum the old man had gifted him, wondering at the age. Even the reclusive High Desert People had used parchment for many years. It crackled, fragile and thin. He opened it carefully with the least amount of pressure he could manage against its edges. Dull brown markings flowed across the vellum made by an artist with great skill. Many small squares formed a systematic map. Each contained a drawing of reference points and direction arrows pointing into and out of its square. The whole formed a detailed map depicting the dangerous and easy places of travel. Lenzel recognized the southeastern hills of the High Desert that he traveled represented in the map's first square. Surprisingly accurate lines pictured a mountain he knew well in the second square. The starting point of the map originated, obviously, from the direction of the High Desert. He folded the vellum as gently as possible and placed it between layers of his clothing wrapped in a waterproof pouch.

The meat tasted good and yet it did not suit his nearly nonexistent appetite. Vibrant images of dying men flooded his consciousness. Human blood dripping from his weapons where only animal blood had previously flavored his steel made an impression that lingered long after he wished it away. The cloying odor of the inn impregnated his clothing. Lenzel stripped and took his leathers and soap to the small stream near his camp. Afterwards, he dressed in fresh leathers and spread the wet ones across branches on the upwind side of the fire. He banked his coals and covered them with dirt. Tonight, he favored a cold camp—fine soft and pliable leather strapped around him, held pouches of Silver Stars in readiness. Light waned and created shadows he welcomed.

Stepping silently, he spiraled outward from his campsite. Cleverly designed noise traps remained behind his journey. He found no one in the area and he doubted anyone would be able to reach him without his knowledge. Challenger softly nudged him with each stroke of a pleasure rub administered to all the right spots. Back at the campsite, the big stallion's soulful eyes followed his retreat to his blankets. Lenzel's last deliberations lingered on a kind man that perhaps had lived too long, as he'd claimed.

Morning brought bright sun streaming through tree limbs and the last of the cold, cooked hare. He broke camp and headed in the general direction of an interception point between the second and third squares depicted on the map. Crossing one road, he then kept going across open countryside, avoiding any land with signs of human occupation. There was little to elude. The sky stayed clear over the next two weeks and small game became easy to find. Sleeping under the stars calmed him and he rose in the mornings feeling good. Challenger seemed the same. On the fifteenth day, lengthening shadows found him at his destination with the next reference point clearly in sight. No signs of habitation existed for many miles. Blackness filled the side of a large hill to his right. He carefully approached the cave.

Light from the torch Lenzel made that he held slightly behind him flowed into the shallow cave. He discovered signs of an animal's home several years old. The white bones of a fox glared at him on his way to the entrance. He gave them a salute and nod. The cave's height and width provided enough space for Challenger to share it with him. The horse drank his fill at a stream about two hundred yards from the cave. Rustling sounds in the underbrush caused Lenzel to quickly produce a Silver Star in his hand. He tethered Challenger and slipped through the trees. Sounds that could be made by man or beast disturbed him.

Soon, he had to hold his laughter at the sight of the peccary rooting its way along a narrow animal trail. Good meat, but the difficulty of getting to it stayed his hand. He bided his time. Then, ill-timed for the peccary, the near dark clouds he'd seen approaching a few hours ago sent his Silver Star flying that resulted in a good, quick, kill. Getting his supplies from his saddlepacks, he dressed out the peccary downstream of Challenger, burying the non-edible refuse. Deadfall limbs and branches quickly filled the front of the cave. Challenger filled the rear much more rapidly. Great lengths of ivy pulled from rock and trees, and varieties of mushrooms and tubers joined the accumulation. Raindrops splattered on Lenzel's head while he brought in the last of the stones for his fire pit.

Challenger could not see the flashes of lightning, and thunder did not bother him. Heavy rain fell for most of the next day. An hour's break in the rain gave Lenzel enough time to let Challenger drink his fill at the stream that had grown considerably. The horse dined on tender new shoots of grass while Lenzel mucked out the ivy strands laden with dung. Light rain followed that night and the next day, conveniently stopping for brief forays outside the cave. Lenzel smoked the last of the peccary and prepared to leave the following morning. He stopped often to check and clean Challenger's hooves.

Reaching the third point on the map at midday a week

later, he stopped for hard bread, cheese, and the last of the peccary. Deep blue water, wondrous to see, fed from a deep spring in an almost complete circle. Jagged rocks jutted out into the water from the sides of the lake's basin as deep as Lenzel could see through crystal clear water. A ten-foot trough of rock formed the direction to the next point on the map where the overflow from the lake rumbled into a fast and deep stream. Lenzel marked a mountain peak faithfully portrayed on the ancient map. Woodlands and several smaller mountains lay between him and his objective.

He neared the foot of that objective two days later. Challenger would shortly be of no use. The stallion devoured tender grasses while Lenzel placed him on the longest tether he had. Access to a stream lay within his range. He found a perfect place to stow his saddle and saddlepacks in an outcropping of rocks that would keep them dry and out of sight. Then, he filled one saddlepack with those things he believed he needed for the climb: rope, hand hatchet, water, a blanket, hard bread, cheese, and several knives.

He carefully covered the trail to his hiding place and started for the mountain. Sweat rolled off him and he found the cool crisp air uncomfortable. Three huge ledges jutted out overhead, each one higher than the last.

Cold wind bit at his bloody knuckles when he reached the top of the first crag. He rested for an hour and then continued toward the second crag that set off to the right. Blood from his fingers and palms made his grips tenuous, at best. Three false starts had him tired, hungry, bloody, and cold. Challenger morphed into the size of a child's toy far below. Notions of returning lower plagued him and he finally set them aside.

He'd made this his quest and he would honor it, as it had been the old man's desire for him to make the trip. He expected nothing at the end of the climb except a small cave and perhaps the nest of a large predator bird. Small strips of cloth that Lenzel carried for bandages fulfilled their purpose on his hands and right knee.

The fourth start offered success and the bandages might have made it easier if the mountain only cooperated, yet his muscles corded and cramped at the most inconvenient places. Genuine fear froze him more times than he could count. Searching hands found handholds while tired feet followed. He breached the top of the second crag while the last rays of sunlight slowly sank over the horizon. Memories returned of climbing the rocks and mountains leading to the high plateau with boys of his clan. *It seemed easier then,* he thought. Bright notes of water flowing over rock from the vast snowfields farther up the mountain provided a welcomed find.

Cold water gradually freed the bandages from his hands. Shivering muscles replaced the last bandage when the old one won free. Lenzel dragged the saddlepack that caused less trouble than he imagined behind rocks that protected him from the wind. That helped, but he soon discovered the rock held no warmth from the sun. He would have to put something between the rock and his body to keep the numbing cold at bay. Trembling fingers removed the contents of the saddlepack. Gelid hands hardly felt the soft fibers of the one blanket he'd brought. The empty saddlepack provided a cushion between him and the rock, as did the blanket across his shoulders. He could not remember being so cold. *It certainly got this cold on the High Desert, but at those times, I had enough sense to be properly dressed.* Near-exhaustion overcame him. He forced himself to eat some cheese and drink some water. Amazingly, the air currents brought the song of a nightingale to him. He found rest and sleep with the help of the small thrush.

The sun woke him and, more importantly, it warmed him. Implements filled the saddlepack rapidly. Lenzel left the blanket for last, wrapped his fingers and palms in bandages and started out as early as possible to take advantage of the sunlight on the rocks. Hand and toeholds became easier to make out as he scaled upward to reach the top of the third crag shortly before midday. When he arrived, he stood as still as the rock, unable to believe his eyes.

A pathway cut into the rock and steps hewn in a gentle curve leading to the mouth of a cave not much bigger than the width of his shoulders. The wind swept him in torrents of currents until he stepped three feet toward the pathway. The warmth and stillness shocked his body and mind. He held out his arm from the calm air into the blast of the wind, and chuckled when its force nearly threw him off his feet.

He followed the pathway to the first steps and wondered at the tricks of the wind that allowed them to remain with so little erosion. A circular slab of flat rock formed a few feet below the entrance to the cave. He stripped off his wet leather top, replacing it with an almost dry vest. Placing the shirt on the warm rock, he faced back toward the cave. Three vertical lines, neatly chiseled above the cave, formed an equilateral triangle where top or base points connected. The writing carved into the rock at the side of the cave had been hewn as sharply as the steps. "Let only the Just Warrior enter on peril of Death." Lenzel read the words the third time, bewildering him. He approached the cave and stopped in his tracks. A prickling of energy flowed over him. It stopped with the next step toward the cave. He looked over his shoulder to observe any visible effect and halted, again. A skeleton's head smiled at him. Caught in the crevice of the rock, the head, along with the remainder of bones piled below it, had found the same protection from the winds that he enjoyed.

Warm golden light formed and increased to a pleasant

brightness from inside the cave. Lenzel stepped through the opening into a large chamber. The air became cool and perfectly still. Scrolls filled a ten-foot high case. Waxed seals lay unbroken and neatly penned writing that made no sense to him flowed across the top of each scroll. Nothing inside the cave showed the slightest amount of dust. A large chest sat beside the scrollcase with light pouring from its open top.

Lenzel looked into the chest and gasped. Precious gems of several kinds winked at him. He put his hand out and two stones rose up. He grasped them and pulled his hand from the direct light pouring out of the chest. One stone, a large ruby, the other, a deep blue sapphire, rested on the palm of his hand, both fashioned with many beautifully cut facets. The light faded when he stepped toward it again. A second chest sat in the rear of the chamber with its lid closed. No manifestation of energy emanated from its resting-place. Lenzel approached cautiously and raised the lid. No force threw itself at him and he neither felt nor saw anything out of the ordinary, except that the chest nearly overflowed with large gold nuggets. The ore looked pure, from what he could tell. Nothing hampered him when he reached in and took a handful of the precious metal. It soon felt warm to his touch. *The cave accepted me. I obtained two stones without ill effect and there seems to be no restriction on the gold.*

About ten pounds of the ore would fit nicely in his saddlepack. Lenzel felt any additional weight would be more than he wanted strapped to him on the climb down and that amount equaled more gold than his whole clan would see in a lifetime. Only one problem remained. The saddlepack refused to pass through the cave's entrance. Lenzel removed one nugget at a time and tried again, again, and again... Expecting the force to contain the saddlepack, Lenzel nearly fell out of the cave. No resistance whatsoever came when the saddlepack held three nuggets. Three rather large nuggets, but they did not weigh anywhere near ten pounds.

He scurried down the path from the cave to examine his treasures in bright sunlight. As he held the ruby in his right hand, he felt a slight tingling. He stood dumbfounded while his wounds quickly healed. The same healing coursed through the rest of his body while he stood there, watching. Strength poured through him and he felt as brilliantly alive as the stone's sparkle. He placed the ruby within the folded blanket and closed his hand tightly around the sapphire. The effect became immediate and binding: his heart soared, self-assurance flooded him, and he felt good, really good. The air around the cave stayed calm and he experienced no sensation when he ventured away from the path into the cold winds.

The direct light of the sun no longer beamed on his side of the mountain, but the wind died to a nearly nonexistent force. Hand and toeholds came easily to him and he traveled farther than he believed possible. He reached the second crag by mid-afternoon and the first crag an hour later. Grayness faded into night when his foot touched the base of the mountain. Challenger gave him a curious look and then continued his lastmeal.

4

HIGH Lord Kyle Byrne, formally the Apex Captain of the Zenith's Guard, settled into the cushions of his favorite plush chair. He ruled the realm of Stonecrest, once known as Mountglen. High Lord Mountglen had died at the hands of his son who then took his own life after he and his father succumbed to the Dark Source.

Kyle and Jarod, the Zenith Lord shared a deep love for each other. Both had lost their mothers; Jarod's mother had died during childbirth, while his own had died from consumption that she caught from him. His father and older brother blamed him for her death and abused him badly. The Zenith Lord, Jarod's father, had heard of the mistreatment and ordered Kyle to the Spires as a companion to Jarod when he was four and Kyle, ten. Kyle won many honors for his service to the Seven Realms. Jarod elevated him to Apex Captain of the Guard, second only to him, in command of five hundred thousand men.

The day had been long, but fulfilling. He read again the message from Jarod and smiled. The Zenith Lord had finished another round of training by the High Desert People in psychic and martial arts and would visit Stonecrest—Kyle assumed, on his way to the Spires, a vast complex outside his capital city of Stonefire and his seat of power.

He had sparred with Jarod in sword practice since childhood and they advanced together, evenly matched. No man could equal Jarod's martial skills since he *joined* with the Sire's Stone: the brilliant emerald embedded in his chest with a golden fire behind it pulsing in time with his heart that gave him physical and psychic powers. The Protector, His Grace Deion Russell, warrior priest, who would train Jarod's son Marc, the Darkslayer, currently came closest to his prowess. Their swords would flash in a blur of constant motion and the ring of steel against steel would not cease until the exercise ended when Kyle last saw them spar.

Deion had studied for his role as the Protector since childhood and became a gifted physic. He received the Guardian's Stone in a ceremony shortly after Marc's birth. Marc's mother, Maress, died a horrible death by poison, from the hands of the minions of the Dark's Source led by Mountglen. Segquo, leader of the High Desert People, assisted Jarod on the astral, Gray Plane, during the first battle of the new war between Light's Source and Dark's Source. They had won that battle at great cost. Deion became a close friend to them in a surprisingly short period. Kyle hoped that Deion would accompany Jarod until the time for Marc's training that would soon begin at the Tower crater, the seat of the religious order of the Seven Realms. He doubted he would see much of him after that. The Tower crater's location remained a closely guarded secret of the religious order of the Seven Realms and the one place in which Marc remained safe from the minions of Dark's Source. His training would take place there until he reached his Age-of-Man time and set out on the quest to find his Great Stone.

Jarod oversaw the care of the remaining six Great Stones from the last Great War that occurred two thousand years earlier. The Sire's Stone and the Guardian's Stone had been reawakened and given in service to Jarod and Deion. Kyle did not understand how the Stones functioned and he would never ask Jarod to explain. His presence when Deion received the Guardian's Stone and when Jarod *joined* with the Sire's Stone produced sharp memories. Kyle witnessed the awesome power the Stones provided their recipients. He remained unsure if he wanted to feel such immense raw energy surging through his body as Jarod described. His Privy Council, the six High Lords, and a few others knew the Stones existed.

Kyle started at the sound of a fanfare, not heard in three years. It sounded clear and crisp from the forward battlements and immediately picked up by more trumpets around the newly finished walls of his keep. The Holy One, Travis Grant, spiritual head of the Seven Realms, arrived for an unannounced visit, a highly unusual occurrence. Kyle worried.

He waited at the entrance of his keep while the Holy One rode through the main gates. His white war-horse pranced at the attention of the crowd that gathered to receive his blessing. Travis dismounted at the steps while Kyle kneeled and took the proffered hand and touched Travis's ring to his forehead, while the assemblage cheered. Rising to his feet, he followed Travis midway up the stairs, a step behind. They stopped and Travis gave his blessing to the crowd. Prelate Daniel, two secretary priests, and four Guards of the Order made up his entire party. Travis preferred as few traveling companions as possible and the priests' robes carried no rank.

Kyle led the way into the reception chamber. The keep's doors swung shut. The coolness of the stone became a welcomed relief from many days in the saddle during summer. Kyle faced Travis and the two men embraced. The Guards of the Order became instantly alert.

"It is good to see you, my son." The warrior priests relaxed a bit. Travis chuckled when he saw their reaction. "These fine warrior priests are my keepers. I must confess they are zealous in their charges." The priests did not smile.

Kyle did smile. "I never imagined I might be hosting

the Holy One as a High Lord of the Seven Realms when you and Mother Mavis scolded Jarod and me for misbehaving." Kyle became aware of his major-domo, Bantel, standing nearby, slightly nodding. He sent Travis and his party off to their rooms for hot baths and refreshment. Then, he asked his guest to join him in is study at his convenience.

Diffused light streamed across the study from a stained glass window ten feet high and five feet across. A skylight, twenty feet square, provided additional light from high above. Bookcases lined three of the walls, from the top of the window to the floor fifteen feet below. The bookcases surrounded the door into the room, which showed no other exit. Four, soft multicolored rugs depicting the four seasons quartered the room. Plush chairs with coordinating colors were placed in convenient groupings and three more were arranged in front of a large desk, inlaid in rich woods forming a woodland scene. The desktop held a candelabrum, ink and glass pens, and a large book that drew Kyle's interest. He had changed out of the formal robes of a High Lord he'd hastily thrown on to greet Travis, into dark gray trousers and a burgundy wormcloth shirt with flowing sleeves. The shirtfront gathered across his chest with ties matching the trousers. He looked and felt at ease.

A servant opened the door with a look of awe on his face for Travis to enter. Kyle motioned him to a plush chair in front of the desk and ordered cool orange juice that he knew Travis preferred. The Holy One projected a look of pleasure and satisfaction. "I came here once, many years ago. The parts of the keep I have seen are a marked improvement from that time."

Kyle smiled. "I tried to reduce the garishness from Mountglen's time. I actually got a good deal of gold coins for all that cynosure. I redid his monstrosity of a bedroom into a war room and took over Clarence's rooms for myself. Clarence actually used good taste. I changed the draperies and uniforms to my colors. I put together a Guard for Stonecrest from Mountglen's old Guard and weeded out troublemakers and flunkies.

"The walls went up smoothly and are well built. I made a few architectural changes. The old boltholes are sealed and a couple of new ones added. I improved the grossly inefficient kitchens, stables, and practice fields. I never knew building caused such a noise from the inside. We have enjoyed a little peace and quiet for only a few weeks." Kyle could hold his suspense no longer. "I know you find all this interesting, but I am sure you did not travel all this way to see what I accomplished with a keep."

Travis looked perplexed. "I thought you would be telling *me* why I'm here. I received a message from Jarod requesting me to make the journey. My Stone is still growing in power, but it is certainly not one of the Great Stones. I could not answer him or ask for the reason of this summoning."

Kyle was just as perplexed. "I received word today that Jarod is on his way here. It came through a bird and the resident priest retrieved the message with his graystone. That message gave no reason, either. I assumed it to be too difficult or long for a bird's mind to handle. I thought it might be to discuss the training sites I established. Now, I don't know."

Both men sat a moment in contemplation and then the conversation settled on pleasant subjects, including an update on Marc's progress.

* * *

THREE days later, a man in the battle dress of the Zenith's Guard approached the main gates of Stonecrest. A warrior rode behind him, to his right. Kyle's lieutenant challenged them. They spoke briefly and the lieutenant saluted and sent runners to the keep and walls above. The

Zenith's fanfare sounded while the two riders made their way toward the keep's main entrance. Blackwind, Jarod's horse, pranced and then settled. People stopped what they were doing and stared at the odd couple. Not many of them ever saw their Zenith Lord and they did not expect a travel-dirty warrior. The ones that knew him bent their knee, crossed their arms over their chest and bowed. The rest of the men followed suit while the women curtsied. Illche missed none of the commotion caused by the fanfare. She entered the bailey before her sex became obvious and then, to only a few. Her trousers and shirt ranged in variegated sand colors. A light brown wide belt with pouches comprised the closest thing to ornamentation she wore. No metal gleamed from her. Deeply suntanned skin made her brown eyes look nearly black. Her closely cropped, light brown hair might easily be mistaken for a man's style. Jarod and she dismounted in unison and in the same fluid motion.

Kyle and Travis emerged from the large double doors and hurried down the steps. Travis stepped forward and embraced Jarod before he could kneel. Illche became immediately alert and her hands opened a pouch with a practiced ease that seemed natural. Kyle became the next to greet Jarod in an embrace; Illche became highly irritated. Jarod faced the keep's personnel and motioned them to rise. He took a saddlepack from Blackwind before a groom led him away. The small crowd gave a cheer and returned to their duties while Jarod climbed the steps of the keep.

The doors closed behind them before Jarod spoke his first words. "This is the Holy One and High Lord Byrne. Gentleman, this is Illche. She is a bodyguard and will not speak unless there is danger."

Illche ignored both men and silently revolved in a circle. She noticed each door, window, and person. She bowed her head to Travis and then to Kyle without discontinuing her surveillance. The overall effect became quite eerie.

Kyle led the way to his study. Illche made a close survey of the room, bowed toward Jarod and left, closing the door quietly behind her. Jarod noticed Kyle's concern when he took a plush chair opposite him as Kyle settled behind his desk.

"She is quite good at what she does. I never would have believed there are so many ways to kill someone without normal weapons. She has weapons, too, of course," Jarod said, gently dropping the saddle pack beside him and spinning his battle sword athwart his lap. The motion proved so smooth, Kyle wondered if he ever took it off.

Travis took the lead of the conversation and spoke first about how well Marc fared. Jarod asked a few questions about his son while some of the tension drained from him. Travis then described his journey and a brief report on the readiness of the warrior priests and their training. He promised a demonstration at Jarod's convenience. Travis could not hold his question any longer. "You traveled here without the Guard?"

Jarod smiled and relaxed, a little. "There are four more like Illche camped nearby. I changed into battle dress from clothes similar to hers before we rode in. The Sire's Stone shields me from Shadure. I saw no reason for a large company. We came across country for the most part and the people we met did not know us. Most didn't get close enough to see our faces. The ladies are most adept at unobtrusively keeping people away. We made good time and bought provisions as we traveled. Illche usually went into the villages or towns to take care of our needs. You may be assured that no one approached me."

Kyle produced a sly smile. "Ladies? You crossed nearly the breath of the continent with five ladies?"

Jarod chuckled. "Five bodyguards that happen to be

ladies. I would not like to approach any one of them with an ulterior motive. You may rest assured that I have never had a more chaste two months." Jarod shifted his position and eyed the room. "I approve of the changes you made, especially the walls of the keep."

Kyle's smile widened to its fullest. "Thank you, my Zenith. Might I inquire why you and the Holy One are here?"

Jarod laughed. "You held out longer than I estimated you would. Are you two telling me you have not figured it out on your own?" Jarod raised an eyebrow and looked to Travis and then Kyle, seeming quite pleased with himself. "The two of you are to be joined to Stones this afternoon." The color drained from Travis' face and Kyle's jaw sagged. "Travis will join Wisdom's Stone and Kyle, the Warrior's Stone."

Travis became the first to recover. "I assume you had another vision?"

"No, the decision is mine to make and the choice of candidates is also left to me. I believe that this is the right time. I need you at the caves in the High Desert and you will need some of the attributes the Stones will give you. We start in three days. I chose Stonecreast for the ceremony because I wanted it conducted as far away from the High Desert as possible and still be reasonably convenient. The joining of two Stones will set off a monstrous and loud psychic vibration. I do not want Shadure to have any idea where we are going after the ceremony. He should not be able to pinpoint the location of your joining, but he can get a general idea..." He paused briefly before continuing.

"You both are already shielded from Shadure's surveillance on the Gray Plane by the High Desert People and after the ceremony, he will not be able to determine which Stones we used or to whom they were given—and the Stones will shield you afterwards."

Jarod looked at the saddlepack lying at his feet, "I have the Box of Stones. I do not believe any, or all, of the minions of the Dark's Source could have caused me harm on the trip here. They probably got a headache just thinking of me. Moreover, I *do* have a little power of my own, you know. The giving of the Guardian's Stone to Deion and the joining of the Sire's Stone to me caused huge expenditures of power that Shadure could not miss. I believe he caused the disturbances during the ceremony because the remaining Stones lay dormant. I do not understand exactly how the power from the Stones works, but I do know that when Deion *became* the Protector, the powers of the other Stones became manifest. Today's joining is not prophecy and certainly will not cause a reaction from the Dark's Source, itself. The only thing Shadure will know is the great power we used today. I think we might as well get this over with while we are alone. Illche!"

Emotions of surprise, disbelief, and resignation mingled on Kyle and Travis' faces.

The door opened immediately. Jarod ignored his companions' unease. "I will seal the room." Illche bowed and closed the door quietly behind her.

"There is not much to the ceremony. I ask each of you if you accept the Stone and the service to the Light's Source. The Stone will join with you when you accept it in your heart. Oh, and you will have to remove your shirts if you do not want a hole in them." It became obvious that Jarod thoroughly enjoyed himself, immensely. It took only a moment for Kyle and Travis to regain their composure to their credit. They looked a bit more resigned than happy.

Travis responded first. He stood and shrugged off his outer gray robe. He opened his shirt and pulled it aside, leaving his chest bare. Jarod removed the emerald from around Travis' neck and the Box of Stones from his saddle pack and loosened the protective cloth from around it. He faced Travis, all of the casualness he'd projected before, gone. He was the Zenith Lord; every fiber of his being proclaimed it. What he did clearly became of the utmost importance, and his manner changed to all seriousness.

Jarod held Wisdom's Stone over the huge center diamond embedded in the top of the Box of Stones. The effect came immediately. The Stone floated up to the level of Travis's heart. Jarod asked, "Do you, Travis Grant, freely accept the power given by the Light's Source to wage war upon Dark's Source?" He'd taken a similar oath of duty and responsibility long ago in his service to the Light's Source.

Travis's answer sounded firm. "Yes!"

A column of power shot upward from the Box of Stones to the emerald, encrusting it with gold.

"Do you freely accept the Stone of Wisdom and its power to be used against the Dark's Source?"

"Yes!"

The emerald moved slowly at first and then completed its journey to Travis' chest in a millionth of a second. Travis felt no pain or impact. The emerald simply appeared there, embedded in his chest, the outside edge even with his skin and a golden light, pulsing in time with his heart, sparkled behind it. It produced no blood or any other sign of a foreign object invading a human body. Travis pulled his shirt together and donned his robe. He sat down in awe of what had happened to him and the feelings coursing through him were written across his face. Jarod returned the chain to Travis with an enigmatic smile.

Jarod faced Kyle who had removed his shirt. His smooth, muscular chest lay bare. Jarod repeated the ceremony and the Warrior's Stone, a sapphire of the deepest blue and the same size as Travis' emerald, accepted and joined with him. Kyle felt the Stone's outer edge lying seamlessly imbedded in his chest over his heart.

"I do hope you do not feel cheated from the lack of a more involved ceremony?" Jarod smiled. Travis and Kyle, remembering the dramatic joining of the Sire's Stone to Jarod and the Guardian's Stone's acceptance of Deion, slowly shook their heads. "You will feel some strangeness for a few days while your bodies adapt. I will instruct you on the Stones' use while we travel to the High Desert People."

Jarod raised an eyebrow at the smug smile on Kyle's face while the latter finished stuffing his shirt in his trousers. He chuckled. "I just decided you certainly know how to make a memorable visit." Jarod and Travis joined in Kyle's chuckles and the final strands of tension left Jarod, for a while.

However, the pounding on the door did little to continue the mood. A little sheepish, Jarod released the seal of power he had placed on the room.

The door crashed open and four warrior priests and Prelate Daniel stumbled through. Jarod countered the shields they hastily tried to erect around their charge and smiled. Prelate Daniel became the first to recover.

"Gentlemen, cease your effort. This is the Zenith Lord."

The priests became aware that their shields had not formed and looked quite disquieted.

Prelate Daniel nodded to Jarod. "My Zenith Lord, it has been long since we last met. I trust you are well."

Jarod laughed. "Daniel it is good to see you, too. I wonder how we might survive the efforts of our perspective bodyguards during this war. Gentlemen, please try to resist using the power of your Stones until we work a few things out."

The priests nodded and said as one, "As you will,

Zenith Lord." Their training had got them through the experience when each of them became overawed at the power they felt and then encountered. The Prelate ushered the priests out, being not the only one that noted the amused look on Illche's face.

Jarod had set the time for departure at three days hence. He watched with Kyle when Illche called in her companions with a shrill whistle from the walls. Four riders appeared almost instantly; each of them led a packhorse and rode for the keep.

Before Kyle could ask, Jarod commented, "They are known as 'Desert's Ire.' Their history goes to the Great War and they have been trained much like the Order trained Deion. Their abilities are rooted out in childhood and they receive basic training in using their gifts. They are given the choice to work on the Gray Plane or become part of Desert's Ire's force. Relatively few take the warrior's path. They have twenty-five completely trained members and roughly three times that number in various stages of training. Desert's Ire has had two thousand years to train and refine their killing techniques, physically *and* psychically. They can use the power of a small graystone to explode a man's skull and they can kill barehanded in any number of ways. Do not underestimate them; they are most effective. It is becoming a problem." Jarod acknowledged the question on Kyle's face. "It is simple. I have too many bodyguards. Darth, would you say hello to your old friend, Kyle?"

The air shimmered with a slight greenish tinge while the simulacrum of the Captain Lord of Angels and Captain Lord of Death formed with drawn sword. Kyle had raised the ancient guardians three years earlier at Jarod's command and remembered how effectively Darth deflected an assassin's arrow at Marc's Naming Day ceremony. The beings still raised the hair on Kyle's neck.

Darth nodded to Kyle. "High Lord, you have done

well in the redesign of the keep's defenses. It is a dramatic improvement over the last High Lord's efforts."

Kyle returned the being's nod. "Thank you, Captain Lord." He did not want to ask how long that had been. Darth sensed Kyle's uneasiness and a smile appeared on his face while Kyle slowly watched Darth fade from view. "I think I see what you mean."

"The Guard has fits when I leave the Spires with under a Boulder of guardsmen. I draw the line at eight hundred and fifty men trailing along everywhere I go. Deion gets apprehensive when I am not in line of sight. One more year, and he will leave to start Marc's instruction, but until then, I have to *order* him to stay away when not needed. He does not take it well. I will have the warrior priests angered when I am not overjoyed at the contingent of protectors they present to me. Kyle, you cannot guess what a pleasure it is to stand here with only you and Darth beside me. I know they all mean well and are trying to do a difficult job, but…" A slight movement caught Kyle's attention when Illche slightly moved into the shadows. He decided not to mention it to Jarod. "…I would like to have some time alone with those I love without feeling like I am giving a performance." Jarod started toward the stairs leading down to the bailey. "Come along, Illche," he said, tossing the comment over his shoulder.

Jarod did find time to visit with Kyle and Travis that evening, alone except for Darth. Travis promised a demonstration of the warrior priests' abilities the next day. Jarod retired early. His guest suite contained three rooms: a reception room, a small study, and the bedroom.

Illche slept on a pallet against the inside of the bedroom door. Her companions slept on the inside of the other doors and one stood guard outside the entrance to the suite.

The member of Stonecrest's Guard that shared the

guard duty with her soon found conversation was not part of Desert's Ire's charm. It became a long night, spent next to a beautiful, if somewhat rugged, woman, and the guardsman showed visible relief at the first signs of dawn.

Jarod woke refreshed. He bathed and dressed in battle dress. Illche had done the same and he found her in the reception room of his suite looking out the window. She turned and followed him quietly. He had firstmeal with Kyle and Travis in a small private dining room. Travis reported that the warrior priests were ready to demonstrate their skills at his convenience. They had been somewhat deflated by Jarod's ease in countering their efforts the day before. Jarod felt sure they did not understand his abilities, or what they were truly capable of achieving themselves. Today would be a memorable one for the Guard of the Order.

The midmorning sun shone brightly in a blue sky with wispy clouds. A cool breeze blew from the northeast that provided comfort from the summer heat. The warrior priests stood at the edge of the field closest to the keep while Kyle escorted Jarod, Travis, and Daniel to join them.

The demonstration began with hand-to-hand sparring with Kyle's guardsmen. The priests held their own and both groups escaped serious damage. The guardsmen reflected a new appreciation for priests, who more than competed with practice swords. The guardsmen were defeated handily, except for one match that Jarod considered a draw. The guardsmen dismissed, the leader of the warrior priests walked to Jarod and bowed his head, briefly. "My Zenith, how may we demonstrate our psychic abilities?"

Jarod recognized the priest that had become the most irritated the day before when Jarod had negated their attempts to raise shields around Travis. Jarod motioned for all the warrior priests to join them from where they hovered about ten feet away. They looked a little less tense after the formalities of introductions concluded.

Jarod stood apart a pace and looked each priest in the eye. "You fought well." The priests began to relax. "I have placed an armed force of men at a distance from here. High Lord Byre has no patrols out this morning. I would like you to locate the hidden men and give a count of their number without leaving the practice field. Another *shielded* force hides in the area. See first if you can locate them and then, if you can slip inside their shields without their knowledge. You are not to hurt anyone with your powers. You are to work alone and not join talents until each of you has explored all other options. Prelate Daniel will take your answers."

The priests bowed as one. "As you will, Zenith Lord." They moved away separately to start their deliberations. Jarod did not psychically follow their progress. He did not want to produce distractions, even though he felt sure they would not know.

One priest, Cordel by name, closed his eyes in deep concentration. He shook himself as if he had awakened from a dream. He made his report to Daniel and returned to the circle the priests had formed. The remaining priests followed suit, one by one, within a few minutes. They joined hands and bowed their heads in concentration. They reported to Daniel again after a few minutes and then stood aside.

Daniel approached Jarod to report. "My Zenith, one priest did all you requested except penetrate the shields of your bodyguards. The others located the hidden men and correctly identified their number. I asked them to jointly locate the bodyguards and try to penetrate their shields. They were able to find their location with Cordel's aid, but they were still unable to get around their shields."

Jarod turned to Illche and nodded once. She closed her eyes and, a moment later, her four teammates trotted from behind the stables and took up an unobtrusive position around Jarod. He called the priests to his side. "You did well for the strength of your Stones and your training. Your abilities will continue to grow while your Stones increase in power. I understand that you have been taught to probe a person for signs of strength." The four priests nodded in acknowledgement. "I want each of you to quite gently probe the Holy One."

The priests, taken aback, proceeded when Travis nodded his acceptance. Their discoveries awed them.

Travis picked up the conversation. "You will travel with me to the High Desert where you will receive additional training. You will then return to the Tower crater to instruct your brothers. You will follow the Zenith's orders in these things as if they came from me."

The warrior priests were surprised and, Jarod noted, not happy.

5

SHADURE watched the war tactics meeting unseen. Daktar was smoothly interjecting Shadure's suggestions into their planning. More than one of Daktar's generals found new admiration for their sovereign.

Sudden pain seared Shadure's mind. He immediately escaped to the Gray Plane near Wathdure's position.

Wathdure looked up. "You felt it?"

"I was on their plane. The force was considerable and the pain severe. Do you know the location?"

"Somewhere in the lower portion of the Seven Realms. I am sure it was not at the Spires." Wathdure reflected Shadure's concern. Shadure vanished.

* * *

SHADURE'S thoughts drifted back over the sensations he had felt earlier. Light's Source released great power. He had used his abilities to search for the disturbance without finding anything. The lower half of the continent was a blur. He was sure of the source, but where it originated, he did not know. This proved the second time he'd felt those sensations in two thousand years. He did not feel the pain some of his lesser beings had, but it was anything but pleasant. The thought that it might have been from the accursed brat, he pushed from his mind with a shudder. Jarod's son, Marc Greatstone, known as the Darkslayer, filled Shadure with anger and pain. His counterpart in the last war was an adult when he received his power from Stones provided by the Light's Source. Yet, the brat would have been only three years old. The thought that he held such power at so early an age was one he could not grasp. It was abhorrent to him. Shadure was wrong in his belief.

His thoughts drifted to Daktar. He had spent much time in cultivating him. Unknowingly pressured toward his natural leanings for conquest, Daktar was a tyrant in his heart and his actions. Shadure's influence merely urged him forward in his desires for terror at an accelerated rate. He would be able to amass a huge army when his conquests were complete on his home continent, Kelor. Sison, Daktar's kingdom, fell under his rule when he'd quietly thrown his father from the highest tower of his keep in the darkness of a moonless night. He'd covered his tracks well and no one suspected until his ambitions became evident. Then, it proved too late to challenge him. Daktar would have been the first to be surprised that an outside force he did not know and could not perceive directed his actions. It amused Shadure to watch his machination's effects on his chosen tools. It would not have amused Daktar.

Kelor had eleven kingdoms. Five of those had fleets of ships used in trading with Serarelique and Stonefire. More importantly, they had shipwrights and expandable shipyards. The treasuries of the kingdoms he conquered would go for warships bound for the Seven Realms. The seas between Serarelique and Kelor were heavy with gales. Few captains, or crews, would take the risk to travel to Serarelique. Those that did made huge profits from spices, fine gold works, rare perfumes, incomparable wormcloth, and the best weapons available. Stonefire's weapons were slightly better but not traded at any cost—a problem Shadure would have to solve. Daktar was not yet up to the logistics of a large army. Shadure was not upset at that. He had vastly more experience than needed for Daktar's beginning intrigues and adventures and he would be there to nurture his minion along the right path. His thoughts then ranged on to Ozlid's problems.

Wathdure's rule of the kingdom for over three hundred years was more than adequate. The battle three years earlier had a high cost for the Dark Source's necromantic army of ten thousand creatures. He had slowly replaced some of them, and had close to five thousand ready to do Shadure's will. The people of Ozlid knew nothing of the undead beings beyond the frozen passes of their northern mountains. The energy Wathdure pulled from the Dark Void to animate his creatures cost him little of his powers.

Shadure reveled in the thought of completely controlling the three kingdoms of the island continent off the Seven Realms' western shores. Wathdure could comfortably maintain a hundred thousand beings, and he would, when he dominated Ozlid's two neighbors, Arestead and Hamptor.

These thoughts proved much more pleasurable than thoughts of Jarod and the brat. Shadure relaxed as much as he ever did. It was not much.

6

VA-A'CIL, Empress of the Aviaries of Heaven, known to the outside world as Serarelique, emerged from her sedan chair. The radiance of her jewel-encrusted platinum headdress, cuffs, and belt awed the large crowd that had gathered to see the rare appearance of their empress in public. Her guard of thirty men escorted her onboard her personal ship, *Serarelique's Majesty*. Ta-Cern firmly supported Ca-Ra'IL up the gangway, his silver clothing and headdress contrasting with her black robes. Her long silver hair shimmered in the sunlight, fashioned into a headdress with jeweled pins and combs. Four Imperial Nobles followed.

Va-A'Cil's entourage and guards formed up behind her on the upper stern deck. She stepped forward and raised her arms outward to the vast crowd. The silence, broken by only a few babe's cries, ceased, while thousands cheered their empress when she raised her arms in greeting to her subjects.

Va-A'Cil lowered her arms and followed her escort to the main deck where she disappeared into her private suite. Ten longboats, each manned by forty oarsmen, took in the slack on their lines to *Serarelique's Majesty*. Powerful arms and torsos glistened in the sun while the huge ship slid smoothly out into the harbor. The ship caught the wind when great sails unfurled from its three thick masts. *Serarelique's Majesty* expertly sailed to the middle of her six escorting war ships. The cheering of the crowd carried to her for a long distance.

Later that evening, she continued the Seven Realms'

language lessons that Ta-Cern taught.

* * *

KYLE'S father, Lord Cartwell Byrne, lord of Bramble Keep, sat at his table nearly drunk. His son, Peter, finished his lastmeal and raised his glass to his father. Cartwell liked his oldest son. Not loved, but liked. That troubled him tonight. He looked at his offspring sitting opposite him and knew the assessment of his feelings to be correct. His deliberations on the contentious proposal he would make continued while he and his son completed the weekly ritual of discussing the keep's business, alone. He raised his glass to acknowledge his son's salute.

Peter takes after my side of the family, after all. He stands relatively short: five and a half feet tall. He met his son's dark eyes and drank in his countenance. *He is pensive, always ready to do my bidding, always ready with pleasing words for me, always determining what will keep me away and what will keep him in my good graces. He is different from Kyle!* Anger flashed through him as it usually did when he considered his youngest son. *Perhaps that is best.*

Cartwell Byrne had abused and tormented Kyle. His wife died from an illness she contracted from Kyle. Irrational pain struck at his heart when he remembered his wife's death. The arranged marriage became the shining achievement of his father's design for expanding their line's station and wealth. She came from a wealthy family with lands three times the size of his, and she'd been the only offspring. He would have inherited through her. He ought to have achieved great wealth. His conclusions progressed down a well-traveled road to despair: *The old fool left everything to the Zenith when she died. He blamed me for his daughter's death! I sent for the best healers. Is it my fault they arrived too late?*

He'd once admitted to himself that the fault belonged to him for waiting so long before sending the message. He buried those feelings deep and had not acknowledged them in years. He would never admit that the cost of her care had become a factor; he'd hoped she would recover like Kyle.

He saw Kyle many years after he left for the Spires at the age of ten by the order of Jarod's father. Kyle rode through Stonefire in the full dress uniform of an Apex Officer of the Guard while he watched as a spectator in the crowd. Kyle sat tall in his saddle, blond, obviously muscular and a handsome countenance that came to him from his mother. He'd earned his position, graduated from the Academy with the highest honors, and had provided great service to the Seven Realms. All his accomplishments shunted from Cartwell Byrne's mind into oblivious nothingness. He'd attributed Kyle's success to his closeness to the Zenith Lord. He'd been wrong.

His voice took a tone that his son knew well and immediately put him on guard. "Peter, what would you think of offering your services to your brother?" Peter's shock took no acting on his part. That proposal encompassed the remotest idea he'd probably ever expected to hear his father say. He tried to mask his surprise without much success. "Oh, come now; do you really believe all this *war* gibberish they are feeding us? I talked to men who were at the so-called battle with the Dark's Source."

His sly smile made Peter more on guard. "I think we will have an opportunity to advance our station and wealth. Kyle has Stonecrest and no heirs! Men get killed in war, if indeed there is a war." He said the last with a sneer. "We would have a claim if he were to die, bravely of course, in any conflict."

Peter's response came immediately and his voice held a strength his father chose to ignore. "Father, do you think there will not be a will, or do you think Kyle has forgotten his treatment here?" Peter knew he walked on dangerous ground. It would be quite dangerous ground indeed, if his father exploded in rage at his last question.

"Ah, but wills can be changed. Especially, if a loving brother is at his side through good and bad. We have seen no sign of war and I doubt if there will be any." He sat back into the cushions of his plush chair and poured another glass of wine, feeling pleased with him. *I will say no more tonight. I think it is best to let things boil a little.*

Peter had talked with men from the battle, too. What he heard rang true; he had no doubt that the battle had been horrible. The son of a tenant farmer had spoken calmly when he told what happened. His wounds had been real enough to cast any doubt from Peter's mind. *I did not treat Kyle too badly, for our ages at the time and the intervening years may have softened my brother's opinions.* Peter sensed where his father headed and wanted no part of it. He could not imagine killing his brother and he knew that must be his father's goal. Peter feigned a stronger bout of intoxication than he felt. He had done so for years when he and his father had their private dinners, without servants attending. *I wonder if he plays the same game.* He fought back a smile at the certainty.

Cartwell Byrne rang for the servants and leaned heavily on his valet's arm when he left the room. Peter looked on with closely hidden amusement. His father's acting didn't match his own, which he'd honed with practice. He waved the servant's attention away and sat on a window seat looking at the dark clouds.

A quarter-moon shed little light during breaks in the overcast sky. He considered what his father proposed and said, "Old man, the only one you are going to get killed is *me*," then made his way to his rooms. His father had deftly turned his attention to other subjects, but the thoughts of his possible participation in Kyle's death would keep him awake most the night.

* * *

THE small private dining room measured roughly

twenty feet square. It had scarlet draperies with matching upholstery on the chairs around the table and a few plush chairs in front of the fireplace. Dark stain covered the wood floors and furniture. Several hunt scenes displayed in various paintings around the room did little to cheer the setting. Alex Careform moved away from the spy hole that lay in shadow of the frame above one of the larger paintings. He eased the stone stopper into the wall matching the grooves that would ensure it became invisible from the other side. Easing along the small, pitch black, passageway, he listened closely for several seconds before sliding the panel open in the darkest corner of the broom and cleaning supply closet. The familiar noise of the kitchen's staff in the adjoining room performing their last duties of the night hid his egress through the hidden hall door. He would not sleep well, either.

Three days dragged as if they were a week. Alex prepared to leave for the Order's enclave ahead of time. He would have three days away from the keep and be hard pressed to return in time. His contact, the local priest, had died a month ago. His replacement did not have the ability to imprint a message on the mind of a bird and direct it to its destination. The enclave would have men with graystones that would send the message and never mention his visit.

At least, the weather held. He struck out on the road from Bramble Keep with a walking staff and meager provisions. He had coin to supplement his provisions and expertise in cracking skulls with the staff if the need arose.

* * *

SHADURE was weak. He would not admit it, even to himself. The activities of the night had drained him and he would not recover for several hours, perhaps days. Outwardly, he appeared the same, or so he believed. He had brought four beings across the void to the Gray

Plane. One would become Gangedure, Plane Master and keeper of the Gray Plane. Shadure knew which it would be. He strongly shimmered in Dark Power; he had served The Dark One well on the other side. Raising his arms, he formed the last thoughts that gave the being a persona. His predecessor destroyed and Shadure weakened in the battle three years earlier had made the replacement necessary.

Shadure never discovered how Jarod had penetrated the Gray Plane, if he had accomplished it. The bare possibility of Jarod's power, conveyed through Gangedure's vortex to transport Wathdure's army to Stonefire from their hidden enclaves in Ozlid, constantly perplexed him. It became even more remote that he continued the attack after the destruction of the vortex. Still, a presence had materialized on the Gray Plane and done him great harm.

Could he possibly have access here? Preposterous! Did Jarod destroy the Dark Stone Mountglen wore upon his death, have it thrown into the ocean, and causing me loss of power and agony in the void? The Dark One brought me from my suffering and made a new Dark Stone from the essence of Eric Mountglen's spirit; the same Dark Stone I will use with great pleasure to entrap a new pawn near the Zenith. Who shall he be?

The new Gangedure's groveling at Shadure's feet pulled him from his unanswered questions.

"Rise, Gangedure." Shadure pointed to a podium where a large tome rested. "It is opened to the beginning of your efforts. Learn your skills well or risk the wrath of the Dark's Source." The other three would remain where they were until he gave them each their personae, which he would hold captive until his powers returned in full.

Shadure's remembrances drifted over the sensations he'd felt earlier. The Light's Source had released power on a magnitude he found incomprehensible. He used his powers to search for the disturbance without finding anything; the lower half of the continent had become a blur. He felt sure of the source, but where it originated, he did not know. The notion that it might have been from the accursed brat prodded his thoughts producing a shudder. Jarod's son, Marc Greatstone, known as the Darkslayer, filled Shadure with anger and pain.

7

JAROD, standing alone on the walls of Stonecrest, looked out on the false dawn that promised to be a good day for traveling. A faint sound of a galloping horse came to him and he looked into the gloom. He let his senses stretch through the Sire's Stone. He located the guardsman about two miles away. Illche stood at a respectful distance while the other Maids of Desert's Ire readied their mounts and packhorses. Jarod motioned for her. She walked the few spaces to his side.

His words carried as a whisper on the breeze. "A messenger comes. He is about two miles out."

Illche whistled a perfect imitation of a warbling wren. Two of her group detached from the rest and rode out the gates.

* * *

TRAVIS emerged from the keep with Prelate Daniel and the four warrior priests to check the journey's preparations. Kyle, his arms master, and two of his guards had completed those tasks and left the others to wait in the dining hall. It would be a fast trip if he knew Jarod— and he probably knew him better than anyone did. Travis' strength and stamina belied his years and white hair, and the power of Wisdom's Stone would do much to increase his physical abilities. Kyle felt no anxiety from that quarter. He expected that the women of Desert's Ire would outshine them all, except him and Jarod. He had observed them on the practice fields and the way they melted together with their horses lay beyond his experience. Jarod rode with them one day. He had accomplished the same excellence of horsemanship, but then, Jarod had been the finest horseman he knew. He looked forward to learning their techniques. *No, there will be no one to slow this journey.*

The only sign of their wealth or station would be Jarod and Kyle's battle swords. A leather cover recommended and made by an enterprising member of Kyle's staff, after the subject came up during lastmeal two nights previous, proved the answer. The waterproofed and easily discarded cover would hide the quality and jewels of the sword's hilt and scabbard. The priest's robes were devoid of rank, with Jarod's battle dress and hair pulled into a warrior's knot with tail perhaps the only thing that might bring comment or question.

The women did not flaunt their sex, nor did they try to hide it, attractive in a no nonsense way. Their lean whipcord muscles, confidence, demeanor, and fluid grace spoke of hidden abilities that should give a man pause before making advances. Their eyes alone could deter anyone stupid enough to get that close. Not that Kyle expected to visit that many inns on the trip. They all could certainly live off the land and avoid villages and towns, and groups did not mingle much on the well-traveled roads without need. Their provisions would last and the need to hunt for their meals would provide recreational benefit.

The travelling group entered the dining hall. Kyle's eyes fell on Jarod standing apart from the others. He had expected changes in Jarod. The Zenith Lord now chose his words wisely after deliberation, did not answer first when new subjects arose, and much of his youthful spontaneity had vanished. Both his voice and attitude projected command, as Kyle admitted they should. The pressures and demands of the last three years had brought out his well-hidden maturity into plain view. Kyle found that disturbing and then realized he had changed in much the same way over the years. Jarod nodded once to Illche and they followed him into the bailey without the need of his authoritarian voice.

The messenger rode in with the two women of Desert's Ire flanking him. The guardsman dropped from his horse and a groom took the animal away for a well-deserved fare of water, oats, grains, and attention. He spun around, surely expecting to run to the keep, and found his Zenith Lord standing a few feet away. He snapped to position and saluted. "My Zenith, I carry a message from Master Gaz."

Kyle joined them and the guardsman again snapped to position and saluted the High Lord out of habit. He had been the commanding Apex of the Guard. He returned the man's salute as if nothing out of the ordinary had happened.

Kyle watched as Jarod dismissed the guardsman to find food and rest after receiving the messenger's pouch. It contained a packet that he recognized as daily updates containing information of current interest, along with a slim, sealed message. Jarod cracked the seal and read the contents, frowning at the outset. He gave the message to Kyle and waited.

Kyle showed his surprise. "Jarod, I do not think Peter would do such a thing. He treated me as a younger brother and most of the things one might call abuse happened only around my father and he pulled his punches. He would not have tried to hurt me at all if Father had not ordered it done."

Jarod considered a moment before he spoke. Clearly, he did not want to place emphasis on surveillance of his father and brother. "Kyle, that is something you must determine. I do not trust your father, but I have an open mind regarding Peter." Kyle took the statement with good grace. He did not trust his father, either.

Jarod set a ground eating pace the first day and Kyle felt sure it would become the norm. He felt surprise by only one thing. Jarod planned to stay overnight at inns once or twice a week. That would allow them to carry the minimum number of packhorses and keep up their brisk pace. Travis, the most recognizable one in their party, took pains to stay unnoticed. Broadric, Kyle's arms master, made the arrangements when necessary and the trip started well and without undue notice. Kyle prayed it would remain that way.

The priests became quite efficient at setting up and breaking down their campsites. They would not accept help from Jarod or Kyle and flatly refused Travis' attempts to do any physical labor. Travis bore the pampering with good grace and a sly smile, his only comment being, "I guess they think I am getting old."

*   *   *

KYLE found Jarod practicing with his sword, working through the various forms for attack and defense. His speed increased until the sword became a blur of silver motion.

A question brushed against his consciousness. *Do you want to join me?* Kyle held himself in check and the memory of Jarod's first sending to Deion came to mind. Jarod had nearly done great physical harm to Deion with the force of his reply.

He cautiously sent a reply. *Yes!*

Jarod's exercise slowed while he finished an attack form. Pecquin, one of the women, emerged from where she stood hidden in the shadows, startling Kyle. She held two blunted practice swords. Jarod sheathed his battle sword and removed it from his baldric. He held the sword in both hands outward to Pecquin. She quickly handed Kyle the practice swords and took the battle sword in both hands, bowing her forehead to it. This remained the only sign of obsequious behavior Kyle had witnessed from any of the women to anyone except Travis. He'd wondered if they showed their respect to

Jarod or to the sword.

They started slowly with a form Kyle knew well. Jarod stopped the spar in less than a minute. "Feel your Stone; search for the warmth and feel of its pulse. Let it flow with your thoughts."

Kyle relaxed a moment, searching. When it exploded into his consciousness, he staggered a step. He wrapped his will around it and marveled at its obedience.

Jarod stepped aside. "Try it."

Kyle thought of the form they had just worked. He raised his sword and started again. The sword lightened in weight and his strokes and countermeasures danced flawlessly through the form. His speed increased until, with a powerful upward cut, the sword flew from his hand and sailed over the nearest tree. It came down and stood buried halfway to its hilt a few yards away. Pecquin actually smirked and Jarod held an amused look on his face. Kyle raised an eyebrow.

Jarod's response held no contempt. "That is the trick! The power you have is far beyond your imagining. It will obey you within the restraints you set and you must concentrate on using the right level of power for the task at hand. It will easily let you put your hand through a heavy oak door; however, it will not keep your bones from breaking when you do it! The practice forms will flow effortlessly as you have discovered. You must limit the power while it transmutes from the Stone to your physical use of it. That is the real practice. You and I know the practice forms as well as any arms-master in the Seven Realms, better than most of them. Our practice is not in the forms, but in restraint. Let us try again."

Kyle turned to recover the practice sword and found Pecquin pointing it toward his chest. She tossed it in the air and caught it gracefully; the hilt quivered mere inches from his hand. He took the proffered sword and raised it to her in salute. Her manner changed to all seriousness.

She bowed her head in a slight nod.

"You honor me, High Lord."

Then, she darted away, concealed in shadows, before Kyle could respond.

The practice continued without further mishap. Kyle became completely engrossed in wielding his new power. *He did well, but he did not approach the speed Jarod displayed earlier.* Kyle started at the stray thought, wondering where it formed; when he turned and saw the audience that had gathered a few yards away. The warrior priests looked dismayed, to say the least.

Firstmeal had finished and Kyle noticed Jarod and Travis in a serious discussion apart from the others. Travis nodded when Jarod spoke, but said little. Kyle helped with the final packing and found that most he tried to do was politely taken from him to be handled by Pecquin or one of the other women. He finally raised an eyebrow in question.

"You are now a true High Lord," she answered, sounding like a nurse might prompt a small child. "The Highest One works with his power ceaselessly to perfect that, which will defeat the Dark's Source. I have noticed it takes a toll that I believe you will soon know well. We may not ease that effort, but this may help."

She turned and briskly went on with the last chores of packing. Kyle wondered if that comprised the longest speech she had ever made.

* * *

THEY approached Boswell after hard days of riding. Its name had originated from the lord who'd developed the area's trade three generations earlier. Boswell had grown into a prosperous town of some ten thousand people. Kyle had met the current Lord Boswell two years ago. An outwardly jovial man that, Kyle's counselors had informed him, hid the traits of decisiveness and many skills. They planned to stop early that afternoon and let the horses and themselves have good food and rest. They would continue after firstmeal the next day, entering and leaving quietly.

But, it was not to be.

Broadric galloped up the hill leading into the town from the west and reined in next to Kyle while they spoke briefly. He bowed stiffly and let others ride by until he reached Jarod. "My Zenith, every inn in Boswell is full! The mayor's daughter and the son of the largest farmer in the area, other than Lord Boswell, marry tomorrow. The farmer and mayor planned a festival for the wedding and combined it with a fair displaying the area's produce and manufactured items. Traders from half of Stonecrest are in Boswell."

Kyle signaled a stop when Broadric started talking to Jarod. The ones ahead turned in their saddle and the ones behind bunched up.

They had been on the road for a week and the horses needed rest and good grains to continue at the pace Jarod set. The need to rest and getting something to eat other than travel fare called also to the humans. Jarod took only a second to decide but did not speak for a moment.

"Ride to the keep and ask Lord Boswell if Prelate Daniel and his party may stay overnight. Impress on the lord that Prelate Daniel is on a long journey, did not come for the wedding, and would like to remain apart from the festivities."

Jarod nodded once. Broadric started to raise his fist to his heart in salute, caught himself in mid-action, turned a little pink, and started off at a cantor toward the town. The commanding voice Jarod used, though soft, brought responses and not questions. Jarod turned to Travis with a slight smile.

"Nicely done," the Holy One said.

Broadric had no way of knowing that, in that short minute before Jarod spoke, Travis and he had had a rather long mental conversation.

Travis smiled. "I think I am getting the hang of it."

"That you are, Father. That you are."

Travis basked in Jarod's praise.

Tents appeared on the outskirts of town in the short time it took for them to reach its edge. The odd group of women, priests, and guards caused a small stir when they turned from the western road onto the northern road leading to the keep located on a hill outside of town. Evidence of the fair showed everywhere along the main street and stretched to the fields behind the town.

Indication of the local ale showed on the drunk who slightly staggered toward Pecquin. "Ah, my strange and pretty girl, would you be so kind to sit *me* as well as you sit that horse?"

Several men coming out of an inn laughed and one started to approach. Pecquin moved so fast that most of those on the road missed her actions. She leaned down to the drunk and her arm swept down and up. Her horse did not break stride and the man wondered what had happened until his pants and privatecloth fell around his heels. No one had seen the small sharp knife, now sheathed beneath the cuff of her left wrist. Another man, who'd started to approach, stopped in his tracks and soon, raucous laughter followed Jarod's party.

Three women formed a protective shield to Jarod's front and sides that went unnoticed at the first sign of the commotion. The gait increased to a trot and they came quickly away from the disturbance.

The gates of Boswell keep stood open. Lord and Lady Boswell stood at the bottom of the three steps leading to the main entrance of the keep. Prelate Daniel stopped and dismounted while pages and stable boys hurried forward. Jarod and Kyle hung back, surrounded by the women. The Lord and Lady knelt on cushions placed before them and each took hold of Daniel's proffered hand and touched his ring of office to their foreheads. Daniel whispered to the lord when he rose. Boswell looked startled for a brief moment and swept Daniel toward the doors and quickly inside. Lady Boswell's look of bewilderment promised a few stern words for her husband while she and the rest of the party followed his hasty retreat.

Boswell stopped at the rear of the reception room and the entrance to the great hall with his wife hot on his heels. She turned to apologize while Travis removed the cowl from his head. Lady Boswell looked back to her husband and then whipped her head around to face Travis again. Her mouth fell open. Travis stepped forward when the lady fell to her knees.

Boswell looked on at his wife's strange behavior. His gaze lifted to Travis' eyes and the color drained from his face while he joined his wife's obsequiousness. They repeated the ritual done with Daniel and started to rise. Lady Boswell struggled, so Illche grasped her elbow in strong support. She started to speak her thanks when her eyes took in the countenance and sex of her helper that left her speechless. Pecquin joined Illche and half-carried the woman to a nearby chair.

Kyle stepped forward. Lord Boswell recognized the High Lord, who he had met once. He started to kneel again and stopped at the motion of Kyle's hand. "Lord Boswell, I have the honor to present your Zenith Lord."

Boswell knelt, crossed his arms to his chest, and bowed low in time-honored tradition. His wife looked from Kyle to Travis to Jarod and promptly fainted.

The gates to the keep were closed with orders that no one may leave, including those that returned from town. Guards assigned outside the exits of the keep leading to the bailey had orders to turn people away. It was an unusual and strange order for Lord Boswell to give. The main gates stayed open, but with an increased guard.

The Great Hall reflected the wealth of the lord's lands. The high table had been covered in a linen cloth bleached to the purest white. Candles in profusion blazed light throughout the hall. Fine porcelain plates and gold flatware reflected on clear crystal goblets. Musicians provided a soft background to the sounds of the hall. Jarod sat in the lord's high-backed chair with Kyle to his right and Travis to his left. Illche hovered behind Jarod with Pecquin and her twin, Secquin, close behind her. Their looks made the staff nervous. They might have been more nervous if they knew the women's abilities.

Kyle had explained their predicament: they had not planned to stop at any of the nobles' keeps on their way; they had not traveled with court attire; they needed their visit hidden until they were two days away; and they had to leave the following morning as quietly as possible. Lady Boswell quickly understood and made her guests comfortable without much ado.

She wore a gown of hunter green—eloquent, sophisticated and flattering to a lovely woman in her prime—paired with an emerald pendant on a gold chain with matching earrings. Lord Boswell sat next to Kyle, in a dark blue suit of clothes with a white wormcloth shirt.

Travis wore the gray of the Order with the Tower emblazoned above his heart in golden threads. Prelate Daniel wore the same, while the warrior priests had on gray with black piping, the Tower stitched above their hearts in black with a white deathcat at its base. Kyle donned trousers of dark gray with a burgundy wormcloth shirt; Jarod, black trousers with a shirt matching Kyle's— their colors.

Jarod's blond hair, pulled into a warrior's knot, glistened in the candlelight. His sapphire blue eyes missed little of his surroundings. Kyle's short black hair reached just below his banded collar. His soft brown eyes contrasted Jarod's blue but remained equally observant.

Lord and Lady Boswell kept their conversation light, without probing questions, much to their credit.

Finally, the most important guests the Lord and Lady Boswell had ever hosted retired early.

* * *

MASTER Michael Gaz, spymaster of Stonefire and the Seven Realms if the truth were known, read again various reports from agents in Arestead and Hamptor. The knock at his door made him cognizant of the time.

"Come!" he called out and sat back in his chair.

His best agent, Zack, and his now constant companion, Currat, entered and sat across from him. He was the first to penetrate Ozlid's seat of power and had brought word of Wathdure and his necromancy back to Stonefire. Jarod had been able to connect Wathdure as the same being he had witnessed on the Gray Plane.

Currat and Zack had traded saving each other's life on several occasions. A former officer of Ozlid's forces, he recognized the evil in Ozlid and when his father was killed during Zack's escape, he knew his life was forfeit and agreed to meet Zack at Hagan's End, Hamptor's port city.

Doris, a woman Zack had saved from murderers and thieves, had cared for his wounds. He sent one of his men, Ursel, to find Currat, who had been caught and was being tortured by Ozlid's agents when Ursel tracked him down. Ursel affected his rescue and Zack, Currat, Doris, and her young daughter sailed for the Seven Realms. Doris had been rewarded by Jarod and now owned a high quality inn in Stonefire.

Zack and Currat could have passed for brothers, so identical were they from the neck down, the same height, and similar countenances. Currat had joined Gaz's network of spies and had well learned the craft. He became an expert swordsman and discovered he had a great talent for forgery. Zack had insisted that the two of them be paired on assignments. Gaz thought that had been a good idea at the beginning of Currat's new career, but Zack still insisted on it now that the spy was fully trained. They would certainly complement each other on the assignments he had for them, but normally, they would have been working alone over a year ago. Gaz knew their dependency on each other had nothing to do with their skills and recognized the great friendship they shared. Still, it was an unusual attitude for Zack. Gaz cleared his throat and got to the point. That, on the other hand, was not unusual.

"Gentlemen, I sent two operatives with Ambassador Openhand when he left for Hamptor and Arestead. Our offers of exchanging diplomats were rebuffed. We did succeed in opening a small trade office in both kingdoms. My man in each office has sent information that warrants investigation. There has been a general upheaval of advisors and some ministers in *both* kingdoms, *and* we've not heard from them in too long of a time. I would not question one of these occurrences, but three at the same time and at the same high levels forms a rather large question in my mind. You know how I hate unanswered questions."

Zack and Currat tried not to smile and failed.

"I want you to do the investigation as quickly as possible." Gaz continued, focusing on Currat. "How are your accents?"

Currat spoke first with the Hamptor twang and then with the Arestead curtness. He would pass as native in either. Gaz directed his attention to Zack and he matched Currat's performance. Currat would not have lived long using his native accent from Ozlid in either kingdom. "You will travel as gem merchants and carry sufficient stones to show perspective merchants. You will travel and dress well, but keep it understated. Four other agents will travel with you."

Zack's surprise was easy to see and Currat caught it.

"I know; it would look strange if you did not have bodyguards and they have to be sensitive to your needs. You can not afford a drunken man telling things he heard or saw out of the ordinary."

Gaz reached below his desk and placed a beautifully detailed leather case on the desktop. "The jewels in here are fake. You will carry the real ones in your boots' heel. They also can be hidden in your belts. The appropriate clothing will be sent to you after midmeal, today." Gaz handed a sheaf of papers to Zack. "These are copies of the reports I received with their identity and the location of our offices. Study the reports and then burn them. The information about our offices and personnel are innocuous and would not be unusual for you to have."

He stood and Zack and Currat followed suit. "You will leave in the morning. A ship from Outreach will be waiting for you at Elizabethville. A coach with a few special improvements will be aboard. The men traveling with you look their part and I believe you know them all. You will collect three homing pigeons at Elizabethville. The ship will return for you one week after they are sent. Guard the birds well unless you want to try your luck with the local ships."

That was a development Zack and Currat did not want to think about. Neither Hamptor nor Arestead had shipyards and the ships there were in pretty bad shape, making a crossing to Elizabethville an event to remember except for one captain's ship. Captain Briggs had helped them and company escape from Hamptor with a new, fine ship provided by the High Lord of Deepwells at Jarod's request.

The spies did not speak as they walked to their quarters, adjoining rooms in the officer's living floors of the Spires. Currat entered Zack's room and went through the connecting door, leaving it open behind him. He heard him call an officer's valet with the bell pull that always squeaked. Zack ordered hot water for a bath when the valet arrived and he ordered the same.

Hot water steamed around Currat's head, relaxing his tense muscles. He did not leave the tub until he heard Zack emerge from his. Tossing a large cloth over his shoulder, he walked to where the other man stood beside his tub drying with an equally large cloth. Zack faced him with a questioning look.

"Would you have gone without me?" Currat asked, his voice low and firm.

He did not know what to expect when Zack barely whispered, "No," as he dropped his towel onto the bed. Currat's towel slipped off his shoulder landing next to his, and he stepped forward into Zack's arms. Currat pulled apart and gently kissed him on the mouth.

Zack's face softened. *We have depended on each other for our lives and our trust in each other was not mislaid and has continued to grow over the years. Currat suffered horribly during the torture he received from his former men and my orders had saved him. I treasure those orders. I cared for him and paid handsomely for the trouble with my own injuries. He helped my emotional scars heal, something I couldn't do or even knew I had suffered from them. We have sparred at arms together, worked assignments together, watched each other's back, killed enemies of the Seven Realms, and shared women. My love for Currat confuses me. He is more than any brother in arms has ever been. We know each other's secrets, hopes, and desires.*

His mind raced. *He always touches the now hard to see scars that I blew greatly out of proportion, making me eventually see their true minor lines, healing more than my body. I don't know what to feel! Is this the kind of love I really have for him? I remember seeing him after the Ozlid officer had tortured him so badly. I didn't know if he would survive. I knew then the depth of my love for him. Is it this kind of love? I remember his care and concern when we left Ozlid, when I was wounded and I could hardly ride. Was the love in his eyes* this *kind of love? What would happen if he married and had children? Could I be happy in a similar life after my wife and daughter's brutal murder with the constant worry for their safety? I can always protect him.* The realization hit him like a sword's powerful blow. *No! I don't think I can live without him. I don't want to live without him. I've thought about his body so many times, the sensations running through me when we touch. Are they the love for him as a lover? I think now, they are.*

It was a long night of gentle and passionate kisses, exploration, powerful releases, exhaustion, and finally, peaceful sleep.

Currat woke early and looked at the powerful body lying naked beside him.

We have seen each other naked often while caring for our wounds and hurts, and in the normal daily encounters of close friends living side by side, swimming in the pool at the palace in Ozlid and when we stripped, pulling our clothes over us with whatever cover we could find to keep from freezing. We are not shy. We both have commented on how much our bodies match. His blond hair and my black hair, his sapphire-blue eyes and my black eyes, mark our only differences. We laughed once when he noticed our ears were mostly identical. Our hard muscles are defined from constant exercise, training and sparring, and I like touching the fullness of his. That is this kind of love? I wonder how the cold light of day will shape his emotions and if I acted wisely on my feelings. I think it might be best to let him have some time. I'm not sure how I feel, but I have imagined being with him for years. I'm sure my actions must have surprised him.

Currat slipped quietly out of bed and walked to his room. He sponged himself clean with cold water, shaved, and dressed. Then, he sat next to the small window and watched the Spires come alive. He wondered how many of the men below, hurrying to the first duties of the day, felt as he did about another man. It was not uncommon, even between some of the fiercest warriors. He had just never thought of himself in those terms until recently. His doubts raised questions he did not want to answer.

He felt Zack's presence before he heard him. Currat turned to face him. Arms embraced him and his doubts were assuaged from the kiss he received.

Zack released him with a slight smile. "Shall we go find our bodyguards?"

They turned and walked from their rooms like nothing different had happened in their lives. *Not much happened last night,* Currat thought. *Nothing more than an avalanche of new and strange emotions, desires, and tactile experiences that could be emotionally compared to several tons of rock!*

Their detachment met them at the stables and they knew and respected them. They were all larger than their new charges and Zack and Currat had seen them in action while training; they had worked together to bring down a gang of smugglers. They were smart, effective, and very strong. The quality of the men Gaz provided emphasized the importance he felt this mission deserved and was not lost on anyone in the detachment. Guardsmen brought their horses out with bulging saddlepacks and two packhorses fully loaded. Gaz came from the main entrance of the Spires with the leather case in one hand and two pairs of boots in the other. The case, he ordered packed with the packhorses. He watched as Zack and Currat struggled to find space to pack the boots in their saddlepacks.

Gaz did not smile when he said; "It will make a rather large dent in my budget if you loose your footwear." Then, he grasped forearms with each of them and waved them toward the gates without further comment.

* * *

WATHDURE sat in shadows with candles strategically placed behind him, scanning the thoughts of the men in front of him. No light source sat in front of him and the twenty men looking at him believed the ebony face hidden beneath the deep cowl was covered in black wormcloth. He knew they would not have cared if his face were purple. The pouches containing five gold coins bought their time and attention, at least for the present— their expenses now paid to travel from large cities throughout the Seven Realms. These men were the heads and overlords of bandits, murderers, and thieves numbering over three thousand.

Wathdure felt Spercine's presence sitting next to him. He loved the perversions her mind gave him as she looked at the lustful stares from the men before her. The lust he enjoyed from them, not nearly as strong or perverse as her sexual concoctions, added to his pleasure. The men compared her with memories of beautiful prostitutes they had had in the past, some much more filled with debauchery than others. From the men's minds he knew they'd never seen her equal. He had approved of her choice of dress to provoke the emotions they desired. Sheer, white material covered her perfectly proportioned body. Hard nipples strained the seams that, no doubt, the men hoped would not hold. They could not know that more than thread held the illusion before them.

Wathdure loved Spercine's skilled illusions.

Heavily armed guards stood behind her, unneeded. Any man would have been dead before he rose from his chair without the aid of her guards. Spercine had her own defenses that would prove more than equal to those of the men before her, alone or together.

Wathdure listened as her voice carried the promise of heat and passion. Each man had the impression she spoke directly to him. "My Master bids you to join forces for the mutual benefit of all as I have described," she said. "His motives are not ones of avarice. You will have the gold and other things of monetary value you reap from your efforts. You will strike as stated with the coordination and times provided. The Guard pulled in every direction at once. Trap after trap will decimate them with little casualties to your bands. Your chief goals will be to keep order and prevent unrest between your men. My Master is aware that some of you have been enemies in the past. Infighting will not be tolerated and dissension within your groups will be met with death!"

Wathdure smiled his approval.

He had monitored the bandits' thoughts over time. No one hearing Spercine's words had doubted her for a moment after seeing a few examples of the power she wielded. They did not know or care how she accomplished the killings she used to demonstrate her effectiveness. Their concern lay with their greed and the possible gains in wealth and power, more than how she had been able to kill exactly when and who they requested. They filed from the hall at her signal.

The overlord of the largest band, Gangkor, returned to the rented hall to seek out Spercine. The empty hall surprised and troubled him. Wathdure smiled from the shadows at the murderer's trepidation. Consternation grew on the bandit's face when his guards reported no one leaving the hall other than his peers. He joined several others talking in a group a short distance from the hall, but did not participate in the discussion other than to acknowledge their greetings. Wathdure watched as his mien masked any troubled feelings. Neither Gangkor nor Wathdure missed one of his many bodyguards.

Wathdure, a shadow within shadows, watched unseen and became amused at the conversations of the various small groups of men. He marked well the ones he decided would be of the greatest value to him. He believed Shadure would be pleased. The first raids would start on schedule.

8

LENZEL struggled. He moved through the brush and high grass silently without giving his position away. He no longer envied those creatures that moved with stealth on the ground. His stomach hurt! This did not number among the official tests; he had completed those. He must reach his objective undetected and take an item of note to this encampment. His light skin and red hair had been altered for the first time to match other members of his clan. No one would suspect he might do so. He advanced on the camp of the mock enemy. The ground remained rough. Stones and thorns punctured through his shirt like his concentration.

He stilled, slowing his breathing and heart rate as taught. Peaceful power flooded him. He opened his clenched eyes and sent his awareness outward. Amazement filled him while he identified the stimuli that returned to him. He knew the men and dogs' positions. Odors drifted to him for analysis, giving him the position of the cook's fire and the latrines. The horses' picket line lay to his left. He crawled in that direction.

His own odors were those of the clan and he had ridden some of the horses. Equine curiosity became their only response to his sudden appearance. He tied a slipknot to the picket line that held tightly to a thin, dark-stained cord, then repeated the procedure at the other end of the rope. Orange powder spilled from his pouch to form a small mountain on a cleared piece of ground to his side. The fuse would not give off light and the flint spark caught on the first try, much to his surprise. The ground around the encampment proved rough like his approach; by the time he crawled behind the operations tent, his shirt practically had no front left and several scratches to his abdomen bled and became quite irritating. His diversion proved to be more than adequate. The explosion sounded louder than he had anticipated. The horses thundered off at a full gallop, warriors ran from their tents to put out the fire and search for horses in the dark, and at last, he heard the voice of the clan leader, Rulac, in the distance.

A shuddering lamp provided little light inside the operations tent. A large map with the strategy of attack for the next day's planned exercise covered the lone table at the center of the tent. Lenzel rolled the map, slid it into the leather container across his back, and replaced it with blank paper. Fire spread quickly from the lamp oil he spilled along the top and sides of the table as he quickly left, again on his belly. Finally, trees surrounded him and Challenger whuffed a greeting. Lenzel led the stallion for a mile before mounting and riding to his encampment.

His commander's eyebrows rose when pulled from sleep and his tent. "Lenzel, you best have good reason for this!"

Lenzel smiled and pulled Mecqua hastily toward their operations tent. Mecqua's eyes narrowed when he saw blood on Lenzel's rippled abdominal muscles and scratches across the taut pectoral muscles. He made no comment.

Lenzel brought the lamps up inside the operations tent and spread the map and plan of attack across a worktable. He explained his actions during the night. His final words filled with enthusiasm and mirth. Mecqua's eyes sparkled when the ramifications of Lenzel's timing registered in his mind. Their camp already stirred for a new day of battle games—games in which he must defend. Rulac had beaten Mecqua's warriors badly last season. They remained longtime friends, but Rulac had teased Mecqua unmercifully. Now, with little time left, Rulac would not be able to change plans and Mecqua became certain, from the difficulty of the plan, that Rulac did not have a contingency plan. Mecqua questioned Lenzel several times about the fire. Lenzel's answers assured that Rulac had been in the operations tent and had rushed out during the diversion. A jostling of the table could well have caused the *accident*.

Mecqua gave a happy snort and walked to a chest along one side of the tent. He withdrew one item that Lenzel could not see and returned, grinning. He held his hand out. Lenzel put his hand under his leader's hand. The warrior's band dropped into his hand and he let go a warrior's cry of joy.

"Lenzel, your first order as a true warrior of the clan is to rouse my captains and send them here. The second order is for you to see the healers when the first order is accomplished. I have great joy in your deeds, but it may not be good to boast of them for a few weeks. I will make sure you get the credit when the time is right."

Lenzel left at a run on hearing Mecqua's chortling, turning into a full-breathed laugh at his yipping sounding through the camp.

He approached the healer's tent feeling more confident than he had ever felt before. His blood did not come from the High Desert People's clans. His infant cries had brought a warrior to investigate and found him in a covered portion of a wagon, not long after bandits had slaughtered his parents. They caught the bandits several days later. A Spirit Worker of Desert's Ire had easily pulled the memories of the bandit's leader from him. She brought him to tears by revealing those things that tormented his mind and drove him with hate. He welcomed the warrior's blade that cut his throat. The clan's Hide of Spirits received the name given to the infant, Lenzel.

His red hair, blue eyes, and light skin made him a social outcast and Lenzel's youth did not proceed with pleasant experiences at times—many times, in fact. His slight build invited provocations from stronger boys. In answer to his tormentors, Lenzel instinctually did the right thing. He exercised his muscles, learned the many ways of fighting that the clans used for defense and attack, and cheerfully tackled the hardest chores. Over time, he became an integrated part of his peers. Albeit, not before imparting several black eyes and bloody noses on his challengers. He became accepted; however, he never found that acceptance in himself. He entered warrior's training at the earliest possible moment.

Lenzel's smile reflected his joy at seeing Ellrill checking the supply of herbs used for poultices when he entered the healer's tent. He entered silently and watched her from behind. He believed her to be the most beautiful of the maidens in a people known for pleasing features.

She straightened and her lyrical voice drifted to him. "Lenzel, you can come the rest of the way into the tent if that is your goal."

Lenzel sputtered. He had never realized his body gave off a different odor than his companions'. No one would have noticed the difference without being very close and intimate. Ellrill had an advanced and well-used sense of smell. It provided her with a talent for identifying and using herbs. Her mixtures became the best found in the clan. Lenzel shook his head in dismay at her abilities and walked to her side of the tent. Ellrill gave a small cry of alarm when she turned to him. "By the Sprit of the Holy, what has happened?"

Lenzel said nothing. He opened his hand revealing his warrior's band. Pleasure escaped Ellrill and enforced Lenzel's joy. Her smile suddenly reflected shyness she had never shown before. "Let me tend your wounds and then I will tie your warrior's knot."

He smothered his joy while removing his shirt—or what was left of it—and turned to Ellrill, hesitantly. Reserve did not number among his accomplishments. Offering to braid his first warrior's knot revealed her gentle feelings for him in a new way.

Lenzel felt his muscles tighten and relax while Ellrill gently bathed his chest and abdomen. Fingers lingered lightly on his muscles a few seconds more than necessary. Lenzel felt one set of muscles rising he definitely did not want Ellrill to notice. A thin line of perspiration formed on his brow. He jumped from the table when she applied the last bit of ointment and gave thanks that his leathers were tight and well made. Her grin made him wonder if she had noticed his discomfort...

She turned away and motioned him to a chair.

Lenzel sat without talking while Ellrill washed out the dye and combed his long hair. She hummed while she worked. He recognized the song and felt color rising on his face and ears. Slowly, he relaxed his mind and body. Ellrill took a long time to complete his warrior's knot, something he knew she had done often and quickly for her father. He had no experiences on which to base the time required and quietly enjoyed the attention he received from her. Suddenly, he tensed. *This is Ellrill...touching...me. Her hands are soft and feel so good.* He remembered his earlier embarrassment.

Ellrill's hands stopped. He felt coolness across the back of his neck and belatedly realized the lack of his thick hair that no longer went to the middle of his back. Ellrill's voice had none of her usual assurance. "Lenzel, I have a warrior's gift if you will accept it."

Shock registered in his mind. She offered a commitment not given lightly. It made his heart soar. He looked up into large brown eyes he had drowned in from afar. "How, how, did you know?"

Some of Ellrill's natural assertiveness returned. "You

think I did not notice the way you looked at me? You think I did not know who left me flowers and spice cakes?"

Lenzel rose from the chair and took her into his arms. He hugged her gently and rubbed his hands across her back. Their kiss felt of testing and newness. The second kiss came heartier with emotions neither of them completely understood, but enjoyed all the same. He broke contact with her and held her at arm's length. Then, looking at him longingly, she pulled him in for another kiss.

Lenzel's voice cracked with tension. "Your father!"

Welquo stood high in the clan's leadership, adept in the mysteries of the clan. He had lately spent much time in service, a service that many rumored to be to the Highest One's benefit. He projected a stern countenance and was known to be protective of his daughter.

Ellrill displayed a degree of coyness Lenzel had never seen. "My father gives his blessing in my warrior's gift."

That relayed all the information he needed. He swept her into his arms and they resumed learning the ways of kissing.

Nudity did not concern the High Desert People in bathing or swimming, but was never used provocatively. He had watched her watching him swim and sunbathe without her knowledge, he thought. Knowing she knew his body well and feeling the hardness of his strong body pressing against her became a heady brew, indeed. He felt hardness against her thigh that increased the power of the brew. Wisely though, he adopted a casual attitude.

Lenzel watched while she worked at her bench with his warrior's band, her gift. She crouched over, blocking his view. Shortly, she rose and held out his head strap with the deep red ruby that matched the color of his hair, expertly worked into the weave as if made with the stone in mind. She turned him away from her while she worked the band through the multiple braids of hair and tied it securely at the back of his head. The band placed a new pressure and weight; it pleased him as a physical reminder that he had completed his training well ahead of his peers.

He turned to the maiden that had captured his heart years ago. Bending forward, he gently kissed her lips. The words he found did not please him, but his mind had become nearly a blank. "I have a maiden's gift for you if you are desirous of it."

Her eyes gave him the answer he hoped for. He opened his pouch tied to his leathers. She inhaled sharply when he slowly pulled a chain of gold links from the pouch. She caught her breath and lost it again when she saw the brilliant multifaceted sapphire held by a finely worked gold frame. He offered it to her and knew then, he offered his heart as well.

"Lenzel, you know what it means if I accept such a gift?" she said, stunned.

"I have loved you ever since I can remember. It is merely a poor expression of my feelings."

The sapphire's size easily surpassed any she had ever seen, and proved similar to the ruby in size. Its worth soared high in her expectation and she never dreamed Lenzel had acquired such wealth.

"I obtained them on my warrior's journey. I was lucky. I have more gold that will give us a good start and I have the skins for a fine tent. I have broken a mare for you and I think you will like her. She is a deep brown with a white blaze on her face. I…I love you, Ellrill. I yearn for your love in return."

She answered in a soft whisper, "I do not know when I first knew I loved you. Three years ago, I realized I had loved you for some time. You have always amazed me. And this, with all else that you achieved…" —She held the chain and pendant of azure fire to the light streaming into the tent— "…is more than I could have ever imagined."

He took the chain from her, placed it over her head, pulling her long black braided hair through, and settled it on her neck. The heavy chain and stone nestled between her breasts, revealing more than she wanted. "Maybe it would be best if I wore the sapphire inside my shirt."

"Maybe it would be best if you showed it only to your father?"

Ellrill started to protest, but then, Lenzel's wisdom must have become clear to her and she nodded her acquiescence. "I will come to you when your tent is raised. It will be with father's blessing."

The sounds of much activity reached them. Lenzel left her with another gentle kiss and hurried to where he knew he would be of use. He found it hard to concentrate.

The day passed in a blur of images and things done that he seemed to complete in a daze, or so he believed. In reality, he performed his assignments as he received them with alacrity. Moreover, if it counted as the best day of his life, it became Rulac's worst day. He did not change his battle plans, accepting the fire as an accident. The damage became clear before he realized his mistake. His warriors returned covered in the yellow dust of blunted arrows used in the mock battles.

It came as no surprise when Lenzel arrived at Mecqua's tent and found Rulac's totem mark before him. He and his captains would have made their way to Mecqua's camp and joined in their celebration as expected. Mecqua would be gracious, as he had been in the past. They would both drink too much of the strong brandy from Wellsport and regret it in the morning. The day after next would be time enough for him to start planning the next battle.

9

JAROD'S party made their way onto the plateaus of the High Desert. They traveled less than a mile before warriors met them. Each approached him on horseback and made the same proclamation: "My blood is yours, Highest One." Then, they went on to Travis and exclaimed, "My Spirit is in your keeping, Highest of Light." By early evening, the warriors led them to a box canyon where a large camp had been prepared and the smells of the spicy recipes made their mouths water in anticipation.

They traveled from camp to camp for a week before arriving at the large City of the Desert. The thick walls of the buildings with their elaborate ventilation would be a welcome change from the blazing sun and the cold desert nights. Paint did not weather well in the High Desert. Buildings painted only with one to three horizontal stripes, one foot in height and in the brilliant colors of desert flowers, spread out before them along precise geometric lines.

The warrior priests had never seen the City of the Desert and were awed by its rough splendor. They followed a wide avenue to the center of the city where Segquo's palace and administration buildings stood behind a wall twenty feet high built in a perfect circle. Four gates rose, spaced at the cardinal points of the world: north, east, south and west. The insides of plain buildings came alive with vivid colors expressed through fired tiles on the floor and parts of the walls in pleasing and often amazing patterns. Graceful pottery in startling hues accented rooms with desert flowers and cacti. The men were sent to private quarters with waiting baths.

Segquo joined the party and personally escorted Jarod to his suite that he had come to know well. Their conversation remained light and Segquo gave none of the polite signs of the High Desert People that would indicate an emergency.

Jarod would receive a full report after he bathed and rested. Rich, spicy foods with cool wines presented in an amazing variety waited for the evening and afterwards, they would meet. They would travel on to one of the battle camps within a day, two at the most, and the priests would be given over to training they had never imagined. It would be bewildering and difficult on them. Their loftiness would be short lived with a strange, new way of thinking and use of their physic skills. Travis would stay behind at the palace and consult with Carille, Spirit Leader of the High Desert People. Jarod had promised Kyle an interview with Carille if she permitted it. Jarod held her in his highest regard and spoke of her in reverent terms, always quietly, gently. *Will this at least, go as we plan?* he wondered.

* * *

JAROD finished his first glass of wine long after the feasting concluded. Kyle, too, had imbibed sparingly. Jarod started and sucked in a deep breath, then whispered to him, "Carille will see you now."

Kyle felt his surprise turn to anxiousness, while he followed Jarod through several long corridors. The colors gradually softened when they approached a large door worked in brass and decorated in gold and silver geometric designs. Two Maidens of Desert's Ire stood before the door and quietly opened it for them to enter without a word. Kyle remembered Jarod's description of Carille as being breathtakingly beautiful and felt delighted to meet the mysterious woman.

They entered a room several degrees cooler than the rest of the palace. A woman floated above a bed behind a sheer curtain in the well-lit room. The curtain divided and drifted to the sides of the room, apparently without human intervention. Kyle had seen Jarod float while asleep and meditating, but this impressed him. Her head rose and she came to an angle that allowed her to see her guests easily and then—Kyle saw her! He did not hide his shock like he believed. It mattered not one bit. Carille read his emotions like a clear sign in the heavens.

Her high cheekbones and beautiful facial features became evident, or rather spoke of a beauty held long ago. She appeared the oldest person Kyle had ever seen! Jarod bowed his head in response to her acknowledgement and belatedly, Kyle followed suit.

Jarod's voice sounded as no more than a whisper— "Open your mind to her the way I showed you."

Kyle's vision blurred for an instant. He saw the most beautiful woman he could ever imagine when his vision cleared.

Her voice carried as tonal chimes, perfectly pitched. Words of a beauty Kyle could hardly believed formed in his mind.

"I welcome you, warrior. A danger comes from a person known but not seen for many years. The danger will pass with your compassion and a warrior made and bound to you. You will be at grave risk if your heart hardens. Your life will be long once you have passed this hurdle and the Dark's Source is defeated. The love you share with the Highest One does you great credit. Alas, you will find woman's love late in life. Fear not! One moment of love that great will last years before your rebirth and years after your death." A feeling of well-being fell over him so strong, it brought him to his knees. "Be well, warrior."

Kyle came away, barely aware that Jarod led him from the room with strong support. The loss of the beneficent emotions made him want to cry out in great despair.

Recovering quickly, he sucked in a lung full of cool air. He still could not talk; it would be impossible to voice his thoughts.

Jarod's smile remained sly, like his voice. "Do you think you could lose your heart to her?" Kyle nodded, weakly. "Well, you would not be the first, but I must warn you she is well over three hundred years old and does not get out much, at least, physically." Jarod chuckled at the amazement on Kyle's face. Then, his tone plunged in gravity. "Remember Wathdure's age and balance your desires."

* * *

JAROD stood silently in a shadowed alcove overlooking the main courtyard of Segquo's palace. He saw faces he knew come and go. Forrest Workman looked harried and sleepy. The man had wanted adventure when he and Gaz had recruited him three years earlier for service to the Seven Realms. Jarod expelled a sigh and wondered if his desire had found fulfillment.

Gal Jerome Kess delivered a pouch that Jarod knew would surely be in his room when he returned. Jerome had secured the evidence against High Lord Eric Mountglen in the murder of Jarod's wife. He also had been the one to find Mountglen's minion, Thord, who preyed on children, giving them to massive dogs to be pulled apart and eaten. Thord met his death by those same dogs. Jarod shuddered at the unpleasant memories and turned to deal with the contents of the pouch and messages the man, no doubt, had left behind.

His suite of rooms stayed cool and a welcome relief from the blazing sun's heat. Cool wines whet his palate and he partook of the beverage, feeling the heat of the day drain away. He found the pouch on the large desk in his reception room. As he reached for the bindings, an insistent knock pulled his eyes to the door.

Segquo entered and immediately bowed his head.

"Highest One, I despair at intruding. A dire message has arrived. Bandits have murdered the Lord of Boswell and his Lady." Jarod rose while the image of the lord and lady formed in his mind. "It becomes worse. This is what happened... Bandits cunningly set ambushes a few miles from the town. They killed and robbed the merchants that had been in Boswell for a regional fair and wedding. Many merchants have been slaughtered and few were left living. A merchant's bodyguard escaped and made his way to Lord Boswell's keep.

"Lord Boswell rode out with thirty men. The bodyguard led him to the ambush site, but they were hugely outnumbered. Lord Boswell sent his man to the keep to get his wife safely away. Lady Boswell refused to leave the keep. The messenger accompanied his lady to the high wall. They saw three large forces converging on the town. She sent Rakin, the messenger, to find the Guard.

"Rakin circled the keep and hid in the valley several hundred yards from it's walls. A servant escaped and found him there. The servant told Rakin that Lady Boswell had been set afire and thrown from the high wall. He also said the bandits bragged that their band numbered a thousand men."

Jarod closed his eyes and cursed to himself.

Segquo's voice held sadness. "Rakin left at once to reach the Guard. He found several detachments of guardsmen; they lay dead, robbed, and many had been mutilated."

Jarod opened his eyes and Segquo paused at what he saw in their depths. "No stray horses remained. Rakin arrived here an hour ago. Warriors brought him in and he could hardly speak from exhaustion. He rode his horse to death and they found him on foot at the edge of the rises to the plateaus. The healers are with him. He will recover. I have warriors outside to carry any messages you might need to send, Highest One."

Segquo bowed his head, appearing more distraught than Jarod had ever seen the High Desert People's Leader. He motioned him to a chair and waved the warriors standing in the corridor to enter.

"Have the gal by the name of Jerome Kess brought here." One of the warriors left at a run. "Have the battle groups brought in." Kyle nearly got run over while the warrior and High Lord contested for the same door. Kyle stepped aside and let the warrior run. Jarod waved him to a chair. "Alert your Birdmaster that several messages will be sent shortly."

Another maiden took to the halls at a run. Jarod sat— or rather, collapsed—into his chair. He drained the rest of the wine and looked at Kyle when he lowered the cup, following his gaze to Segquo. The old man's eyes had glazed over and he sat deathly still. He stirred after a moment and slumped against the chair's back.

"Highest One, Carille has received a most unusual dream message. Seven ships, larger than any ever seen before, approach Wellsport. Six war ships escort a truly marvelous ship. The richness of the ship has never been encountered and High Lord Wells is most impressed."

A Lieutenant of the Guard stood at the door, trying to recover his breath. "My Zenith, messages have arrived from the Spires by bird. They report two major attacks by large bands of bandits in Eastfall and Trueridge. Each band numbered a thousand men, or more."

The lieutenant suddenly realized he had interrupted his Zenith Lord without permission and groaned softly to himself. Jarod paid no mind to the man's distress, remaining deep in deliberation.

A familiar twinge pulled at his mind, moments later. He opened himself to his power and followed the thread of thought to Deion. *My Zenith, I am on my way to the Tower. Gaz intercepted me. Taylor, the bodyguard of a bandit chieftain named Gangkor, who has previously sold reliable information to Gaz, came with him. He reports a gathering of bands numbering over three thousand. Wathdure directs their efforts, planning, and coordination! I mind-linked with Taylor and can locate him when needed.*

10

LENZEL gingerly felt in his pouch and withdrew a Silver Star, silver in color, but made of steel. Its finely honed star-points bit deep into its target. Lenzel's hand flowed from the pouch, a bright arc of silver light shot to its destination, and struck solidly into the pattern of previously thrown slivers of death. Mecqua approached from the south, smiling when he saw the results of Lenzel's practice.

"A nice pattern. Few of us have attempted to master the art of Desert's Ire's weapons. You have done well, Lenzel."

Flashing white teeth spread across the new warrior's smile. Mecqua rarely gave compliments and he basked in his commander's praise.

"Lenzel, I have requested the honor of bestowing upon you the battle cuffs you have had made. If you agree, the ceremony will be held tonight." This amounted to great honor, indeed. A warrior's father or brother usually acted the part. Lenzel, having neither, gave little consideration to the ceremony. Its importance had grown in the past few weeks while Ellrill spent more time with him. Battle cuffs held beauty and death. Each supported a brace of throwing knives and a garrote, tightly fitted to the warrior's forearm. Constructed of strong, sturdy leather, a flap covered the weapons when not needed. Lenzel's expertise with throwing knives and Silver Stars marked him as a dangerous warrior. Mecqua's countenance took on an air of seriousness that belied the happiness of the coming ceremony.

"Ellrill has given you a warrior's gift." Mecqua eyed

briefly the sparkling red stone in Lenzel's warrior band.
"You have given her a maiden's gift and both have been
blessed by Welquo. I spoke with Welquo today…" The
smile vanished from Lenzel's face. "We depart for the
City of the Desert late tomorrow and will go with the
Zenith's Guard and the warrior priests to do battle with
the enemies of the Seven Realms. Welquo gives his
blessing to Ellrill and your declaration of oneness if you
and she wish to forego the usual period of waiting."

Lenzel's head swam in delirious joy and elation. He
knew Welquo would never have given his blessing if
Ellrill had not agreed. "I…I…must go to Ellrill. I am in
favor of making the declaration tonight if she agrees."

"Well, young wolf, gather your stars and see to your
needs. The ceremony will happen at sunset."

Lenzel, seeing the sincere pleasure expressed on his
commander's face ran before Mecqua finished speaking.
He barely escaped cutting his hands on the Silver Stars,
more than once.

He easily found Ellrill; he knew she would be sorting
herbs in the main healer's tent. She rushed into his arms,
tears sweeping across her face. Lenzel kissed her and
tasted the tears. "You cry?"

"Oh, my warrior, my love, I cry from great joy that we
will declare our oneness and I cry with great sorrow that
you will leave for the path that death often frequents."

Lenzel closed his arms around her and ached to make
an enclosure of protection that would shield her forever.
They held each other briefly and then made their separate
ways to prepare for the ceremony.

Three families had participated in raising Lenzel. The
matriarchs and patriarchs of each family would play parts
in the ceremony. Ellrill's mother had died. Welquo and a
niece would play the required roles for her. A flurry of
activity stirred the camp. Preparations got under way not
only for the ceremony, but the uprooting of the camp had

begun.

Lenzel found the three matriarchs waiting for him at his tent, one he had known as Grandmother and two he had known as Mother. They each gave their blessings to Lenzel and then surprised him with two sets of warrior's leathers. The workmanship and leather of one set had been fashioned of the highest quality and beautifully tooled with a deathcat design that covered his left arm and back. The other set came from the same high quality, but looked plain and stained with earth colors for stealth. Each family wanted the honor of providing the one thing that expressed his stature as a warrior. Thus, they combined their resources and had the leathers made.

The three patriarchs presented him with a long knife, a longbow with a quiver full of arrows, and a full pouch of Silver Stars. The leathers had overwhelmed Lenzel; the new weapons presented to him by the men that had influenced and taught him the values of a warrior nearly brought him to tears. They had profoundly honored him with the gifts, beyond his expectations. He rushed to dress in his new leathers and wore the set with the deathcat. Emerging from his tent at sunset, he hurried to the center of the camp. The warriors had gathered and Lenzel became surprised to find many of his peers had joined the ceremony to wish him well.

Mecqua arrived when the last rays of sun showed on the camp. The brief ceremony held Lenzel in awe while he repeated the oaths to the Light's Source, the Highest One, and the clan. Each warrior locked forearms with him and they swore to protect each other in battle. Afterwards, the young men Lenzel had known all his life gathered around him, their respect for his new status plainly evident. This not only pleased him, but also profoundly affected him. Their obvious pride in his accomplishments sent his confidence soaring. The noise of the celebration quieted with a piercing note from a silver disk suspended by a leather thong struck by Welquo.

He stood on the northern side of the blazing central fire pit. Lenzel's companions parted and he made his way to Welquo from the eastern side, dropping to his knees on the fine blanket woven with a vivid scene of a sunrise using many desert colors. Welquo struck the silver disk again and all eyes turned to the west. Ellrill walked from the shadows with her cousin as escort. The clan members sighed almost as one when they saw her. Her inner beauty glowed and enhanced her physical beauty all the more. She wore a buttery soft leather gown, bleached white. Fine blue embroidery sculpted the mirror image of the deathcat worked into Lenzel's leathers. She knelt facing Lenzel when her cousin moved to the right and behind Welquo.

That ceremony, too, completed in moments; they each declared their oneness with the other and recited the vows of fidelity. Their kiss at the end of the ceremony brought sighs from the older women and whistles and loud yips from the younger men.

Much remained to be done before leaving the next day. The prepared feast included many delicious favorites. Normally, the feasting would have gone on throughout most of the night with much wine consumed. Lenzel and Ellrill left after the toasting had finished among the many barbs of good-natured comments. Lenzel, glad that he must not wait to join with Ellrill, loathed the need for leaving her after only one night.

They tied the tent flap closed and stood looking at one another for a moment. Their smiles melted into kisses and gentle caresses. Then, pulling apart, Ellrill began to remove Lenzel's leathers. She pulled at the ties of her gown when he stood bare above the waist. Her gown dropped to her hips and she gasped when he pulled her back into his arms. The rest of the undressing became a blur of emotions, caresses, and passion. Their coupling came at times ardent and at times gentle. They continued their lovemaking in a satisfying blissful response to each other's needs until they held one another, with him curled around her still body. Sleep found them quickly and peacefully.

He woke with the first sounds of the camp coming to life in the false dawn of the first day he would leave his life's mate. After dressing in the second set of leathers, he neatly and carefully packed his warrior's leathers. Ellrill woke when he finished and pulled him to her. Their embrace and kiss communicated mutual happiness and joy.

"My fine warrior, if we have too many nights like last night, I may never leave the tent."

Lenzel's quiet, pleasant laugh charmed her. "My beautiful mate, if we have too many nights like last night, we would be run out of the clan for never completing our parts of clan duties."

She had promised him that she would not make a fuss over their circumstances and joined him in the packing of their belongings. He struck the tent and settled their packs and tent on two packhorses, then leaned down and whispered he would return shortly. Ellrill watched in confusion while he rode Challenger away from the camp. Her mother and father approached and they quickly fell into conversation.

Lenzel returned, leading a sand colored mare with a white blaze on its face without her notice. She turned when they were almost on top of her and stopped speaking with her mouth left open. Lenzel dismounted his huge dun and red colored stallion and pressed the reins into her hands. When she stroked the mare's face, she received a mild whicker for her trouble. The mare nudged her when she stopped, begging for more. Her laugh and obvious joy brought a warm glow to him.

She whirled to face him and hugged him fiercely. "Lenzel, she is beautiful. I had no inkling of her beauty."

Lenzel helped her mount and her happy smile overflowed through him. He prayed that his gift diminished the hurt of parting.

Welquo called the warriors to him. "We ride to battle! Clear your hearts and minds, resolving to our purpose, and know you are in the care of Light's Source."

The warriors rode out toward the City of the Desert, while the rest of the clan rode toward their summer village.

Lenzel wondered when they would see each other again.

11

Two years later

JAROD sat at his desk making notes for the conference that would convene in an hour. Attendants busily packed the things he required for the journey immediately after the event. He felt Kyle's presence and waved him in before he could knock on the open door.

He wondered if Kyle would ever be able to become that sensitive to his surroundings. His daily practice with his Stone's power had increased his abilities, but he had much to accomplish to match Deion's abilities or me. *Perhaps, that too, would become possible.* Kyle stopped in front of the desk and bowed his head.

Jarod looked up, nodded, and waved Kyle to a chair beside the desk. He finished his notes a few minutes later and gave the other man is full attention. Kyle's voice still held tinges of surprise that none but Jarod might have noticed. "I received a message from the Spires a few minutes ago. My brother, Peter, presented himself at the gates requesting to see me. Gaz told him my location and Peter stated he would look for me here. A fast courier bringing the other dispatches brought the message to me. Peter should arrive before we leave if your schedule remains the same."

Jarod smiled. "Then prepare to meet your brother; the schedule remains the same. I will leave immediately after the conference for Wellsport. You will take command of our various groups. Have the battle groups arrived?"

"The last group reported in as I came here. They are a remarkably, trained force, physically and mentally. We believed that the training we received over the last three years came from a few masters of their techniques. Most of the men I saw practicing from the battle groups over the past few days are nearly their masters' equal and the Maidens of Desert's Ire are unbelievable, but then, you already knew that. One could not ask for a better force.

"Much of the training had been passed on to the Guard through Zack and Currat. I understand my spies are glad to be back in the Seven Realms. Ursel has remained in Ozlid to lead efforts there. He has done well and I'm quite pleased with him. Their new methods included in the overall training are well received. There have been fights over which boulder will get the training next. Your overall plan has prevailed and proven quite efficient.

"Forrest has done well in integrating skills throughout the different forces and he's biting at the bit to see some action. He may yet live to regret those sentiments. He has outgrown some of his impulsiveness to jump in over his head." Kyle chuckled and Jarod smiled.

Jarod tapped the glass pen he had been using against his chin before speaking. "Our main problem is stealth. Gaz' plan is good and I have faith in it. I want you to stay in close contact with Segquo as things develop. This will be the first challenge operating with so many varied groups. It is essential that we keep Shadure from discovering what we are about until it is too late. We have set out the bait; now let us see how many rats we can kill.

"Deal with your brother as you see fit. You will have my backing in whatever you decide. Now, I have a few things to accomplish before the conference."

They rose and left together.

Jarod went to Segquo's reception room and found the old man in a trance. Sitting down in a plush chair, he quietly waited for it to end.

Segquo raised his head and smiled a greeting at him.

"It is as you suspected, Highest One. The wonderful ship carries a sovereign of great wealth and beauty. She has remained aboard her ship and High Lord Wells has sent your instructions. Ta-Cern will act as translator if that pleases you. I believe you have quite a treat awaiting you at Wellsport, one that you deserve and need. Carille and I think you have been pushing yourself too hard. We are concerned for you."

Jarod had come to love the old man in the last three years and would have hugged him if it would not destroy his reserve before an important conference. The High Desert People maintained quiet formalities underneath a veneer of coolness. Their devotion to their Highest One bordered on obsession, but then, they understood that the future of the Seven Realms rested in his and the Darkslayer's hands alone and if they survived, it would be through his efforts and those of his son when his time came.

"I suppose we should convene the conference and let me be on my way to Wellsport."

They walked together to the large conference room, speaking little.

As they approached the double doors, two Guardsmen snapped to position and saluted. They stood, already nervous from Kyle's presence, waiting on the Zenith Lord.

Kyle spoke softly when they drew near. "Everyone is here. I think there will be few questions." Jarod nodded and the guards opened the double doors.

"Focus on the Zenith Lord!" rang through the room as Jarod entered. The Apex officers snapped to attention and the various groups in the room paid their obsequious movements as their protocol demanded. Jarod nodded in recognition and walked directly to his plush chair—nearly a throne—and sat. The men and women, arrayed before him at a large semi-circular table, did not speak.

Jarod sat facing them with Kyle at his right and Segquo at his left. He nodded again and the rest of the members of the conference took their seats. Jarod's eyes fell on each man and woman as he swept the table from left to right. Cordel, the warrior priest who had proven to be the most talented under Deion, sat with two priests to his right that Jarod did not know. Next was Debgril, leader of Desert's Ire, with two maidens to her right.

Jarod had to suppress a chuckle at the visual differences between the groups. The warrior priests in their gray robes with black trim looking as if they had never done a day's work—far from the truth—and the women of Desert's Ire looking as if they could kill you in an instant, which proved quite true. Each of the Apex officers crossed their arms, their fists at heart level, and bowed their heads. Jarod knew each of them quite well, as he knew all of his generals. Mecqua and Lenzel came next. Lenzel's question of the need for his presence showed quite evidently on his young face. The remaining battle group commanders followed and Forrest Workman hastened to the last seat. Jarod suppressed another chuckle at Forrest's demeanor. The adventurer who wanted and begged for excitement looked as if he'd found all he sought and then some.

He cleared his throat. "The false information is disseminated as we planned. Segquo will brief the battle commanders immediately following this meeting. High Lord Byrne will meet with Lenzel shortly for a special assignment." Lenzel stared wide-eyed for a second at the pronouncement. "Are there any questions about the plans?"

Debgril looked to her sides before speaking. "Highest One, Desert's Ire's role is somewhat limited in scope. We would like the Highest One to know that we stand ready as needed."

Jarod smiled. "Debgril, believe me; you have not been

slighted." He waved away her protest before she could speak. "Desert's Ire will have a large role in the battles to come. Like Lenzel, Desert's Ire will play a part that will require formidable skills that it can perform better than anyone here."

Debgril bowed her head with pride.

If I must take you kicking and screaming myself to the duty you may not want... Jarod mused.

"You have labored hard on these plans and have coordinated your individual strengths to form a stronger whole. I will return here as soon as I have completed the State's affairs at Wellsport. We wish you well!" He rose and departed the room before most rose from their bows.

* * *

THE members of the conference went their separate ways to prepare to leave on their missions. Kyle stopped Lenzel on his way out, looking at the ruby in his headband. "That is quite a nice stone. I did not know that those were mined near here."

"High Lord, I am honored that you noticed. It is a rather long story of how I came by it. It is a reward of sorts."

Kyle looked perplexed and wished that Jarod had not left, yet. "Lenzel, have you noticed anything unusual since you put it on?"

Now, Lenzel looked perplexed. "High Lord, I have not thought much about it, but I know that in my recent practices I have not missed a throw." Lenzel looked a little sheepish. "I am good with bow and arrow and Silver Stars, but I *do* miss now and again. Lately, even on a bad toss, I hit my mark. It is a bit uncanny and I do not know how to explain it."

Kyle considered for a moment before speaking, making Lenzel a little nervous. He feared he might have done something wrong in taking the stones.

"Lenzel, I want you to try something, for me." Lenzel

nodded his agreement before Kyle finished speaking. "Let me start by saying that I am not an expert in Stones with power, although, I am joined with one of the Great Stones and am still learning more of its uses every day." Lenzel's eyes widened. I received my Stone shortly before coming here with the Zenith Lord. He has been teaching me in its use. I want you to concentrate on a single item that you think is pretty: a flower, a piece of art, or perhaps one of your people's fabulous sand paintings. I want you to relax when you have it firmly in your mind and let your consciousness *float* above it."

"I know; it is a technique we use in our meditation."

"Good, once you feel relaxed, *float* downward, into yourself. Search for a feeling of power and wellbeing. Let it flow into your body."

Kyle sat back and watched the young man sit cross-legged and close his eyes. It did not take long for a reaction to occur. Lenzel's eyes popped open with a look of disbelief. Kyle chuckled. "Well, my young warrior, I believe you have a Stone of power! The problem is that we do not have time to train you properly in its use. I can only tell you to let its power sustain you in times of stress and use it as you have been doing, albeit unknowingly, to guide your weapons. I will arrange for your training as soon as this current problem is settled. Just realize that the Stone will not hurt you and wear it wrapped around a part of your body that keeps it hidden. Your warrior's band will suffice for now. The Zenith will want a report on how you came to own it."

The question on Lenzel's face became easy to read. "Let me tell you about your mission." They both smiled when they exited the room an hour later. Lenzel went to join the two members of his party and Kyle went to take the last leisurely bath he would have for a long time.

After soaking in the warm water for a while, he reluctantly left the tub and dried off. He put on a clean privatecloth, threw the drying cloth over his shoulder, and walked toward his bedroom when a knock came at his door. He stuck his head into the small reception room and called, "Enter!" The door opened slowly and a man stepped into the room, closing the door behind him. Kyle stepped farther into the reception room. He believed he knew who'd called.

Peter Byrne watched as Kyle stepped into the reception room. "By the Light's Source, Kyle, you are beautiful!" He stood there looking at Kyle with his mouth slightly open.

"Make yourself comfortable, Peter. I will be with you in a moment."

His brother fell into a plush chair and Kyle retreated into his bedroom. He glanced into the mirror, making sure the drying cloth had covered the Warrior's Stone. He dressed quickly in his uniform and returned to the reception room.

Peter rose as Kyle drew near. He looked up into Kyle's eyes, stepped forward, and embraced him. Kyle felt strange, having physical contact with a brother he had not seen in nineteen years. Still, he found himself returning the embrace. Peter broke away and sat back into the plush chair. Tears streaked his face, surprising Kyle. Peter did a poor job of trying to relax. Kyle sat back and watched him struggle with something important. Peter jerked once as if an insect had bit him, and then seemed to come to a decision made.

"Kyle, there is something I must tell you and afterwards, I will leave if you wish." Kyle gave him a wary look, but said nothing. "Father sent me here to get into your good graces and fight alongside you in battle. He..." Peter looked squarely into his eyes. "He wants me to kill you when we are fighting." It took all Peter could do to get the last of his words out and then, they were a soft whisper. A whisper Kyle had no trouble hearing.

He did not take his eyes from his brother. "Go on," he said, his voice distant and quiet.

Peter sat on his hands, a habit Kyle remembered him doing under stress. "Kyle, I treated you badly, but I have never hated you like Father does. I could never do anything to harm you, much less kill you. I have been so proud of your achievements." He looked at his brother with new eyes. "Kyle, you are…radiant. An aura around you exudes power. I have never seen anything like it."

Kyle clasped his hands with the index fingers pointing up and tapped his chin in a slow, calming rhythm. He did not speak for several moments while his brother squirmed.

Peter's thoughts came erratically to Kyle, something new he didn't expect. *Great Light's Source, I walk into the Seven Realms' second most powerful man's rooms and announce that I am sent to kill him! How stupid can I be? I could have at least gotten to know him before he has me thrown into a cell. I never should have come! I should have taken Father's wrath and stood up to the conniving bastard for once.* His thoughts stopped when Kyle rose.

Kyle opened the door to his suite of rooms and motioned for one of the warriors that stood on guard duty. He whispered for a long moment. The warrior's eyes widened and she went off at a run, barely making a sound in her soft leather boots. Kyle walked to a credenza. "You must be tired. Would you like a drink, perhaps some food?" he asked over his shoulder.

Kyle heard a weak "Yes," in reply. He poured them each a tall mug of white wine and handed one to Peter.

Walking to where Peter sat, he commanded, "Stand up!"

Peter complied, looking up at a man that could easily kill him, instantly. Kyle put his arms under his brother's armpits and easily lifted him until their eyes were level. "I have never hated you, big brother." Then, he kissed him on the cheek while Peter relaxed and tears rolled down his cheeks once more. Kyle placed him back on the floor.

Peter laughed. Kyle looked questioningly at him. "You would make three, or more, of me and you call me, 'big brother.'"

Kyle chuckled. "Let us go and find some food, brother," he said with a grin. He opened the door to the corridor and found four warrior's waiting. Kyle nodded once. "This is my brother; he is welcomed here."

The warriors relaxed and melted away.

12

A Desert's Ire Maiden rode at a canter toward Jarod's party. She stopped and flashed a hand signal to Illche, principal bodyguard to the Highest One. Jarod had learned much of the unspoken language and got the gist of the message. A detachment of High Lord Well's guard awaited him over the next hill. Illche smiled when she noted the understanding in Jarod's face.

The detachment dismounted, dropped to their knees, crossed their arms across their chest, and bowed when Jarod came into sight.

"Rise!"

The Captain of the Guard for Deepwells strode forward. "My Zenith, High Lord Wells awaits your pleasure. The Empress of the Aviaries of Heaven awaits your arrival on her ship. She has entertained High Lord Wells on two occasions when I came here to await you. The empress eagerly seeks your presence. My lord asks if I may send a bird to announce your arrival."

Jarod nodded his permission. The escort mounted and rode behind while they continued toward the ocean at a brisk pace. Jarod knew the rise of the next hill provided a view of Wellsport's harbor and he felt the impatience of seeing the Aviaries of Heaven's ships, not unlike the empress' desire to see him.

Jarod's sharp intake of breath, seemingly noticed only by Illche, sent a warm feeling through him. He found the magnificent ships before him beyond his expectations. They proceeded to High Lord Well's keep sitting on a hill at the base of a sheer cliff.

Jarod motioned the High Lord to rise before he had a

chance to kneel properly and the two men grasped forearms. No fanfare sounded his arrival, as ordered, and many of the keep's staff wondered whom the visitor might be. Wells ushered Jarod into his private study. Illche followed, satisfied herself of the room's orientation and withdrew, closing the door behind her.

High Lord Wells beamed a smile after Illche. "She seems quite efficient, my Zenith."

Jarod nodded as he took a plush chair. "She and her team are remarkable to say the least. Speaking of *remarkable*, tell me about the ships and the empress."

"My Zenith, that word does not go far enough to describe either of them. The ship's design is beyond my shipwrights' understanding. However, the empress commanded her captains to answer our questions and they are beginning to make sense of it. The empress is a competent ruler from what I have been able to understand from the men I have spoken with through Ta-Cern. Of course, his loyalty belongs completely to the empress. I found Ta-Cern to be an honorable man when he served as my Captain of the Guard and I do not believe he would lie to me concerning his empress. She holds you in awe and refers to you as the Visage of Visions. I am not sure what that means but she promised to explain everything once you arrive. I found no evidence of deceit. If she is lying about anything, she is far better than most."

Lord Wells' seneschal, who carried a tray of crystal wine decanters and crystal goblets, followed a knock at the door.

Wells raised his glass to his Zenith Lord after the fellow left. "My Zenith, I am honored to have you as my guest. How may I serve you?"

Jarod smiled. "Please send a message to the Empress of the Aviaries of Heaven announcing my arrival and my desire to meet with her at lastmeal, tonight. I need a bath and your seneschal's help to get my uniform in order. Will she request me to go there or are you to be host?" Jarod produced a sly smile that cut the sharpness of his words.

Wells chuckled. "My Zenith, I have the honor to host the two rulers of the majority of the landmass residing on this planet, if that is your wish." Jarod's raised eyebrow requested a response. "Serarelique is approximately the same size of the Seven Realms, from what I have been able to gather through Ta-Cern. They know of no other landmass that approaches our size. One of their ships sailed from the east and circumvented the world slightly below the equator. The captain stated he did not run into anything of magnitude on the five-year journey of exploration! They charted many islands and subcontinents."

Jarod could see that Wells greatly enjoyed himself. "Roberd, you are having much fun with this, are you not?"

Wells chuckled again and a warm glow of pleasure infused him from Jarod using his given name. "My Zenith, how can I not? These are truly dire times and one must find what amusements one can, while one can."

Jarod agreed while Wells led him to his suite of rooms and made the arrangements he'd requested. His bath, quickly drawn, relaxed him. He reached inside and let the familiar warmth of his power further assuage his tension. His uniform lay clean and crisp when he went from the refreshment room into the adjoining bedroom. Illche stood by the window.

"Highest One, the suite is secure." She turned around and faced Jarod's dripping body wrapped in a large drying cloth. She calmly walked to him, removed the cloth, and briskly dried his back without embarrassment to either of them. Part of their training required swimming in different scenarios. The High Desert People's casualness to nudity amused Jarod, as he envisioned his chief steward's response at such actions. He was not certain which would shock Rolo the most: The nudity in itself, or someone touching him in a familiar way without his express permission.

Jarod put on a privatecloth and black trousers, stockings, and highly polished boots. He slipped a crimson wormcloth shirt over his head and sat while Illche expertly sleeked his long sandy blond hair back and into a warrior's knot. A thought came to him that he decided he must share with her. "I suspect there will be a great show of pomp tonight. The empress will undoubtedly have honor guards and I am sure that High Lord Wells will provide the same for me. In other words, there will be a lot of bare steel around me tonight if Serarelique's protocol is anything like ours. You and your team should expect this and not become concerned. I do not think the Empress of the Aviaries of Heaven traveled this far to cause me harm. Indeed, I represent some type of almost religious personage to them. I do not know exactly what to anticipate."

Illche thought a moment before answering. "Highest One, Desert's Ire will do nothing to cause you embarrassment. We will be discreet." Jarod knew no other concessions would be forthcoming and he did not want to order them to withdraw for the evening.

They would disobey me if I ordered them away and that may cause more problems than if they come. Perhaps they will fade into the background; the Light's Source knows they can when they wish to.

Jarod finished dressing and Illche had just hung his cape on his shoulders when Pecquin entered and signed that High Lord Wells awaited the Highest One in the outer room with a strangely dressed man.

He walked into the reception room of his suite and did not recognize Ta-Cern until he rose from his bow to the floor at his signal. The man wore his traditional dress as

Seeker of the Empire that Jarod found quite remarkable. Intricately woven platinum threads formed a headband holding exceedingly brilliant, long, and quite slender feathers in hues he had never seen. He wore a shirt and trousers made of a silver wormcloth. Platinum cuffs with a row of sapphires matched his belt. Boots, stitched with silver threads and silver metal tips and heels shimmered in the candlelight. A matching cape lined in black wormcloth completed his uniform.

"Ta-Cern, you look a little different from when we last met."

"Zenith Lord, I am again in the service of my cousin Va-A'Cil, Empress of the Aviaries of Heaven, known in other lands as Serarelique. However, the empress orders me to carry out your commands. You are the Visage of Visions that I may explain at your pleasure. My Empress sends her regards and, at your invitation, attends you tonight."

Jarod nodded and smiled.

"Zenith Lord, my empress seeks to offer you the wealth and power of the Aviaries of Heaven. These are as considerable as your own resources. There is one point she insists on before making this offer that I sincerely hope will not cause you embarrassment."

Ta-Cern paused until Jarod nodded for him to continue, wondering what condition she might place on her cooperation. Her wealth did not concern him. Her ships did.

"Zenith Lord, my empress must see the emerald in your chest for herself." Ta-Cern looked like he might have just asked for the wealth of the Seven Realms. His speech faltered as he hurried on. "Zenith Lord, please know that my cousin, the empress, means you no embarrassment. I am aware that the Seven Realms are not as casual about such things as our lands. We mean no disrespect!"

Jarod chuckled. "Ta-Cern, you are not familiar with *all* of our people. We take no offense and we will grant the empress' request." Ta-Cern looked as if the weight of the Seven Realms and the Aviaries of Heaven had disappeared from his shoulders. "Perhaps, you might inform us of the protocol we might follow to make the empress more comfortable in a strange land. We would not like to see her distraught."

Ta-Cern immediately recognized the use of what would be an Imperial Command in the Aviaries of Heaven. He relaxed considerably and chuckled, surprising Jarod and, it seemed, himself, too.

"I am sorry, my Zenith. I have spent the last several weeks teaching the Empress Va-A'Cil the protocol of the Seven Realms and some of the language. The empress is a quick study and I hope you will find her charming."

Jarod gave him a sly smile. "I appreciate your efforts. There is only one thing I must insist on."

Ta-Cern's expression changed to one of concern.

Jarod continued to smile. "I expect to meet your empress as an equal. I do not expect any obsequious display on her part."

The man's smile widened fully. "My Zenith, you do the empress honor. I will impart your desire to her and I am sure she will be most pleased."

Jarod then sent him off to confer with Lord Wells' seneschal and staff. He requested Lord Wells join him in his reception room and spent several hours bringing him current with events. He also outlined a plan that would require Serarelique's cooperation. At a certain point, one of Wells' staff arrived with a message that the Empress approached the keep. Neither had heard a fanfare and looked questioningly at one another. They left the Great Hall of the keep while Wells' seneschal whispered what to expect.

Jarod reached the hall and his fanfare sounded. All

those present bowed or saluted. Jarod wore the uniform of the supreme military commander of the Seven Realms. His hair shimmered in the candlelight and his eyes missed little. Several of those closest to him started when the force of his countenance fell on them. They blanched under the intensity of his eyes and many reevaluated their thoughts about their Zenith Lord, raising his status to awe-filled reverence.

A table covered in a linen cloth of the purest white sat on a raised dais with two ornate plush chairs of light oak with gold inlaid wood and crimson cushions, seat and back. Clear crystal goblets, gold utensils, and white plates resting on gold chargers and white napkins that matched the tablecloth lay folded in an elaborate design that piqued Jarod's curiosity. The doors to the Great Hall opened when he took his place before the dais. Two silver cushions lay on the floor in front of him.

Maids of the Empire entered and went to their covered harps while their male counterparts settled behind instruments unfamiliar to the people of Deepwells and Jarod. A strong mellow sound rose with a deep surging rhythm. Flutes joined in counterpoint with other string instruments. The full-bodied sounds floated across the hall and held its occupants spellbound. The size of the harps had caused a stir as their covers fell away and the maidens made ready to play.

Two of the honor guard entered in their traditional fustanella with only a full cape in silver to protect them from the chill. The long red, orange, and yellow feathers of their headdress barely moved. They marched with their swords held at arm's length lying across their palms. Jarod knew what to expect and still, the presence of the guards impressed him. They dropped in unison onto the cushions and bowed to the floor with their swords held out before them for five seconds. Jarod touched their swords when they rose. Each guard bowed their heads and then carefully sheathed their swords, unaware that five Maidens of Desert's Ire held Silver Stars at the ready.

The guards moved back approximately twenty feet and faced each other standing at position. The music changed to a smoother tempo and two nobles appeared at the doors.

High Lord Wells' major domo struck the floor three times and announced: "Ta-Roul, from the Noble House of the Heron, Noble of the Empire. Ta-Zeul, from the Nobel House of the Flamingo, Noble of the Empire!"

Jarod had never seen such fine wormcloth dyed in equally marvelous colors. The nobles walked at a stately pace to the cushions, dropped to their knees, placing their hands on the floor in front of them, and rested their heads on their hands for five seconds. They rose, nodded, and positioned themselves beside the guards, facing each other some ten feet apart. Their movements held great dignity that Jarod knew took a lifetime at court to accomplish.

The major domo's staff boomed against the marble floor. Ta-Dren, from the Noble House of the Swift, Noble of the Empire, and Ta-Yoon, from the Noble House of the Falcon, Noble of the Empire, followed their fellow nobles' example with the same time-refined grace and dignity.

Two of the large harps sounded with the other instruments, bringing lushness to the music. Jarod looked at the doors and smiled at Ta-Cern's entrance. He found the man's titles impressive: Ta-Cern, from the Noble House of the Hawk, Seeker of the Empire—and was not surprised when the Nobles of the Empire bowed as he walked toward the silver cushions. He held his bow for exactly three seconds, then rose.

Jarod's voice rang across the room with immediately recognized authority. "Ta-Cern, Friend of the Seven Realms." The proclamation seemed to take Ta-Cern by surprise and his eyes alone showed his joy. He moved backward and stood even with the nobles in the center, facing Jarod.

Lord Wells' honor guard entered in front of a draped sedan chair made of platinum inlaid wood with encrusted jewels forming fantastic designs of long feathers that Jarod knew must be accurate representations of beautiful plumage somewhere in Serarelique. Ten guards carried the sedan chair and set it at an angle behind Ta-Cern.

The harpists started cascading melodious notes that entranced their audience. String instruments began to fill in while the wind instruments chased them in intricate passages flowing together.

When the music died, Ta-Cern said, "Ca-Ra'IL, from the Noble House of the Stork, Truth Bearer of the Empire!"

A maiden approached and helped Ca-Ra'IL out of the sedan chair. Her resplendent countenance inspired more than a little envy from the ladies of the Seven Realms. Her beauty and figure presented a woman not yet past her middle years. Ta-Cern had told Jarod her age of over a hundred years and he looked on with amazement and thought of Carille. She wore a black dress with diamonds sown into the bodice that trailed into a feather design to the floor. Her silver hair, held in complicated woven braids with jeweled hairpins to form its own headdress, flared loose to her waist at her back.

She moved forward with stately grace. Jarod stopped her before she could kneel on the cushions with a light touch on the arm. She looked at him and Jarod saw her shock when she recognized the power within him. Jarod's majestic voice carried throughout the room. "Ca-Ra'IL, Friend of the Seven Realms." She bowed from the waist and joined Ta-Cern.

The music soared into waves of lushness never heard in the Seven Realms. Two Maids of the Empire gently pulled the sheer wormcloth panels aside. Va-A'Cil, Empress of the Empire, set foot on foreign lands for the first time. Her brilliance matched the stunned approval of the guests. Jarod watched the empress' beauty wrapped in platinum and precious jewels emerge from the sedan chair. Her headdress awed everyone, with its magnificent feathers made of platinum, diamonds, rubies and emeralds. The same stones formed a flowing feather pattern designed in her dress and trailing to the floor. The dress didn't leave much to Jarod's imagination. A large necklace of diamonds, set in platinum so well the metal could hardly be seen, spread across her chest.

High Lord Wells stepped forward and bowed from the waist. The guests bent their knee. Wells rose and looked upon the empress' great beauty. "Va-A'Cil, Empress of the Empire, I am High Lord Wells and it is my honor to welcome you to my lands. I'm deeply honored to present you to the Zenith Lord of the Seven Realms." He presented his arm, bent at the elbow and parallel to the floor. The empress lightly rested her hand atop his white gloves. Wells walked and the empress seemed to glide to Jarod.

"My Zenith Lord of the Seven Realms, Jarod Greatstone, I'm deeply honored to present Va-A'Cil, Empress of the Aviaries of Heaven."

Jarod took Va-A'Cil's hand, stopping her from bowing and slightly nodded to her. She nodded back and raised her head to meet his eyes. Startled, she drew in a deep breath. Lord Wells stepped to stand behind his chair at the head of the guest tables while Jarod led the empress up the steps to the top of the dais. He turned to face her and she to him. Jarod raised his left arm, lifting his cape with it to make private his actions. With his right hand, he quickly opened the laces of his shirt and pulled the cloth away from his left breast, exposing the emerald with its dancing golden arcs. This time, he couldn't stop her deep bow. Jarod pulled the cloth back over his chest and moved his left hand to her arm, allowing his cape to drape freely from his shoulder, to urge her back up, and stand at her full height. Her eyes became moist and her lips slightly quivered.

Walking her to her seat, a maiden of Desert's Ire pulled her plush chair back and another maiden readied his. Jarod looked into Va-A'Cil's eyes, projecting calmness and happiness to the empress. Shock registered on her face, after which she gave Jarod a brilliant smile. After they sat, Lord Wells seated himself at his table with the rest of the guests following suit.

Va-A'Cil's melodic voice surprised Jarod with her pleasing tone. "My Zenith Lord and Visage of Visions, I look forward to discussing your needs with Ta-Cern to help."

"It will be my pleasure, Empress."

She looked perplexed.

Smiling, he said, "Good."

Va-A'Cil smiled back and nodded her approval.

13

CALBRIS, the resident member of Gaz's network in Elizabethville, played his role as the town's drunk to perfection, and that ability singled him out as one of the primary people to deliver misinformation. He also knew the exact place and person to take it to. Sitting a table away from that man, he sloshed his ale about, giggling in that way drunks do, chuckling to themselves like they know the world's secrets. In this case, he did know a lot of them.

"All...all that pretty gold," he slurred, and giggled some more. His antics had the desired effect. The Guard had stepped up its activities and a large number of bandits were in prison.

Dugwar had been the mastermind of many of the robberies in Stonecrest over several years. He sat across from Calbris, who did nothing to acknowledge his presence. However, he did giggle again.

"What gold are you talking about?" Dugwar asked, barely above a whisper. His voice came shrill and menacing at the same time, making a somewhat unusual mixture.

Calbris looked up, startled. "None...none you...you could get." He giggled again because he knew it irritated Dugwar.

"What is it you are talking about? I will not ask again! Now! Lay it out for me." Dugwar leaned sideways, against a floor beam supporting the ceiling.

Calbris cocked his head sideways; matching the angle Dugwar made, and nearly fell off the bench. He caught his elbow on the table. "What...what is in it for...for me?"

Dugwar's scorn plainly showed. "You know I pay ten per cent for good information that proves out and we make a profit."

Calbris waggled his finger at Dugwar. That action would have gotten him a black eye, or worse, if Dugwar had already pried out what he wanted. Dugwar sat up in ill temper, an act, which elicited a deep breath from Calbris. "No...no...no." Dugwar drew back to send him to a peaceful, but painful, sleep. Calbris started talking as if Dugwar had done nothing. "Way too much...much gold for that." Dugwar lost his impetus to strike and dropped his arm by his side. "And...and I will...will not tell you all of it right...right away. Besides, it is too...too big for you to hand...handle."

Calbris promptly crossed his arms on the table and fell asleep in a heartbeat, or so it seemed. Dugwar's men carried him a few doors away to the bandit chief's rooms.

Dugwar looked down on Calbris with distaste. "Get a healer here to sober him up."

"Not necessary." Calbris yawned. "You think I am as drunk as I seem all the time. I do not remember being completely sober for years, but I am not completely drunk, either.

"I want twenty per cent of the whole take, not just your part. And, I will not give you the final details until you have made certain arrangements."

Dugwar looked on, shaken. No one had talked to him that way in years; well, almost no one.

"Dugwar, you are good," Calbis continued, clearly aware how Dugwar remained a pushover for praise. "This little adventure involves too many of the Guard. Two boulders, possibly more; that is seventeen hundred men in case you forgot."

"I know how many are in a boulder," Dugwar snapped. "What is so important that requires that large of a guard?"

Calbris sat further back in the plush chair he had been unceremoniously dumped in. Dugwar, one of the worst sorts, had surprisingly good taste.

"Have you heard there is a strange ship, or rather seven strange ships, anchored at Wellsport?"

Dugwar gave no sign of what he did or did not know. Calbris shrugged and went on. "There are seven ships at Wellsport from the empire of Serarelique."

Dugwar actually took a step back. No one in Stonecrest, except him, should yet have that knowledge. Serarelique had been completely unknown in the Seven Realms until Wathdure passed the information to the united bandit gangs that had taken on the fanciful name of "Relievers."

Calbris continued, knowing Dugwar's mind must churn. "The main ship—I hear it is something to behold— is trading the plans for a weapon that will give the Guard complete dominance over everyone, including bandits, or whole armies for that matter. The cost for those plans is what two boulders of guardsmen will be watching over from the Spires to Wellsport. I understand the price is in the range of a hundred thousand golds and ten pounds of emeralds!" Dugwar had to sit down, reduced to speechlessness.

"Now, I suppose you want to know how good *my* information is. Let us say that it comes from within that big, fancy, main ship. My cousin, *Jarvark*, made the mistake of going to the eastern lands and got caught up in a sailor's sweep. The captain meant to sail to the empire of Serarelique. There are monstrous storms on the way all year round. Most sailors know enough to make the trip only one time; at least, the ones that make it back. Jarvark has no skills at much of anything and the captain sold him for a slave. He is a good looking and strong man. They put him to work on that big ship."

Calbris looked around, searching for a drink.

"He jumped ship when he got here and saw an acquaintance on shore." Calbris looked forlornly at Dugwar. "He got captured almost immediately, but not before he threw a message wrapped around some cheese to a man on shore and yelled, 'He will reward you!' to him. The man—I never did get his name, not one of my best nights—had someone read my name and where to find me written on the outside of the message. Jarvark's ideas that I would know how to turn the information into gold and buy his release won't happen. Unfortunately for Jarvark, I hate the bastard!"

"Let me see the message."

Dugwar fought not to sneer; he failed. Calbris knew he would be dead the minute Dugwar had it in his hands.

"Come now, Dugwar, I am not the drunken fool you and the rest of this town think I am. Most nights I have no more than one mug of ale. It took me two years to get used to my stench. My preparations were worth the effort. I can cut purses left and right. No one ever looks at me. Through me, yes, but not at me. Oh, by the way, here is yours." Calbris' slid his hand into his rags for a second and gingerly tossed Dugwar's purse toward him. "I decided you might want some proof of my talents."

Disbelief covered Dugwar like a shroud. He yanked the cords holding his purse and two bare ends of leather offered no resistance. He sat, looking astounded and at a loss for words a second time.

Suddenly, he laughed and threw the purse back to Calbris. "You earned it; you keep it."

Calbris caught the purse with a smile and an off-hand salute. He pretended to be deep in thought for a moment. "You are not going to like this next part!" Dugwar's eyebrows did a short dance on his forehead and settled in a definitely, downward, position. "Do you remember the merchant's ledger?"

Dugwar raised his hand and Calbris stopped talking. "Yes, I know of what you speak," he snarled. He did not want anyone to know about that ledger, especially the men in the room. It contained damning evidence that would ultimately relieve him of his head's weight.

"I have provided for a person in this town for years. The reason for my largess is unimportant and not one that would interest you. He or she lives and works inside the garrison and has the ledger. It will be given to the garrison commander if my smiling face is not seen stumbling around Elizabethville for more than twelve hours." Dugwar edged his hand toward the knife on his belt and then thought better of it. Calbris stared at him in a way that made him squeamish like shivers ran up his spine. *No one has done that in a long time,* Calbris mused. Dugwar looked as if he did not enjoy the evening and the way it was progressing.

Calbris pitched his voice and spoke barely above a whisper, "Good decision!"

Anger surged through Dugwar. Then, he realized his men had not heard the words and Calbris had meant it to be so. His anger ebbed.

"Look, Dugwar," Calbris continued in the same quiet tones. "I have the information and you have the means to put it to use. I would not live two minutes if I did not take precautions. You gather the men required and negotiate my percentage and I will return the ledger to you when I get my share."

Dugwar would have many things to do if he grasped the opportunity. Calbris' information seemed immense in his eyes and although he hated to admit it, he began to enjoy trapping the man more than usual. He did not have time for long decision times. "There are time restraints in this.

"Can you show me something?"

Calbris kept his face neutral. He knew he had Dugwar

where he wanted him, but it would not be good to let him know that. He fished around in his rags and produced a paper that had all the earmarks of his story, but ripped across the end. He passed it over to Dugwar. The paper backed up every part of the story, including the amount of money, down to the smell of cheese. The words stopped abruptly at the end of the page. Dugwar looked at Calbris.

"The location and time of the exchange are on the rest of the page. It is with the ledger and I purposely did not read it any more than to satisfy myself of its nature. It goes with the ledger to the garrison commander, should my health suddenly fail. I repeat myself, Dugwar. We do not have to be enemies and we should not be, if this plan is to work. You are highly regarded by your counterparts in the other realms. I am worth nothing to them. I will give you a third of my share when done. You will be richer than the High Lords and possibly the Zenith! Who knows how much he has stashed away? Would any ruler not give half he had for such a weapon? Think of the rewards. None of us will ever work again if it is our wish."

Calbris made a show of relaxing and taking his ease. He actually did relax when he saw Dugwar lower his guard and called out for one of his men to bring some wine. *Avarice is a powerful emotion in a man like Dugwar.*

* * *

TWENTY minutes later, Dugwar watched from his window as Calbris staggered up the street in his perfect imitation of the town drunk. He shook his head in wonder of the many years that he had looked on Calbris as nothing more than he seemed. He had ordered his men not to disturb him for any reason and laughed at the thought.

Calling Wathdure might be the most disturbing thing I ever witnessed or have done. The sweat on Dugwar's face reflected the effort and his retching gut gave all the evidence he needed for his concern. Plush cushions and wine had done little to relax him.

Black pools formed in his mind's eye. A force pulled him toward the middle pool of darkness. Suddenly, he became enveloped; his consciousness dove through worlds of blackness. A harsh voice he had never heard started the sweat flowing again.

"Dugwar, why have you called me?"

Dugwar jumped several inches off the cushions, his mind locked in the void. Strangeness and the over-whelming feeling of power pulled his taut muscles into knotted spasms. "I have information that I believe deserves your attention." He started when he realized he had not used an honorific. A presence raped his mind.

"You were right to call me. Calbris will get his twenty per cent and you will have the third of it as he promised. Raise your men and send them to the point where the borders of Stonecrest, Deepwells, and Stonefire intersect. They are to make no attacks on anyone as they travel. Groups should number no more than fifty men. Choose your groups wisely. Strive not to send a man that may have issues with another in the group. Food and supplies for two weeks must be available at the end of their journey—bought, not stolen on the way, and they are to avoid villages or towns. They must buy extra for the two weeks as they travel and not wait until they reach the end of the trip. Gangkor, Burstead, and their men will meet you within the two weeks. Camp your men in an area large enough for the three groups and away from prying eyes. Set out guards and kill any males approaching that cannot identify themselves as belonging to one of the groups. Use any woman as you will, but they must be dead when you leave the area. Hide your presence well. All is the same as it happened at Boswell except the number of men is larger and the chance for discovery is greater. Your men must be in place in two weeks. You will join them on the way once you have the route the treasure will take."

Dugwar jerked his head, suddenly aware that he alone occupied his thoughts and memories. Knotted, painful, muscles took nearly an hour—and a few glasses of wine— to relax. His guards stood mystified by his countenance when he sent them for his lieutenants. Dugwar remained supremely mystified, for reasons they would never discover.

* * *

WATHDURE easily found Shadure on the Gray Plane. He allowed Shadure to obtain his recently gained information by mental transfer. Other memories and thoughts he held jealously guarded behind weak shields. He could not keep Shadure from taking his thoughts, but that way he would know what shields he breached. He needed not bother as Shadure withdrew from his consciousness.

Shadure seemed pleased. A financial defeat remained as good as a military one in many cases. The loss of such an amount would limit the men the bastard and his brat could keep in the field. Perhaps not immediately, but the effect would be strongly felt. Shadure's smile pleased him and the tone of his voice filled him with pride.

"Excellent! Excellent indeed, my friend."

Wathdure watched his Master wave his right arm in a circle and an oval faded from the nearly uniform grayness of that plane to form a view of a part of the world below. The forest ranged northward to the foot of two small mountains and several streams. One of the mountain's crests, shaped like an unshod horse's hoof with no sign of habitation for several miles around, stood stark and bare. Shadure let the image fade.

If Wathdure had been able to focus on a certain part of Segquo's palace moments later, he might have sensed a telepathic message from Segquo informing the Highest One that he would receive a dream message that night.

* * *

JAROD woke just before dawn. The dream remained vivid and he remembered every detail. It left no doubt of the location Shadure had focused upon. Jarod had camped in the hollow of the horse's hoof while on camping trips with his father and some of the lords and high lords. The location remained one of three logical choices for the information passed to Wathdure. Jarod became somewhat disconcerted over the rapidity that the message took to reach Wathdure and filed that bit of knowledge away.

He had nearly dressed after bathing, when his most trusted advisor knocked lightly on the door. Jarod opened the door from where he stood across the room.

Kyle shrugged his shoulders. "It still makes me squeamish when you do that!"

Jarod motioned him in with a chuckle. "You will get used to it when you learn how to do it. What brings you out so early?"

He finished dressing in desert warrior's leathers and motioned Kyle to a chair. Kyle closed the door the conventional way and joined him at two plush chairs looking out on the desert, brought to life by a vast array of battle groups. Groups of warriors were already practicing various forms of individual combat at measured intervals throughout the huge encampment.

Kyle shook his head. "I would never believe the desert harbored so many. How does it support them?"

"The forest surrounding the High Desert on three sides is owned by High Lord Wells. It provides much and poaching by one other than the High Desert People is severely punished. Many of the people think the forests are haunted. Segquo and his people's abilities make a poacher quickly known to Lord Wells who acts just as quickly. The reputation keeps most away. The various lords in the surrounding lands receive a terse message of the incident, naming the poacher, the date of the incident, and the poacher's current location. The lords of Deepwells hold their high lord in considerable awe. In addition, the desert holds many secrets. There are fertile places in the high desert that you would not believe. Their existence is highly guarded. There is more too, but that is not what brought you here. Is it your brother?"

Kyle chuckled. "Is there nothing that escapes you?" He continued, knowing Jarod would not answer, and described the conversation between his brother and him. "I believe him. I remembered many of his idiosyncrasies as we talked. His actions matched his words and I think the tears real. That leaves my father to deal with. Peter disliked Father before I left for the Spires and it has not diminished, but I do not know if he would testify and Gaz's agent's statement alone would not be enough evidence to try him for treason."

Jarod tapped the arm of his chair with the middle three fingers of his right hand as his father had done before him in times of concentration. Kyle seemed uncomfortable with this conversation. "You may do as you please with your brother. I will take care of Cartwell. I would leave your brother here to be trained by the warriors, if you do not mind a suggestion." Kyle appeared to immediately see the sense of such a plan. His brother would be a realm away and get the training he no doubt lacked.

He nodded his acceptance and went on with the second reason for his visit. He expressed his unease concerning the number of bandits that Wathdure had been able to bring together.

Jarod laughed, eliciting a surprised look from the other man. "Kyle, I will lay out a scenario from information that you know well. The Seven Realms has a population bordering on one hundred million people. I would not be too concerned over a bandit group of three thousand. The problems will arise when Shadure and his minions insidiously subvert the lords of the realms. It will require guardsmen to put down a fight even if it is one lord against another. The Guard numbers five hundred thousand; each high lord has a force up to ten thousand and each lord a force up to a thousand. It has not changed in the three short years since you became a High Lord. One might ask what is the problem and the answer is that the lords, or high lords, may involve the people. It happened in the last war and I believe we will see some of the same tactics this time.

"We can defeat all the fighting men the realms can muster. However, we cannot hold a million mobilized troops assembled through Shadure's coercion! And, therein lies the problem."

Kyle thoughtfully nodded. "Oh, I forgot! Lenzel wears a Minor Stone."

The speech the Zenith Lord just gave, completely escaped his mind.

14

LENZEL practiced with deadly Sliver Stars, each one hitting the target perfectly. His talent with the Stone encased in his woven headband increased daily; his distance from the target grew to a hundred yards, amazing those who watched him on the sidelines of the large field used for archery. The Silver Stars weighed a pound and he had never been able to throw one so far with any accuracy before thinking of the Stone as he threw. When he depleted his stash of stars, he ran down the field to collect them and carefully place them in the specially made pouches attached to the right side of his leathers at his thigh.

Gal Aston approached as he seated the last star in its holder. "Lenzel, the Zenith Lord needs you at once. I'll take you to him." After he recovered from his surprise, Lenzel hurried to catch up to the gal that walked at a pace closer to a run. They entered Segquo's palace and walked hurriedly down magnificently decorated halls depicting scenes of desert life in colored tiles. Two of Desert's Ire stood alert before a large carved door of fighting men in curious uniforms he had never seen. He felt their eyes scan him and stopped at his thigh. They looked at each other and then back to the gal, who said, "He is the one the Zenith sent me to bring here. He has the Zenith's trust."

The women seemed to know Lenzel, but looked closely at the weapons he carried once more. Nonetheless, one pulled the door open and said, "The Highest One is waiting for you."

Lenzel entered the room alone, finding Jarod sitting

behind a large desk and Lord Byrne sitting in a plush chair to the right side of the desk. He bowed low to the Zenith Lord and then to Kyle.

The command in Jarod's voice jarred him. "Lenzel, sit in the chair facing me and Lord Byrne." After he obeyed, Jarod continued, his voice softer, "Tell me how you found the stone you wear."

Lenzel took off his headband and gave it to Jarod, who examined the stone, feeling its relatively weak power as he told how he received the drawing to the cave of Stones. He carefully removed the map from the secret pocket inside his leathers and put it on the desk, gently unfolding the ancient document, pointing to the mountains and telling their location. "My Zenith, the cave allowed me to take two stones and some gold from the horde I found. I gave the second stone to my wife and she told me it helps her in healing."

Jarod and Kyle leaned over the vellum. Jarod touched its corner and channeled his Sire's Stone's power to it. Within a few seconds, it looked new and in much greater detail formally lost to age. Lenzel's eyes widened and he sat back into the pillows of the plush chair, looking at Jarod in awe.

"I know this mountain range," Jarod said, "but I've never climbed any of its mountains. Traveling at our best time, it would take eight days there and back. Nonetheless, we can't afford to wait." He rang a small bell sitting on his desk.

The oak door flew open and the two Desert's Ire maidens and the gal entered with their hands on killing weapons. Jarod didn't let his amusement show. "I need to know if anyone in Desert's Ire knows of this mountain range."—and he told them its general location.

The maids studied the chart, memorizing its details. They took only a minute before one answered, "Highest One, we will take this information to our leaders and return within the hour." They left the study, flashing hand signals to the maidens who took their place when they entered the room.

Jarod continued—"Aston, we'll want a small Boulder with full support men, horses, and supplies for the fastest travel. Send men and relief horses out at once to be stationed at proper internals for the most efficient exchanges. We'll leave at first light tomorrow and we will rotate the horses both ways, so include the wait time in their supplies. We'll also need a small, empty wagon that must be heavily guarded on the return trip and able to carry a heavy load. Aston, select the best and strongest men you know personally to guard the wagon. Blackwind and Challenger will not have to be relieved. Kyle, any suggestions?"

He replied with one word: "Deathcats."

Gal Aston started out of the room as Lenzel replayed the conversation in his mind. *I'm glad I don't have to make these decisions!* He looked up as he heard Jarod say his name.

"Lenzel, you'll be coming with us. You, Lord Byrne, and I will be the only ones climbing the mountains. Get your gear together for the journey."

Lenzel let out a large breath, pushing up from the plush chair. He bowed to Jarod and Kyle before nearly running out to the hall. He didn't see their smiles.

* * *

JAROD sat in Segquo's study, watching him analyzing the vellum chart. Lord Wells peered over his shoulder. They stopped at the sound of Jarod's voice. "Segquo, I'll need the assistance of your followers from the Grey Plane. We know the bandits have taken the bait and they'll travel to the site they think we'll pay for the weapon. Some may travel near where we'll be and we cannot run into them on our trip. Can your watchers scout the area and let us know if any will intersect us?"

"I'll instruct them to start at first light. One group will hover over the three mountains and another will scout around you and your men."

"Wells, how go the efforts of Ta-Cern and the empress' ship building?"

"Her shipwrights are working well with ours. Our men are amazed at the advancements being taught. We are felling the trees and replanting as we go. We're using several of the surrounding forests and we'll not deplete any one of them. The first two ships have the keel in place."

"Does she remain at your palace?"

"Yes, she has my best suite of rooms and seems to be comfortable, as does Ca-Ra-IL."

"Send word to Va-A'Cil that I'll be away for ten days and I'd like to see her on my return."

"At once, my Zenith."

As Lord Wells departed, Jarod turned to Kyle. "Am I missing anything except the deathcats?"

"I don't think so, my brother. Do you foresee problems?"

Jarod liked when Kyle called him "brother." He had not used the familial name in a long time. "There will always be dangers when the Dark Source is involved. Segquo's watchers will give us warning and our stones will block Shadure and his minions spying on us, but if he notices an area of land he can't see well from the Grey Plane that travels in a logical path, he could cause trouble from above or direct men to intercept us. I don't imagine he can get to the cave, but I don't want to underestimate him. We don't know how powerful he is at this point. Our Stones are growing in power; I'm sure his abilities also increase."

Jarod ordered midmeal for Kyle and him. He leaned into the pillows of the plush chair. "Kyle there are several hidden sites of stones. There is no documentation on their location, if one ever existed. I suspect our ancestors never made one for fear it would fall into the wrong hands or a Zenith collecting them for his own use. I've been trying to locate them with my Stone, but without success. Travis may have more information, but I'm reluctant to send a message on the off chance it will be found by the wrong person and it would mean disclosing the location of the crater to the carrier."

"Do you think MomMav could make the trip?"

"She is still at the Spires and a courier leaves tomorrow morning. That may be the safest way especially if she stops at hospices along the way."

Kyle tapped his hand on the desk. "Travis might still be at the Spires."

"I doubt it. He should be overseeing the training of the priests."

They talked for a few minutes more and then Kyle left to make arrangements for their trip.

* * *

JAROD penned the note to Mother Mavis and asked the courier to be brought to him. He wrote simply, "Have your husband contact me." *Very few know MomMav has a husband and fewer know who he is.* Jarod worked on future plans, making a list of dangers and obstacles that might arise when the courier's knock sounded.

"Come!" he ordered.

The courier walked past the Desert's Ire maidens, oblivious to the fact they followed him into the room. He stopped three feet in front of Jarod's desk and saluted.

He looked up at the courier and recognized him, then returned the salute. "This message must be highly guarded. I'll give orders for a pebble to ride out of uniform in front and another behind you in addition to your regular escort. If you're attacked and cannot get away, tear the message to shreds. Do not read it." Jarod turned the envelope over and sealed it with his ring and hot wax. The wax dried quickly and he handed it to the courier.

The man took the missive and read the address:

MOTHER MAVIS
THE SPIRES

A look of curiosity flashed across the courier's face before he saluted. "I'll see it safely there, my Zenith."

"Tell no one you carry anything special. Let it be known all you carry is soldiers' letters and receipts." Jarod's commanding voice visibly jarred the courier who saluted once more and hurriedly left. Jarod smiled. *He wanted out of here before I gave him something else out of the ordinary.*

He finished his notes then sat back, resting his head against soft cushions, and gently massaged his temples.

Kyle slipped into the study and took the seat across from his desk. "You're tired," he said softly.

"It's been many long days. I'm hoping there will be something in the cave that'll point us in the right direction to the other caves' locations. The cave gave him two minor stones. Do you think Lenzel could wear a stronger stone?"

"I hadn't thought about the possibility. Even I can feel his devotion to you. I wonder if that might help."

Jarod smiled. "I think he is in as much awe of you as he is of me."

* * *

THE column moved out as the sun glowed eerily behind overcast skies when darker clouds scudded from east to west. Two hundred and fifty troopers led by Jarod, Kyle, and Lenzel riding before the small wagon to be used on the return trip were followed by the remaining troopers. A column that size normally wouldn't move rapidly, but these men had much experience and the word passed between them: "The Zenith is in a hurry."

Jarod liked the pace. "If the weather holds, we'll make it back in seven days. If it rains, it could be two weeks," he said to Kyle.

Kyle motioned to the support group riding forward off the side of the road to find a campground for the night and have a hot meal waiting. Jarod nodded.

Lenzel had travelled with hunters in small groups of never more than twenty men. He saw troopers coming and going from the High Desert, but had never been close. His head turned from side to side taking in all the actions going on around him. He looked impressed.

Approaching Jarod, he spoke when recognized. "Highest One, I would like permission to range outward from the column to find game and clear water. The food and ale supplied to the troopers doesn't agree with me. I'll dress out my kills and give any overage to the cooks."

Jarod seemed to think for a few seconds before replying. "I'll want you to have two guards go with you. They can remain behind when you dismount to hunt. They'll take a packhorse in case you find large game. Lenzel, you are an essential part of this mission. You are not to engage anyone if you can help it. I know your fighting skills and your valor, but the information that someone is in the area is far more valuable than a dead body, especially your dead body. This area is sparsely populated, but some locals live here. Be careful to remain invisible."

"Two guards, Highest One?"

Jarod partially hid his smile. "One will assist you if you run into trouble. The other will ride for reinforcements. Lenzel, you're a well-trained warrior. It is important for you to not be seen. Additionally, I have men scouting the area who are not in uniform. You and they must be careful. I'll send word that you might be in the area and to signal you with a hawk's cry if they spot you. You do the same if you spot men in the area and see if they answer your call. I'm allowing this because I know our food could make you sick and that's not a good thing to happen while climbing mountains."

Lenzel started to protest until he saw Jarod's smile. He bowed his head and went to prepare for an afternoon hunt. It didn't take long and as he finished, two large, heavily armed troopers rode toward him. Their size impressed him.

"Lenzel, I am Garret and this is Marson. The Zenith ordered us to travel with you on your hunts. I'm looking forward to seeing what you can do and we like the idea of being away from the damn crowded column once in a while."

Lenzel grasped arms with the speaker and then the other trooper. He mounted and struck out west of the column toward dense woods. He could partially hear the troopers talking behind him.

"Do you think…good…they say?"

"I heard Lord Byre…to…he's good."

Lenzel put the idle comments out of his mind as he approached the trees. Ten feet into the forest, the column disappeared from view. He dismounted and tied Challenger to a low tree limb. Checking his weapons, he opened the pouch holding the Silver Stars.

"What are those?" Marson asked.

Lenzel gingerly lifted a polished star from the pouch and held it out toward the men. "Killing stars. Careful, they're very sharp."

Garret took the star and immediately dropped it with a yelp. A few drops of blood dripped from his palm. "Hells to the Dark Source! I barely touched it."

Lenzel picked up the star and carefully wiped the blood away before putting it back into the pouch. Marson placed a cloth over Garret's wound while Lenzel silently disappeared in the woods. Lenzel soon found an animal trail and followed it until he sighted a wide stream. A large, ten point stag bent its neck to drink water. The first arrow dropped him without a cry, a clean nearly painless death over in a second. Even with his skills, it took a good hour to dress out the stag and bury the awful and head, leaving the horns beside the stream in remembrance. He hefted the remaining meat, wrapped in its skin over his shoulder, and somewhat staggered back to the edge of the woods.

Marson spotted him first and dropped his mouth in mid-sentence. The men rushed to help him tie the remains to the packhorse and settle him from the smell of blood. Lenzel drank some of the cool, clear stream water and plugged his water skin. Pulling his bow, strung at his waist, over his head, he replaced it and his quiver of arrows in holders on his horse's tack.

"Will we have venison tonight?" Marson asked.

Lenzel nodded and rode out to find the column.

* * *

LENZEL approached the officer's cook. "I have this venison for the Highest One and Lord Byre. I would like portions for the three of us. Give whatever remains to whomever you decide appropriate."

"You are Lenzel?" the cook asked, then continued when he received a nod, "I got word you might bring something in. I had no idea it would be anything this size. I should have it ready in about an hour. I'll have your lastmeals brought to you. I imagine quite a few men will find favor with you. There must be two hundred pounds here!"

Lenzel chuckled. "It felt more like four hundred carrying it out!"

"Oh Lenzel, you and your men are to eat at the officer's mess by order of the Zenith."

* * *

LENZEL drank a mug of water with Garret and

Marson drinking ale in the officer's mess in a dark corner, trying to be inconspicuous.

"How did you get two lowly troopers in the officer's mess?" Garret asked him.

They gulped when Lenzel answered: "The Highest One's orders."

* * *

THE weather held for the first four days, but the sun did not break through the overcast sky on the fifth day, making Jarod uneasy. He looked at the mountain range and the three tallest peaks. His ascent would start when the skies lightened the next morning. As he turned, he saw a scout riding toward him at a full gallop. Jarod mounted Blackwind and rode toward the scout at a canter.

He returned the scout's salute when they met.

"My Zenith, one of your outriders found me and told of a group of fifty-six men camping in the valley a mile from the tallest mountain. He stated they showed all the signs of a bandit band. When he got close enough, he reported they didn't practice at arms and their supplies looked low and their horses are not the best."

They can't be part of the bandits grouping for our trap. They're completely in the wrong area. "Tell the outriders to send two men to watch them. We'll arrive at the base of the mountain by midmorning. I'm sure they'll scatter when they hear us." Jarod smiled. "Five hundred men on horseback make a lot of noise. Get a fresh horse."

The scout grinned and saluted. He trotted toward the picket lines before Jarod finished returning his salute. Jarod nudged Blackwind to a trot on the way to his command tent, then sent Kyle and Lenzel a mental message to meet him there. He wondered if Lenzel's stone was powerful enough to allow him to receive his thought.

One guard took Blackwind and two others pulled back

the tent's flaps. Kyle and Lenzel rose from camp chairs and bowed their heads.

"Come," Jarod said. The High Lord and the young warrior followed him.

He walked to the table where the larger map of the area sat, supplied by Lord Wells.

"There is a report that fifty-six men are camped within earshot of the base of the peaks. They certainly won't attack six hundred troopers, but I want them rounded up, placed under guard and bound away from sight. Kyle, put a gal in charge and tell him to take one hundred troopers to surround the men before first light; get a man in to cut the picket lines. Take a bugler; have him sound a charge as a man shoots a fire arrow into the biggest tent. The men will not charge, but slowly tighten their circle with drawn swords. I don't want a fight, but if a man starts to draw a weapon, have an archer take him down. Assign three of them with the group. If the horses don't scatter at the sound of the bugle, have the archers put a few fire arrows in the ground at the picket line. Kyle, any thoughts?"

"Could these men be travelling to join up with Dugwar's group? We expect men to come from all over the Seven Realms."

"That *is* a good thought. Before we start back, interrogate them. Do you think Gal Aston should be the man for this?"

"He's a good choice. I'll get him started on putting his men together, if we are done here."

"Highest One, may I speak with you?"

Jarod nodded for Kyle to leave and when the tent flap closed, he led Lenzel to the camp chairs and motioned him to sit beside him. "What is it?"

"Highest One, how did you summon me? You did it, didn't you?"

"What did you hear?"

"I heard nothing. I had a vision of this tent and felt a strong desire to come here."

"Interesting. Do you know I've joined with the Sire's Stone?"

"No, Highest One."

"You know how the stone you wear assists you in using your weapons?" Lenzel nodded. "Well, that is known as a Minor Stone. There are three types. The Minor Stones are the most plentiful and are fairly weak. The Channel Stones vary in strength based on the ability and bonding of the wearer. The last group is the Great Stones. There are seven and we don't wear them. They are embedded in out bodies." Jarod unlaced the top of his shirt and showed the gold-arching emerald.

Lenzel's eyes popped wide open. "Highest One, does it hurt?"

"No, it feels good and it's very beneficial. It is the power of the Stone that allowed me to send you your vision. As your Stone increases in power, you may be able to hear the thoughts I send to you."

"Highest One, I hope it increases soon!"

Jarod chuckled. "I do too, Lenzel. I do too."

* * *

JAROD had dozed off when the bugler sounded the charge. *Great Source of the Light, they must have taken a pebble of buglers!* Jarod rose as Kyle entered the tent dressed in a heavy brown wool shirt under a thick leather jerkin; a heavy cape hung on his shoulders to the heel of black leather boots. Jarod grinned as, except for the color of the shirt, they wore the same set of clothing and boots. His own white shirt peaked out at his throat. Neither man wore a symbol of rank. Lenzel entered with strips of cloth the width of a hand. He held several out to Jarod and Kyle.

"Highest One, my hands became swollen and bled from the rock. I thought these would help."

"Thank you, Lenzel." Kyle nodded his approval.

The three left the tent to where troopers held their horses at the ready. A pebble of men, mounted and alert, joined them and they rode toward the base of the mountain a mile away.

They arrived as troopers set about erecting a fortified encampment. The small wagon was positioned closest to the mountain behind Jarod's command tent. A cry went up and men parted as a male deathcat slowly meandered toward Jarod and the command tent. Jarod kneeled and held out his hand. The deathcat sniffed once and gave the hand a lick with his rough tongue before pushing his head against Jarod's forehead and uttered a purr that sounded more like a growl. When Jarod rose, the deathcat circled once and lay down at the entrance to the command tent. Jarod sent a vision of welcome and pleasure; the purr became louder, then collapsed into silence when Jarod sent visions of him going up the mountain and a deathcat waiting at the base of the mountain. The big animal looked agitated, but went to the mountain's base and curled up.

Jarod, Kyle and Lenzel rechecked their backpacks, wrapped the cloth strips around their hands and started upward. As Jarod passed the deathcat, he scratched him behind the ears and received a vision of a deathcat rising up to fight enemies. He smiled and again scratched him.

* * *

THE first two hours went smoothly until they reached the steeper part of the near vertical rock. Lenzel led, using the path he'd first traveled. He reached his third handhold when the first drops of rain hit him. He looked back and saw Jarod and Kyle pull cowls over their heads. Lenzel did the same and kept climbing while tightening his safety rope to Jarod below him and Kyle below Jarod. The rock bit into Lenzel's wet, cloth-wrapped hand. An hour later, he felt the cold air rushing past him as he bounced off the side of the mountain. A strong arm caught him around the waist; his eyes looked into Jarod's chin.

"Hello, Lenzel! I'm glad you dropped by."

Fear and then confusion flashed through him before his laughter boomed off the rock. Then he did something he'd never dreamed of doing—he hugged Jarod.

"Oh, Highest One, I shouldn't have. Please forgive me!"

"Lenzel, there is nothing to forgive, but my arm is getting tired. Let's see if we can get you climbing again."

"Highest One, there is the first stopping space about fifty feet up." Lenzel caught a hand and foot hole and scampered upward.

The three of them settled on the narrow ledge with their feet dangling over the edge and their back against the rock. They fished food and water from their packs and rested.

"Lenzel," Kyle asked. "How are your hands?"

"Much better than on my first time here, my Lord. I think my stone helps."

The rain slacked off and the men let out a sigh. Lenzel spoke about the rest of the trip. "Highest One, I think we are over half way. We'll reach the cave much before nightfall, but the return shouldn't be attempted in the dark. Unfortunately, the hand and footholds are smaller and it took a lot of concentration for me to continue. I found little scree, but the rock is sharp. I'm going to change my hand wrappings and the dry ones should work better, at least for a while." The rain had completely stopped by the time they again started upward.

Lenzel's observation about the mountain proved correct: The indents in the rock for climbing became smaller. Still, they moved faster and reached the terrace with the cave two hours before nightfall. He looked over the cave's entrance and remembered seeing the stylized marking of three tors; he smiled.

Kyle's voice broke Jarod's concentration. "By the Light's Source!"

Jarod turned around looking at the entire terrace bathed in golden light. "You're right, Kyle; it *is* the Light's Source."

Lenzel walked toward the cave's entrance and stopped. "Highest One, the shield protecting the cave is gone." He took another step and the stone in his headband flew into the cave and a larger ruby floated to him. He took the stone and his mouth gaped. "Highest One, I feel a great warmness and power flowing in me!"

"May I touch it?"

"Of course, Highest One." Lenzel held his hand out to Jarod.

Jarod barely brushed the stone. "Lenzel, do you remember my explanation of the Stones?" Lenzel nodded. "This is a Channel Stone. It gets its name from compacting power in several ways. It's much stronger than the Stone you had. It will grow in power as you continue to feel the purity of the Light's Source and live for the destruction of the Dark's source. It'll lose its power if controlled by a dark heart. When we return to the High Desert, you must start a new line of training for leadership. You have the potential to command a tor, over five thousand men, many of whom will have their own stones. And, you should have much less trouble on our descent."

Lenzel sat down looking at the stone that nestled in the palm of his hand emitting golden arcs into his body.

Jarod bared his chest, allowing the Sire's Stone to be seen. The back wall fell away to open a much larger room.

Kyle opened his shirt to let the golden light touch the Warrior's Stone. A wall adjacent to the larger room fell away exposing weapons and scrolls. In the center of the largest room, a large trunk sat with its top thrown back and a smaller one behind it. In the weapons room, another large trunk set away from the weapons. They all looked empty, but after seeing and using various boxes Jarod had given him, he pushed the thought aside.

Kyle stepped to Jarod's side. "Why am I continually amazed? This is unbelievable! He went to the wall and reached for a strange weapon.

"I wouldn't do that," Jarod said. You should read the scrolls before handling these weapons. They might bite."

Kyle touched the nearest scroll and jerked his hand away. "Great Source of Light!" He quickly felt the edge of each scroll. After the last one, he looked around to see Jarod smiling. "You could have warned me!"

"What, and spoil the surprise?" He fingered each of the parchments. "Mmm interesting, I knew of some, but not all. Lenzel, step in here."

Lenzel walked in the weapons room fastening his headband in place. He had cleverly woven the ruby allowing only a small part of the stone to be visible. "Yes, Highest One."

"Touch the edge of a scroll and tell me what you feel."

Lenzel looked somewhat concerned, but did as ordered, and then turned back to Jarod with a question showing on his face. "I felt the parchment. Should I have felt more?"

Jarod came beside Lenzel and took his hand. While still holding his hand, he grazed the scroll. Lenzel jerked his hand away, looking dumbfounded. He walked to a particular weapon on the wall and pointed to it. "Highest One, I know all about this weapon!"

Jarod smiled and repeated the process on the rest of the scrolls except the last one. "Touch this one without me holding your hand."

Lenzel obeyed and turned back to Jarod, smiling. "It worked! Why?"

"Your stone grows with use and you with it. You could manage it eventually on your own. I just gave you a little help. You are a very important warrior, as I have told you. You will need this information for tasks and battles to come."

15

KYLE scratched his chin. "Jarod, in all the seven hells, how are we going to get this down the mountain? The gold alone must weigh a thousand pounds!"

"No, only eight hundred pounds according to my records. Do you remember finding me floating above the bed?"

"Uh, yes. It scared me more than seeing my first deathcat."

"Two weeks ago, I tested my skills. With a safety rope, I jumped off a three hundred foot cliff. I fell normally for about fifty feet before I figured out how to channel my stone's power. After that, I floated down at the speed of a rose petal in a light wind. I tried it with various weights and none seemed to make a difference. I tried to go upward and could rise only a few feet. I think the floating is one of the protections of my stone. The smaller chest should hold the gold and stones. The larger chests are for the contents of its room. I should also be able to handle your and Lenzel's load. You and I will carry the chests."

Kyle looked at Jarod like he had lost his mind. "Are you serious? This is not one of your jokes?"

"Yes to the first and no to the second. We'll test the actions first, but I don't think we'll have a problem. The Great Stones have tremendous power. The more we use them, the faster they grow in ability, but remember, as they increase, so does the Dark Source's influence. The first Zenith Lord barely won the war with the Dark by using its greed and blind aggression against it. I don't think it's changed from its true nature. Perhaps this time, we can defeat it before millions die. One other thing—

while we have control of our powers and many safe-guards, we can still be killed."

Kyle looked at the cave's entrance where Lenzel lay in the sunlight and lowered his voice. "What about him?"

"I feel he has great potential and he'll be a huge asset. He has two great loves—his devotion to the Light's Source and his wife; we should send a message for her to join him. A minor stone accepted her as one did him. It's possible she has the ability to join with a Channel Stone. If so, I'll arrange training for her with a High Healer, and if not, she can learn much from our healers. I probably should have sent for her before now. Let's see if this will work."

Jarod concentrated on the small box. Slowly at first, it rose a foot and floated next to the hoard of jewels and gold and eased to the ground. A constant flow of gold bars began to settle in its bottom. In less than two minutes, eight hundred pounds of gold fit snugly together. The stones followed in no more than a minute.

"Highest One, is there nothing you can't do?"

Jarod and Kyle turned to Lenzel at the cave's entrance. Jarod smiled. "I can't cause a flower to bloom or a cow to give sweet milk or a woman to feel love for me with my power. You'll find the same with your powers. We are who we are. The stones allow us to do many physical things as long as we remain devoted to the Light's Source and stay true to its values and teachings. We have work to do. It'll be dark before long and thankfully there is no moon tonight."

The rest of the cave's contents filled the appropriate trunks in a half hour as darkness closed around them. Kyle fastened the straps of the trunks. Jarod stacked the large trunks one atop the other at the terrace in front of the cave and then the smaller, but heavier, one on top. Jarod turned to the wide-eyed Lenzel. "It's your turn."

Lenzel's mouth gaped open and his eyes widened as he

slowly floated to sit on top of the trunks.

"Kyle, take hold of the lower trunk's handle. Lenzel, if you're uncomfortable, close your eyes."

"No! I wouldn't miss this for all the gold in this trunk," Lenzel replied.

Jarod smiled and sent a mental vision to the deathcat below to move away from the wagon. He firmly held the opposite handle from the one Kyle held. Slowly, very slowly, the men and trunks began to rise, first, a few inches, and then faster to lift a foot off the ground before floating several feet beyond the sheer wall of the mountain. They descended at half the speed of a normal fall until reaching a hundred feet from the ground where they gradually slowed until easily resting on the bed of the small wagon. Jarod floated Lenzel to the ground. He and Kyle jumped to the ground and then Jarod rearranged the trunks to fill the wagon to one level. They pulled a tarp from behind the wagon's seat and tied it in place over the trunks.

"Trooper!" Jarod called out.

A full pebble of guards rushed from the front of the command tent carrying torches in one hand and drawn swords in the other. They stopped short upon seeing their Zenith Lord.

"My...my Zenith!" the senior man said. He looked up at the black mountain face. "How...when..."

Jarod raised his hand, stopping the trooper's words as Gal Aston came in sight at a run. The gal saluted when he came close and the troopers, looking awkward, remembered to do the same. Jarod retuned the salutes. "Aston, put four pebbles of men in a semicircle from the mountain around the command tent and back to the mountain. Bring meat and a bucket of water for the deathcat. He'll also guard the wagon. Rotate the guards in two-hour shifts. I want all the guards here to be alert and fully awake. Anyone found sleeping or away from their post will be barred from promotion for life and their pay will be docked for six months. The restriction of promotion will be lifted for valor in battle. Where are the captured men?"

"It will be as you ordered, my Zenith." Aston said. "The prisoners are tied and guarded two hundred yards from here and out of sight."

"Fine, Lord Byre will interrogate them momentarily. Pass the word that Warrior Lenzel has the rank of Gal with all its privileges. No one but Lord Byrne, Lenzel and me are allowed into the command tent without permission from one of us three. Ask the cooks for three lastmeals for us. That's all." Jarod returned the gal's salute and turned to Kyle. "Concentrate on your stone and project guilt, remorse and the need to tell the truth to three of the prisoners away from the rest of their men," he said softly. "It shouldn't take long to get the hang of it and you should be back here before lastmeal arrives. I'm starving! You'll find that using your powers will make you hungry and thirsty."

"At once, my brother."

As Kyle left, Jarod motioned for Lenzel to follow him into the command tent where a brazier held glowing coals emitting a warm glow with its heat, and collapsed in one of the camp chairs. He nodded to the chair next to him and Lenzel sat, looking exhausted.

"Highest One, I know nothing about being a Gal."

"When you get back to the High Desert, you'll be trained. You are not used to giving orders and leading men, but I feel you have the instincts for command. It's nothing for you to worry about at this time. How are you adjusting to your new stone?"

"I feel more alert and I seem to hear and see better. I got the feeling one of the troopers didn't like the orders you gave and he didn't like me being a gal."

"The one with the eye patch. He has some deep

resentments. He lost his eye in a brawl he started and won't take responsibility for his actions. He had served the guard with distinction and I learned the man he killed had provoked him in the past and jabbed him in the eye before the fight came to blows. I had to sign off on keeping him in the guard because he killed the man in the fight.

"I ordered we'd start back the morning after I returned from the mountain. It might be a good idea for you to practice some of your skills with the Silver Stars and archery after we stop tomorrow. I would like to see how you've improved and word of your talents will spread rapidly through the men. That'll impress them and they'll feel differently about you."

Lenzel asked about Stonefire and Jarod enjoyed his reactions when he described the city and especially the Spires. It cemented his thoughts about taking Lenzel to his city when the bandits' trap had played out and the matters with Va-A'Cil had been completed. They chatted on and Jarod thought Lenzel began to feel more comfortable around him. A chime sounded.

"Come," Jarod called out.

Two cooks brought in three heaping trenchers of steaming food and two bottles of chilled wine. They placed the meals on a square table with four camp chairs around it.

As they left, Kyle entered. "Food!" He seated across from Lenzel and poured wine for Jarod and himself. Lenzel had his water skin and took a swig.

"Jarod," Kyle said, "my stone's power has indeed grown stronger. I did as you ordered and within a few questions while projecting those feelings you suggested, one dropped to his knees, sobbing. They all confessed to a litany of crimes and admitted they'd travelled to join others for a big robbery. I'm still surprised at how well it worked. I couldn't hear their thoughts, but I think I came close."

Jarod nodded. "Good. Let's eat!"

He hardly had the words out when Kyle cut a bite of venison and chomped down on it.

* * *

AT first light, a courier rode out to alert the support men holding fresh horses and supplies for the Small Boulder's return as troopers broke camp and prepared to march. Four large drays in traces tested the wagon and it moved with an initial groan that smoothed out when a trooper placed grease on the two axels. Jarod ordered the gal to protect the wagon as he would protect his Zenith Lord, which caused more than a few raised eyebrows when the order flowed through the troopers.

That afternoon, Lenzel left the column to hunt. He entered the woods as Garret and Marson took up positions. He made no noise going two hundred yards deep into the forest. He rounded a boulder hiding a dale when he heard, "Who have we here?"

Lenzel spun toward the speaker as several men entered the small valley thirty yards away, drawing their swords. They walked slowly toward him. The leader smirked and several of the eleven men smiled.

"I want no trouble," Lenzel said.

"You won't be a problem once you're dead."

"Why do you want to kill me? I have little of value for you to lose your life."

"We want to travel unnoticed. You may get one of us, but you'll still be dead."

Lenzel smiled. "Oh!" He opened his pouch and removed the Silver Stars, rapidly slinging polished death in ten directions, concentrating through his stone. The men dropped with their throats ripped apart. The eleventh turned to run when Lenzel's knife lashed through his left knee; he fell hard.

Then, he heard a hawk's cry and answered it. A

moment later, three outriders entered the dale a few yards south of where the men had emerged from the woods. The lead man looked at the carnage and said, "You must be Lenzel?" He nodded, then the man continued, "We followed them for the last day, tried to herd them close to the column by closing off trails before they reached them. We wanted to capture them before the Zenith arrived."

It was hard to hear the outrider with the injured man screaming. Garret rushed around the boulder with his sword drawn and stopped short when he saw Lenzel with another knife ready to throw and three outriders with weapons ready. The men put away their weapons. Garret looked anxious. "Marson went for reinforcements when we heard the screams."

Lenzel looked at the man and laughed. "He does have quite a voice on him."

The bandit tried to keep his leg from moving and grimaced with each breath. Lenzel went to each dead man and extracted a Silver Star, cleaning it on the man's clothing before moving on to the next one. When he had all ten stars back in his pouch, he approached the wounded man, who tried to crawl away until he started yelling with pain. Lenzel reached him and in one smooth motion of less than a second, he ripped his knife out of the man's knee. The yelling stopped when the man dropped back, unconscious.

Men running through the woods caused the ones in the dale to take cover. A rocker rushed around the boulder followed by his thirty men. Garret and Lenzel stepped into sight and Lenzel held up his hand. The rocker slowly joined the others. The outriders gave Lenzel a mock salute and went back into the trees from where they had entered. Lenzel finished cleaning his knife and listened with his power as Garret spoke to the rocker, "…no, Lenzel killed them all! One of the outriders said it lasted only a few seconds."

Lenzel finished with his knife and addressed Garret, "The Zenith Lord will want to have the bandits' clothing and what they carried with them examined. I suspect the outriders have gone for their horses and what they had at their camp. Carry them back on their horses. Marson and I will return to the Zenith."

Before they could leave, the outriders returned on horseback leading twelve saddled horses and two pack animals. Lenzel looked at Garret with a raised eyebrow. "Twelve!" he exclaimed.

He felt his stone against his head and focused on the surrounding area, turning as he surveyed the trees. "Garret, wait for my hawk's cry and then come with two men." Before the man could answer, Lenzel slipped silently out of view.

He found an animal's trail and followed it for a few yards, stopping before a thicket fifteen yards away. An arrow slammed into a tree a few inches to his right, even with his head. He dropped to his knee and threw his knife into the thicket. A strangled cry sounded, followed by a body crashing into the brush. Before Lenzel could react, another arrow sliced through the calf of his right leg. He rolled on his left side and pulled a star from his pouch. Discerning a slight movement down the trail, he threw. Half way to the target, the star veered three feet to the left and slammed into something with a thud. A man holding a bow fell forward onto the trail. Lenzel imitated a flawless hawk's cry and began to tend to his leg, snapping off the arrowhead sticking from it and pulling the shaft free, amazed at the lack of severe pain and small amount of blood. Garret entered the trail and, upon seeing Lenzel, ran to him.

He blanched when he saw the arrow beside his leg. The sight of two dead bodies drew a curse from him.

"There may be more and the one down the trail wears a trooper's uniform," Lenzel said. "Sound your cry for the rocker. We'll need more men to thoroughly search these woods."

"Gal Lenzel, you're hurt. We need to get you back to the column."

It didn't seem strange when Garret used the honorific, but the awe in his voice did. "No need. Lord Byre is coming with a Trass of men and a healer." Lenzel searched the area with his stone. "There are twenty-six men five hundred yards southeast. They're stationary. They couldn't have heard the violence through the trees."

Lenzel pulled his leather trouser leg up above his wound, regretting the bloodstains soaked into the animal skin. Garret found tree moss with lichen and pressed it against the wound and then ripped a strip from the bottom of his shirt to bind it.

Lenzel kept a mental observance of the men and tried to determine more about them with his stone. He found something strange, which deeply disturbed him. A half hour passed when the sound of horses rushed toward them, faster than a safe pace in heavy woods. Garret started to draw his sword when Lenzel said, "No need; it's High Lord Byrne."

Seconds later, Kyle rode into the small clearing on a lathered horse. His voice sounded with concern. "You're hurt!"

"Not badly. They're twenty-six men and three have a dull blackness surrounding them. Three are dead."

"Yes, I feel them, too."

The rest of the trass caught up with High Lord Byrne and crowed around him.

"Lieutenant, we need to plan," Kyle said. "I'll meet with you and your men momentarily. Gal Lenzel, you need to rejoin the column after the healer finishes with you."

"High Lord Byrne, I ask permission to remain here in case someone escapes and comes this way."

Kyle thought for a moment. "Very well, but stay completely hidden and attack only when you're very sure." He leaned close and couched his voice for only Lenzel to hear. "The three with the blackness are part of the Dark's Source and the dead men are troopers! I can't tell if they're minions of the Dark's Source or controlled by it. If they are minions, they could be powerful. Trust your feelings from your stone." Then, he left to meet with the lieutenant and the three rockers as the healer tended to Lenzel's leg.

Lieutenant Jascod with his rockers moved off the trail a few yards into the woods to Kyle, who kept his voice low—"Gentlemen, you know we are facing a new threat from the Dark. The men we are going to capture or kill today are under its influence to probably varying degrees. We must be very careful and it will be best if we can spy on them first to determine how strong they are. Remember, the minions of the Dark *can* be killed! We must move with extreme covertness. Pass the word and be ready to move out immediately after your men understand what we're up against."

Shortly, under a half hour, the ninety men formed up in a small clearing ten yards from the trail. Lieutenant Jascod approached Kyle, "A few of the men are quite nervous, but they'll pull through. The others are just nervous." He gave Kyle a wry smile.

"I'd be upset if they are not nervous. The High Desert People and Forrest Workman have trained you and your men. They need to use their new skills. How many learned the High Desert hand signals?"

"All have the basics," the lieutenant said. "Some are quite fluent with them."

"Good! Let's move out and no talking. Make sure everyone knows that."

Kyle rested his hand over where his stone lay beneath his High Lord's clothing, concentrating on Jarod and replaying the day's events and what he planned. Within a few seconds, the quiet voice sounding in his head startled him. *"Be careful of the Dark's minions. We don't know their power!"*

The men split into three groups and crept toward their goal, staying in sight of each other a few yards apart. Kyle led the center group and felt pleased with his communication with Jarod. A hundred yards in, Kyle became satisfied with the men's stealth abilities; they moved silently and with confidence. A few looked hesitant, but kept up with improved self-assurance the farther they walked.

The next three hundred yards went without incident. Kyle heard camp sounds ahead and raised his hand. All three groups stopped. He gave another sign and the men kneeled on the ground. With the next set of signals, three men crawled forward in three directions: one straight ahead, one to circle left, and the last to circle right. Forty minutes later, the last of the three returned to Kyle's side. They sat in close together and spoke in low, quiet whispers with the lieutenant and the rockers.

"Lord Byrne," the man from the center said. "It is as you said. There are twenty-three who are sluggish. They walk around in a daze. The other three stay off to the left side. The whole camp feels depressed. All are in trooper uniforms, some torn and some with bloodstains, but none of the twenty-three have weapons. The others have swords and knives on them in plain sight."

The man from the left added, "The three alone don't move naturally. They're quick, but it's like they are not used to walking and using their arms. While they look normal, there is a cold eldritchness about them and they stink."

"The main group is like Cardon told you," the last man stated. "They're restless and walk around, but their eyes are constantly jerking about."

Kyle thought for a while. "I don't think the twenty-three are part of the Dark, but are being used by the three others and I don't know the amount of control they might be exercising. They might have the ability to make the troopers—if they are troopers—fight. Have your men try to disable them, but I don't want a single one of them to become injured or killed. Tell them to protect themselves and the rest of us as best they can. I understand we have three archers in the trass. I wish to talk with them and you four."

A rocker rushed away and returned on the run with the three archers. After the salutes, Kyle asked, "Do you have fire arrows?"

"Yes, my lord," the men answered in unison.

"Good," Kyle said. "I want you to split up and be in position to hit the three beings we think are part of the Dark. Each of you decide how you want to accomplish your shots, but I believe it will work best if you hide yourselves and you fire as much as possible. Shoot your targets by rotating the three." The archers showed confusion on their faces. "Let's call the beings dark, darker, and darkest. One of you will shoot a fire arrow at dark, another of you will shoot at darker, and the last of you will shoot darkest, all at the same time. In the next volley, the first of you will target darker and in the volley after that, shoot at darkest. You should be in separate locations so the arrows come from different directions. I want the beings to think there are many more archers than the three of you. Form up; we leave when your men are ready."

* * *

LENZEL pulled branches across the thicket's entrance. The healer repaired the cuts and stopped the bleeding, but he didn't have the skill to heal the torn tissue inside his calf and it ached. He touched his stone with one hand and his injured calf with the other hand. Immediately, the pain subsided to being barely noticeable. Light from the top of the undergrowth allowed him to see and he pulled all ten Silver Stars from his pouch. The star's thin metal belied its strength. He carefully stacked the razor sharp, death rounds in groups of three for easy access and kept the last one next to his hand. Rising up on his knees through the top of the brush, he would have full mobility to throw anywhere along the trail. He heard the men leaving on foot through the woods. Shortly, their sounds disappeared. *They well learned their stealth skills*, he thought.

He leaned back and prepared for a long wait. Thinking over the last few years, he found it hard to put memories in relevant order and importance. His wife cane first and his commitment to the Highest One and the High Desert People came next, equally. *I know nothing of being a Gal. The Highest One says I'll be taught how to lead many men. How will it be to fight the Dark?*

* * *

KYLE eased close to the clearing, lying on loamy soil. The flora around him smelled fresh and showed abundant life. Inside the clearing, he could see nothing green. Rotted plants oozed dark brown and black stinking muck. From the far side, an open latrine fouled breezes and brought more reeking odor flowing over the area. He saw the archers moving into position. Their well-banked small fires, tented with a wet cloth, could not be seen and no smoke escaped.

Lieutenant Jascod make the call of a chukar and seconds later, three fire arrows struck the chest of three *men* lounging away from the *troopers* at the same time. The Dark's minions' outer glamour exploded. Three hideous creatures rose up, snarling, looking from side to side when the second volley of fiery arrows hit them in the chest. They cried out in pain and the twenty-three adjacent men collapsed, sprawling onto the ground. The minions drew swords and searched for an enemy.

Lieutenant Jascod's voice rose above the den, "Advance and surround!"

Memories flooded into Kyle's mind from Wathdure's attack near the Spires. Jarod had gone to the gray plane and destroyed Gangedure, the creature who'd brought Wathdure's creatures from Ozlid, through the gray plane to fight the Guard in an effort to destroy Jarod's son. Hardly anything would defeat the creatures who continued fighting with arrows stuck a hand's depth through them and missing limbs until someone lopped off a head, destroying the false life form.

The ersatz minions, who had been quite saturnine in human likeness, began to fight with alacritous bravado. Two troopers went down, one wounded, one dead. As with Wathdure's other creatures, the cuts inflicted on the creatures caused little damage without oozing any fluids. One went on fighting with a missing arm.

Kyle ran toward the fight. "Make way!" he yelled.

The troopers fell back and the minions centered on Kyle, who concentrated on his stone and sent great love toward the beings. They cried out, collapsing on the ground and writhing in agony. When Kyle approached, they tried to crawl away. His flashing sword took the first creature's head, resulting in its body imploding and the sickening fluids flooding the area around its quickly decomposing substance.

Seeing the effect of Kyle's actions, Lieutenant Jascod and a rocker hacked off the other two minions' heads. Two troopers cared for the guardsman's wound and others prepared to wrap the dead man's body with reverence for the journey back. As they finished, tying the tarp in place, a great cry came from a low, nearby mound. A creature, larger with bulging muscles, its repulsive face bearing tusks upward to a finger's width and fiery red eyes, snarled and ran into the woods. Troopers gave chase, but the minion outpaced them and disappeared in the dense forest.

The tress started back to the trail where Lenzel hid. Kyle sent a mental message: *A strong minion of the Dark is headed your way. Aim for his throat. He won't completely die until he's decapitated.* Not knowing if Lenzel's stone would capture the message, he rushed back with a pebble of men.

Lenzel heard someone traveling toward him from the woods, being nearly silent. Peeking through his blind, he saw an outrider step onto the trail. At the same time, he faintly heard Kyle's communication.

He did not know the outrider, but that wouldn't be unusual; he had met only a few that shadowed the tress. Nonetheless, the way the *outrider* sniffed the air, turning in a complete circle, alerted Lenzel. Apparently satisfied, the creature shook its head violently, shaking off the glamour, revealing its true shape. Lenzel nearly gasped, but caught the action, forcing down a gulp of air. It wore trousers and boots. The creature's upper body, muscled and toned, contrasted with its face's monstrosities. A chill climbed Lenzel's back. The hideous face turned slowly, again sniffing the air, and then turned back to face him, its tusks lowered, pointing outward, then started running toward him from forty-five feet away. He stood, throwing three Silver Stars at one time, concentrating on his stone and his target's neck. They flew at an amazing speed, striking and boring deeply in the creature's throat.

Yet the being tore the stars from its neck, releasing a black, foul smelling liquid arching high in the air. It opened its mouth, but no sound came forth, seeming to infuriate it. When it stopped thirty feet from where Lenzel stood, he could see the rage in its face; its eyes glowed a bright red and it sneered, exposing sharp fangs. It continued its run toward Lenzel. He threw another two stars, targeting its eyes. The beast tried to raise its arms, failing to move fast enough to protect its sight. Stumbling backward three steps, it sniffed the air and again started its run.

Lenzel threw three more stars, which cut into the creature's throat just below the first volley. It stumbled once more; its mouth opening and snapping shut, its teeth making a terrible sound. It moved forward, stretching its hands with three-inch claws stabbing the air in front of it. Lenzel threw his last two stars, landing above the first barrage, deep inside the throat with a satisfying crunch of bone.

The creature's head slid to the side, but it continued on toward the thicket. Lenzel moved across the trail, a few feet inside the wood with only a sword for protection where he could see the thicket. The Dark's minion crashed into the undergrowth, clawing the brush apart. Looking up, it sniffed the air once more.

Perhaps I should have put one of my stars in its nose! Lenzel drew his sword and tested his leg. The minimal pain belied his true condition; he thought it might give way at any moment, but he could stand on it at present. *I'll have to fight. I don't think I can run.* He steadied his sword and stood partially hidden by a tree.

It sniffed the air once more and crossed the trail, its head slipping from side to side as its right hand tried to hold it in place. It stumbled unerringly toward Lenzel, who waited, ready to strike with his sword. Taking a small step on his bad leg, he collapsed to his side. The creature struck, cutting through his trousers and deep into his leg above his wound. He cried out and rolled to the opposite side of the creature, swinging his sword into the beast's knee. As it fell, Lenzel kneeled on the good leg and brought his sword across the minion's neck. It tried to rise up at the beginning of the cut, only to fall away in the other direction of its rolling head. Great globs of putrid substance oozed from its neck. Lenzel rolled away from the filth to a tree and tried to use it to help him to rise when a strong arm lifted him to an upright position. He turned with his sword ready to strike to look into Kyle's worried eyes. He relaxed and felt the full extent of the creature's claws, falling forward into Kyle's arms, fighting not to scream.

"In your condition, you did very well," Kyle said, then pulled Lenzel's cut trouser leg apart and gasped as he suddenly bore all of Lenzel's weight. He settled him to the ground. The creature's claw cuts had already festered, dripping a bad smelling substance—not blood, but black. Kyle concentrated on his Stone and touched Lenzel's leg above the claw marks. The cuts foamed and frank blood began to flow in small amounts. Unfortunately, the area around the cuts stayed a dark gray. He concentrated on his Stone and Jarod. *Lenzel hurt badly by Dark's Source minion. I'm bringing him into camp. Have a healer ready.*

An answer came immediately: *We'll leave now and meet you on the way.*

The tress, Kyle, Lenzel, the cart, and the captured men met Jarod's men half way to the palace. The healer reported he didn't have the power to mend Lenzel's wounds and he put him to sleep, hoping the rest would do some good.

The caravan reached the palace in record time and Jarod handed Lenzel over to High Healer Sternwood.

* * *

WATHDURE walked toward his workbench when he slumped forward, reaching out to a table to steady him. His scream ricocheted off the cave's walls, his dead army not hearing. Pain ripped through his senses. He counted three of his minions destroyed. He tried to relax on the bench when, after several minutes deep, unrelenting and savage agony tore at his very substance. An upper minion's torment on its way to the Dark's pool savaged his being, bringing him to his knees.

Not only Wathdure, but Shadure also favored the

tusk-beast. It would take time and much energy to replace it and Shadure's wrath would be exceptional, as was his torment.

16

HIGH Healer Sternwood grasped his stone, concentrating on Lenzel's calf, healing the muscles and closing the wound. Minutes later, he wiped the sweat from his brow, drank water, and ate bread with a slab of cheese. He attacked the beast's claw wounds when he felt better from his refreshments. He managed to repair the muscle damage fairly rapidly. Nonetheless, the poison fought any effort to remove it. The healer tried to destroy it only to find it moved to another location. He knew he had more power from his stone than ever before and it had been growing in the last three years. Trying something he had never done, he encapsulated the toxic substance, pulling it from the cuts. He tired quickly, but finally when he thought he would pass out, the substance popped into the air above Lenzel's leg and then dissolved away. Sternwood motioned for his assistant to wrap the damaged leg.

"Lenzel," he said. "Stand and tell me how you feel."

When the assistant finished, he helped Lenzel to his feet and he took a few steps and smiled. "High Healer, you did a wonderful thing. My leg is a little tight, but there is no pain and it feels strong. I'm sorry your effort tired you so much."

The high healer made a dismissive gesture with his hand. "Lenzel I don't think I could accomplish it without the power from your stone. It worked in conjunction with my Stone and added its strength with mine. I felt its force radiate through the damage and I couldn't expel the beast's substance without your stone's influence. I've never felt a Channel Stone; it's quite remarkable."

LENZEL walked in a circle, still smiling. "It's fantastic!" After another circle, he stopped and faced the high healer, "You have my thanks. I don't know your fee, but whatever it is, I'll pay it."

"There's no need. The Zenith pays me."

Lenzel nodded. "I must go. Lord Kyle wanted to see me when you finished. Thank you!"

Sternwood gave a rare smile and motioned Lenzel away.

When he left the hospice set up in Segquo's palace, a Desert's Ire maiden moved from the shadows. "Lord Kyle is in the Zenith's study."

"Thank you, warrior. I know the way." Lenzel grinned when he noticed she followed him. He stopped before the beautifully carved door of blooming cacti to the study given over for the Zenith to use and started to knock.

The Zenith's voice sounded, "Come in, Lenzel."

Lenzel entered to find Jarod and Kyle looking closely over the map table. "Highest One and Lord Kyle, how may I be of service?"

Kyle spoke, "First, your stars have been carefully cleaned and a healer could not find any trace of the beast's poison. They are on the Zenith's desk. Second, you did wonderfully killing the creature. How did your stone help you?"

"I felt greater power and my stars found precise targets," Lenzel answered while putting stars in his pouch. "My swordsmanship became quicker and I seemed to have a stronger force using it. I don't think I could have been so effective using my old stone and I wouldn't have defeated the beast."

Jarod nodded. "Good. That's what I wanted to hear. I've sent for Ellrill to join High Healer Sternwood and study under him and I want to see if the stones will select them."

Kyle chuckled at Lenzel's expression of joy.

"When will she arrive?" he asked, hardly containing himself.

"Arrive? She's waiting for you in your quarters and yes, you're excused," Jarod said. "I'll want to see you both tomorrow for midmeal."

"Yes…yes, my lords, thank…thank you!"

Jarod and Kyle only smiled, but the Desert's Ire maiden laughed when Lenzel tore by. Men, women, and children moved out his way as he ran through the palace halls. He found Challenger in the stables and galloped a half-mile to his tent. After tying his stallion next to Ellrill's mare with a long lead, he turned and saw his wife, smiling at the tent's entrance. She slipped into the tent and by the time she settled on the furs, Lenzel stood before her. He sat beside her, took her in his arms and kissed her passionately.

Between the second and third kiss, he whispered, "We are expected for midmeal tomorrow and we have no duties until then…except our duties to each other."

His soft laugh matched the joy in her eyes. They spent the afternoon in each other's arms, touching and caressing each other, skin to skin, and much more.

At the time of lastmeal, the chime at the tent's entrance sounded twice. Lenzel pulled a fur around his nude body while Ellrill stretched another one over hers. He opened the tied tent flap and folded it back to see two Desert's Ire maidens, one with a covered tray and the other with a skin, filled to the brim. They entered the tent as if it belonged to them, placing their burdens on a low table. Turning, the taller of the maidens said, "Compliments of the Highest One." Then, they left with no more words, but a sly smile they didn't try to hide. Lenzel thanked them and retied the flap closed after they were gone.

Lenzel uncovered the tray while Ellrill got mugs. She

gasped when she saw the tray laden with braised lamb, root vegetables, a loaf of bread, and honey cakes, on platters. A slip of parchment, partially exposed under the platter holding the honey cakes, caught his eye. He read the note and looked up into her eyes. "The Highest One wants us to join him for midmeal tomorrow, as I said before, and we should plan on being with him the rest of the day."

"I don't know what to expect. Is he a nice man?" she asked.

"He and Lord Byrne are pleasant and they have treated me well. The Highest One had a high healer tend to my wounds."

She squeaked. "Wounds? I saw no signs of wounds but a few scratches…and I have looked you over pretty well." Her smile came with a giggle.

"That's why he's called a High Healer. They cut deep."

"Tell me!"

"No, not tonight. I'm well and that's all you need to know now. I don't want anything to spoil this night. I want only you…and maybe this meal."

She looked perturbed, but said nothing while she pulled on a shift and Lenzel climbed into his leather trousers. When seated across from each other, she ventured, "Should I wear my joining dress? It's the nicest one I have."

Between chomping down on a lamb chop, Lenzel answered, "No. You shouldn't wear what you do when you search for herbs, but nothing fancy. I wear my hunting leathers. The Highest One and Lord Byrne will be in everyday dress. I don't think the Highest One likes a lot of formality."

The rest of the evening went much as the afternoon and Lenzel slept comfortably next to a seemly equally pleased wife.

* * *

THE next morning, they rode to the palace and stabled their horses. Ellrill's face filled with wonder when she saw the extent of the palace complex. Lenzel took her to a square building, two hundred feet per side.

"This is the hospice. High Healer Sternwood is here to teach. He works with a stone and is powerful. I hope you'll be able to meet him. Has the Stone I gave you helped your healing?"

"Some. I find my herbs much easier than before and when I concentrate on my tasks, my medicinal poultices seem to work better."

"I have a new Stone. It's larger and the Highest One called it a Channel Stone. I'm not sure what that means. It's much, much stronger. When I have time, I'll tell you how I got it. Now, I want you to see the palace complex."

They walked by the armory and the smithies behind. The mess hall had been built to serve hundreds of warriors at a time. Various shops selling everything from weapons and leathers to fancy dresses surprised Ellrill. Lenzel paid a silver for a beautiful wormcloth scarf she had fussed over. He ignored her dismay at the price he paid.

"Why are you upset? I left you with gold and I have more."

"Yes, but it has to last a long time!"

"The Highest One made me a Gal and I draw that rank's pay. It's enough for us to live well without paying from our gold. Where is your gold?"

"Late one night, I buried it a mile from our tent at the Clan of the Cat. Do you remember the large oak you could see from the archery field?" Lenzel nodded. "It's buried twenty paces north of there. That night, only a quarter moon showed and I made sure no one saw me and I covered my trail back to the middle of the field. I went back a few days later and discovered no sign of anyone and only the track of a small fox."

Lenzel laughed. "I too, buried mine in the middle of the night and made sure no one followed me." A bell chimed from over the palace. "It's time to go to the palace."

Lenzel wore his leathers, which provided no sign of him belonging to the Guard, but the trooper at the door saluted. He returned the acknowledgement, thinking, *Word travels fast.* Ellrill seemed to look in every direction at once. He tried to explain some of the murals' stories as they walked. When they reached the personal quarters for Segquo, Jarod, Kyle, and other important guests, a Desert's Ire maiden stepped out of the shadows, startling Ellrill.

"Warrior Lenzel, the Highest One awaits you in his study."

"Thank you, maiden," Lenzel said. She nodded and returned to the shadows.

When they reached the study, Jarod's voice could be heard through the door. "Come in, Lenzel."

"How did he know it's you?" Ellrill whispered.

"He senses me or my stone; I don't know which."

They entered and once again Lenzel found maidens setting up food for midmeal while Jarod and Kyle stood by the map table. Jarod looked up. "Lenzel, you never told me Ellrill is so beautiful. Do the introductions."

"Highest One, this is indeed my wife Ellrill. Ellrill, I present to you the Highest One, Lord Kyle Byrne, and High Healer Tobias Sternwood."

Ellrill looked dumbstruck, but recovered quickly. "Highest One and my lords, I'm honored."

"We have much to do this afternoon, but let's enjoy midmeal first," Jarod said.

After seating, Lenzel looked down on a platter of a small fowl of some kind stuffed with pleasant smelling herbs, mashed and creamed root vegetables, some type of bean Lenzel did not recognize, and bread. The maidens finished pouring chilled wine in mugs and left, leaving a full beaker on a side table.

The conversation flowed easily on mundane subjects when Jarod asked Ellrill if she wanted to know something he could tell her.

"Oh, Highest One, I would like to know about Stonefire. I've heard it's wonderful."

Jarod smiled. "There are two Stonefires. One is the name of my realm and the other is its capital city. My realm is one of the smallest and the city of Stonefire is the largest in the Seven Realms with a population of over four million people. The Spires is a large complex that is the real seat of my power, located on the outskirts of the city. It gets its name from three seven hundred foot spires that form a triangle with the walls connecting them. Each spire is a mile apart. We don't know how they came about; we just know the first Zenith Lord built them. Other lands call the Seven Realms by the name of Jewel because the realm of Stonefire mines precious jewels. It is one of our few exports."

Jarod started to say more when a Desert's Ire maiden knocked lightly and entered carrying a message pouch. She took it directly to him, gave a slight bow, and left without speaking.

* * *

JAROD read through the missive twice before looking at Kyle. "Several groups of bandits have been caught while traveling in this direction. Other groups have been seen, but disappeared in the countryside before the Guard could arrive. I gave orders for the Guard not to search for them if that happened. I don't want to capture too many and have Gangkor call off the robbery."

"Gangkor?" Kyle asked.

"He's the leader of the largest group of bandits. Gaz found that out a year ago, but he's as elusive as Gaston before Zack Stand killed him. Oh, Zack and Currat Duval are on their way here at my request. He knew many of the bandits when under Gaston plus several more from his work. He's still the best spy we have and Currat is a close second.

"You haven't said what happened in Deepwells."

"I had lastmeal with the empress and she left on the morning tide. The shipbuilding is proceeding well and the empress left shipwrights to continue helping us. I'm pleased.

"Now, it's getting late and we have a lot to do. All of you will be going on a trip this afternoon and I want to be back before dark. Unfortunately, for your future protection, all of you except Lord Byrne will be blindfolded. Your questions will be answered when we arrive at our destination."

Kyle had arranged the trip. The traveler's horses waited for them at the private exit from the palace with plenty of water, bread, and cheese in case it took longer than Jarod thought. Jarod knew Tobias disliked horseback riding and after all the years, he still found it difficult. He thought about bringing a Desert's Ire's maiden to ride double with him, but Tobias' pride would get in the way. As they cleared the complex, Jarod and Kyle blindfolded the rest of the group.

"Is this really necessary?" Tobias whispered to Kyle.

"Yes, it's for your protection. If you're ever caught by our enemies, Wathdure's minions will search your mind and realize your don't know the way. That just might save your life and possibly allow you to be rescued." Kyle could see Tobias' frown, but the healer couldn't see Kyle's smile.

The trip ended an hour later. "You may take off your blindfolds," Jarod instructed.

Kyle retrieved torches from his saddlepacks. The group saw a mound in front of them and Jarod led the way to the top. He reached inside his shirt and touched the Sire's Stone and concentrated; a portion of the mound disappeared leaving steps into the ground. Kyle lighted two torches and gave one to Jarod, who led the way down. With the other torch, Kyle took the rear position. They descended below ground level to a cave some twenty feet square. Jarod walked to the far end of the cave and again concentrated on his stone. An illusion floated away, exposing an even larger room. In its middle sat the trunk of Stones. Ten feet behind it sat the other trunks and scrolls and weapons.

"Lenzel, walk to the edge of the trunk holding the Stones."

When Lenzel reached the trunk, the effect happened immediately. The Stone in his headband ripped free and disappeared among other stones in the trunk. Stones rustled in the trunk and a gold chain with a large emerald attached with gold wires floated free. Jarod stepped to the emerald and took the chain. He touched his stone once more and a golden glow surrounded him and Lenzel as he placed the necklace over Lenzel's head.

"Lenzel, this Stone is the most powerful except for the seven major stones like the one embedded in my chest," he said softly.

Lenzel's eyes widened, clearly not knowing the Highest One had a stone in his chest.

"Once I let it fall onto your shoulders, it can never be removed except by one with a major stone," Jarod continued. "Before the stone will accept you, you must silently or vocally declare your devotion to the Great Creator and the Light's Source and to the Major Stones."

Lenzel appeared to be in deep concentration for several minutes before he spoke in an even voice, "I, Lenzel, warrior of the Clan of the Cat, turn over my life to the Great Creator, the Light's Source, and wearers of the Major Stones until death." He seemed to concentrate further and after a few seconds, the chain rose from

Jarod's hand and settled over Lenzel's shoulders.

Jarod grasped Lenzel's forearm. "Lenzel, you'll have much more power and it'll grow. Take off your shirt."

Lenzel blinked, but did as Jarod bid while he reached toward Kyle, who handed him a new leather shirt. When Lenzel laid his shirt aside and turned back to Jarod, he blinked once more upon seeing a shirt made of beautiful leather with the emblem of a crouching deathcat sewn over the left breast.

"You now hold the rank of Apex. Congratulations."

"Highest One, I had trouble thinking of myself as a Gal. I have no idea what to do as an Apex!"

"You will intensely train with Lord Byrne for three months, which will be only the beginning. Afterwards, you'll learn a lot by leading your men or from your experience working in small groups or alone. On the occasions when not commanding thousands of men, you should wear leathers without your rank. Now, please rejoin Ellrill."

Ellrill embraced him. "I'm so proud of you, my love."

"I'm glad, but this will make it even harder for us to have time together!"

Lenzel's words sobered her.

"High Healer Tobias Sternwood, approach the trunk and remove your stone," Jarod somberly instructed.

Tobias complied. A large citrine rose from the trunk and in a blink of an eye, the stone on Tobias' chain lay in the trunk and the citrine occupied its former place.

"Tobias," Jarod said. "You've made the oaths to the Light's Source many times. The stones know of your devotion. You now wear a Channel Stone. It will allow you more power and skill. Please step back."

As Tobias retreated, examining the stone and slipping it over his head, he looked amazed.

"Ellrill from the Clan of the Cat, come to the trunk."

Ellrill's stone exchanged in a second for a gold chain

with a large amethyst in a procedure like Lenzel's.

"This, too, is a Channel Stone. I've asked Tobias to work and train with you and he's agreed. We should go; we've been here longer than it seems."

The return trip seemed even farther to Jarod. They were set to arrive at the palace in time for lastmeal and his stomach let him know how much it wanted food. He had spent a great deal more energy than the others observed. His lack of energy, even now, grew back to normal, but left him strained. Kyle removed the blindfolds when they neared the palace compound.

A tress of mounted men approached. "Focus on the Zenith Lord!" the lieutenant yelled. He leaned forward, staring at Lenzel's chest and then to Jarod, who slightly nodded. The lieutenant added in the same voice, "Focus on the Apex of the Guard!"

Several of the men looked surprised, but recovered quickly. Jarod chuckled in a soft tone no one could hear. Lenzel frowned. Ellrill beamed with pride. Tobias and Kyle held their mien as if nothing happened.

They encountered several other guardsmen's surprise on the way to Jarod's study where two Desert's Ire maidens finished setting the table with steaming platters. They slightly bowed to Jarod as they left and Jarod motioned his companions to sit.

Little conversation flowed, but all ate large portions. Jarod and Kyle forewent the wine and drank cool water, as did Lenzel and Ellrill.

The lastmeal neared its end when Jarod spoke, "For the next three months, Lenzel will work with Lord Kyle; Tobias and Ellrill will work together. I must go back to see the empress at Wellsport. Lenzel, Ellrill, and Tobias, you're excused when you finish your lastmeal. Kyle, I wish you to stay." Jarod rose and went to stand by the window looking over a garden of cacti flowers in shades of yellow and orange. Only when Lenzel, Ellrill, and

Tobias left and he sensed Kyle behind him did he turn and took his chair at his desk, motioning the other man to sit across from him.

"I sensed a great ability within Lenzel to learn. The growth he's gone through over the last three years has amazed me. You may be surprised at how fast he develops. Keep him learning at his peak and devise ways for him to become comfortable giving orders—the right orders. Also, provide a path for him to earn the guardsmen's respect. If done properly, the men rotating back to Stonefire will carry the right kind of information to other guardsmen. Lenzel has a natural stealthy capacity he absorbed in his clan training. It will be interesting to see how it affects his battle plans and lesser operations."

"I think I'll enjoy this more than I thought I would."

"Work him hard over the three months, but let him have some time with Ellrill when he reaches a block in training. I hope to return before his training period is over. Now, I need to sleep."

"I'll meet you in the morning, brother."

Jarod nodded and both men smiled.

17

KYLE watched Lenzel pouring over maps at a table set aside for him alone. Jarod had been right about Lenzel's progress. In the past two months, the young man had completed nearly a year's training at the academy in the subjects that really mattered in a war. He had led several war games tor to tor, to familiarize men with larger encounters than they had participated in before the current troubles. Lenzel faced seasoned commanders and, by using different strategies than the old and true stratagems, he won every confrontation. *Later tonight might be different.*

Lenzel would lead a trass to infiltrate the *enemy's* camp to gather information. *Ninety men against a full tor of twenty-five hundred and fifty men should be interesting,* Kyle chuckled at the thought. When he reached Lenzel, he saw him studying the several formations used for a tor's encampments. He felt a little better about Lenzel's chances.

"Lenzel," he said. "I see your scheming side is well and good. May I ask what is in the box you've been hiding behind your desk all day?"

"Lord Byrne, you harm me to my very core," he said before softly laughing. "I seem to have come across ninety-five insignias of Looker Jeroam's tor. Luckily, I found horse glue so they can be applied quickly on unadorned shirts. My men will all be of the lower ranks, at least for tonight."

"I don't want to know more until the exercise is over. I wish you well."

LENZEL watched Kyle leave. *I wonder what the Highest One will think of the efforts of my men and me. Lord Kyle doesn't give compliments often. Tonight, I hope to earn one.* Lenzel gathered his notes and supplies, and left for his first clandestine meeting. He found Lieutenant Momets waiting at their arranged staging area, a box canyon not far from Looker Jeroam's encampment.

The lieutenant snapped to position and saluted. "Apex Lenzel, I'm honored you chose my tress for this exercise."

"Thank you lieutenant, but I didn't choose you; your actions on previous exercises and the performance of the men under your command made that choice for me. This will be a difficult mission; we have to collect a tor's information from within its encampment. It will take cool heads. In the last two days, the tor has been rotating men in and out of the area for leave. There will be men the tor's remaining men won't recognize and that is the only thing in our favor, but it will help greatly. I need a man to survey the encampment and return with its formation. Of course," Lenzel said with a smile, "without getting caught. The top of the backside of this canyon will allow a view of the encampment, but it's a difficult climb. Select your man wisely."

"I know just the man. He's a skimmer under my best rocker and he climbs mountains in his off time. All the rockers should be here within a few minutes."

Even as the lieutenant spoke, three mounted men entered the box canyon and rode toward them. When they dismounted and saluted their lieutenant, Lenzel turned toward the rockers from looking over his notes. The men snapped to position and saluted, a look of surprise across their faces.

Lenzel returned their salute and appraised the three men, each in turn, before saying, "Stand at ease. I understand one of you has a competent man to climb rock."

One man stepped forward. "Skimmer Amdrose Cammeron, sir."

"Will he have any trouble going up the backside of this canyon?" Lenzel asked.

The rocker took a few steps away to get a better view and looked over the near sheer wall about three hundred feet high. He turned back. "Apex Lenzel, from the Clan of the Cat, from what I see from here, he shouldn't have too much trouble."

Lenzel smiled. "That title is for formal occasions. Apex Lenzel will do."

Three guardsmen rode in showing the rank of skimmer. The rocker motioned one of the men over and introduced Skimmer Cammeron to Apex Lenzel.

After the salutes, Lenzen said, "The parchments over here are the four approved formations of a Tor." Lenzel pointed to the documents on the desert floor, held down by rocks. "Familiarize yourself with the formations, and then climb the back wall to see which configuration is being used. You must not be discovered! Stay only as long as you need to correctly identify the formation. I'll wait until you return to explain our mission. Lieutenant."

While waiting, Lenzel went over some of the plan with the lieutenant and the rockers and asked for any suggestions before he explained the complete plan. The men studied the formations of tor encampments.

"I know they have new men and there will be many they don't know, but they'll recognize our uniforms," the lieutenant said.

Lenzel smiled. "Open the large crate and then the small box."

Momets looked puzzled for a few seconds before a wide grin spread across his face. "Apex, you're a clever man. Will all the shirts fit?"

"They should. I got the sizes from stores last night

without being seen. It was easy to find the shirts and proper insignias. By the time the shortages are found, I'll have an order for the missing items. At some time in the future, I'll have others trained to do these types of things. Now, Lieutenant Momets, you should look over the overall plan while we wait on Cammeron." Lenzel handed the lieutenant a sheaf of parchments.

The rockers seemed to like the small part of the plan Lenzel had explained and Momets smiled broader, knowing what Lenzel planned. The sound of Cammeron's horse came close and he dismounted near his lieutenant. He saluted Lenzel, who returned the gesture with a questioning look.

"Apex Lenzel," Cammeron said. "It is the formation with the command tents against the other side of the wall I climbed. Looker Jeroam must think the formation is protection enough. He has only a pebble on guard in front of the command tents." As he finished, the remaining members of the tress began arriving and their rockers admonished them to make as little noise as possible while forming up.

Momets addressed his men. "We are to complete a mission tonight I think you'll enjoy. I remind you to make little noise here and on your way to the object of our mission. Now, focus on Apex Lenzel."

True surprise showed on many of the men's faces as they came to position. In unison, they saluted and Lenzel returned the gesture as he came before the center of the formation.

"Gentlemen, you are not here and you have not seen me or your comrades tonight." Several of the men smiled. "Our exercise is to infiltrate Looker Jeroam's tor and replace certain documents in the command tent, which I'll do. The job of you ninety men is to make distractions for me to accomplish my part. There will be little moonlight tonight, to our advantage. Our exercise will start at midnight when most of the encampment will be sleeping. You each will have leave slips signed by Looker Jeroam. Once you're inside the camp, you'll throw them into campfires. There are nine pebbles among you and each pebble will have specific orders. We have approximately six hours before midnight and you may think you have a lot of time to get ready, but don't be so sure. It's important you did not know the plans before now. After a few ales, tongues might wag and I couldn't afford that to occur. Lieutenant, distribute the orders to the appropriate rockers. Every one of you must know your actions to the least bit. I'll be available to answer questions. I'll leave you to your planning."

As the men settled down poring over their orders, a wagon with its load covered by a tarp rolled to a stop ten feet away. The driver saluted Lenzel and began bringing water off the wagon for the horses and men. Next came a lastmeal of bread, cheese, and slabs of peccary wrapped in cloth. Marked crates followed and the lieutenant helped the driver take them to the appropriate pebble. When the last load had been taken from the wagon, Lenzel waited on the driver at the wagon.

"Are there problems?" he asked the man when he returned.

"No, Apex. I found everything in its hiding place and the transit pass you gave me raised no questions. I don't think anyone paid attention to me."

"Good, you're the only man outside the men here that knows something is planned for tonight. You did well and I'll let your superiors know your participation. You're dismissed until later."

The implied threat did not look lost on the driver. He saluted; Lenzel saluted back and the man climbed onto the wagon and turned the team to return to the palace complex.

Lenzel looked over the men and saw two of the

pebbles had joined, talking amongst them, referring to the orders. Again, smiles flared from time to time. *Yes, I think I picked the right men.*

The lieutenant approached. "Apex, my men are pleased with the assignment, as am I. It'll be a story told for some time."

"No, lieutenant. The story cannot be told for at least two weeks and perhaps longer. Form up your men."

Within three minutes, the tress stood at position and, at the lieutenant's command, saluted when Lenzel drew near.

"Gentlemen, stand relaxed. This is a direct order. You are not to discuss tonight's activities with anyone, including your wives or lovers, until I give the order in two to three weeks!" Lenzel smiled. "Don't let that spoil your fun tonight. Dismissed to your duties."

As Lenzel walked back to his horse, he immersed himself in his thoughts. *I can't imagine how this exercise will grow from the truth by the time I allow it to be talked about. Actually, I must let Jeroam agree to the information's release.* He approached Challenger and opened the saddlepacks, removing a dark cape with cowl, and walked back to the men; he found Skimmer Cammeron and motioned him over.

After the salutes, Lenzel said, "You'll be with me tonight on top of the canyon wall."

Cammeron's expression fell.

"Look at it this way. You'll be in a position to see how it all unfolds and have my life in your hands." Lenzel didn't tell he had practiced with levitation and, while he did not come near Lord Kyle's, and certainly not the Zenith Lord's ability, he could land from a high fall with little more than his breath knocked out of him. He could fall, but not rise; he needed Cammeron.

The man's smile returned.

"Do you feel your second in command can lead your

men?"

"Yes Apex, he's due to take command of a pebble of his own, although he doesn't know that yet. He can lead the pebble inside the camp and he knows the rocker as well as I do."

"Good, it's near time to deploy. Find the lieutenant for me."

Cammeron ran back toward the staging area and, within a few moments, the lieutenant stood before him. "At your command, Apex."

"Cammeron will be going with me. Are your men ready Lieutenant?"

"Ready with a few gangling nerves, but that's expected."

"Are their instructions clear and well understood?"

"Yes Apex, your orders are well written and the men didn't have many questions. I've heard several say they would enjoy this exercise. All the shirts are swapped out with appropriate rank and insignia."

"Very well. It's close to midnight. Start the infiltration and begin the exercise in two hours."

"At once, Apex."

After the salutes, Lenzel and Cammeron mounted horses and rode to the back of the box canyon to where Cammeron had previously climbed to the top. Lenzel pulled his cloak around him and started up, concentrating on his stone. He reached the top and looked down to see Cammeron at about the half way mark.

The skimmer crawled onto the top ridge. "Apex, I've never seen anyone climb so fast. Do you climb often, sir?"

"I've climbed one or two mountains," he said with a chuckle.

"Apex, your cloak is marvelous. I could hardly see you and I looked. From farther away, you won't be noticed."

"We have a while to wait."

As midnight neared, men started penetrating the encampment's three entrances. Lenzel removed his spyglass from one of his cloaks' inner pockets and searched the area. Small groups of men passed the guards, showing their passes; some seemed drunk, some walked slowly, while some ran to meet the midnight deadline.

The encampment had posts driven in the ground with three equally spaced ropes connecting them. Anyone found outside the fence would be hunted after midnight when all passes expired. Lenzel gave Cammeron the spyglass and watched the satisfaction on his face as his men took up their places at the line of paddocks containing a thousand horses, one hundred per paddock.

Lenzel put the spyglass back and watched men working their way around the guards to the outside edge of the paddocks, and started loosening the ropes. Other men silently began tampering with the ropes of the major tents, while others settled by campfires. Lenzel found Lieutenant Momets walking toward the main campfire located in the center of the encampment. He nudged Cammeron and pointed. They watched as he walked by the fire and then circled back the way he came. Lenzel slowly counted to twenty when an explosion of fiery sparks shot upward with a loud explosion. The large tents began to fall and the horses began running amuck escaping the new explosions erupting from the smaller fires at various points around the area. The mounts cleared the paddocks at a gallop. Stampeding horses' vibrations and thunderous sounds struck the canyon wall.

Officers shouted orders and Looker Jeroam appeared outside his tent, half dressed. The other officers began to converge on him at the run. Soon, a bugle sounded across the desert, repeating the call three times. Riders from the outer paddocks would be arriving shortly.

Lenzel patted Cammeron on the shoulder and dropped the rope over the side of the canyon wall.

Cammeron checked the ties and nodded and watched as Lenzel nearly disappeared against the stone. After the first fifty feet, he let himself go and floated downward at only a little more speed than he wanted. He landed behind the command tent without injury and waited for the order he knew would come. It did not take long.

A lieutenant ran toward the command area shouting, "All men to the paddock area!" and repeating the order as he ran down the string of tents. Men exited the tents and ran to their assignments. Lenzel waited a few heartbeats to loosen the lower ropes and slip into the command tent. A brassiere burned, emitting a golden glow around the space. He went to the large trunk at his right and, touching his stone, grabbed the lock. The lock began to get warm and, after another few heartbeats, slipped open. He replaced several packets with others from his cloak's inside pockets and then slipped back outside to retie the lower tent ropes. As he approached the rock formation, a guardsman appeared ten feet away to relieve himself. Lenzel stood still and concentrated through his stone. The guardsman finished and looked past Lenzel before returning the way he came.

Lenzel found the rope and yanked it once before starting the climb upward. Cammeron's pull on the rope helped and he reached the top, rolling over face down on the ridge. He took the spyglass and searched the fence farthest from the paddocks. He saw men slipping through the fence and rounding behind a rock formation to their horses.

Several moments later, they rode into the staging area as Lenzel and Cammeron returned. Lieutenant Momets gave orders to change shirts and put the others in the large crate. As they finished loading the shirts, the wagon swung into the box canyon.

Lenzel approached the driver as he pulled next to the crates. "You arrived on time."

"Its easy to know when to come when fire shoots up into the sky," he said, and chuckled.

Lenzel smiled and the man seemed to relax. The lieutenant gave more orders and men loaded the crates on the wagon. When the wagon returned the way it came, back to the complex, men spread out, erasing any sign of its being there. They continued, leading horses and wiping away their signs. A half hour later, they reached the main trail, mounted, and rode back to the palace complex.

* * *

LENZEL answered the message brought by a Desert's Ire maiden and made his way to Lord Kyle's study. He arrived and started to knock when Kyle's voice came through the door—"Enter."

As he reached for the door, he realized the command had sounded in his head and not in his ears.

He found Lord Kyle behind his desk and Looker Jeroam red-faced and pacing between the desk and window. His mind held a smile that did not show on his face. When Jeroam saw Lenzel, he turned to Kyle. "With respect Lord Kyle, why is *he* here? Arrogance dripped from his words.

"Jeroam, Apex Lenzel deserves your respect. It's been reported to me on numerous occasions of the remarks you made demeaning a superior officer. You don't seem to respect him for his accomplishments. His last one defeated you in the recent war games!"

"What…what do you…" Realization dawned on Jeroam's face. "You are the…the one that caused the disturbance at my encampment! But…but how did that cause me to lose?"

"Jeroam," Lord Kyle broke in. "If you had personally examined your order's packet, you might have discovered it's not the packet and plans outlined to you before the exercise. Even after you fell into Apex Lenzel's trap, he let the other Lookers defeat you without putting a man in the field."

Jeroam sputtered spittle and started to speak, but Kyle raised a hand to stop him. "Not a word, Jeroam. You don't know all that took place that night. A tress of imposters under Apex Lenzel's command infiltrated your encampment and caused the havoc you refer to as a mere disturbance. Apex Lenzel lowered himself from the top of the canyon's ridge behind your command tent. He slipped into the tent and exchanged the packets, and then climbed back to the top of the rock wall, something I doubt you or your men could do in daylight. Over the last few months, Apex Lenzel planned the winning orders for every exercise."

"It's not my fault; he sabotaged me!" he said through gritted teeth.

"It's never your fault Jeroam, not when you served Mountglen and later, when you served after Mountglen's treason and I took ownership of his realm and renamed it Stonecreast."

Jeroam started to sputter. "I'm not under your command." His face burned with anger, "I serve in the Guard"

"Not any longer!"

Jeroam stopped and turned toward the new voice, finding his Zenith Lord. Then, he did have the presence of mind to salute and keep his mouth shut.

Jarod spoke softly yet with command, which made his tone menacing—"My personal detail with three maidens from Desert's Ire has searched your quarters. They are still searching, but I'm sure you know all they'll find."

"Zenith Lord, I can explain... It's not what your think."

"Oh." Jarod's voice still carried ominous tones. "Do you mean the messages between you and Thord? Even a fool would've destroyed them." Jeroam's face went white. "Your fate is sealed. You plotted in the death of my wife.

Your trial will be held tomorrow morning and I expect you'll be dead by sunset!"

Jeroam spun, bringing out a knife hidden in his jerkin, and shoved it upward and under his ribs, then dropped to the floor, his eyes dead.

* * *

JEROAM heard a terrible voice in his dead mind. "Welcome to the Dark. You belong to me for all time."

"NO! No my lord, I worked on your behalf by doing what Wathdure commanded."

A foreboding laugh tore at Jeroam's mind. "Yes, you tried, but you failed. You escaped punishment on the physical realm, but this is the Dark. I don't permit failure!"

Jeroam's screams rose until they faded as he descended into the void. Shadure's laughter followed close behind.

* * *

"MAIDENS," Jarod called out.

Four Desert's Ire maidens burst through the door and quickly took in the scene. Their hands held knives while crouching in an attack position.

"Highest One, did we fail you?" the tallest one said.

Jarod chuckled. "I can't imagine a maiden failing. No, Looker Jeroam committed treason and took his miserable life when we discovered his deceit. Remove him and perform a traitor's cremation on the body."

"At once, Highest One," the same maiden said. "The head will be severed, cremated separate from his body, and the ashes buried apart in an unmarked grave. No one outside Desert's Ire will know the graves' location." She slightly bowed and the four maidens began removing the body.

"You're back, obviously," Jarod said to Lenzel.

"It's not what I expected on my return. Thinking on it, Jeroam stayed far away from me. I suspect Wathdure had a hand in that."

"Lenzel, I heard the conversation earlier and I'm pleased with your progress over the last three years here. You found the first cache of Stones. You may not repeat what I say next." Lenzel nodded to the Highest One. "There are six more hoards of Stones. I have an assignment for you. You are charged with finding the remaining Stones."

Lenzel gulped and then smiled. "You honor me, Highest One."

"You may pick a pebble of men and four maidens of your choice from all who are here. You'll have orders allowing you to draw men and supplies from all garrisons and the realms' High Lords. When you find Stones, concentrate on me with all your might while holding your stone. Guard them until I arrive. Do not let any but those under your command know what you're about and only when it's absolutely necessary. I suspect the caves will all be located in mountain terrains. If you need men from an outpost, keep them at the foot of the mountain and let them know only that you wait for me. Go at your best speed without overtiring your men and horses. Allow a day in ten for rest. I think your stone is powerful enough for the Dark not to track you, but take no changes. I'll inspect your men and maidens before you leave. I'll detect any who have a dark tinge around them.

"Lenzel, I consider you a friend to me and the Seven Realms. Lord Kyle must return to Stonecreast and I've been away from Stonefire too long. Pick your group carefully, but as quickly as you can. Lord Kyle and I will depart shortly after their inspection…"Now, let's have a meal; I'm starved."

"Highest One," Lenzel said. "You honor me greatly."

Jarod smiled as maidens filed into the room with steaming trenchers giving off aromas of herbs and spices.

PART II

18

LENZEL sought out Segquo, knowing he knew of his mission, asking for recommendations for maidens to join him on his search. He received the names of eight maidens and sent messages for them to meet him in one hour, three hundred yards north of the palace.

He rode out to arrive early and found all the requested maidens awaiting him. They sat in a circle, legs crossed, a few yards from their horses, and rose as one when Lenzel dismounted and approached them. They held no weapons and did not speak.

"Honorable Maidens of Desert's Ire, I'm pleased you answered my call," he said.

The oldest looking maiden took a step forward. "We know of you and your exploits and we, too, are honored to be in your company. Honorable Segquo impressed on us the importance of your mission. We feel privileged to be here for your selection."

"I'll not make the selection; you will, based on the criteria I give you."

"You are wise for your years, warrior. What skills do you need from us?"

"My mission must be done in great secrecy. There will be a need for mountain climbing at times. It would be good to stop at only Guard garrisons and High Lord's estates, but that's not always possible. A maiden familiar with lowland villages and cities would be a great asset. I've selected a group of men to form a pebble who will be assigned to our mission. The men are competent with arms and with being on a long mission, but I don't think they can match your tracking and stealth abilities. Those attributes may be greatly in need. These guardsmen are not used to our people and any untoward advantages or remarks must be handled firmly, but with care not to disturb their egos."

All but one of the maidens smiled; the remaining one laughed. "I am an Apex in the Guard and a sketch of me has been distributed to all garrisons, outposts, and forts. I will wear my rank only when needed. The guardsmen will wear their uniforms only in the same situations. They and you must be able to not cause undue notice. I'll wear leathers and I think it'll be in your best interest to do the same, but you should be comfortable in the clothing aside from ours. This last requirement I know will not be a problem for you, but perhaps for the men. We must travel at best speed without overtiring our mounts and ourselves. We must be ready for an attack at any time."

The oldest maiden said, "Honorable warrior, you've given much to consider. Allow us time to do so."

Lenzel nodded and the maidens withdrew to reform their circle on the ground. Lenzel moved away out of earshot for anyone who didn't wear a Channel Stone. He listened long enough to be satisfied the maidens understood the seriousness of their tasks and studied maps of the Seven Realms he carried in his saddle packs. An hour passed before Lenzel sensed the older maiden approaching from behind. He turned to face her.

"Honorable Warrior, we have selected four who best meet all your requirements. The remaining four have great talents, but are not necessarily what you need. It would be my pleasure to introduce you to our choices for your approval."

Lenzel walked beside the maiden to those standing in a line.

"Honorable Warrior, I am Kaarill. I'm the oldest, but still an excellent fighter. For a time, I lived with lowlanders and I know their ways."

Her words were stated as fact, not with conceit, Lenzel sensed.

Kaarill pointed to the tallest of the maidens. "This is Rystarill; she is the best at tracking among us and is almost never noticed."

The next in line stepped forward. "This is Kelosrill. She is a strong fighter as we all are, but she is excellent with archery and Silver Stars. We have watched you at practice and are not nearly as good, but she is much better than the average."

A forth maiden stepped forward. "This is Syrill. She is the best fighter among us and, perhaps as important, she is the best cook in Desert's Ire."

"Kaarill," Lenzel said. "You do me great honor with your wisdom. Now, we must hurry; the Highest One awaits us." Lenzel addressed the remaining maidens, "I sense you are all a great benefit to Desert's Ire and, if permitted, I'd be honored to take all of you."

The maidens smiled and nodded to him.

On the way to the palace complex, he listened to the maidens' remarks.

"He respects our ways."

"Yes, and he's the best warrior in all the clans. I hope our service to him and the Highest One will be what they need."

Lenzel closed his mind to them and mentally reviewed the maps he'd studied earlier, weighing the routes to mountainous regions around the Seven Realms, and deciding the best start would be Stonefire. He increased the pace, not wanting to be late for his meeting with the Highest One. Rounding the palace corner leading to the stables, he saw the pebble he'd put together. He asked the maidens to wait with the pebble until the Highest One arrived.

I wonder what the pebble will think when he arrives.

He moved to the corner of the palace and met Jarod

as he came from the private quarters.

"Highest One, the men I selected stand ready with the maidens chosen for me."

"Chosen for you?"

"Yes, Highest One. Honorable Segquo selected eight maidens for me to choose from. I explained the nature of the mission without mentioning what we searched for and let them decide who should go. I believe they selected the best for the mission. Desert's Ire training precludes making decisions based on personal interests."

"There are times when you continue to amaze me, my friend. I know you used your Stone when selecting your men, but let's see what I can discover."

"Highest One, there is something you should know. While scanning the guardsmen with my Stone, I found several with a dark edge around them."

"That's interesting, Lenzel. I think I'll have time for a general inspection before I return to Stonefire in a few days."

"Highest One, I selected Stonefire as the first realm to search."

"Lenzel, two men, Zack Stand and Currat Duval, are arriving tomorrow. I want them to join you. I'll explain later. Now, let's see your group."

As they approached, the skimmer yelled, "Focus on the Zenith Lord!" The men snapped to position.

Jarod approached the women first. "Maidens of Desert's Ire, I am pleased maidens of your talent have joined Apex Lenzel on this mission. He, and you in turn, operate under my direct orders. Kaarill, you and your maidens follow me." Jarod moved out of earshot of the pebble. "This mission is of the highest importance and secrecy is even higher. Apex Lenzel's talents are best suited for what is to come, better than those of anyone in the Seven Realms. He has unique talents and his life must be protected."

"Highest One," Kaarill said. "I am honored you know my name. The Honorable Segquo has sent word to all the clans that Honorable Warrior Lenzel's life is the clans' responsibility and he is raised to the rank of Apex in the Guard."

Lenzel didn't let his surprise show on his face, but Kaarill's words jarred him. The elders had talked about such a scarce decree happening over two hundred years ago. *Segquo must have informed the Highest One before he sent out a message so unusual.*

"I am happy for the clans' involvement. Now, let's join the guardsmen." Jarod said, then he, Lenzel, and the maidens walked back to the men standing at position. Jarod stopped in front of the skimmer. "Your name, Skimmer."

"Zenith Lord, I am Skimmer Lorell Andress."

Lenzel could feel the power emitting from Jarod.

Jarod repeated the inspection for each man in turn: Guardsmen Roush Letern, Sorrel Billon, Dusten Remming, Daniell Respecton, Larrell Sontos, Stevemon Surron, Davad Drosh, Richmon Userron, and Charlos Mattene.

"Skimmer Andress and Guardsman Userron, I've read of your valor while fighting bandits. I'm sure the rest of you are as brave and will do your duty. Listen well! Any mention of your mission outside your pebble will be regarded as high treason and carries with it a death sentence. That includes members of the Guard, best friends, wives and lovers, or any other person."

Jarod's words had a visual effect of surprise and then resignation on the men.

"Apex Lenzel is an important man in the fight against the Dark. Your greatest duty is to keep him alive and in doing so, you'll save the lives of thousands, perhaps hundreds of thousands. We leave for Stonefire in two days and join two Mounts for part of the way. There will be an action you'll not, I repeat *not*, take part in. Apex Lenzel may lead you to an advantage point, but you're not to engage under any circumstances. It would be an unnecessary danger to you and the Apex. Two men will join your team. You are not to ask them about their past or their orders. They will help your mission and should be treated as full members of your group. These men are proficient in battle and many other areas. One last point, you must act in concert and harmony. You are dismissed to Apex Lenzel's commands."

"Salute!" Skimmer Andress shouted.

Jarod returned the salute and then walked to Lenzel. "My study in two hours," he whispered.

Lenzel nodded while saluting and turned back to the pebble. "Meet me here in the morning at sunrise. You should stay together as a group when eating. Drink no ale. You're dismissed to consider the Zenith Lord's words."

After the salutes, he turned to the maidens. "My Honorable Sisters, until this mission is over, we'll use no honorifics. Outside our lands, most women wear long dresses, but it's not too unusual for a woman to wear trousers and carry weapons. You may wear your leathers until the need to change clothing. The men I chose are very disciplined and I don't expect problems, but if anyone makes advances toward any of you, I must be told, and please don't kill the offender. I'm aware and understand Desert's Ire's codes. I doubt the pebble even knows you have codes. I thank you for your participation, until the morning."

"Hon…Lenzel, we are glad to be a part of history," Kaarill said.

Then, as one, the maidens turned toward the road leading to their tents.

Lenzel thought, *I never considered this mission as a part of history in the future. May the Great Creator allow our kind to survive.* He shook his head and went to the officer's mess for midmeal.

* * *

LENZEL arrived at the Zenith's study two hours later and heard the now usual command to enter in his head. He found the Zenith with Lord Kyle and two men who must have been twins, but with different coloring.

"Lenzel, these are Zack Stand and Currat Duval," the Zenith said. "Except for their names and their ability to fight, you're not to reveal their true purpose. They are the best spies in the Seven Realms."

Zack grasped Lenzel's forearm. "Zack."

Lenzel grasped Currat's forearm. "I know, you must be Currat."

Lenzel looked at them while concentrating on his stone. *Something different.* "Are you sure you're not brothers?"

Zack smiled. "Brothers and more."

What Lenzel sensed became clear. *They're lovers!*

"We've heard of you, Lenzel. You killed one or the Dark's beasts. That is something I would've liked to see. I assume the hideous face, tusks, and overly muscled body are not inflated rumors?"

Lenzel chuckled. "The wounds seemed inflated to me."

"They always do!" Currat said.

"Lenzel," Jarod said. "Zack and Currat may leave your group for days at a time. They must know your plans and the direction you'll take. Also, warn your group that their horses don't like strangers, and they are big horses."

"Highest One, as big as yours?"

Jarod developed a glint in his eye and smiled. "Well, almost. The last time we raced, Blackwind won by a nose; Snowflake and Spellbinder tied. Zack, tell Lenzel your plan."

"It's a simple plan and most good plans are. We've made arrangements to have three tinkers' wagons and a supply wagon ready by the time we reach Stonefire."

How did they know I'd go to Stonefire first? He looked at Jarod and saw him smile.

Zack continued—"The wagons will get us to the mountain ranges and carry the equipment and supplies we'll need. It's better than a line of packhorses and they will hide our group's true numbers. We will ride ahead from time to time to gather information about the area. It'll be good to know if bandits are in the vicinity, and if there are any left after our Zenith Lord's little trap."

"The information has been leaked that the gold and jewel transport will arrive at their location in four days," Jarod said. "We'll have time to set up for them before the *treasure* arrives."

Lord Kyle rose and walked to the window. "Zack, what have you heard from the Tower?"

"Not much, High Lord. The Holy One keeps a close rein on his priests. I do know he pays a good amount to keep herds supplied for the deathcats. There seems to be an unusually high number in the forest around the crater. I saw Mother Mavis in the Spires and she said Marc grew at an alarming rate and his mind is crisp, always looking for new things to discover, and the priests have a time keeping him in check. I would love to see him scampering about and the priests' flapping robes while chasing him." Zack laughed and the others chuckled.

"High Lord," Currat said. "I did hear your realm is well run and hasn't suffered in your absence. I didn't hear of any unrest."

"Yes," Zack said. "The people seem happier than when Mountglen ruled."

Kyle gave Jarod a firm look. "In case you're wondering, I'm leaving for Stonecrest when the Zenith leaves for his adventure."

"Our High Lord Byrne thinks I'm putting myself in unnecessary danger."

"I don't think, my brother; I know. You're going to worry me to my grave."

"Kyle, I'll be well away from the action and protected by men and my Sire's Stone."

"My Zenith," Zack said, "have you heard anything from Ursel's activities in Hamptor?"

"He still faces some of the problems you're familiar with when you were there, but he continues to make progress. Wathdure hasn't targeted him as a major threat, yet."

Zack's face showed no emotion. "Thank you, my Zenith."

For the first time, Lenzel felt truly included and a personal bond formed between him and the men in the room. *They speak of personal things they would let few hear. The emotions I feel between the Highest One and Lord Kyle are those of true brothers. Zack and Currat have the same love, but theirs goes deeper into a lover's passion. Theirs is the love I have for Ellrill.*

As if reading Lenzel's mind, Jarod said, "Lenzel, you'll likely be away for a long time. Go spend time with your beautiful wife."

"Highest One, you're most kind and I'm on my way." His words brought another chuckle when he nearly raced for the door.

Challenger waited for him at the palace entrance and he rode the stallion home at a full canter. Ellrill pulled the tent's flap open while he unsaddled, groomed, watered, and fed him. Walking to her, he took her in his arms and kissed her.

"I have to leave early tomorrow, as usual." Disappointment bled through in his voice. "We leave soon and I will be away for a long time, probably well over a year."

Ellrill smiled and pulled the ties of his leather shirt. "Then we shouldn't waste time."

Her smile melted Lenzel's knees.

19

LENZEL woke two hours before sunrise. He untied, and raised a window flap high up on the tent to check the stars for the time. The breeze entering the tent, crisp and cool with little moisture, promised a nice day. He had about finished bathing, the water cold, when Ellrill's warm hands took the cloth from his hand and washed his back, continuing down to his half-moon buttocks and between his thighs. He turned, pulling her nude body into the shallow tub, and wrapped his arms around her. He kissed her passionately then lifted her to his height and kissed her again, their stones touching. Each felt the emotional and physical sensations of the other. When it had happened the night before while making love, Ellrill nearly fainted and Lenzel's body shook violently. After that initial experience, they had a time of wonderment, exploration, and awe.

While he dressed in freshly oiled leathers and later started his daily routine of sharpening knives and Silver Stars, she built up the low-burning fire with dried dung and started water to boil in a small pot hanging over the flames. Lenzel pulled on his boots as Ellrill scooped oats into a bowl and poured honey over the top, prized foods in the desert. He finished, and placed the bowl on a low table when he heard horses approach their tent. He untied the tent's flap, and looked out. In predawn light, Zack and Currat sat on magnificent steeds, a hand taller than Challenger. Lenzel stepped out to greet them and Ellrill stood in the entrance to the tent.

Zack grasped Lenzel's forearm and said, "Are we too early?"

"No," Lenzel said. "Come meet Ellrill."

The two men dismounted and walked with him to the tent. After the introductions, Zack commented, "Ellrill, the Zenith said your beauty is remarkable. He's right. It's a pleasure to meet you. Currat and I will do our best to keep Lenzel safe."

"For that," she replied, "I'll always be in your debt."

Lenzel went to saddle Challenger. Zack and Currat chatted with Ellrill for a few moments before joining him as he finished watering his horse.

"We greatly value our privacy. At times we'll be away from the group, and we'll always sleep apart from you and the others. Does that present a problem?" Zack spoke softly and almost conspiringly.

"No, the Highest One said it would be what you wished. One or more of the maidens may seek you out once or twice due to their nature. Even if they do, they'll not care that you're lovers and would never mention it."

"What? How did…" Currat sputtered.

Zack's raised hand silenced him. "Who told you?"

Lenzel reached inside his shirt and pulled out his Stone. "This did. It has great power and many advantages. You know for what we search; the pebble doesn't and shouldn't be told. The Highest One believes you two will be presented with your own Stones. They may be less or greater than mine, but I, too, believe you'll get yours and probably strong ones. There's another thing I wanted to talk to you about in private. When I found the first cache of Stones, I thought its size of stones and gold large, but when the Highest One and I went back for them, we found several times that amount. We must get word to the Highest One for him to provide the Guard and wagons for transport. I can probably do that with my Stone, but I'm not sure. It'll be up to you and the maidens to guard the treasure until reinforcements arrive, and we probably will find it at the top or near the top of a mountain. The pebble is only for our protection."

Zack looked deep in thought before asking, "How far will we eventually travel?"

"The Highest One hasn't said, but I think there's a cache in each realm. It makes sense; the first Zenith Lord and six High Lords each received a realm. It would seem appropriate that each realm would contain the Stones their men wore. We found a cache here in Deepwells, and we go next to Stonefire. I would like to use Stonefire as a base of operations, but it would lengthen our time of searching a great deal and that makes it out of the question. The Dark grows and we must grow with the Stones or we'll soon be overmatched. I think it best if we go in this order—Stonefire, Eastfall, Northmount, Trueridge, Stonecreast, Westwood, and back to Deepwells or Stonefire…probably Stonefire."

Zack nodded. "That certainly would keep us from crisscrossing the realms."

"Shadure and Wathdure cannot sense the Great Stones. My stone is called a Channel Stone and I don't know if they can sense me or not. If they can, going to the realms in order would allow The Dark to know where we're going next, and if that happens, this is going to be a long search. I'll discuss this with the Highest One and see if he has a way of finding out what they can sense."

"He can do that?" Currat asked.

Lenzel cocked his head. "I know he has many documents copied from the first war with the Dark, and I believe Segquo has powers I know nothing about. It's getting light; we should go."

Lenzel kissed Ellrill goodbye, and then he mounted Challenger to catch up with Currat and Zack at a canter. They arrived as Andress formed his men and yelled, "Focus on the Apex!"

Lenzel, Zack and Currat dismounted. They dropped their reins, and the horses stood still, something Lenzel knew would not be lost on the men. Few horses had that training. Lenzel returned the men's salute and motioned Zack and Currat to follow him to stand before the pebble.

"Men, this is Zack Stand and Currat Duval. They'll join us in our journey. From this afternoon on until I tell you different, you'll wear regular clothing; no uniforms or anything that might lead anyone to think you're in the Guard. Master Stand, and Master Duval will counsel you this afternoon on ways to disguise your involvement in the Guard. If all you have is a Guard baldric for your sword and knives, let your skimmer know and one will be supplied that is used and shows wear. The same goes for boots and your horses' tack. The maidens and I will wear leathers, but as you can see, mine is without my Apex insignia.

"As your Zenith Lord stated, this mission is highly secret and I can't impress that too much. Nonetheless, I'll not repeat it again. We will be together for a long time and we must live in harmony. If problems arise between any of you, come to me and I'll help you work it out. Do not let your resentments fester if you develop any. If we find ourselves in a confrontation with the Dark, we must fight together, and protect each other. You can't do that well if you're angry with a fellow guardsman, and that may cost a life.

"You are released to Skimmer Andress to sort out your clothing, gear, and tack. Meet me in the officers' mess after midmeal." The last sentence widened some guardsmen's eyes.

Lenzel turned to Zack and Currat when out of earshot of the pebble. "The Highest One is reviewing the men this morning. You might find it interesting."

* * *

THE immense review field held a full mount, the hundred support men, with their support wagons to the side of fifty-one hundred men. Gleaming brass glinted in the sun as the men tried to keep highly polished boots free from desert sand.

The Zenith Lord stepped out on the reviewing stand. The mount commander, Apex Roller called, "Focus on the Zenith Lord!" the order repeated in turn by Lookers, Gals, Throwers, Lieutenants, Rockers, and Skimmers.

Jarod returned the salutes, surveyed the men, and spoke to Roller for several moments, at times gesturing with his hand. Roller signaled for four skimmers and gave them orders. The men spread out to various points in the huge field. Soon, four pebbles headed for the reviewing stand at the run, forming up below Jarod. Two tresses divided into four groups, separated the pebbles, and surrounded them, keeping a five-yard space from each group of men and the pebble.

Jarod descended the stand and walked to the first group. The tresses' men drew their swords, as did Jarod.

Men stepped aside and then reformed after he walked into the space before the pebble and ordered, "Skimmer, remove all but this man from this formation."

Jarod pointed his sword at one guardsman. As the men left the formation, the one before Jarod stood stark still, his eyes bulging. Jarod concentrated on his Sire's Stone. In a few heartbeats, the man fell to the ground, writhing with a pained expression on his face. The glamour dissolved, leaving a Dark's minion, snarling and trying to stand. Jarod's sword swung in a powerful arc, decapitating the creature's head. Foul smelling, black fluids gushed out on the ground. Several men came to the creature with a tarp and carefully moved the body and head onto it, vigilant not to touch the liquids or any part of the creature with their skin.

The Dark's minion's snarling produced the only sound during the whole procedure after the rest of the pebble left. Before wrapping the monster, the men opened the square they had formed, allowing the first ranks of guardsmen to see the body and head. Jarod nodded and the men picked up the tarp and moved it to a viewing area for the men to see when released from the formation.

Jarod moved to the next formation in line with gore still dripping from his sword. He pointed out one man and the rest of the pebble left, as the first had done. He again concentrated on the Sire's Stone and after a moment, the man fell to his knees, screaming.

"It's not my fault! Wathdure egged me on and tormented me for years!"

"Did you kill your wife and child before joining the Guard?" Jarod asked.

"Yes, but my daughter just got in the way. I didn't want to kill her." Tears flowed over the man's face as he sobbed.

Jarod flipped his sword, sending some of the creature's gore into the murderer's face. He screamed for several moments before falling dead on the ground, his face melting away where the black fluid touched him, spreading across his upper body. Men again entered the square, removed the body, and placed it next to the creature on the tarp.

In the next formation, one guardsman confessed to murder, and men escorted him to the complex's small prison to await trial. The fourth formation yielded a bandit in disguise. Jarod sent him to Lord Kyle for interrogation.

He climbed back on the reviewing stand beside a white-faced Apex Roller. Jarod concentrated and spoke in a normal speaking voice that carried to all five thousand, two hundred men, minus four. "I order you to march by the Dark's creature and the murderer who touched the monster's fluids. The remaining men have confessed to crimes and they will be tried. There are no more of the

Dark's minions in your ranks. When we engage the bandits, there may be more minions among them. I will be greatly surprised if that's not the case. They can be slowed with swords and arrows, but you can kill them only by taking their heads."

The men quick marched by the bodies and the second full mount took their place and Jarod found two minions, another bandit hiding in the Guard and a thief. Most men seemed not to conceal their revulsion when seeing the bodies.

Lenzel motioned Zack and Currat back toward the palace. He had given orders for the men in his pebble to see the bodies and saw them some twenty yards away going toward the tarps.

"Do you know how the Zenith knew they had infiltrated the mounts?" Currat asked.

"I told him," Lenzel said on a matter-of-fact tone.

"What?" Zack asked.

"I saw the men getting into formation yesterday. My Stone allowed me to see a dark edge about some men and I told the Highest One."

Zack smiled. "Now, I do hope we get a good strong stone."

Currat nodded and Lenzel smiled to himself.

Lenzel, Zack, and Currat ate midmeals in the officers' mess. They each chose a hearty stew with root vegetables, herbs, spices, and bread; it was filling and tasty. Lenzel had water; Zack and Currat stayed with ale. They kept the conversation light.

Lenzel then saw Andress enter and motioned him and his men to a private room near where they sat.

The men filed in and Lenzel, Zack, and Currat followed them inside the spacious chamber used for special occasions and private lastmeals. A large oval table sat in the middle of the room. Lenzel took the head chair with Zack on his right and Currat on his left. The remaining men sat five on each side of the table and waited. Jarod entered and Lenzel stood, pleased the skimmer did not give the Guard's command to focus on the Zenith Lord.

"My Zenith Lord, welcome." he said.

Jarod nodded and Lenzel sat down.

"You men saw the Dark's minions today." The room became somber at Jarod's words. "They fitted in with other guardsmen without giving themselves away. Apex Lenzel has the ability to sense the Dark's creatures. Your lives depend on keeping him safe in a situation where the Dark is involved. I believe you'll likely die of boredom than the Dark's minions, but that's no reason for being lax. Many in the Guard and, more importantly, some outside the Guard have underestimated your Apex. Don't make that mistake; he's very powerful. Zack and Currat have also done amazing service for the Seven Realms. I came here today to restate the importance of your mission. We move out in the morning for a separate mission. You'll accompany us part way and you'll have the chance to watch the culmination of work done by Zack and Currat. Another man set the plan in motion, but Zack and Currat have monitored it and kept it working. You have physical strength and excellent fighting ability. Do not become physically soft and keep vigilant of your surroundings on your journey. We leave at sunrise." Jarod nodded to Lenzel and left the room as unceremoniously as he had entered.

Lenzel looked at the closing door and then around the room. *He knows how to make an impression.* His guardsmen stirred in their chairs before settling once more. Lenzel regarded them in turn, making eye contact.

"It will be interesting to see how many of the Dark's minions you'll see tomorrow, and remember well not to mention your mission to any one. There is not much else to say. I'll leave you with Zack and Currat for their consultation."

Lenzel mounted Challenger, and rode to his and Ellrill's tent. She met him at its entrance, smiling. She ducked back inside as Lenzel took Challenger to water, feed, and groom him. His thoughts wondered while doing the chore. *These days have been my happiest since I last saw Ellrill. I'll miss her just as much as before.* Challenger nudged him, perhaps thanking him for a good brushing. *Yes, my ole friend, I love you too.*

When he entered the tent, Ellrill lay on furs in a sheer shift. Lenzel knelt before her and smiled as she sat up and started slowly untying the cords to his shirt and then pulling it over his head. He lifted her shift and pulled it free, softly cupping her breast as he leaned forward and gently kissed her. Two hours later, they lay with legs and arms intertwined, breathing hard. Ellrill recovered her shift and Lenzel lay still a while longer.

"Ellrill, my love, we've spent more time apart than together since we married. Now it seems we'll be separate again for a long time. My heart is heavy." The sorrow in his tone surprised him. He looked at Ellrill to see a tear form and spill down her cheek. He went to her, embraced her, and whispered in her ear. "You are my greatest love. I'll miss you more than life."

"No, my love, not more than life or you might not make it back to me. I love you as much, and I'll miss you terribly."

They spent the rest of the afternoon talking about remembrances of their life together, their life in the clan, their wedding, and their times apart. Most of the latter, neither knew of the other. Talked out, and with a stomach filled with a special lastmeal Ellrill made, they settled down on furs and drifted to sleep.

* * *

SMELLS of honey cakes woke Lenzel. When Ellrill walked by, he pulled her to him. Their lovemaking didn't last long, but knowing each other when their stones touched, they melted in luxuriated satisfaction. Ellrill brought the cakes and desert tea to Lenzel. They ate firstmeal with little conversation, but a good bit of soft touching. All too soon, Lenzel dressed, and left to prepare Challenger for the day. In predawn light, he kissed Ellrill longingly and then rode toward the palace complex, looking back once, answering her wave with his own. Great distress and sorrowfulness overcame him for several moments. He shook it off and continued on.

I've been away from her so much. Will we ever have a peaceful life together?

The two Mounts had formed on horseback. Lenzel found the sight of ten thousand-four hundred mounted men with their two hundred support wagons amazing. Zack, Currat, the maidens, and the pebble rode to his side and watched as Jarod and Kyle, swallowed up in the vanguard, rode to the south, the Mounts following. Lenzel's group rode to their small, loaded wagon train, the horses in their traces with trailing leads for the horses of the men on the wagons. They moved out and joined the back of the last Mount's own wagons. Lenzel knew Jarod planned on a pace to cover the thirty-two miles to the trap's site by nightfall.

The first mount reached the staging point two hours before sunset; the second mount arrived an hour later. Men set up camp rapidly with practiced efficiency. As the first mount finished, their support men went to help the remaining efforts of the second mount. Fires sprang up and a long row of cooking wagons began emitting savory smells. Lenzel received a message for his group to join the Highest One at the command tent for lastmeal.

He heard Userron's whisper to Andress—"I'm beginning to enjoy eating with officers."

"Don't get used to it," Andress replied. "We'll be on our own soon enough."

Lenzel chuckled and walked with the maidens toward the command tent.

"Kaarill," he asked. "How are your maidens in this large group?"

"They don't like it, Honorable Warrior."

Lenzel cocked his head.

Kaarill answered the look. "You are a warrior and in leathers and anyone who knows anything about our ways would be surprised if I didn't address you in the proper way. I understand the guardsmen hiding their life in the Guard, but I think it would be strange if we tried to hide the culture of the High Desert People and it would be odd to those we meet."

Lenzel smiled, and continued walking, only sensing the satisfied expression on Kaarill's face.

Guardsmen pulled the large tent flaps back and admitted Lenzel's group to the command tent, motioning for them to take seats at a large table loaded with food and ale. The maidens, Zack, and Currat flanked Lenzel, and the guardsmen sat across. Jarod, Lord Kyle, and the Apex commanders took their seats.

Jarod took a piece of bread, signaling the others to begin eating. Stewards kept mugs filled with water or ale and Lenzel found the mutton better than he imagined.

The Highest One spoke with Apex Roller and Apex Kenell on how to position their men, placing the archers in high positions over the trap site and the mounted men well hidden behind trees a quarter mile away, finally saying, "I'll be with my van, and then with Apex Lenzel's group above the trap. I'll do my best to expose the Dark's minions. Reiterate to your men that the only way to completely kill them is by decapitation."

The conversation then turned to social subjects and Lenzel concentrated on his men.

Dusten arranged his three-tonged fork and meat knife into its proper setting, "…and we'll miss this food. I saw some of what's in our supply wagon."

"I don't think we need worry too much as long as Davad has his hunting gear," Sorrel said with his usual smile.

"Me?" Davad answered, "Have you heard the stories about our leader's hunting skills. He could kill twice the game I could in half the time."

"I don't think Apex officers usually hunt for their men," Richmon commented.

Sorrel cut in, "Officers always have the welfare of their men at heart."

"Besides that," Stevemon said between gulps of ale. "I bet the maidens could out hunt Davad, but I wouldn't want to ask them to do anything. I hear those ladies could carve your heart out before you felt the cut."

Lenzel observed the maidens on his left to see if they had heard. The stoic expression on their face said they had not; the sparkle in their eye said they had. He looked at Zack and Currat and got the distinct impression they didn't miss anything going on in the room. He felt good about the men he had chosen, and those assigned to him.

20

LENZEL'S mind reflected on his amazing dream of Ellrill and their full night of lovemaking, then waking refreshed and energized.

How did it happen? Can our stones affect our dreams?

A hawk's cry pulled him back to his surroundings.

He looked out at the vista below him. *The Highest One couldn't have picked a better place to entrap the thieves and murderers.*

The bandits would enter the valley from its wide mouth, gradually tapering down to a narrow exit with high ridges on each side. This could enable them to easily handle the men caught in the trap. His smile grew as he continued watching the preparations for the next day when the bandit horde would arrive. Scouts had reported they were on schedule and at their current pace should reach the place of their capture—for the lucky ones—and death for the others at midmorning.

Small platforms rose into the oak trees' canopy. They would be barely seen from the valley below them, and remain unnoticeable if one didn't search for them. He kept looking for holes in the Highest One's plan without finding anything. Still, he continued to study the preparations for flaws or improvements.

He stood on a high, rocky promontory, which gave a commanding view over the valley, next to the Highest One who seemed to be in deep thought. He didn't want to interrupt him, but watched him closely for a few minutes as he scanned the valley and placement of his men's resources when the memory of traps his clan used made him smile.

When Jarod seemed to relax, Lenzel said, "Highest One, have you given thought to digging a ditch in the middle of the valley's tapered end? It could be covered with tarps staked into the ground and covered with matching soil from its surrounds, leaving enough room on the sides for your men to enter the valley. It would be another way of keeping the bandits from escaping."

Jarod's gaze fell on Lenzel, and shortly, he felt a great calmness, and a feeling of deep friendship filled him. Jarod's voice reflected the feelings, "Lenzel, I've made plans to keep the horde from fleeing, but your suggestion is a good one, and one I'll remember in the future. I want to spare as many horses as possible; dead animals will be more of a hindrance than I want. The younger ones will be a way of expanding our herds and the older ones will enjoy green pastures. I meant it when I said yours is a good plan, and I want your thoughts as events progress."

Lenzel caught the sight of Lord Kyle coming onto the overhang from the corner of his eye, and turned toward him. The High Lord looked pleased and refreshed.

"Good morning, High Lord Byrne."

Kyle's smile was infectious. "Good day Jarod and Lenzel. I slept well and feel good, and I trust you both did the same. Somehow I think our Zenith Lord might have had something to do with the night's rest; the dreams were good, too."

Jarod beamed at his friend. "I tried something new, and I'm pleased it might have worked."

"Highest One, you caused my dream? Could you...you see my dream?" Lenzel choked out.

Jarod laughed. "No, my friend, I couldn't see your dream and I wouldn't intrude if I could, but indeed, it sounds like you had a very good one."

Kyle's chuckle ended with a wink and smile at Lenzel. He turned to Jarod. "My brother, I'll soon take my leave. I would like to witness the activities tomorrow, but

Segquo received a message from Stonecrest and had a Desert's Ire maiden deliver it this morning just in time to disturb my dream's end."

His face showed an exaggerated frown. "It seems a fast ship has come into port with reports from Hamptor. A quick ship can only be Captain Briggs. The message was sketchy, but it seems Wathdure is wielding his power in a new way, but no details were given. I'll inform you when I know more. I spoke with Zack and Currat on my way here. Their advice is to proceed with caution. Wathdure has agents in Hamptor, as we know, but he may have started a more direct incursion into his neighbors' lands. As soon as I can get to a priest, I'll send messages for more information and report back to you. I hope this has nothing to do with Ursel's missions."

Lenzel watched Jarod's face change its features from relaxed to concerned. The Highest One and Lord Kyle talking freely in front of him reinforced his feeling of being included as a trusted member of the Highest One's inner circle. Pleasure flowed from his thoughts until the huge responsibility such trust entailed in return sobered him.

"Kyle, you are not to leave the Seven Realms under any circumstances," Jarod said. "You are joined with Warrior's Stone and we have no idea what influence Wathdure could assert over you closer to Ozlid. Currat reported Wathdure's minions lost power the farther from Ozlid they traveled, but we don't know how powerful he is by now. We have men available for an overseas mission and friends in Hamptor to help them."

"Don't worry, my brother. I have no intention or desire to be away from the Seven Realms." Kyle approached Jarod, embraced him and gave held his gaze when he released him. "I think you're in more danger than I am. Oh, not from the bandits tomorrow, but from the Dark's growing power in our lands. You tell me not to take risks. You're much more valuable in the coming war."

"Perhaps, but we must all work in concert to defeat the Dark. By the way, have you noticed skin growing over your stone?"

"Now that you mentioned it, I though I saw some skin encroaching over my stone yesterday, but I dismissed it as a trick of the eye. If it was skin, it was very little."

"Interesting. I thought I saw the same. There is nothing in my records stating the stones became covered over." He grabbed Kyle's bicep. "Be well, my brother, and safe journey."

Kyle saluted and said with a smile, "As you command, my Lord Zenith."

"You have my leave to go, High Lord Kyle Byrne of Stonecreast!" Jarod answered in the same voice of authority.

He and Kyle chuckled once more. Kyle gave a mock salute to Lenzel who returned it in the same manner.

Lenzel acknowledged the brotherly love the two men shared while watching Lord Kyle descend the ridge to his waiting mount. He felt close to a few of his clan brothers, yet nothing as close as what he felt between the Highest One and Lord Kyle. He hoped that one day he would have such a relationship with a friend, someone who garnered that magnitude of trust.

* * *

LENZEL woke before dawn and felt a little nervous about the coming day. He tried to place what upset him for a few minutes until he identified a pervasive heaviness around him. Pulling on his boots over the leathers he'd slept in, he left his tent and went looking for Skimmer Andress. He found him exiting his tent.

When the skimmer saw him coming, he didn't salute and that pleased Lenzel. Farther down the line of tents, Andress' men began to come out, a couple of them stumbling and groggy looking. From another direction, the Desert's Ire maidens loped toward the now forming group. Suddenly, without notice, Zack and Currat appeared next to Lenzel.

He waited until the pebble gathered within earshot and pitched his voice to them alone—"After your firstmeal, get food for midmeal from the cooks. If they give you a problem, tell them it's my order. Take your horses and hide them from a view of the valley, behind the south ridge. Then, make your way to the overhang near the top of the ridge. If the Zenith Lord arrives, do not engage him other than to acknowledge him with a slight bow of your heads. Move back on the ledge to give him room to meet with those he summons. Once the battle starts, do not interrupt either of us, or those others that might be there. If the need arises, be prepared to be a runner for messages. We should be in position shortly after daybreak. Don't try to climb the mountain in the dark. I'm just beginning to know you; I don't want to go to a cremation so soon. Be on your way."

As the disguised guardsmen left, he motioned for Lorell to remain. "Andress, keep a watch on your men," he said to him in a near whisper. "We need to know who gets restless, and any that act on their feelings no matter what they are...fear, excitement, shock or anything else. We must ascertain how our men will react in different circumstances. You understand your men best; notice any changes in their normal behavior. I'll discuss what you find in private and do not let your men discern what you're doing."

"I don't know Surron or Sontos that well. They joined the pebble three months ago, when two men were promoted to skimmer. I wish I had those men now. I feel the new men are good, but we've gone on only one exercise together, and while I believe they'll perform well, I don't have the experience with them that I had with my former men."

"I understand. You'd better join them. We'll talk after the trap is completed."

Lenzel again liked the nod he received rather than a salute as Andress left. He spoke in turn with Zack and Currat, and then the maidens, telling them much the same. He watched them go, wondering what the day would require of him. A part of him didn't want to know and the majority of him looked forward to the experiences to come.

His stomach full, he secured Challenger, hidden behind the ridge, and was not surprised to see Blackwind already grazing on a long lead. He started his climb. He felt scree through his leather boots and slid it off the trail as best he could for it not to hinder his group's ascent. The mount had two rough spots for climbers. Nearing the overhang, he looked back to see the maidens easily making their way toward him. Behind them, the pebble had started their rise. Looking above, surprise registered when he saw Zack and Currat observing him.

Currat reached out to grasp Lenzel's hand, pulling him onto the ledge. After expressing his thanks with a firm grasp of forearms, he walked toward Jarod. Lenzel noticed a line of solid colored flags in different colors, leaning against the mountain at the back of the overhang.

Jarod nodded. "Good morning Lenzel. I'll try to communicate to my men with my mind, but if there are problems, I can use the flags to convey my orders. Tell me the gist of the orders you'll give your force."

"Highest One, I'll direct the maidens to watch how the bandits fight and their general abilities, or lack thereof. I'll ask Zack and Currat to comment to the maidens and the pebble on the nuances of the bandits' leaders and how their commands seem to be carried out. If, or perhaps I should say *when*, the Dark's minions are discovered, I'll direct them all to watch the creatures' movements and the method of their deaths."

"I would add only one other directive. If they notice you working with your Stone, they're not to interrupt you, and they're not to interrupt me at any time. You must be ready to assist me with your Stone if I stretch out my hand to you. All you need do is touch me and think of your power merging with mine. I may not need your help, but it is prudent to prepare for any situation."

"I'll do all I can, Highest One."

* * *

LENZEL thought of the overall plan as he ate midmeal with his group. *It's not much different...*

The sound of many bugles in the far distance jerked his attention away from his thoughts. *Apex Kenell's mount must have started its run from the bandit's rear.* The air seemed crisper; Lenzel's mind cleared and his heart pounded in his chest. He felt immense power flow from and to the Highest One.

Jarod moved to the ledge's edge, and Lenzel moved to join him. Looking back, he saw the guardsmen walk to the center of the projection, out of the way, but able to observe the fight. The maidens hugged the mountain at the end of the outcropping against the rock wall. Zack and Currat faced them at the other side of the ledge. Everyone had a commanding view of the valley from its wide mouth—over a mile away—to the narrow end below them.

Lenzel watched as archers settled on wooden platforms, and began their ascent into the forest's canopy. Horses' cries rose from outside the valley. Jarod faced the sound and Lenzel could see beads of sweat on his brow. The cries subsided and stopped within a few moments. He wondered what could have spooked the mounts so badly when he saw over fifty deathcats enter the valley and disappear into the edge of the woods.

He looked at Jarod, who smiled and said, "I can have a

surprise or two, can't I?"

Once the last of the huge cats could no longer be seen, Apex Roller's mounted men took up their station across the narrow end of the valley. Lenzel looked over the upper wooded area; he could not see the hidden archers. He observed the Highest One searching the bandits as they entered the valley and watched them beginning to draw their swords. A foreboding darkness among the bandits' ranks jolted his mind.

The Highest One slid his hand into his shirt; Lenzel felt even more power leap outward. He followed its direction and saw seven brigands' forms slowly fade into black creatures as their glamours fell away; screeches pierced the air while they urged their mounts forward. The narrowing of the valley and the thieves crowding behind them slowed them to a crawl. Finally, within range, volleys of arrows peppered the bandits, and then a voluminous number of bolts flew into the Dark's minions. A huge roar went up, scattering horses as six deathcats leapt forward toward Wathdure's creatures. Working in pairs, the enormous cats sprang over the minions' mounts, knocking the riders to the ground to rip off their heads.

Other pockets of the Dark's beings began to lose their magic coverings, adding a cacophony of diabolical screams to those men and horses' mortal cries. Apex Roller's guardsmen rode forward to engage the oncoming thugs. Many bandits tried to turn or escape into the thick forest. Those who turned fell to their own men; those moving toward the trees became shot through with arrows or rather large bites from a deathcat. The horses of those fallen began to cause more disruption to the horde.

A new roar, more intense, more evil, rose from the middle of the valley. Lenzel saw three tusk-beasts strike out toward the trees. Their long claws wounded a deathcat that forced a death scream as its body turned black and began to dissolve. Riders moved away from the rapidly dying animal.

Jarod turned toward the deathcats on the field below him. Lenzel watched his look of deep concentration. Suddenly, the cats moved away from the tusk-beasts and rushed the few other minions remaining. Jarod looked toward Apex Roller's position on a low hill just outside the valley. Only a moment later, a bugle sounded and Roller's guardsmen stopped advancing and stood their ground, letting the bandits come to them—many of which wanted only to lay down their weapons. When the advance stopped, it allowed the archers to come back into play, not having to worry about shooting their own men. More and more thieves fell.

An immense sound assaulted Lenzel's mind and ears. The tusk beasts converged at the valley's middle. They joined, their bodies assimilating into an expanding blackness, rising twenty feet into the air. The miasma coalesced into something Lenzel thought not seen for two millennia. Its head centered fiery eyes on the ledge. He felt the beginning of the attack and reached out for Jarod's waiting hand.

Feeling his power explode exponentially, a shield—felt, not seen—formed before the outcropping. The force directed toward them bounced off the barrier. He watched archers' bolts shoot through the Dark's creation as if it were composed of smoke. Its arms swung from side to side in uncoordinated sweeps, killing several bandits. Two more thugs dissolved into minions and joined with the substance of evil. The latter rose another ten feet in the air, centering its attention on the ledge once more.

Jarod fell to one knee, Lenzel on both his. Indescribable pain in nature and force ripped through him. He saw Jarod start to crumble. Then, another hand grabbed his free hand and the power flowing through him into Jarod increased a hundredfold, then a thousand times over. He could not gain his vision, but envisioned streams of power in his mind, arching outward to the evil at the center of the valley. The force tried to return the attack, but slowly, too slowly, it began to dissolve into vapors that tried to reform without success. Unexpectedly, a disc of black light swept through the bandits, killing over a thousand men, horses, and two deathcats before dissipating into nothing, fifty yards before the forest. Lenzel felt his head fall backwards before consciousness left him.

* * *

LIGHT patches swam before Lenzel as he opened his eyes. Finally focusing, he saw the Highest One looking down on him. His first words sounded weak. "What...what happened."

Jarod's infectious smile beamed at him. "He happened!"

Lenzel turned toward Jarod's gesture, smiling when he saw High Lord Kyle Byrne doing the same.

Jarod's mien became serious. "Lenzel, it's true that the power comes from the Stone you wear, but it's also true that use of the power it brings to you will deplete your body's strength. Use too much and you could die. There is bread, cheese, and juices in the horses' saddlepacks. You must replenish your body after a fight like we've just been through. It seems when the power is directed to do good, the body improves and your strength with it grows, which is why healers and priests rarely have this problem. They are performing well in their expenditure of power. Kyle didn't have a problem when he fought the Dark's minions before you encountered the beast you defeated on the trail because he sent feelings of love to them, causing them to self-destruct. Using that technique wouldn't have worked today as too much hatred and death happened around them for them to draw from to keep them strong. You must remember to keep nourishing food and water with you.

*   *   *

LENZEL had never felt such hunger that plagued him as he waited for a trencher of food in the Highest One's command tent. The smells entering the tent made him stifle a groan. A guardsman set a platter of mutton, root vegetables and bread before him. He noticed neither the Highest One nor High Lord Byrne spoke before attacking their lastmeal. Following suit and after a few bites, he thought he might live.

Jarod spoke first—"I didn't want to talk in front of the others on the ledge. Kyle, what brought you back?"

"Yesterday, after traveling twenty miles, I felt a great depression in the air around me and the Warrior's Stone pounded in my chest. I didn't know what to make of it and continued on another twenty-five miles. The heaviness in the air became most uncomfortable. I ordered my guard to return here. The closer I came to you, the less the discomfort. We stopped at sunset and started again at first light. When we arrived, the battle raged. Apex Roller briefly filled me in and I went directly to the ledge, and I saw you sag as I came onto the outcropping. Lenzel had your hand and I felt an urge to take his free hand. The accumulated power made me feel awed and very small. After the creature—if that is what it's called—dissolved, I realized great power returned to me, more than I had before the battle."

"I, too," Jarod said, "feel much stronger."

The two men eyed Lenzel. "Yes," he said, "I do feel I hold more power than before. Do you think it'll remain part of our ability or dissipate over time?"

"The force that escaped from the Dark's evil, I think, was pure power—neither good nor evil, just power. I believe our Stones depleted state attracted it and sucked it in…Kyle, I assume you'll start out again in the morning?" Kyle nodded and Jarod continued, "Because of the archers, deathcats and the Dark's force fighting against its own, we lost only three hundred and forty-three men with another seven hundred and twenty-six wounded out of ten thousand guardsmen. And three deathcats died out of fifty-two. The main reason for such few losses is, our men never had to infiltrate into the horde. They saw our numbers and didn't try to attack toward our men, and the valley became a killing basin. I think we were incredibility fortunate."

* * *

SHADURE slid upright in a circle, cursing with the foulest obscenities. Wathdure stopped short, next to him on the Grey Plane.

"I came as soon as I felt our minions' destruction. What happened?"

"I'm not sure! I sensed a measure of discomfort, and then the distinct loss of our tusk-beasts. It came from one of those areas we can't penetrate with sight. I sent a force essence into the middle of the area and a directive to any minions there to join with it. Suddenly, the power evaporated and I lost it. I felt many men join the void. At least, their screams brought me pleasure."

21

LENZEL woke early and had firstmeal with his group. The spies and maidens said little, but the guardsmen chattered amongst their companions, mostly about the battle. Without the use of his stone, he would not have been able to hear their whispers.

"What was that thing?"

"Stevemon, how many times are you going to ask that question?" Dusten said. "None of us had an answer last night and we still don't. I'm not sure the Zenith Lord knows what it was or what caused it, other than it came from the Dark's Source. I just hope we don't meet any others like it!"

"I wouldn't want to guess what the Zenith Lord knows or doesn't know," Roush interjected. "We saw a great deal of power being used, not only from the Zenith Lord and High Lord Byrne, but also from our Apex. I've heard men say they didn't think Lenzel should have such a high rank. Do you believe our Apex isn't powerful enough, or smart enough to lead a mount? I think he is, and I don't know another Apex that can accomplish what he has done. I also wouldn't want to second-guess the Zenith Lord's decision in giving him the position. I do know this, if we have to travel all over the Seven Realms with just our numbers, other than the Zenith Lord or High Lord Byrne, I don't know anyone I'd rather lead us."

Davad nodded. "I heard how he fooled Jeroam and helped expose him as a traitor. I also heard he's a skilled hunter and that is something I respect. I don't know what we encountered yesterday, but I feel safer with our group than with a whole mount without Lenzel there." The pebble fell silent with a few nods.

It was *from the Dark's Source. I think every man and woman there realizes what caused it, and whatever it was, it had great power,* Lenzel thought. *I don't want to even think about what we seek by name. If the Highest One can hear our thoughts, can the Dark's minions do the same?*

A messenger eased a note beside Lenzel's hand, saluted, and walked away. Lenzel read the missive and knocked on the table three times with his knuckles. When the men quieted, and looked at him, he said, "Gather your belongings; we ride with the Zenith Lord in one hour."

Lenzel watched the expressions on his group's faces. Most looked eager; the maidens showed slight smiles. Zack and Currat simply rose and left, wearing expressions of resignation.

He left the table and walked briskly to their supply wagon. After checking his snugly packed belongings wouldn't become dislodged over rough roads, he disappeared into his tent, emerging a few minutes later in lowlander clothes and boots. Returning to the wagon, he added his leathers to his other belongings. The hat he wore completely covered his red hair.

Larrell nodded as he walked by. Two steps on, he stopped, turned, and retraced his steps, stopping in front of Lenzel. "Sir?"

Lenzel couldn't help a low chuckle. "Yes, Andress. I don't know who my parents are, or if they are still alive. The Clan of the Cat adopted me, kept me safe, taught me the clan's ways, and trained me to be a warrior. I'll miss my leathers, but I'm the only High Desert warrior with red hair. Explain to the men not to think of me as a clansman on this mission. We have taken many steps to be unnoticed; this is just one more. Reinforce that on the men from time to time. Get the men and wagons formed up and follow the vanguard. Zack and Currat will ride wherever they desire. I doubt you'll see the maidens, but don't think they're not nearby. I'll be with the Zenith Lord."

"Sir, do you think your name is well known by our people?"

"I see your worry. The Guard outposts are the only places where my name is listed. It is with my picture among the other Apex officers. Remember, there is a general order that guardsmen do not discuss Apexes at any time except when required. I could be compromised if that order is not followed, because, as you know, the Dark has infiltrated the Guard's ranks. This is another reason why we will not be stopping at the Guard's outposts unless absolutely necessary. If we should run into guardsmen, I'll stay in the background and I doubt they'll see the maidens anywhere in sight. If, for any reason, someone wants to inspect us, or our wagons, quietly bring the guardsman in charge to me. Such an inspection team should be led by a lieutenant or higher ranked officer, but you know that." Lorell nodded before Lenzel continued, "I think you get the idea. We *must* keep our mission and our identities secret."

"I'll see to it."

Lenzel watched as the skimmer trotted off toward his men. *I don't like going forward with so many variables.* He turned at Challenger's nicker, mounted, and rode to the front of the vanguard.

* * *

LENZEL thoroughly enjoyed High Lord Byrne's banter and running commentary on the countryside's history. When the High Lord turned off toward Stonecreast, Lenzel wondered when he might again see him. The Zenith Lord carried on brief conversations and answered his questions, but most of the time, he seemed deep in thought, and Lenzel didn't want to disturb him.

Meals provided a much different experience. Lenzel's group no longer ate with the Zenith Lord except for Zack and Currat. The conversation between him and his vanguard's officers covered subjects he had not thought of, the strengths of the realms' private armies and how they were used, among other more personal activities of the High Lords. They added to his concerns. Two officers from the Zenith's planning staff held Looker rank. They took time with him, explaining how the realms interacted, and some of the High Lords' idiosyncrasies. They didn't mention High Lord Byrne, or the Zenith Lord. He committed their comments to memory for when he would meet them, if he met them. He also learned a good deal about the realms' terrains, which became part of his concerns, especially in Northmount. He didn't like the idea of climbing mountains in freezing weather. Summer would definitely be scheduled for it.

There's so much I don't know, Lenzel thought. *I'm glad Zack and Currat are with me. From what the Zenith Lord said, they've been to each of the realms, and I'm sure they know much more than the lookers do.*

* * *

LENZEL continued to enjoy the countryside. He spent time riding with each of the pebble's men, and while he knew they didn't speak much about their ideas on the mission, or their attitude toward the Guard, he did learn more about the men, their thoughts on daily things, and their backgrounds.

A messenger told him the Zenith Lord wanted him at the front of the vanguard. As he rode along side the Highest One, Jarod said, "I would like to hear your comments when we crest this hill."

Lenzel didn't quite know what to expect. He wondered if a natural wonder might be on the land ahead, but all thoughts flew from his mind except for wonderment when he reached the hilltop. A huge valley contained a city larger than he ever thought possible, and on a plateau to the northwest, three huge spires rose high in the sky, their bases connected by buildings several stories tall, all surrounded by manned outer walls and gates.

"Highest One, I realize this must be Stonefire and the Spires. I thought I had anticipated what I would see, but this goes far beyond my imaginings. I predicted buildings three or four stories high, but there are many twice that size, and the Spires' buildings are massive. I'm truly amazed."

Jarod chuckled. "I grew up at the Spires and saw Stonefire daily, but when I've been away for a while, it always amazes me when I return. The city continues to grow, and while there are many miles of the valley untouched by the city, I wonder how much more it can expand."

As the vanguard crested the hill, a watchtower two hundred yards to the east raised the Zenith's flag. Almost immediately, fanfares ricocheted across the valley. A scree of men rode from the Spires with pennons flying the Zenith Lord's colors toward the outer perimeter road, the same road the vanguard approached, and then turned onto.

"See the second perimeter road in?"

Lenzel nodded.

"It was built when my father reached his tenth year. The Spires ordered the construction of this road in my tenth year. As you can see, the city has grown beyond it in the east and west. It is said the city here before the Great War spread over the entire valley, making it many times Stonefire's current size. Afterwards, the entire city lay in ruins with only the Spires remaining and remarkably untouched. Most of the other cities in the Seven Realms lost at least two-thirds their scale, many completely destroyed. Disease and famine ruled for many decades.

We don't know exactly how many died, but the deaths numbered many millions. This, Lenzel, is what we must keep from happening again."

"I understand, Highest One," Lenzel replied.

* * *

THE group settled on the tenth floor of the Spires. Lenzel gave orders they would move out at sunrise two days hence to the northwest toward the deep forest and small mountain range where the Highest One suggested they start. He allowed the pebble to visit the shops and inns inside the Spires, but ordered them not to go outside the walls. Lenzel forwarded an invitation for Zack, Currat, and the maidens to reside in guest quarters on the twelfth floor.

His mouth gaped open when he saw the main doors to the Zenith's private floor. Recovering, he approached the Guardsmen at a table near the entrance. The guardsmen rose and saluted. "Welcome Apex; your quarters are ready. A steward is waiting for you inside and he'll take care of your needs while here."

Lenzel returned the salute, wondering how they recognized him so easily before seeing his portrait on a sheet of parchment lying on the table. Then he marveled at the workmanship of the life-sized deathcat carved into the entrance's doors. Only the jewels betrayed the life-likeness of the trees and feline. As he approached, two guardsmen pulled the doors inward and saluted. He returned the salute, this time wondering how they knew he approached the doors. A man dressed in black trousers and vest over a white shirt approached and slightly bowed his head.

"Apex, I am Curso and I'll be your steward while you're here. If I may, I'll show you to your quarters."

Following Curso, Lenzel continued to wonder at the age and workmanship of the artwork along the corridor, on the walls and tables, some adorned with jewels, some lifelike sculptures so fine they seemed molded out of creamy air, portraits of men resembling the Highest One, other pictures of beautiful women and children, landscapes of different locals—even the high desert, a clock dividing the twenty-six hours of a day into quarter hours and many more objects he didn't recognize. His guest quarters amazed him. What he thought would be a bedroom with perhaps a refresh room consisted of those, in addition to a study and reception accommodations. The furnishings, plush chairs, and furniture of the highest quality surpassed the best suites in Segquo's palace.

Curso said, "You'll find clothing in the wardrobe I believe will fit you, as well as new boots. Your clothing and leathers have been sent for cleaning. The clothing you're now wearing will be sent out once you've changed. There is a bell pull in each room that will summon me if you have any need. Would you like a bath, now?" Lenzel nodded. "Hot water will be brought in for the tub in a few minutes. If you wish, I'll lay out clothing for you while you bathe." Lenzel nodded once more. "I'll have things started at once."

Curso turned on his heel and left the suite, leaving Lenzel wondering how many more surprises the Spires would offer him.

Before he could examine the suite in closer detail, five young men entered, carrying large vessels with narrow necks on top where steam wisps slowly rose upward. On leaving, one of them slightly bowed, saying, "Apex, your bath is ready. We'll remove the water and clean the tub when you're finished. It's been a pleasure serving you." Without waiting for a reply, he turned and followed the other four men out of the chambers.

The bath relaxed Lenzel as no other ever had. He found scented oil that pleased him. Its sandalwood fragrance permeated his skin, leaving a redolence of remembered candles. He soaked until the water had cooled. A large drying cloth gently absorbed the water from his skin. He sniffed his arm, analyzing the slight aroma lingering there, and found it not overpowering and barely noticeable. He liked it.

Entering the bedroom, he found a beautiful, understated light blue suit with a white wormcloth shirt on the bed alongside a new privatecloth. Black boots of the highest quality leather, with black stockings lying across their top, also surprised him. He never wore stockings with his leather moccasins and had none to wear with the down-lander boots, so he wondered if they would help cushion the roughness against his feet. The clothing he'd taken off had disappeared.

Lenzel dressed, feeling the quality of the material soft against his skin. The boots, smoother on the inside than his own, felt even better with the stockings. Looking into the largest mirror he'd ever seen made him smile. The suit's coloring tempered the contrast of his light skin and red hair. No one would ever think he belonged to a High Desert clan.

A light knock followed by Curso entering the reception room called for Lenzel to join him. Upon seeing him, Curso cocked his head and stroked his chin with his right hand. "Apex, you look well. I think the Zenith Lord will be pleased. He asks for the pleasure of your company for lastmeal in one hour. Is there something you require before then?"

"Yes, Curso. Is there a place that overlooks Stonefire? I'd enjoy seeing the full scope of the city."

"Yes, Apex. I'll take you there and come for you at the proper time for lastmeal."

Curso left him on a large terrace above the twelfth floor. The view astounded him. The sun began to set, giving off sparkling and shimmering reflections over the windows, lakes, and streams around and through the city. He couldn't see much of individual streets or buildings from his distance, but on the ride to the Spires, he'd noted how clean the streets and byways remained. The huge horse areas to the side of the Spires left him breathless.

True to his word, Curso arrived at the proper time to take him to lastmeal. The Highest One, the Pinnacle Lord, and Michael Gaz stood talking when he arrived. If this was the small private feasting room Curso had talked about, he couldn't imagine the large one. Beautiful porcelain plates were set on gold chargers, with heavy silver utensils to the right and left. Crystal goblets for wine and tall glasses for water completed the setting. A tray of short-stemmed roses lay in a long, shallow dish of water with greenery interspersed between them along nearly the entire length of the table, giving off a remarkably pleasant scent. The Highest One gestured and the guests took seats at the table as stewards brought in trays of food, making Lenzel's stomach growl. The food included roast fowl, grilled white fish, root vegetables, peas, and a nutty bread.

Everyone spoke on a first name basis, but Lenzel couldn't bring himself to call the Highest One, "Jarod." He listened and observed his fellow guests. The Highest One was unusually quiet. Others in the room noticed and kept the conversation low with a light banter around him. Some stories told that would normally cause a hearty laugh brought smiles and chuckles. The stewards cleared away the platters and made ready for dessert when a light knock sounded. The door opened and a guardsman carried a sealed note to Gaz, and after giving the Zenith Lord a bow, went back the way he came, closing the door unobtrusively behind him.

Gaz read the message twice. "My Zenith, Apex Lenzel and I have a matter to attend to. I beg your permission to depart."

Jarod seemed not to hear until he replied—"Do you

need the Guard?"

"No, Lenzel's men should be enough, my Zenith."

Jarod simply nodded and returned to whatever occupied his mind. Gaz rose and Lenzel followed him out of the room without prompting.

Then, stopping a few feet from the door, he whispered, "One of your men, Guardsman Stevemon Surron, has passed through the outer gates toward the City. Two of my men are following and one will report back his location. We'll probably meet up with him on our way. If not, we'll wait at the City's outskirts. I assume you gave no one permission to leave the Spires?"

Lenzel hid most of his surprise. "No. Their orders are to stay inside the inner gates. Surron likes his ale and women, but his record indicates he's not the type of guardsman to disobey a direct order."

Curso stood a respectable distance for privacy. Lenzel motioned for him and he hurried over.

"Curso," he said. "Send an order for my men to meet me at the entrance below in all speed. Tell Skimmer Andress not to wait if one of his men is not present. Send word to ready our mounts and have them brought to the entrance." He looked at Gaz, who nodded. "And, include Master Gaz's horse."

Curso hardly got the words, "At once, Apex Lenzel," out before hurrying away.

"It would be best if we presented ourselves in clothing for the City streets," Gaz advised.

Lenzel nodded and walked quickly toward his quarters.

22

LENZEL found his pebble minus Surron waiting for him in civilian clothing. Gaz arrived a few heartbeats later as the horses were led to them at a canter.

He turned to Andress. "Have you noticed anything strange about Surron in the last few days?"

"He's seemed withdrawn, but he has those spells."

"He was reported leaving through the outer gates about an hour ago. He's being followed by guardsmen and we need to find him, quickly."

"This hasn't happened before." Andress shook his head as he mounted his horse.

A quarter mile from the City, a guardsman approached and reined in alongside Gaz. He and his horse were sweating. He took a gulp of air before speaking. "Sir, he's at the Copper Tankard Inn. I'm Sreford. Jamison is keeping an eye on him in the common room. He's sitting with a woman, quite a beautiful woman, at that. Do you need help finding the inn?"

"No," Gaz said. "I know it. A little pricey for a guardsman. Follow us back, but rest your horse a bit, first."

Gaz and his men continued on at a canter. The inn, located a short distance from the outskirts of the City in a wealthy area, had a good reputation. Two stable boys made fast work of caring for the mounts. The common room for the inn was outfitted with circular tables and comfortable chairs made of light oak, rather than the large rectangular tables and benches of less opulent establishments that were usually roughly hewn. The large fireplace boasted a welcoming fire and it was well vented, leaving little smoke in the room and few stains around its opening. The serving maids wore attractive dresses of the same color: black with white cuffs and collars and not the revealing bodices worn in lesser inns. They had pleasant demeanors and smiled when attending their customers. A guardsman stood at the long, mostly empty bar nursing a mug of ale. He nodded at Gaz when he entered.

Gaz' group joined the guardsman. "I'm Jamison, sir."

Gaz said, "I remember you."

Jamison moved his chin in the direction of the far side of the fireplace. Surron sat with his back to the bar. Most men would call the woman facing him strikingly beautiful, or other more generous descriptions. Long, raven black hair framed her face, bringing out lush lips, a straight fine nose, and large black eyes and lashes under exquisitely arched brows. A black thin dress fitted her stunning curves and perky breasts, showing large nipples. Somehow, the dress didn't brand her as lewd like it would on other women. Fluid gestures and an animated face brought her whole appearance together, making it hard for any man to resist.

"They have been sitting there sipping ale," Jamison said. "I've seen only one mug ordered since I got here. When I came in, a maid carried plates from their direction; they may have eaten. Surron has been the perfect gentleman and the lady has hardly taken her eyes off him. There is something strange about them; notice how the tables around them are empty. When the serving maid came back from taking them the ale, she shivered."

"Now that is different for Surron," Andress said. "He's usually boisterous and chugs ale like the inn is about to run out of it."

Lenzel tapped his pouch carrying his silver stars. "I think it would be best if I approached him alone. We don't want to cause a scene and it would be good to get him out quietly. That said, be ready to move quickly if there's trouble."

As he moved toward Surron, he felt the air become heavy, dead like—a feeling he'd felt once before while killing a Dark's minion that nearly cost his life. He signaled behind his back and his men spread out, moving toward the couple. When he reached the table, the feeling of the space about him became oppressive. He loosely held a silver star in his pouch.

Standing three feet away, he spoke with authority, "Surron, you're needed at the Spires."

The big man looked up at his superior with a blank expression, his eyes as dead as the air he breathed. "I must kill you." His voice came in loud, staccato slurs. He rose slowly. "I must kill you!" Pulling a knife from his belt, he started to lunge for Lenzel, moving slowly as if in a slight daze. Three men of the pebble and Jamison grabbed Surron before he cleared the table.

The woman growled, making an unworldly sound. Long claws replaced her beautiful fingers. She leapt up as the first Silver Star bit deep in her throat. The second and third followed in a blur of action. The creature shook off its glamour, revealing a black, beastly body in roughly human form. The rest of the pebble moved in to surround the table.

Pandemonium's vehemence spread throughout the common room.

"This is the guard's business. Leave at once!" Jamison yelled.

Most there didn't need the warning as they rushed for the exit. A woman fell and the man behind her stomped on her leg. She screamed. Two men picked her up and carried her out, still screaming.

The beast turned on Jamison and swung arching claws, missing his face by inches. Lenzel threw three more silver stars, burying them deep at the nape of the creature's neck. The stench from oozing gore made a guardsman retch. The monster opened its mouth to scream, but no sound came from its ragged throat. It twisted about, its hate manifested, changing its face to more horror. Two guardsmen buried their swords deep in the beast's chest, but it twisted them out of the guardsmen's hands, pulling them from its body and slinging them across the room toward the bar. Lenzel drew his sword and severed its head in one solid swing, bouncing it toward the fireplace.

The corruption started, disintegrating levels of its body, each fouler smelling than the last, until an ash like material spread over the floor, and then, that too, dissolved into nothingness, leaving six pristine silver stars lying on the floor. Lenzel collected them and, other than being slightly hot, they seemed normal.

At the moment of the monstrosity's death, Surron fell backward across the table, his eyes shut, his breathing labored.

Looking back, Lenzel yelled for the innkeeper to bring water. The man behind the bar stood rigid, holding an axe with powerful arms across his barrel chest, his mouth agape. Suddenly, he shook his head and ran to a back room, emerging a moment later with a pail of water. He brought the pail, sloshing some water out as he ran. Jamison used a napkin to dribble water into Surron's mouth and then rubbed his forehead with more water. He patted the big man's cheek and shortly, Surron groaned.

The innkeeper stood transfixed, looking at the floor where the beast had lain. Coming to himself, he asked Jamison, "You said this was Guard business. Will the Guard pay for my loss of custom? What officer is in charge?"

"That would be me," Lenzel said. "In case you haven't heard, we're at war with the Dark and you had one of its minions in your common room that could have destroyed your inn. That should be payment enough."

The innkeeper huffed. "I want to talk to your superior!"

Jamison spoke up in a flatly modulated tone, "That would be the Zenith. This man who just killed the beast in your common room is an Apex."

The innkeeper's huff deflated and he stomped toward the bar, mumbling under his breath. He laid the axe on the bar, put both outstretched arms on the bar's edge, and started to shake.

Sreford arrived and looked around. "I must have missed the fun."

"Be glad you did and don't ever get in a fight with Apex Lenzel," Jamison said.

Sreford arched his right eyebrow with a puzzled look.

Surron, still slightly dazed, managed to leave the inn and mount with Sontos leading his horse toward the Spires. Andress had taken his weapons and his compatriots surrounded him. He seemed strangely subdued. Lenzel, Gaz, and the two uniformed guardsmen followed several yards behind.

Gaz' commented, "We must learn how the Dark controls our minds."

The comment resonated with Lenzel and he agreed. "Perhaps we can persuade His Grace to interview Surron," he said.

Gaz nodded in agreement.

* * *

CURSO delivered a message to Lenzel from Gaz to meet him in the Zenith's small study at midmorning. Rolo, Jarod's steward, answered his tap on the door, admitted him and then, he left. The Highest One motioned him to a plush chair. "His Grace is coming with Master Gaz."

Lenzel was surprised to find Jarod in full uniform with his battle sword within reaching distance on a nearby table. "Highest One, does this have to do with Surron?"

"Yes. His Grace spent time with him last night and early this morning. On another subject, you are to inspect the guardsmen. Since the Spires' outer gates will be closed during your assessment, you will wear an Apex uniform. The reason for your actions will be to root out any of the Dark's minions that have infiltrated the Guard. The guardsmen will be told it's to familiarize you with the ranks. Do it with no more than one mount at a time. His Grace and I will remain unseen atop the inner walls to provide support in case you find more powerful minions than you can handle. You will be on a reviewing stand surrounded by a trass from those men sworn to secrecy. They will be taught to decapitate any you may find." Jarod chuckled. "Your silver stars might help, as well. Lenzel, the Dark penetrated our ranks at Deepwells. I think the guardsmen here may be better protected due to the Stones in play, but we know the Dark's minions are in the City. We must find an easier way to detect them."

"Highest One, perhaps it would help if the Holy One participated with you on the wall. He has Wisdom's Stone and High Lord Byrne had success by projecting good thoughts at the minions he found before one found me."

"That's an interesting proposal. I'll discuss it with those involved and the Holy One." Jarod looked at the door and opened it with his mind as Gaz reached for the door handle. As he entered the study, he looked behind the door and to Jarod, shaking his head with a wry smile.

"My Zenith, not you, too!"

Deion followed Gaz into the room. "Master Gaz, what makes you exclude my involvement with the door?"

"That's alright, Gaz," Jarod said. "Wait until you master the power. Think how helpful it will be in your capacity. Now, if you'll take seats, I'm interested to hear what His Grace learned from Surron."

"More this morning than last night. He's still under some of the Dark's influence, although it's waning. So far, he doesn't remember going to or leaving the inn. I think his memories are intact, but deeply buried. It's different from Lady Deanna's intrusion by the Dark three years ago; it seems to be another kind of control. I want to study him more intensely. At present, he's under guard and constant watch."

Lenzel felt a presence, one that he knew, but could not completely identify. *The Holy One, it must be him that I feel. Well, if they can do it...* He touched his stone and concentrated on the door's mechanism. It slammed open, hitting the inside wall before a startled Travis, who was about to knock. *Oops!*

"Apex Lenzel," Deion said. "You need to practice that one."

Gaz shook his head; Jarod chuckled. Three guardsmen appeared at the door looking concerned. Deion motioned them away. Lenzel tried to hide his embarrassment and mostly succeeded.

Travis looked a little bewildered, but then smiled. "My Zenith, you called me with your mind, I believe."

"I indeed did so. Lenzel has an interesting proposal. He will inspect the Guard stationed here, one boulder at a time, to discover any minions that might have infiltrated us or one that has a guardsman under its control. He thinks you might be of help in locating the Dark's scum. You have Wisdom's Stone, which is powerful. His Grace and I will be atop the inner walls, watching and assisting Lenzel if needed. You could join us there if you wish to participate. I know the prelates have stones, but I think they won't be required. I would like to have a priest join us who has a minor stone and can channel. Are there any here?"

"I would like to join you, and a group of channeling priests arrived yesterday on their way to the Tower. Prelate Thurston is seeing them this afternoon to judge their individual strengths at the chapter house on the mall level. Do you want to see if one can detect the evil in the creatures?"

"I do. I suppose you heard about the problem with one of Apex Lenzel's men last night?"

"Gaz mentioned it to me when I saw him at firstmeal. I read the report before eating."

"Have Prelate Thurston pick a priest with average ability and the one who is strongest," Jarod said. "And now, gentlemen, if there is nothing else, we are adjourned. Apex Lenzel, remain a moment."

Travis hung back as the others left. He looked at Lenzel and then the Zenith.

Jarod said, "You may talk in front of the Apex."

"Jarod, my son, it's hard for me using titles with you and Kyle," Travis said in a low voice.

"Travis, you know I love you and Mavis very much. In private, when no one is in hearing distance, it's fine to call me as you wish," Jarod whispered back. Then, in a normal tone, he said, "It's a matter of discipline. Our personnel, in and outside the Guard must become accustomed to the fact we are at war, especially the Guard, which is another reason for inspecting the ranks. Once guardsmen see a creature beheaded, they will have no doubts about our war footing.

"You know I don't prefer to wear a full uniform; now, I must, *and* carry that sword at all times, when outside my rooms. I read about the attitude of the innkeeper where the trouble started last night. His concern was about losing his guests, not that a Dark's minion had been in his inn. Gaz learned it had been letting a room there for three days. Shortly after the inspection, I intend to heavily restrict the Guard from visiting the City until we can find a way of identifying the Dark's filth."

"I understand, my son. I will impress the importance of titles to the prelates. They would never refer to you other than 'Zenith'; still, along the lines you mentioned, it would be good for the people to hear the priests use full designations. I'll have the word passed down. The information regarding Maress' death is beginning to travel to populaces of the other realms. I'm surprised it has taken this long. Some priests have reported the people are reluctant to believe the manner of her death."

Jarod nodded and entertained a brief silence before asking, "Apex Lenzel, how do the High Desert clans react in battles?"

"Highest One, we have small clans, but we have many of them as you know. We train as warriors and when we interact with other clans, we use clan titles. I would be called Lenzel of the Cat Clan. If a warrior has a position of importance, like 'Leader of the Horse,' it would be added, and that is different from your custom. Throughout all the clans, Segquo is known by that name alone. No other person can have his forename. We have many warrior maneuvers three times a year to hone our skills. I drew on those experiences from one exercise to the next, and in following your orders. My men and I can wear our uniforms while here, if you wish."

"No, Apex. I believe you will be the exception. It's important you wear it during the inspection, but not afterwards. Your men must stay accustomed to wearing the type of clothing of the realm you'll be in…Holy One." Jarod smiled. "It's hard for me to use titles, too, at times. I'd asked Apex Lenzel to stay to go over what turned out to be the answer to your question. If there's nothing further…"

Travis nodded to Jarod, and Lenzel saluted. The Zenith Lord walked them to the door. On leaving, Lenzel turned back and saw a greenish glow fill the room as the door closed. Alarmed, he started back when Travis' hand stopped him. "No, my son. That is one of the Zenith's protectors, Darth, the Captain of Death. Sarth, the Angle of Death, is with Marc. They are a gift from Light's

Source."

Lenzel looked dumbfounded, but only smiled after a moment.

23

THE lieutenant called, "Focus on the apex!" as Lenzel mounted the reviewing stand. Over five thousand men saluted, fist over heart. He felt resplendent in his dress uniform of black boots over black trousers and crimson coat. He wore a sword Jarod had presented to him earlier in the morning. Centering on the reviewing stand, he returned their salute. The mount's Apex looked at the striking deathcat emblazoned on Lenzel's coat, over his heart. He saluted. Lenzel returned the salute and motioned the Apex closer. "I haven't had the pleasure of meeting you, Apex Nenon. I am glad to do so."

"What I'm about to tell you is to remain secret by order of the Zenith Lord. The purpose of this review is to discover any Dark's Source minions that have infiltrated our ranks or the minds of our men. Of course, if one is found, it'll no longer be a secret; at least, that part. The rest that is to remain between you and your skimmers is that they are to report anyone having nightmares. More will be explained in an upcoming Apex meeting.

"Position your men to the side and order them to the reviewing stand, one boulder at a time. They will face me and stand at position until I order them to pass, at which time the next boulder will follow."

"Apex Lenzel, I assure you that none of my men could possibly be part of Dark's Source. It's not possible; I would know."

"Perhaps. You're dismissed to your orders."

The older Apex didn't like being dismissed, but he saluted smartly and left the reviewing stand to find his next in command.

Shortly, the mount repositioned to the left side of the reviewing stand began to break up into distinct boulders. The first one marched in front of the reviewing stand, turned to face Lenzel and saluted. He returned the salute and, using his stone, projected his voice so all could hear.

"I may wish to inspect individuals. Maintain ranks."

He quickly scanned the men row by row, and found no indication of the Dark's influence. He again projected his voice, "Dismissed to orders." He received a sending from The Protector: *Three in the next boulder.*

Lenzel caught a glimpse of Apex Nenon. He projected self-satisfaction and assurance. Lenzel detected the three Deion referred to before the boulder took two steps toward him. He signaled the trass' lieutenant who immediately came to his side as he whispered, "Three in the next boulder, second scree, first pebble back, standing together." The lieutenant joined his men.

Grabbing his stone, Lenzel projected his booming voice over the field: "*Boulder halt, second scree to the reviewing stand.*" Then, in a normal command voice, he added, "Apex Nenon, please join me."

The two hundred and seventy men commanded by their thrower approached, and saluted smartly. Lenzel returned the salute and quietly said. "Apex Nenon, are you familiar with this scree?"

"Yes sir, I inspect my men weekly. They are excellent guardsmen."

Lenzel spoke out over the boulder, "First pebble, five steps forward. Prepare for close inspection."

The lieutenant's men moved between the first pebble and the rest of the boulder. Lenzel grasped his Channel Stone and projected kindness to the three minions, knowing the three watching from high above did the same. The three became agitated, and within a few heartbeats, they began to move around. Their thrower started to intercede, but the lieutenant spoke quickly in his ear. Lenzel watched as the Dark's minions began to yell oaths, then scream. The lieutenant's men moved the rest of the pebble away. Swords drawn, they surrounded the three yelling creatures. The middle one lost its glamour first. Its black body expanded, seeming to sprout huge muscles. The hideous head with long fangs snarled at Nenon and leapt onto the reviewing stand, reaching for the Apex. Lenzel's sword swung up in an arc to slice through the creature's neck, made possible by the downward motion of its jump. Its head stopped at Apex Nenon's feet. Turning ashen, he threw up his firstmeal, backed away, and then, slumped to the floor of the reviewing stand.

First one, then two guardsmen attacked the remaining monsters and were thrown ten feet with their uniforms ripped. Four guardsmen hacked away at black necks, trying to separate them from each other. More guardsmen speared black bodies with swords. It took a quarter hour to finish them, their heads finally rolling away.

"Sir, we lost one man and five are injured, one seriously. They are being taken through the inner gates," the lieutenant reported.

Lenzel returned the lieutenant's salute. "Replacements are being sent. We still have five boulders to go in this Mount and then four more Mounts to inspect. Have the gal leading this boulder order his men off the field under my command." He grasped his Channel Stone and projected his voice over the remaining boulders. "If anyone tries to escape, capture them and bring them here!"

* * *

LENZEL entered the Zenith's small study when Rolo opened the door. Still in his Apex uniform with a smear of black gore on his right sleeve, he saluted and Jarod waved him to a cushioned chair. He was exhausted and it showed. Rolo brought him wine, bread, and cheese before leaving and closing the door. He took a sip and looked into Jarod's eyes.

"Highest One, we found twenty-four of the Dark's creatures within the ranks of twenty-five thousand men, as I'm sure you know. Gaz asked me to report that his men are interviewing the guardsmen in the same barracks as the creatures. Two of the mounts had no infiltration and the monsters had congregated, usually in groups of threes, within a boulder. Seven boulders were infected with the scum and one boulder had six of them. We lost three men altogether and forty-two were injured, three seriously. Apex Nenon and Apex Jonather were badly shaken by the experience, but seemed to recover. The other three Apex officers took the matter in stride, showing surprise, but commanding efficiently."

Lenzel took another sip of wine before continuing while Jarod jotted notes on a pad. He leaned back in the soft cushions and breathed a sign of relief, and then continued when Jarod stopped writing. "Highest One, the Dark's minions' bodies and heads were placed on tarps beside the reviewing stand and each Trass marched by to view the bodies and heads before regrouping to their boulder and being dismissed to orders. One of the minions had dissolved. It was the only one with which I used my Stone to combat. After all Mounts had seen them, guardsmen poured salted water on them and they too, dissolved. I think they didn't disintegrate sooner due to my not using my stone on them except to identify them."

"I think your assumption is correct. I had instructed those on the walls with me to send only pleasant thoughts and love to the creatures. The Holy One had no trouble recognizing the Dark's minions. The two priests discerned their presence, but could not identify them until they reached the reviewing stand directly below us. The stronger of the two saw the black around them; the other one recognized them from feelings. The Holy One was impressed and the priests were shocked at what they saw. They swore to the Holy One that they would join the fight by searching the peoples' guises in their areas of influence. They were sent on to the Tower and ordered not to discuss what they had seen until they reached the crater. I am greatly relieved at their success."

Lenzel adjusted his posture before asking, "Highest One, what will a priest do when he detects the Dark's minions?"

* * *

LENZEL heard Segquo's voice in his head. *"You did well. Shadure and Wathdure are in pain. They know only that their creatures ceased to exist."*

24

SKIMMER Lorell Andress hurried after Lenzel's retreating back. Lenzel turned at the sound of running boots on the marble floor and waited for Andress to reach him. He felt a hesitation in Andress.

After the salutes, the skimmer said, "I'm preparing our men and ordering the supplies for departure tomorrow morning at sunrise. My anxiety comes from Sorrel's condition. Will he be fit for travel?"

"The Protector will examine him at various times today. If he cannot find remaining evidence of the Dark's influence, I see no reason to exclude him. Have you discussed him with your men?"

"I have. Sontos is concerned how Sorrel will react in a fight and Remming wonders if he should be left behind for the sake of the rest of us. Sorrel wants to try for officers' training. Being left behind would hinder his chances. I'm in favor of his joining us. He's better with a sword than most of the men and he's smart."

"Join me in my study for midmeal. I'll have an answer."

Lenzel had hardly finished returning Andress' salute when he sent a mental message to the Protector requesting an audience. The reply came instantly, a voice in his mind so crisp and clear, it was hard to believe Deion didn't stand next to him: *"Come now. I'm in the Zenith's small study."*

Lenzel approached the door as it slowly opened to admit him, which was beginning not to surprise him. The Zenith returned his salute and motioned him to a plush chair next to Deion. "What troubles you?" he asked.

"Highest One and Lord Protector, some of the men have reservations about Sorrel joining us on the trip. Based on the Lord Protector's statements thus far, I have no objection. But then, I wondered if there might be another way to ensure his state of mind. Do you think he and the rest of my men would be accepted by a minor stone?"

Deion looked at Jarod with a raised eyebrow. "Lenzel, that is an interesting idea. If there were any of the Dark hiding within Sorrel, I'm sure the stone would not accept him. Nonetheless, the stones may not join with any of them. The men would need to be totally committed to Light's Source and to me, which is a fact they should not be told in advance. Assemble your men in the large study in the mid-afternoon. We'll see what happens. The less they know before the meeting, the better."

After saluting, Lenzel managed to open the door with his mind in an acceptable way. He smiled as he hurried down the hall leading to the stairs to the eleventh level to send messages to gather his men, the Desert's Ire maidens, Zack and Currat and ask them to meet at the appropriate time.

* * *

LENZEL'S men looked nervous, arriving in dress uniforms; the first time they wore the outfit since their assignment to him. The maidens arrived wearing leathers, and the spies wore dark blue suits with white shirts and black boots. Only Lenzel's men looked nervous. There was little whispered conversation on the way to the twelfth level and Sorrel didn't speak.

Two guardsmen stood at the entrance to the large study. They saluted the Apex and opened the door for them to enter. The Zenith Lord stood near the other end of the room in full battle dress. Beside him, the Lord Protector stood wearing formal robes. Their attire didn't surprise Lenzel; the two pebbles of men in battle dress with drawn swords did. On the thick, white marble tabletop laced with deep blue veins, a large chest with closed lid sat before Deion.

Lenzel and his men saluted Jarod, who was the first to speak, "Earlier today, Apex Lenzel proposed a thought-provoking idea. He suggested all of you be tested for a minor stone. If the stone selects you, it will improve your natural abilities, coordination, strength, and perhaps offer other attributes as well. These stones can be used for many things besides healing. There is nothing to fear. If a stone doesn't choose you, nothing will change and you'll not be less thought of in your assignments. Only someone embedded with a major stone can open the chest."

Deion rested his hand on the lid for a moment and took it away as the chest's top rose to provide full access to its contents. He looked at a mixture of expressions on the faces of Lenzel's men, ranging from shock to surprise, from anxiousness to bewilderment. He performed a light mental probe on the men confirming his thoughts. The Desert's Ire maidens seemed non-affected, but their light analysis resulted in some of the same feelings as the men.

He addressed the room; no one person in particular— "There has been some trepidation concerning Guardsman Sorrel Billon after his encounter with an agent of the Dark's Source. I can assure you he has no remaining influence from that creature. Nonetheless, I'll start with him." Deion's voice softened a bit, "Sorrel, come stand before the chest."

Lenzel could feel the shock rise within Sorrel, but the man cast a pleasant smile to the room. His stance and stride showed confidence Lenzel knew he didn't feel. He wanted him to receive a stone.

Deion said, "Before a stone will accept you, you must silently or vocally declare your devotion to the Great Creator and the Light's Source and to the Major Stones."

Lenzel remembered those exact words said to him when he received his Channel Stone. *Will a Channel Stone be awarded today?* The thought increased his wonderment. The memory struck him of the increased power the Highest One obtained when Lord Kyle grasped his hand to float the chest sitting before him from the mountain. *Such control would certainly be an advantage.*

Sorrel closed his eyes, standing before the chest. Several long minutes passed before he looked at the treasure of gold and magic. A grey minor stone floated to a few inches of his chest. He hesitantly closed his hand around it. His eyes widened.

Deion smiled. "Keep the stone on your person at all times. I suggest you make a necklace with a pouch to hold it. If you had any of the Dark's influence left in you, the stone would not have picked you. I'm happy for you."

Deion went on to call the rest of the pebble. Skimmer Lorell Andress received another minor stone, a blue one. Deion next called Zack and Currat forward. Lenzel felt their surprise. The two men stood together in front of Deion, facing the chest. From Lenzel's advantage point, only he and Deion could see them gripping hands, interlacing their fingers. They looked at each other for a moment and then, at the chest. Their eyes remained open. In a short time compared to the long moments the others took, two Channel Stones floated forward captured in gold wire fastened to a gold chain, and settled on their shoulders.

Jarod and Deion said in unison, "Congratulations!" Deion went on to add, "I'll speak with you later today. There are things you need to know."

Lenzel wondered if one of those things was how to properly close a door and he smiled as the two spies walked back to the other end of the table, looking perplexed. Next, Deion started calling the maidens, one at a time. They each received a minor stone—fiery red ones.

Lenzel thought the color appropriate. The maidens didn't show emotional feelings, but he detected floods of emotiveness raging within them.

Deion's voice registered in Lenzel's mind—*"Will you train the ones with minor stones?"* Lenzel looked at Deion and nodded before responding, "I'll meet with those of you who obtained minor stones this evening. Still plan on leaving tomorrow morning."

25

LENZEL met with Sorrel, Andress, and the maidens after lastmeal. "What sort of things have you noticed since receiving your stones?" he asked.

Andress answered, "I feel more alert and stronger."

The others nodded.

"Good," Lenzel said. "You'll find your skills with the weapons you favor will increase. I know some of you practice those skills amongst yourselves. Be careful until you discover the new maximums on your abilities. It takes a little time to focus on your objective and your stone at the same time. You'll realize the results easily. Do you have questions?"

Lenzel expected the litany of queries that followed. The guardsmen centered on the social and working parameters of being in the Guard. Lenzel assured them their use of the stones would not be perceived by anyone other than their capabilities had increased and that could be explained as the results of renewed practice in most cases.

The maidens' inquiries focused on personal combat and working as a team. Lenzel explained they should become familiar with each other's new characteristics and what to expect. He ended with, "I strongly suggest you keep your stones a secret; in fact, it's an order that might well save your life."

* * *

SITTING in his room with the door closed, he sensed the men approaching and used his mind to open the door. Zack and Currat looked confounded upon seeing Lenzel sitting cross-legged on his bed across the room.

Lenzel smiled. "It's one of the new things you'll learn.

Didn't the Protector explain?"

Zack answered, "He said he had never had a Channel Stone and that you could answer our questions better than he."

"Ah," Lenzel said, "I remember you're good with knives and swords. Do you remember how the Highest One and the Protector practiced swordsmanship and how their swords were almost a blur of motion?" They both nodded. "You probably won't become that good, but your skills will increase well past the point of secrecy. Practice away from outsiders of our group.

"You will begin to communicate with your minds. Your deep love for each other will facilitate that ability faster. It did with my wife and me. You will find your lovemaking spectacular."

Zack and Currat looked very uncomfortable. Lenzel continued in a softer voice, "Gentlemen, as you well know, the love between two men or two women, while frowned on by some, is not forbidden in the realms. I *do* understand your desire for secrecy and I agree with you. Still, any of us with a Channel Stone or Great Stone will know of your love for each other and I'm sure it will not be discussed unless necessary for your safety.

"You will also begin to be able to do some things with your mind like sensing someone and opening the door for them." Lenzel went on to tell of his first experience opening a door and how it almost knocked a hole in the Zenith's wall.

Lenzel's visitors seemed to relax and they talked well into the night.

* * *

THE next morning at daybreak, Lenzel's group with supply wagons and a packhorse met at the entrance to the Spires. Lenzel became gladdened when he saw the Highest One riding toward them.

The Zenith Lord reined in and pitched his words for

all to hear, "Your stones will afford you some protection from detection by the Dark's Source, but do not become complacent about not being discovered. Our proficiencies will grow with the power of the stones, which means the strength of the Dark will also grow. It will not be possible to hide every portion of your mastery of the stones. Nonetheless, I command you to conceal as much as you can. Set aside time to practice each day that you're able. May Light's Source protect and keep you and the countenance of the Great Creator shine upon you. You are dismissed to your duties." The Zenith Lord wheeled away before the salutes finished.

That was short, but then, he sounds more and more like a commander than a friend. I must learn from him.

As the group passed through the outer gates, Lenzel used his heightened senses to judge the people they passed going into the Spires. A few men looked at the women, but no one seemed to peer overly long at the wagons or the men. Their response pleased him.

The team circled around to the mostly unused road leading to the forests and mountains located in the northwest portion of Stonefire, a trip of five hundred miles, or more, depending on how far into the mountain range they traveled. Lenzel set a goal of reaching the range's foothills in fifteen days, barring inclement weather and unforeseen obstacles. His team seemed to find the goal an easy one. Lenzel was not so sure.

The first three days went well. Lenzel ordered his men with stones to an hour's practice session at daybreak and another before lastmeal. Sorrel and Andress grumbled at first, seemingly not knowing Lenzel would detect their feelings. Once they discovered how improved their skills became, they showed their eagerness to continue and complained if their time was cut short. The maidens practiced away from the guardsmen. Lenzel had no worries that they would not train. Then, the rains came.

26

LENZEL cursed the rivulets of rainwater streaming down his face on the fourth day. His large leather cloak with cowl kept most of the water off until the wind changed direction, driving raindrops into his eyes. The cloak covered around him snuggly, but still left his lower legs and boots exposed, which felt like he had waded into a lake up to his knees. The oil-slicks over their supplies did their job and at least they were dry. One hundred and ten miles outside Stonefire, the road turned to little more than packed dirt with stones removed. Shallow ruts, due to the road's little use from travel wagons, quickly filled with water. The rain didn't entirely bog them down, but Lenzel had doubts the weather would soon clear.

In the few areas black clouds didn't abound, the sun dipped toward the horizon. He had sent Larrell Sontos and Davad Drosh to scout for a space to stay overnight. The guardsmen had not returned and he became anxious, although his fears were short-lived when he saw them coming down the long hill in front of him.

Sontos did the reporting. "Master Lenzel, we found a cave leading down into the hill thirty yards off the road and twenty-five yards below the crest of the hill. We explored it a bit and discovered it had been used before, but the signs are at least a year old. The mouth of the cave is big enough for our horses and wagons. We didn't go far into it. The rooms we saw are large and the passageways between them are wide. The ground leading to the cave seems well packed with a lot of rocks and very large oaks. It's passable."

Lenzel thanked Sontos and gave orders to make for

the cave. He felt better even though he feared the rains would last longer than he wished. *To the seven hells of the Dark, one afternoon of this rain is more than I'd wish for.*

The cave met their requirements, and more. Disappointingly, the distinctive carving above the mouth of the cave was not present. The ground to the cave held the wagons without much trouble other than moving a few rather large rocks. Luckily, they couldn't be called *boulders*. The wagons barely made it into the mouth of the cave. A wider and taller passageway led to a large room with plenty of leeway for the wagons and horses. He ordered men to gather any dry wood they could find and to make torches and fires for warmth and cooking. Davad Drosh asked permission to scout for game and Lenzel agreed. As the hunter left, he saw Zack briefly speak to the guardsman and point in the direction of a spot farther down the road.

The entire group worked well together performing orders. Lenzel yearned for that level of cooperation to continue. He had no doubts about the maidens or the spies; the guardsmen caused some concern. He sensed their feelings of strangeness about the mission. They were used to the tight structure and discipline of the Guard. The control and strictness remained, but geared toward *not* looking like a guardsman. Zack and Currat still talked to the men every day; it helped some but not enough, in Lenzel's estimation. He motioned Zack to his side away from the others.

"Yes, Lenzel," he said.

"How are you and Currat coming with being able to sense the men's feelings?"

"Your talks with us have helped and we are beginning to sense each other and you to some degree. I don't know what the upper limits of that talent will be, so it's hard to say."

"I've found it keeps growing. I can communicate well

with Ellrill. Interconnecting with the Highest One and the Lord Protector is somewhat overwhelming. I would like you and Currat to let me know if you discover unease in the men. Your and Currat's counseling is important and it needs to continue."

Zack nodded. "I agree."

"You talked to Drosh earlier."

"Yes, I do pick up on game. I felt deer in the direction I pointed him to go. I also felt wolves to the north. If this rain lasts, they will be hungry. It would be good to be aware of the packs' whereabouts."

"That's an interesting talent and one I don't possess. Can Currat do the same?"

"No, but he told me about the weather yesterday. He got it right down to the direction of the wind and the severity of the rain. He mentioned earlier that it would not stop tomorrow."

"I couldn't sense that in such detail. I did have a feeling it wouldn't soon stop."

Zack lifted his chin toward the cave's entrance. Drosh stood with something large wrapped in oilcloth that loaded him down even with his massive frame. Sontos, nearly as strong as Drosh, rushed to help unload the guardsman's burden. They unwrapped the oilcloth as others surrounded them to watch, exposing a dressed-out deer, bringing congratulations and a few tired jokes playing with the words *deer* and *dear,* which also elicited a few groans.

Syrill stepped forward; a knife appeared in her hand in a blur of motion. She made quick work of slicing off a large portion of venison. Putting the meat in a basket, she headed toward the cave room set up for cooking, saying over her shoulder, "Lastmeal will be in two hours."

Zack turned to Lenzel. "Kaarill was right when she said Syrill is the best cook in Desert's Ire. I've not tasted any other of the maiden cooks' food, but I can't imagine better. I watched when she loaded their supplies and there are a lot of herbs and spices on that wagon. I don't think the men will complain."

Lenzel nodded his agreement.

"Now, with your permission, I need to find Currat and practice our skills with our new stones."

Lenzel merely smiled and nodded. He motioned for Andress and Sorrel to join him at a private corner of the cave and counseled the men on the use of their minor stones and what to expect. After nearly two hours, he praised their efforts and suggested ways to discover what other talents they possessed. The smells coming from the cook's fires and Syrill's call to lastmeal ended their practice session.

*   *   *

LATER that night, Lenzel lay content on his sleeping furs with one pulled over him, still in his leathers to help fight the cold, remembering the wonderful lastmeal he enjoyed. He heard Ellrill's soft whisper in his mind—*"I love you."* Lenzel answered in kind. He started to send more thoughts to her when the alarm sounded. He quickly pulled on his boots while half running to the entrance to the cave.

Zack, Currat, and guardsmen Daniell and Andress got there before him, holding torches in their hands, waving them toward the outside of the cave. Lenzel stiffened slightly at the first snarling sounds, pulling Silver Stars from his pouch; he loosened into a battle stance. A long, loathing howl sounded a bit farther away from the torches, answered immediately by two wailing calls even longer away.

He moved swiftly to the start of the cave, slightly in front of the torches, which allowed him to see into the darkness before him. Five pairs of feral eyes reflected the light from the cave. Lenzel thought of his Channel Stone and concentrated on the scene in front of him. Instantly, he saw the wolves, ranging back and forth, glaring at the men. They looked thin, their fur hanging from them with rainwater running off it while matted blotches covered them in other spots. One larger animal charged the cave. Two Silver Stars cut into its head and chest. The wolf collapsed in mid stride. Lenzel looked to his right where Desert's Ire maiden Kelosrill crouched with another star ready to throw.

The largest of the wolves charged the cave's entrance, meeting a similar death. The remaining three slinked back into the woods before emitting a long, keening cry. Soon, wolves, some near, some far away took up the vowling. Lenzel ordered fires built across the front of the cave, but still under the overhang.

Zack approached him. "They looked diseased, scrawny and malnourished."

"I agree," Lenzel answered. "There's something else, something strange and wrong. I doubt they will try to attack again tonight. I believe the last one killed was the alpha male. I want to look at the carcass in the light. Meet me here at sunrise. I'll have guardsmen wake us."

*　*　*

LENZEL woke when the guardsman entered his sleeping area. "Is it first light?"

After the man's nod, Lenzel shucked off his furs and made for the cave's entrance. Zack and Currat arrived a few heartbeats later. They gathered around the largest, a male. Lenzel stepped back and touched his Channel Stone. He stood straighter and whistled a low note. Black fog formed around the beast and black gore oozed from the wounds. He released his stone and the blackness disappeared. Its back leg jerked. The wounds pulled in, closing. Lenzel didn't have a sword strapped on him, but Zack and Currat did. "Zack, take its head."

As Zack drew his sword, the creature began to rouse. Rising up on its haunches, Zack's sword flashed, reflecting the sun, and cut through the matted fur, skin, sinew, and bone, flapping the head to the side where it hung before the body toppled over. Without waiting for an order, Currat's sword sliced through the remains of the creature's neck. Lenzel held his stone and saw the blackness fade from the lesser beast. Within a few heartbeats, both wolves' bodies started to decompose, bringing forth the stench and rot of Wathdure's makings. Lenzel retrieved the Silver Stars carefully, not touching the now visible black gore excreting into the ground. He grabbed a torch and touched it to the remnants of what had once been wolves. A blinding flame shot up into the air with a strong sucking sound. When they were able to see again, nothing remained of the beings' bodies.

Lenzel noticed the shocked faces of the guardsmen who'd witnessed the destruction of the beasts. His words pitched low, "It seems the Dark has a new trick; nothing we can't handle." In the distance, the ferocious screams of animals sent a chill up Lenzel's spine. "Zack, you and Currat take as many men as you need and investigate."

Kelosrill stepped out from the cave's entrance. "I'll go."

"The three of us should be enough," Zack said.

Lenzel nodded and, as they left, he turned to Guardsman Roush Letern giving instructions on how to clean the Silver Stars lying on the ground. He stood just inside the overhang watching the rain pouring over the rock from above. Composing a succinct message in his head, he tightened his fist around his stone and sent his thoughts describing the incident to the Highest One. The Channel Stone vibrated with his effort.

The Zenith Lord's response came almost instantly. *"I'll alert all concerned."*

Lenzel followed with, *"The rain could hold us up a week after it stops for the roads to dry up."*

The answer—*"Understood."*

* * *

THE rain took two days to stop and another nine days for the road to dry up for travel. Three other wolves, infected with the Dark Source's evil, died at the hands of Zack and Currat. They reported the animals near death and could hardly move. Other wolves spotted in the area seemed malnourished, staying away from men and running in a large pack.

At sunrise of the twelfth day, Lenzel approached Zack and Currat. "I'm glad to get away from this cave. It gave us shelter and protection, but I prefer the open sky."

Zack and Currat nodded. "The wagons are nearly ready for the road," Zack said. "We'll ride out and scout ahead. If we find nothing, we'll meet up with you toward sunset."

Lenzel followed the spies toward the front of the cave, where he encountered Sorrel and Skimmer Andress, both holding their minor stones. "Have you noticed differences while using the stones?" Lenzel asked.

"Yes," Andress answered. "Our reflexes are faster and our swordsmanship has improved a good bit. We both have noticed being able to tell when you are in close proximity."

"It seems our eyesight and sense of smell have improved, also," Sorrel added.

"Good," Lenzel said. "The more you work with the stones, the more uses you'll find. Keep alert to them, but it's easy to read something ordinary into thinking it came from the stone. You need to learn the difference and sometimes that variance is light. Try seeing if you can move small objects that weigh little with your mind. It will likely take a lot of trying and I'm not sure it's possible, but it could become useful if you can master doing so. Work with your stones often during the day. You may be surprised at what you find."

Once on Challenger and leading his group forward,

Lenzel felt better. The sun showed bright with few clouds in the air, which was sweet with the smell of freshness from the flora. A family of rabbits at the side of the road scattered as Lenzel approached. Andress, riding beside him, chuckled. The area filled with rolling hills and few cleared areas, mostly along the side of the road for resting overnight, and those were poorly maintained. The road continued to show little use. Large evergreens with thick undergrowth grew a few feet from the road's shoulder. A trench, hard to see from green growth and the only thing stopping the encroachment, kept the road from becoming part of the woodland. Men and horses seemed glad to be rid of the cave. He had heard guardsmen complaining about mucking out the animals' area and had wondered how they would've liked sleeping in rain and mud. But then, lowlanders seemed to like to grumble. Lenzel was thankful for it.

The unit passed a much better maintained road running east and west. A little way north, they found an unusually large roadside clearing and, shortly after setting up camp for the night, Zack and Currat rode in, dismounted, and went directly to Lenzel.

"About five miles farther, we could see three mountain peaks," Zack said. "We didn't see a road or trail leading to them, but they fit the criteria you spoke about when briefing us. I think it's worth investigating and perhaps we'll find a trail beyond where we left off, but even with a trail, the wagons wouldn't make it. The woods looked to be the same as we've seen here."

"I agree," Lenzel replied. "Let's see how it looks when we reach the area. I've been thinking of whom to take in this kind of circumstance. My initial idea is to take the maidens, you two, and the strongest guardsmen, Santos and Drosh. Desert's Ire has a broad, short sword used for cutting through dense brush—we call it an undercut knife. Sounds like it'll be needed. I want the wagons protected at all times and the rest of the pebble will stay behind. What is the better road just south of here? I didn't see it on any map."

Zack looked around before answering, "It's the road leading to the Zenith's mines. There is a garrison at both ends. We spotted guardsmen several yards off the north road a mile before reaching it. They must have been told we would be coming through. They saw us. A lieutenant I knew came to the side of the road. He asked what detachment we belonged to. I asked him what he expected. He was hesitant, but finally described our group. I told him you would be about two hours behind us. He waved us on. That road is not known to many and rarely spoken of, and then, only between those who are detailed in its security. Discussing it where outsiders can hear is considered treason."

"I understand," Lenzel said. "In a day or two, I'll impress the importance of not saying anything about our duties and, as you know, that too, if violated is punishable by death. On another subject, have you picked up on any nearby game?"

Zack smiled. "There is a lot of small game such as hares and, farther into the woods, some larger game, bigger than wolves. I suspect the undergrowth must thin out about five hundred yards in. We have about two hours of daylight left; if you want, I'll get Drosh started in the right direction."

Lenzel thought for a moment. "Ask Kaarill to assign Kelosrill to go with him. She is proficient with Silver Stars and I imagine she's just as good with their undergrowth knives. Tell them not to get caught in the dark even if they have not made a kill."

As Zack left, Lenzel asked Currat, "Did you see signs of water? We have plenty to drink, but it would be nice to find some to bathe in."

"We didn't cross any streams. There is a fair amount

of game; water must be available to sustain them."

"Do you sense any weather problems?"

Currat smiled. "No heavy rain or storms. I don't think I can detect light disturbances; perhaps with more practice. I'll let you know if I feel something."

* * *

LENZEL watched Kelosrill cutting through the first few yards of heavy growth as Kaarill came next to him. "The knife works well," he said.

"Yes," she answered. "They take off the heads of wolves rather satisfactorily, too."

Lenzel laughed. "They do work as good on desert brush. I had not seen them used, but I did see the results from time to time."

"High One, I've noticed some discontent among the guardsmen."

The honorific surprised him. It was used for clansmen whose duties affected all the clans. The idea weighed on him. Dismissing it, he answered the leader of Desert's Ire's detachment, "The lowlanders do not soothe their mindsets with calming routines as we do. Since I've been working with the Guard and in the Highest One's service, I've noticed they work out their quarrels in a boisterous and sometimes physical way, not to the death as we do when a matter rises to that level. We talk more than fight; they fight more than talk. Thankfully, the Highest One and his close companions I've met are more like us."

As the maiden walked away, Lenzel's thoughts nagged at him. *The Highest One gave me the rank of Apex. I have the duty to command many men and in some cases, other Apex officers. I never thought of it in our way. I don't know if I like it or not. I wish the communication between Ellrill and me was better. I'd like to discuss it with her.*

* * *

AS the sun set, Lenzel saw Kelosrill and Drosh return with a young stag over Drosh's shoulder and what looked like a full quiver of arrows. The question in Lenzel's mind was answered when Kelosrill went to a basin and started cleaning her Silver Stars. Under Syrill's direction, two guardsmen helped butcher the venison while Lenzel watched the other maidens arranging the fire pit. He looked forward to a good night and interacting with Ellrill.

27

GRADUALLY, the terrain began to rise as they approached the three mountains Zack had reported. There had indeed been no trails leading toward the peaks. At a stop for midmeal, he climbed a giant oak, taking forty minutes to reach the top even with his Channel Stone's help. Back on the ground, he reported to Lenzel.

"About a half mile ahead, the lay of the land seems the best approach to the mounts. The trees parted for a distance and I think there must be a wide watercourse on our way."

At the location Zack described, Lenzel gave orders for the guardsmen to remain behind on guard duty. The maidens, each with an undergrowth knife, started hacking away, cutting a trail wide enough for two to pass without a problem. Some hundred yards into the forest, the brush thinned, leaving space to walk with seldom need for knives.

The watercourse turned out to be a river of sorts. It flowed gently and only calf high at its deepest. Lenzel felt pressure on his right boot as shining steel passed his head, going downward. Kelosrill reached down and pulled a viper's head, the size of two hands across, from the water, venom still dripping from large fangs.

"Did the serpent puncture your skin?" Kelosrill asked.

Lenzel lifted his foot from the water, showing impressions of two points in the leather.

"Run!" Currat yelled.

The group raced for the far bank without looking for the danger. As they ran three yards back on solid ground, Lenzel spotted a large disturbance in the river where the attack on him took place. Several of the vipers tried to make landfall as tiny fish leapt in the air, sharp teeth glinting in the sun, then dove back, biting into them, tearing them apart.

Being unfamiliar with rivers, Lenzel stared at Zack. "Is that normal?"

Zack chuckled before answering, "No."

"I thought not."

Zack and Currat scouted ahead as Lenzel and the maidens continued northwest, the mountains looking larger. The evergreens gradually gave way to tall pines and the land became rocky with boulders scattered about. Through the trees, Lenzel made out the beginning of small foothills not far from the base of the mountains. The highest peak called to him. He knew the jewels slept above him. An hour later, they found Zack and Currat waiting at the base of the tallest mountain.

Lenzel moved apart from the maidens. "Concentrate on the highest peak with your stones and tell me what you feel," he told the two men.

He could see the effort on the spies' faces as they looked above. After several moments, Zack replied, "Nothing." Currat shook his head.

Lenzel sighed. "I was hoping you could feel what I do. The Stones are there; they summon me. You two come with me and use your Channel Stones to help the climb. As soon as I confirm our find, I'll send the Highest One a message. He'll send troops and he may come, too."

He motioned the maidens to him, who gathered around him. "Become inconspicuous and don't let anyone follow us. Kill any who try if you must." He didn't expect any show of surprise on the maidens' faces and there was none. They dispersed and, in a short time, they couldn't be seen, but Lenzel could still feel their presence.

The ascent went well for the first two thirds of the

mountain. Then, the rock surface seemed to fight their every move. The skies darkened and a heavy rain started.

Lenzel thought, *Not again!*

Sharp scree plagued them, causing cuts and slippage downward. Other loose rock looked attached until touched, nearly triggering several falls.

Currat fell past him, horror masking his face. Lenzel grasped his forearm as he passed, downward, his hold slipping to his wrist, onward to their hands clasped painfully. Lenzel's shoulder hurt, muscles cramping, the torture increasing; his cheekbone slammed on the rock. Not knowing how long he could hold on, he strained, until boots landed close beside his head, very close. Kneeling beside him, Zack shot an arm past his eyes, and locked his hands onto his and Currat's wrist. He could feel heavily muscled arms sliding against him, pulling them back from the precipice. He lay back, closing his eyes against the rain, feeling Zack and Currat's bodies half on top of his.

No one moved for a hundred heartbeats. Zack stood then, using rock to steady him; Currat followed. Powerful arms lifted Lenzel from the ground to his feet. His shoulder jerked in spasms, and he felt dizzy for a moment. Concentrating on his Channel Stone, the seizures stopped; his head cleared.

He sensed the concern for him from the spies. "I'm fine," he said.

Without further words, they started to climb.

Near the top, the cave reminded him of the other one he found. The three vertical lines carved into the rock above the entrance made him smile. The same *shield* made his skin crawl and the men's faces showed surprise.

"It's a type of protection for the cave. I don't know how it works, but if you take your shirts off and lay them on those flat rocks, they'll quickly dry."

He pulled his leather shirt off and followed his own

advice. Zack and Currat followed his example. Never seeing the men shirtless, Lenzel marveled at the exactness of their bodies, down to the sparse hair under their arms, and even their nipples, except for the color of hair and eyes. *How can they not be brothers?*

A foot farther on, the cave began to glow, lighting the interior where three familiar looking chests rested along the room's wall. At the back of the cave's room, a small, closed chest sat on a rock pedestal, the precious jewels on its lid sparkling from within. Lenzel touched his Channel Stone and the closest chest opened, uncovering gold and more jewels. He chuckled to himself at the expressions of awe on his companions' faces.

Standing to the side, he clutched his stone and focused on the Highest One. *"We found the cave in Stonefire."* He went on to describe its location and the trouble at the river.

Jarod's answer was immediate. *"I'm sending the Guard and I'll be there at best speed."*

As had happened before, when passing the shield, the rain slacked to a drizzle, and then, as they went back out the entrance, it stopped, returning blue sky. Inside the shield, before the cave's mouth, warmth flooded through them, seeming to ease Lenzel's soreness. In an amazingly short time, the shirts dried. They stripped down to privateclothes to let the rest of their clothing and boots dry. Lenzel liked not having to feel the wet clothing.

After a while, dressed again and comfortable, they started the descent, Lenzel knowing full well it would be much easier…and it turned out that way. The maidens, except Syrill, came out of hiding as the men reached the last few feet to the base of the mountain. None of them showed concern.

"Any problems?" Lenzel asked.

"No," Kaarill answered. "We did find game. Kelosrill brought two hares down with one arrow each. Syrill is roasting them. We started when we saw your descent, figuring you would be hungry. We also saw Master Currat's fall and his rescue. High One, you did well; we are proud."

"My stone helped me a great deal. I've sent a message to the Highest One. He will send the Guard and he will join us. Send a maiden to our guardsmen telling them to watch for the Guard's arrival. Have her return with supplies with the help of a guardsman. I'm worried about the river."

"High One, Rystarill is our best tracker. She found a crossing where the water rushes through a narrowing in the river. She was able to cross back and return without much trouble. It's not too much deeper and neither the fish with teeth nor the snakes seem to go there. I'll send her."

"Good. Once she and the guardsman cross the river, have her send the man back. Leave a message for the Guard to come only to the river crossing and sound the call-to-duty. We should hear the trumpet well enough from here. There is no need to mention the Highest One will come. Now, food."

28

RYSTARILL left at first light and the supplies arrived by mid-afternoon. The maidens brought them across the river and sent the two guardsmen back. Lenzel faced Rystarill and raised one eyebrow.

"High One, it seemed prudent. We don't know when the Highest One will get here. The guardsmen seemed surprised and not to like it when I told them to watch for a detachment of men. Guardsmen Surron and Mattene must have fought from their looks and demeanor. Skimmer Andress and guardsman Billon spoke with me away from the others. All they said was there had been a scuffle, but the men had settled down. They also said that, thinking about those two when using their graystones, they felt uneasy, and using mine, I felt the same. I don't know if it's the Dark One or not. I didn't mention the Highest One would come."

"He will sort it out. I don't know how long it'll take for the men to get here and I don't know how many will come. If they are sent from the detachments at the ends of the east-west road, it won't be long. Determine the best route for wagons to reach the river and the effort it'll take to clear the undergrowth."

Lenzel waved Zack over and repeated what Rystarill had said about the guardsmen. "I want you and or Currat to see what's going on with the men."

"We'll both go to observe them from both ends of their camp."

"Fine," Lenzel answered, "Stay until the detachment comes and lead my pebble here. Rystarill found a crossing that is safe. She can show you where it is located."

Zack smiled. "No need; we found it yesterday, assuming you mean the spot where the river narrows."

Rystarill looked startled. "I didn't see your tracks!"

Zack only smiled.

"On second thought," Lenzel said. "I'll come with you. I want to be in uniform when the Highest One and the detachment get here."

"We can bring it to you," Zack said.

Lenzel shook his head. "No; if the Dark's influence or beasts are in the area, I may be needed. Zack, you Currat and the maidens are the ones I completely trust. I sensed a great deal from the men coming here and in training. I don't expect anything is amiss, but I'd rather be safe. Andress and Billon are inexperienced in using their graystones and probably wouldn't feel the Dark if it's there. We will."

"When do you want to leave?" Zack asked.

"At first light."

*   *   *

LENZEL pulled closer to the fire and tried to sleep. He couldn't. His questions raced from subject to subject.

What is the small box on the stone pedestal with jewels on top and what's the preternatural light shining from inside them? Is the Dark One or his minions at work around us? Can we beat them? When will the Highest One be here? What's happening with the guardsmen, if anything? How far can we get a wagon into this terrain?

Lying on the ground, squirming to be comfortable and feeling cold, he grasped his Channel Stone and called to Ellrill. *"Are you awake, my love?"*

A few moments passed and he thought she must be asleep, but then he heard her thoughts. *"I'm awake and wanting you. How are you?"*

"Troubled, but there's nothing to do but wait. Otherwise, I'm well. I couldn't sleep and I missed you."

"Shall we make love?"

Lenzel chuckled. *"You have no idea how much I want to. I don't think it would be a good idea. I'm at a campfire, surrounded by men and women who are trained to wake at the slightest disturbance that is out of place…and I'm sure the sounds I would make would qualify for unusual."*

Ellrill's laugh chimed gently in Lenzel's mind.

"How is your training coming with the High Healer?"

"Very well. I was able to use my mind to remove a blood clot in the leg of an injured man. It was a thrilling experience."

"You'll be a High Healer soon."

"That will take a while. I must be up before sunrise tomorrow; let me sleep."

"I too must be up before sunrise. Sleep well."

"After communicating with you, I always rest well. You, too."

"I will."

Interrelating with his wife calmed him. Tonight was no different. He slept.

* * *

LENZEL stirred to see Zack and Currat coming back into camp. It was the sound of their relieving themselves that woke him. He felt safer with them there and found the Highest One's order for them to join the group, wise. Following suit of the men, Lenzel returned feeling refreshed. Interacting with Ellrill had indeed worked its magic. He chuckled at the pun.

Syrill had prepared firstmeal for them and packed food for midmeal. Lenzel took the food and thanked her. She hurried away to start again for the maidens. He watched for a moment, realizing how efficiently she made every movement with no need to retrace her steps when possible. *That could become a good training program.*

Lenzel didn't like wearing his sword. He strapped it to his back, knowing he must attach it to his waist belt if trouble came. *At least, it'll be away from my pouch of Silver Stars.* He did wish he had his bow and arrows. He decided to bring them back to the mountains.

They moved away from the road side of the river and soon found the cleared trail. The sun shone, trees blocking its warmth with light patterns reaching the forest floor in irregular designs. He also decided to take his furs back to subdue the night's cold. They made good time and he enjoyed the banter between them. Zack raised his hand; they stopped. Lenzel went north with Zack as Currat went south, approaching the road through the undergrowth. Lenzel searched for any sign of the Dark's minions or authority. He sighed with relief upon finding none. Yet there was something, a feeling of disquiet...a disturbing sensation.

Lenzel used the clans' hand signals to inform Zack he would return to the trail. He entered the encampment without notice until Drosh looked in his direction. The man looked astonished. "Andress, Lenzel has returned," he said.

The pebble leader hurried over.

"I'm glad to see you." Lenzel ushered his skimmer back up the trail and spoke softly, "There is something wrong and I don't know what it is, more of a feeling than anything. The men are edgy."

"Gather them and we'll talk after my remarks to them."

Moments later, the guardsmen stood in a loose line in front of Lenzel. "You have done well in your pretense of *not* being in the Guard. Now, we must revert back to being guardsmen. Detachments will arrive soon and later, the Zenith will join us. I imagine the men will be led by a gal or higher. You need to be in uniform and ready to greet them. I suspect the Zenith will be in the Guard's uniform. I don't know how many are coming, but I believe a Tress is the smallest number and there could ultimately be a full boulder. Do not mention the Zenith Lord is on his way here. I consider you well trained and disciplined; show it. Keep your uniforms in inspection condition.

"Now, I want to know of anything out of the ordinary that you've experienced over the last few days, no matter how trivial or strange it may sound." He offered Billon a direct gaze.

The man, who yearned for officer training, started slowly, "Apex, I feel a heaviness around us like we are in the middle of a major storm or before a battle." Gathering confidence, he continued, "It's hard to explain. I think all of us are agitated. Tempers are short, but not because of infractions between men. It's similar to the nervousness when you know you might be in trouble with other men in a common room. Something *could* happen, but it's not certain."

Lenzel noticed a few of the men nodding in agreement. "Has anyone else felt that way?"

"I did not know how to say it as Billon did; he's right, at least for me," Surron said hesitantly.

Lenzel sensed the general agreement from the pebble. He concentrated on his Channel Stone and let his mind float over the area. The response nearly brought him to his knees. He sent out one emotion, love, and called to his protectors before saying, "Gentlemen, we are about to have company."

Moments later, Lenzel saw the first deathcat, a very large male, come through the brush and directly to him. He calmly scratched the animal behind the ears, causing a loud purring, growling sound, and felt at peace with the beautiful encasement of powerful muscles before him. Its eyes seemed to devour him, the feeling of protection growing until its power matched its strength.

Farther north, another male bounded from the brush onto the road as a female casually walked toward them from the south. A total of seven deathcats formed a semicircle around the men—three males and four females. The large male stayed at Lenzel's side, the others settled facing outward, in a circular defense, no one noticing his slight hand signal. Whatever emotions the deathcats projected, the horses barely noticed the great felines.

Zack and Currat soon emerged from the trail with two male deathcats following close behind them. The men's smiles well communicated their acceptance of new benefactors. As with Lenzel, the males settled at the spies side. Zack bent to one knee, having to look upward to behold golden, orange eyes, the black pupils not stirring from him. He leaned forward and laid his head beside soft, luxurious fur. That, too, brought a purring roar.

Currat sat cross-legged and held his arms out to his male. The response caused chuckles and laughter from the men when a furry forehead knocked him backward and an enormous tongue slurped across his face. Coughing, he tried to rise until nearly fifteen hundred pounds of deathcat decided to lie next to him and plopped its head on his chest. A somewhat strangling sound escaped from Currat, startling the animal; rising to a sitting position, it gave him another wet kiss on his face.

Lenzel felt the heaviness lift from the men.

* * *

OVER the afternoon, four deathcats left in ones and twos for a short time, returning with game kills not over a day old. They placed two does and a peccary on the far side of the road, delivering a stag to the encampment. Drosh and Santos moved the carcass and began dressing it out. Two of the male deathcats watched with a distinct, questioning expression before moving to their own lastmeals. Deathcats are solitary animals; Lenzel sensed them working together and not fighting over their kills. It amazed him.

Later that evening, he settled down on his furs; the deathcat with whom he'd developed an attachment looked on from a few feet away. Lenzel concentrated on his Channel Stone and formed an image of himself in his mind. Speaking mentally and normally, he said his name. The deathcat cocked its head. He formed another image of the deathcat and repeated the name, Dark-killer, as before. Each time he focused on his stone and sent loving thoughts, the deathcat purred.

Lenzel slept well, dreaming of romping through trees and forests, swimming in streams and rivers, catching game and fish, seeking a mate and lovemaking, now knowing more of the life a deathcat led. He wondered if the dreams had transferred to Ellrill, then discarded the idea; he would have heard from her, otherwise. The deathcats meandered out of camp, Lenzel sensing they never wandered far. He packed supplies like Zack and Currat, adding his uniform.

Lenzel told the spies about the exercise he performed with Dark-killer the night before and suggested they try it with their deathcats. "The tricky part is forming the images in your mind and projecting them. Touch your Channel Stone when communicating with them if at all possible."

"Will they ever get angry at us?" Currat asked.

"I haven't heard it mentioned, but remember, these are still wild animals. They love us and I don't think they would attack as long as they feel those emotions returned. The stories I've heard tell of them bonding for life with the human they feel an affinity for, an attachment that is repaid. The Zenith told me they are extremely loyal and protective. For such a large creature, they have a long life and they will probably outlive us. Always, always treat them well and you'll be greatly rewarded."

Zack chuckled. "I feel like I just gave birth without the pain." Currat looked at him with a raised eyebrow.

Ready to move out after giving the guardsmen their orders, Lenzel told the spies to think of their deathcats and picture the trail ahead, not forgetting to send a little love with the message. A hundred yards farther on the trail, Dark-killer sprang onto the trail while the other two appeared behind them. The men had not seen or heard them in the underbrush. Lenzel felt love and protection surround him and projected the same back to Dark-killer.

"How did they do that?" Zack asked.

"Do what?" Currat replied.

"Get here without us hearing or seeing them; they're huge!"

"I've heard," Lenzel answered, "as we get certain powers and abilities from our Stones, they have other talents given by Light's Source. We combine our abilities when joined and it is in a way similar to a marriage. I'm not sure Dark-killer and I have united, but I do feel more from him and for him than the other deathcats. I feel a slight loss when he's not near me."

"You think we should attempt to name our deathcats?" Zack asked.

"I do," Lenzel replied. "I think it tightened the bond between Dark-killer and me." When he said its name, the deathcat let out a throaty purr.

Approaching the river, Lenzel sent a mental picture of the snakes and flesh eating fish to the deathcats. They immediately went into a low crouch, muscles tensed. He went to the edge of the river and called all three deathcats. Again, he projected the images and what had happened when they first tried to cross over. Then, he walked to the narrows and projected safety and an image of Zack and Currat wading across the low rapids.

He started to enter the water when Dark-killer nudged him aside and seemed to study the river. He put his giant paw into the water, claws extended. Slowly, he waded in, looking from side to side, his neck fur raised and tail slowly moving with his head. Lenzel followed and sat near a tree on the other side. Dark-killer came to him and he projected all the love he could muster to the feline. Ropes of emotions encased him—feelings of security, protection, and love so strong he nearly fell to his side.

Something has happened; combining, joining, marriage or whatever we are!

He put his hand to his head and it cleared as quickly as it had become muddled with strong emotions. Dark-killer looked at him as if nothing had happened.

One day later, in the morning, Lenzel heard the Guard's bugle call announcing a small boulder. Two hours afterwards, the same call sounded once more.

"Two small boulders of six hundred men?' Zack asked.

"It would seem so," Lenzel answered.

"Did the Zenith send so many men when you showed him the first cache?"

"No, but this cave has something new I didn't see in the first one." Lenzel let the subject drop and Zack didn't ask for more information.

A few minutes later, Lenzel appeared in the full Guard uniform of an Apex officer with a springing deathcat emblazoned over his left chest. He gave orders for Zack and Currat to scout ahead and spy on the formations to find anything out of place. A few moments passed before they left and started to disappear down the trail, deathcats in tow, but somehow looking the other way around.

Lenzel approached the road, Dark-killer at his side, nearly two hours later. A sergeant saw him first. His face paled before he found himself and bellowed, *"Focus on the Apex!"*

The cry was picked up and within a few minutes, ranks of guardsmen and officers rushed to formations. Two gals quickly walked to where Lenzel stood. He judged the two officers whose titles meant iron-bearing rock and decided these men to be aptly named. Dark-killer settled by him, his tail whipping the grass every few seconds. Lenzel sent calm and the deathcat decided it was time to wash its face, ignoring the men. The officers, on the other hand, seemed to find it hard to take their eyes off probably the largest deathcat they'd ever seen; if indeed, they had seen one at all.

The slightly larger of the two men, well over six feet tall, spoke first. "Apex Lenzel, I am Gal Jannus Kritz of the eastern fortress and this is Gal Strufford Sumtom from the western fortress located at the ends of the east-west road. We are honored to meet you and await your orders."

"Are others apart from the Zenith joining us?"

Both officers looked startled, recovering nicely, then Gal Sumtom answered, "My Apex, there is a team of engineers with support men and supplies following us. They should arrive tomorrow."

Lenzel called on his Channel Stone and bore holes into the men's eyes. "You didn't know the Zenith Lord would join us?"

Dark-killer sat up on its haunches.

"No, sir."

"Then, gentlemen, you'll keep that information to yourselves and not discuss it where others can overhear. In the meantime, there is a river some one and a half hours through the forest. The river has hidden dangers. You must give strict orders that none of your men enter the water without one of my party with them, and that excludes the pebble of men you found here when you arrived. We are Master Zack Stand, Master Currat Duval, five maidens from Desert's Ire, and nine deathcats. What do you know about my men and women?"

"I know you outrank all but the Zenith Lord in the Guard. I've had successful missions with Master Stand and I've heard of Master Duval and the maidens of Desert's Ire," Gal Kritz answered.

He looked at his counterpart from the western fortress.

"My Apex, mostly the same. I did meet Master Duval

once, but did not serve with him on a mission."

Lenzel softened his persona and sent reassuring feelings to the officers. Some of the strain left their faces.

"Gentlemen, the knowledge of your fortresses is highly secret and telling of them is treason. Impress on your men that anything they see or hear on their assignment here falls under the same edicts. Inform them that the deathcats will not hurt them if left alone. The Desert's Ire maidens are not to be approached unless specifically ordered. One of these women is capable of bringing either of you down and cutting your throat before your body hits the ground, perhaps both of you. You needn't tell your men that, but a command not to bother them would be in order." Lenzel mentally shook his head and laughed without changing his demeanor. "I don't know when the Zenith Lord will arrive and if you hear, inform me at once.

"The trail from here to the river must be widened to accommodate two wagons abreast. Do you have equipment to accomplish that task?"

Sumtom nodded. "We do. Men can start working on it tomorrow after firstmeal unless there is need to work overnight. We certainly have enough men to work a complete day at a time."

"That's not necessary," Lenzel answered. "We have until the Zenith arrives and I doubt that could be under three or four days. With the men available, the work should be completed within two days at the most.

"Gentlemen, I don't know you and you haven't worked with me. If I say or order something not in the best interest of our goals, I strongly expect one of you to tell me. If, for instance, this work cannot be done in two days, I would want you to let me know. Am I clear?"

"Yes, sir!" Both officers answered in unison, seeming more at ease.

"I'll join you for lastmeal tonight and leave for my

camp at first light. You should also be aware that Masters Stand and Duval are in the area with their deathcats. They'll probably want to join us, too. Will that make a problem for you?"

"No, sir," Sumtom answered. "We each have six wagons of supplies. We can order a large tent constructed for you and your group. If, perchance, you don't need it, the Zenith might welcome it on his arrival, but the men wouldn't know that."

"Go…" Lenzel said.

A bolt slammed into the tree behind Lenzel's head. He ducked as another shot past. It would've found its mark.

"Attack!" Kritz and Sumtom yelled.

Lenzel dove for the ground and rolled away when yet another bolt penetrated the dirt to his side. Dark-killer bounded toward a tree west of the road. From the projectile's path, the archer must have been near the top of the giant pine. He grasped his Channel Stone and projected great fear of heights upward in the attacker's direction. Orange fur caught his eye and he saw Dark-killer a third away up one of the trees.

A man, panic stricken, reached out for a better hold. Lenzel increased the fear of heights. The man screamed, then fell, crashing through branches, breaking limbs, and thudding to the ground, bone sticking out of his right leg. His screams ended in what must have been great dread when Dark-killer landed beside him.

Lenzel called to his deathcat and sent soothing emotions. The great cat looked back to him and cocked its head. He opened his hand flat, and made a gesture downward. Dark-killer plopped down and licked his paw, rubbing it against his fur where he had left off.

Lenzel chuckled, then walked toward his attacker. The gals each ordered three pebbles to scout the area. As they started to form, Zack stepped through the trees with his deathcat beside him.

"Stand down!" both gals yelled.

Waving at them, he continued on toward Lenzel and stopped ten feet before reaching the wounded attacker. Lenzel and the gals joined him.

"I killed two more and Currat wounded one other," Zack said. "I tried to take them alive, but had no choice. They are quite a way back from the road. I started to scout this way when I heard the commotion and saw Dark-killer going up a tree. Currat is guarding the wounded man. One of the men's shirts ripped. His chest is branded with a pattern of an open flame around his left nipple."

They walked back to where Lenzel's attacker lay. A healer stood over the man.

"I put him to sleep," he said to Lenzel. "He'll lose the leg; I don't have the skill to save it. I'm not sure a high healer could."

Zack reached down with his knife in hand and slit the man's shirt. There, surrounding his left nipple, a newly branded open flame, pink and weeping in its newness and looking still painful, seemed to stare back in bold defiance.

"Have any of you seen a mark like this before now?" Lenzel asked the gals. There was no answer. "Have the other wounded man brought in and search the dead for any clues. Send a message to your commands for men, at least a boulder to start searching from the fortresses to here."

"Apex," Fritz said. "That many searchers would leave the fortresses vulnerable to attack. There are two boulders at each fortress. We have standing orders from the Zenith that each fortress must have a compliment of a boulder or more at all times. You, I believe, are aware of what they guard."

"I am," Lenzel answered. "Ask your superiors for them to start a search with as many men as they are comfortable ordering out. Give them all the details of the attack here. Do not let your rider know the Zenith is expected. I'm returning to my camp." The gals saluted and hurried away before Lenzel could complete responding to their gesture. He faced Zack. "We go back as soon as Currat is here."

"Did someone mention my name?"

Lenzel nodded. "Our camp is under-guarded. We must return at once."

It took only a few moments for Lenzel to find Andress. "You are to follow the trail to the river. Do not go into the water; it's very dangerous and men could die. Bring as many supplies as you can carry to bivouac for several days. Engineers will arrive tomorrow and start cutting a road through to the river."

Lenzel returned the skimmer's salute and started back wondering what he'd forgotten, if anything. Dark-killer walked beside him; still, he had a nagging feeling.

29

LENZEL spoke with Zack, Currat, and Kaarill in the grayness of false-dawn light. He still had one of his furs wrapped around him and the others wore blankets or extra clothing over their usual outfits. The night had turned much colder than expected. Currat commented the snap would pass and the day should be pleasant.

Zack added wood to the fire pit while Lenzel collected his thoughts. Dark-killer lay beside him and he absently stroked the animal's deep, soft fur, only realizing his actions when a soft purr sounded. It suddenly amazed him at how normal it felt being beside Dark-killer in so short a time. Within a few moments, the other two males and a female settled near them, cleaning the fur around their faces. Lenzel suspected a nocturnal hunting trip had taken place. The female had come across the river after lastmeal, seeming to know where to go. She stayed near the maidens and before long, purred the loud throaty sounds becoming common among them.

He had sent the Highest One a mental picture of the brand marks found on the attackers. The reply woke him nearly an hour earlier. *"Neither Gaz nor Segquo know of the brand. Others are investigating."* He had sent nothing about when he might arrive. Even if he'd arranged for fresh horses at intervals, it would still be at least two more days before his appearance.

The pebble had started forming a bivouac before resting. Lenzel had unobtrusively watched, seeing Andress and Billon working well together, anticipating each other's needs. Both performed efficiently and interacted well with the other guardsmen. *Perhaps there might be two candidates for officer training,* Lenzel thought. *The Guard will need good officers, a lot of them. I wonder if the Highest One would share the timing required to be ready. I wonder if he knows.*

The banter between the others around the fire pit brought his attention back to center on the day's requirements. He cleared his throat and silence prevailed. Dark-killer settled his head next to his leg. "Zack, I want you and Currat to keep alert to the surroundings here. Put up the alarm traps I've heard so much about. We have much more to do within the Seven Realms. I need the entire group. The cave is the most important, but I believe it will protect itself.

"If additional attackers fire on the Guard at the road, they are more than able to handle the situation. I don't think that'll happen. Those bolts were aimed at me. The gals were not targeted. The men initiating such an attack knew they would not get away and would probably die. Such men are either in fear of what might befall them if they fail, and that circumstance being worse than death, or they are fanatics, possibly both. How old are the branding marks on the men?"

"The two who actually loosed bolts had fresh burns a few days old," Zack answered. "The scars on the two farther away looked two to three months old."

"That means," Lenzel said, "the organization recruiting the attackers is at least that old. It's difficult to keep a group that fanatical a secret. I wonder if they're that tightly controlled or just small in number."

Zack ran his fingers through his hair. "I've not come across the markings before now. If anyone would know, it would be the healers. They see more naked breasts than anyone. Well, perhaps not as many as the prostitutes see, at least the good ones."

"Yes, but the healers work longer," Currat said.

He and Zack laughed, while Lenzel and Kaarill

showed knowing smiles.

"What?" Currat asked.

"The clans are much different than the rest of the realms' populaces," Zack answered. "Their family structure is very close and tight and protected within its clan. Their social bearings would not allow for prostitution to exist. A woman's disgrace, or man's for that matter, reflects not only on him and his family, but the entire clan. Any sexual activity before or outside the joining of two people is highly frowned upon and punished by exile...and how many exiled clansmen or clanswomen have we seen? Did I get that right, Kaarill?"

The maiden looked at the spies, her smile disappearing. "The part about prostitution, yes. We find the idea most disturbing. Sex between two women or two men is considered their business and does not change their status within the clan. Sex between a man and woman before they are joined is permitted if the parents are informed and they pledge to join if a child is produced. Those incidences are most rare. In my life, I've heard of it happening only twice. There were problems keeping the man or woman from joining at that time. The couples did, however, join later. The private actions of our people are preserved closely; a man or woman can be severely punished for telling someone in another clan of any private information that concerns others." She looked at Lenzel.

"Of course, Kaarill is correct. There are other major differences between the clans and the rest of the realms. You may discover those at some point."

In the distance, the Call to Duty bugle fanfare floated through the trees. It got the men across the river rising. Kaarill went to check on firstmeal. Zack and Currat started planning the camp's defenses and Lenzel wondered what the Highest One might want from the engineers.

He walked to the base of the mountain, peering upward. He couldn't see the cave or the ledge before its entrance. *I could order a guardsman to climb the smallest mountain to observe the land. Could he see the cave? Is it needed? These are the mostly guarded and patrolled areas in the Seven Realms except for the Spires. Then, how did the attackers get to us? What's on the other side of the mountains? How long would it take for me to climb the smallest mountain? I need more information.*

He crossed the river with Dark-killer at his heels and found Andress. With the formalities finished, he asked, "Lorell, who is your bugle man?"

"Dusten Remming, sir."

"Have him sound the Call for Counsel. I know Roush Letern comes from a mountainous region. Do you know if he's good at climbing?"

"He's spoken of climbing when a child. I don't know to what extent or his expertise."

"Find out."

As Lenzel reached solid ground, returning to his camp, he heard a sharp and loud bugle blast. He sought out Zack who helped Currat prepare alarms for trespassers. The deathcats watched intently. Dark-killer nudged between the other males. Before he could ask Zack questions, the female bounded up. Things got crowded with nearly six thousand pounds of felines. Lenzel felt a twinge in his mind. He grasped his Channel Stone and concentrated on the deathcats. They communicated in pictures, not completely surprising him. *How much more do I have to learn from them?* They had identified the trap as something not to encroach upon.

Zack finished the trap.

"Given what you know about this area, what advantage would we have if I ordered a guardsman to climb the smallest mountain? The maps don't show this area," Lenzel said.

"It would need to be one of the gals' men. They get

very edgy about who knows what. I don't think there will be a problem if you, Currat, or I went up, but anyone else needs to come from their command."

"I thought as much."

* * *

LENZEL had just finished firstmeal when he heard a commotion at the river. Fritz and Sumtom had arrived with three men wearing armbands with the yellow and black colors of an engineering detachment. Andress talked to the gals and gestured toward the river. They had gathered a few yards north of the river crossing. Lenzel came up from behind them.

"I see no reason why I shouldn't go into the water. I don't take orders from skimmers!" an engineer said.

"Then perhaps, you'll take them from me," Lenzel said.

The engineer turned, startled. "I take orders from..." The color drained from the man's face when he saw the springing deathcat on Lenzel's uniform. His salute lacked fortitude. "A...Apex Lenzel, of...of course I'd be honored to take your orders. I'm Engineer Tallus."

"Don't wade into the river except at the rapids. Those are my orders. *My* skimmer tried to save you from harm. The waters are infested with vipers and they are aggressive." He turned to the gals. "Gentlemen, if you'll follow me to the other side, I require your counsel." Lenzel turned on his heel and led the way to his camp.

They settled around a camp table on stools brought up with the supplies. Zack, Currat, and Kaarill joined them at Lenzel's call. After the introductions to Kaarill, Lenzel asked Sumtom, "Have you received any messages?"

"No, sir. I sent the bodies back to my garrison. The man with the broken leg is unconscious and the healer says he shouldn't be moved. The other prisoner hasn't talked, yet. There's not been enough time for the men to return from the fortress. I expect them at mid morning."

"Do detailed maps exist of this area and do you know what lies on the other side of these three mountains?"

"No maps sir, at least not to my knowledge," Fritz answered. "There are mountains to the north and south of our fortresses, but the land north of here has no more for a hundred miles or more. We send patrols throughout our area and that includes the other side of these mountains for about ten miles."

Lenzel frowned. "I want to establish a lookout on the smallest of the three mountains to see if there is movement of any kind. No one other than those in my group are allowed on those mountains, excluding the guardsmen assigned to me. Those orders now include your men. Make sure it's clear; no one is allowed on our side of the river except by direct order from the Zenith or me. *If* I send a guardsman on the mountain, he'll have to be someone I believe is completely trustworthy to stay where he's sent and not to wander about. I do have one man that may have experience climbing mountains. Skimmer Andress is questioning him now. Do you know of anyone in your boulders who has such experience and one you trust to that extent?"

"I imagine we both have climbers in our ranks. At times, we are asked to guard the way into and out of the mines more than usual. We have men on watchtowers half way up the mountains and one at the top when that occurs. Here, the two mountains alongside the largest one have fairly easy slopes unlike the one in the middle. That one would be very difficult to climb."

Lenzel chuckled. "It was for me." He chuckled again at the expressions on the gals' faces. "Gentlemen, I hold my rank for expediency in dealing with the Guard and High Lords. I don't expect to command armies anytime soon, although the Zenith seems to think I'm capable of that duty. You guard the mines that I suspect few of the High Lords of the other realms know about and I don't think they are aware of any of the details. I assume you've thought of this, but are you privy to something that would bring the Zenith and me to investigate and is of the highest importance? The real reason we are here should not be in your men's minds if it becomes known. Do what you can to drive down the importance of the Zenith's visit. Giving you more information than that will be up to the Zenith when he arrives. The engineer I saw earlier looks like he's the type to brag about things. How did he get here?"

Sumtom sighed. "He's a problem. His cousin has a high position at the Spires and got him the posting. We are trying to think of how to get him transferred before he learns too much. I've kept him away from the mines and working on projects at the fortress. The mine engineers rarely come to the fortress and he's not come in contact with them. He's not very well liked."

Lenzel nodded. "Put him to work on the road to the river. If he objects, tell him it's on my order and he's free to talk with me.

"Frankly, I'm concerned about the attack yesterday on several levels. I'll come to the road after midmeal to talk with the one we caught. I do want increased vigilance at all times. Those young men with the newest brandings had to know they wouldn't live. That kind of devotion, or fear, comes from a cause, not the love of money. Keep them under close watch. I wouldn't be surprised if the relatively unhurt one tries to kill the other one and then, him. If you have to, tie him down. Put a constant patrol on the trail to here…"Now, gentlemen, if you have nothing more, you're dismissed to duties."

After the officers left, Lenzel asked, "Comments?"

"I suspect," Zack said, "the troublesome engineer will be reassigned soon and his cousin may not be at the Spires for long."

"He won't be a problem after this afternoon," Lenzel

said, and didn't answer the questioning look on the others' faces.

"High One, I could climb the mountain. It doesn't seem too difficult," Kaarill asked.

"Your other talents may be needed here, but I'll keep you in mind."

* * *

LENZEL ate bread and cheese while riding Challenger toward the road. When the rest of the supplies came up, the horse came, too. Lenzel sensed Challenger and Dark-killer bonding almost immediately. The deathcat ranged ahead, but never out of sight. He sniffed the air, searching undergrowth and trees. Lenzel also projected his senses outward, finding discord ahead.

Rounding the final bend before reaching the road, Engineer Tallus berated two guardsmen. "No, you must use the pounder before and after trenching." He sounded condescending and angry.

The guardsman, showing a sign of relief, shouted, "Focus on the Apex!"

Tallus jerked around and saluted, his face still dark and with the puffiness of annoyance until replaced with terror when seeing Dark-killer staring at him. He started to speak. Lenzel cut him off. "Tallus, report to camp and await my orders." He motioned for another engineer farther toward the road.

Tallus audibly huffed, saluted, and turned away as the new engineer arrived and saluted. Dark-killer growled; Tallus ran.

"Apex Lenzel, I'm Engineer Jordan. How may I be of service?"

Lenzel returned the salute. "Take over here."

"Yes, sir."

Lenzel and Dark-killer entered the command tent, a guardsman holding Challenger at the ready just outside. Fritz and Sumtom arrived and after the formalities, the three sat at a round table.

"Which of you has Tallus under his command?"

"I have that dubious honor," Sumtom replied.

"Write orders reassigning him to the Deepwells garrison. Send a sealed order to the garrison commander that Tallus is to never have anyone reporting to him and his permanent duties will be cleaning out the sewage tunnels leading to the sea. I'll sign both orders. Have him on the road south in the next two hours. I don't wish to see him...Now, what of our two prisoners?"

"The bigger one refuses to speak or eat. He did drink some water. He did as you suggested. His attempt to get to the other man failed when guards arrived. The man was already dead. The healer said his heart failed during the morning."

"I'll see him now."

As Lenzel left the tent, he heard Sumtom's whisper. "...sewage tunnels. I hope I never piss him off!"

Lenzel stopped beside a tree for a moment to send a message. *"Highest One, I've reassigned an Engineer Tallus to the sewage tunnels at Deepwells. He may pass you on the road. There's something not right about him. My probe returned vindictiveness and a certain evil, but there is something else I haven't encountered before and I don't recognize it. I wanted you to be aware."*

The answer came immediately, *"Understood and I'll investigate. I should arrive in two days. Give no warning to the Guard."*

Lenzel continued on to the tent where the attacker awaited. A sergeant saluted and pulled the flap open for him to enter. Inside, in dim light, the man that tried to kill him sat on a chair, tied and gagged. Two more sergeants came to position and saluted.

Lenzel motioned to the taller of the sergeants. "Take the gag out."

The attacker's wrists, tied with cloth, seeped blood.

"We had him tied with ropes. He struggled to get free

to the point his wrists bled," the other sergeant said.

Lenzel nodded. "Wait outside."

The guardsmen looked uncertain on their way out. Lenzel caught the man's eye. His look held determination and something else. Lenzel gently probed his surface thoughts.

Hate.

That emotion bubbled to his forethoughts, before subsiding, and then, gaining power once more. Over the next few minutes, the routine repeated five times. As the hate ebbed, pain increased, nearly suffocating the prisoner.

Lenzel had little experience controlling a man's mind. He sent good emotions, love, fairness, and kindness. It had little effect, at first. As the man's mind opened more, something dark and ominous rose to the surface, something approaching Dark's minions' degrees, but different. A memory flashed across the man's essence. A flayed child who screamed once and died in horrible pain.

Pain trapped and multiplied in the man.

Pain eating the man's soul.

Pain redirected to an evil purpose.

Pain at the loss of a daughter.

Lenzel called to the outside. "Send for the healer."

Waiting, Lenzel sent every comforting thought he could imagine. It had some effect. A voice behind him said, "Apex, how may I be of service?"

"Do you have syrup of the flower?"

"Yes, of course."

"Give him enough to keep him asleep and pain free, but no more. If his body seems to fight you, send for me at once. Watch him closely. Do what you can for his comfort. When you must sleep, have someone replace you with orders to call you if he stirs."

Outside the tent, Lenzel confronted a lieutenant. "Order a pebble on guard at all times. Keep another two guardsmen inside the tent and rotate them every two hours. Whoever is with him must stay alert. Keep your men fresh. If anyone questions your actions, tell them these are my orders and to see me if they object."

Dark-killer sauntered up and sat next to his master.

The lieutenant looked at the deathcat. "I don't think anyone is going to object, sir." A smile played across his face. "Huh, sir?"

"Yes."

"Can…can I pet him."

Lenzel smiled to himself at the hesitation in the young guardsman's voice. "Kneel down and put your hand below the level of his chin. You'll find out very soon if you can pet him."

The lieutenant followed directions and tentatively held out his hand. Lenzel sent warm feelings to Dark-killer. The huge deathcat smelled the outstretched hand and his tongue slapped across the lieutenant's startled face before the he could move. Dark-killer butted heads, knocking the even more surprised man to the ground. He soon gasped for air with a heavy deathcat's head on his chest.

Lenzel mentally called and Dark-killer followed him back toward the command tent. Behind him, he heard, "Thank you, sir!" He smiled, wondering if the young lieutenant meant it.

Inside the tent, he told the officers the orders he'd given, but little more on the subject. Sumtom proffered two sets of orders. "He's been told he's leaving for Deepwells within the hour."

Lenzel read through the commands and signed them, and then watched as Sumtom sealed the packet to the garrison commander, wondering if Tallus would break the seal and read the contents. He decided he didn't care. If Tallus disobeyed his orders, he could hang. *There's something about him besides his attitude, something wrong.*

Stopping by the mess tent, Lenzel asked for and

received two sweetstones. He offered one to Dark-killer. The deathcat sniffed it and walked away. He found Challenger waiting beside a watering trough. Dark-killer didn't care for the sweets, but he went full charge for the water, and with equal vigor, Challenger chomped down on the sweetstones. On the way back to camp, Lenzel decided he'd climb the mountain, the middle one. It called to him.

30

THE climb seemed easier the next morning. Lenzel reached the cave and went higher to the top ridge. The view caught his breath. The river flowed in a westward direction, through rushing rapids and wide meanderings. The tops of both fortresses reflected the noon sun miles away. Carrion eaters circled high over a valley to the east, while eagles soared higher, wings outstretched, floating on air currents, searching. The north road deteriorated and ended about twenty miles farther along, winding back and forth to the east and west before settling in its general northern direction and dying.

The northwest looked different. Heavy gray clouds hung low to the ground. There was no evidence of rain. Static lightning flashed within its confines, searing, eerily silent. At times, a dark miasma escaped the cloud's upper side, only to settle back into its boundaries. He gently probed the cloud's edges. He woke lying on his side, his mind dazed. From the sun, he knew he had been unconscious for a short time. His muscles ached and his head pounded in a most irritating rhythm.

He stood, mind clearing and the pains gone after a few deep breathes. He sent the cloud's image to the Highest One with a brief description of what happened. Making ready to descend, he heard, *"Is the cloud moving toward you?"*

"No."

"Let me know if it moves."

"Yes, Highest One."

Back at camp, the sun setting, he called Currat to him. Zack came, too. "Currat, do you feel a weather disturbance to the northwest?"

"I feel something. It's not really a storm, but it seems to contain a lot of power. I don't feel it getting closer."

"Monitor it two or three times an hour. Let me know if it moves."

"Is it dangerous?" Zack asked.

"I lightly sensed it and woke up on the ground. I informed the Zenith. He wants to know if it moves. I couldn't feel the Dark's influence, but it's not something I'd want hanging over me. I can't help but think it's a new weapon formed by the Dark's Source."

Rystarill approached. Lenzel motioned her closer.

"High One, Skimmer Andress requests to speak with you."

"Tell him I'll be across the river within the hour."

"Yes, High One."

"Zack, I want you to go northwest for two miles at first light. Climb the tallest tree you can find and report back what you see in and around the cloud. I would guess the cloud is another five miles farther northwest. Unless your life is in danger, don't use your Channel Stone or try to sense inside it. All I could see from the mountain was the canopy of treetops. Look for anything unusual. Currat, you communicate with him if you sense the cloud move and Zack, you get back here as fast as you can if that happens. I spotted carrion eaters to the east, nothing to the northwest. Now, I suspect I'd better see what's on Andress' mind."

Syrill passed him on the way to the river. "High One, I'll have lastmeal ready for you in about a half hour."

"Thank you, Syrill." He had not thought about food, but his stomach suggested he should have done so.

Andress waited for him near the crossing point. "Apex, Guardsman Userron is ill. He's been lethargic all day and he has said hardly two words. I normally can't get him to keep quiet."

"The healer is watching over a prisoner. Can Userron

ride?"

"I think so."

"Are any others sick?"

"No, sir."

"Did he drink from the river?"

"I asked him that first. He said no."

"It's getting dark. Send someone with him. It'll be too late to return tonight. Start back at first light. Ask Gal Fritz for accommodations at my request. Leave Userron there if the healer thinks it's best." Andress saluted, smartly. Before leaving, Lenzel searched out Userron with his senses. The man's melancholy was pliable, but centered deeply within him. His body needed rest.

Lenzel crossed the river. *I don't recall reading of Userron ever being sick. What is causing his sadness? A man filled with pain and rage, the cloud, and now an unexplained illness in a short period of time. Are any of these connected? I don't know which concerns me most, a murdering man or an unexplainable and powerful cloud.*

Reaching the table near the fire pit, Lenzel sat, troubled. Syrill brought over a steaming bowl of thick venison stew with root vegetables and spices. The freshly baked bread surprised him. He looked at the maiden with a raised eyebrow.

"Gal Sumtom sent over a few more supplies while you climbed the mountain. Rystarill found a small creek that runs above ground for only a short distance. The water is sweet," Syrill said.

She looked pleased, which surprised him more. Desert's Ire's maidens rarely showed emotions over trivial things, and making lastmeal would be inconsequential to them. *It's not insignificant to me.* He enjoyed every bite. As he finished, Currat joined him and Lenzel motioned him to a campstool.

"I've not detected any positional movement from the cloud, but there are great currents within it. I'm feeling more heaviness from it. I think that is due to me sensing it so often."

"Cut back to every hour. I don't know if it can locate you from your touching it with your mind, but I don't want to take the chance. Touch it lightly with just enough force to determine its location. See if that weakens the feelings you're getting from it." He saw Zack and waved him over.

Zack sat across from him, giving Currat a concerned look. "I'm fine," Currat said. "I feel *something* from the cloud. That's all I want to feel. I'm not getting inside it."

Zack smiled. "I wouldn't want to be in it, either."

Lenzel related his worries over the three incidences, ending with Userron's *illness,* if that was causing his distress. He wasn't sure. The whole day nagged at him.

Lenzel woke before first light and performed his ablutions before putting on fresh leathers. Syrill brought him food and water as he finished pulling on his shirt over his head. Zack arrived and ate a small amount with him and then left to get supplies for his mission.

When Currat came over, he looked tired. "That accursed cloud hasn't changed positions, but I've noticed its power ebbs and builds back to its former strength. At times, it seems docile and at other times, I don't do more than whisper by it from the power it's emanating."

Lenzel suggested rest and Currat didn't hesitate.

The first rays of sunlight shimmered off the water when an alert bugle blast sounded in the distance.

Lenzel shouted across the river, "Saddle Challenger! Sontos, with me!"

Dark-killer bounded across the rapids before him and waited beside the prancing horse. Lenzel sent a calming thought to Challenger, something he didn't feel. The trail hadn't been widened or fully packed down. He set the pace at a canter, searching the trail before them for obstructions and holes with his senses.

Gal Fritz waited on him just off the trail on the road. He saluted, looking up at the Apex and said, "The prisoner is dead and so is the healer!"

Lenzel glared down from Challenger at the officer. "How?"

"Userron killed them."

"*What?*"

* * *

LENZEL paced inside the command tent. Userron sat in restraints on a chair sturdy enough to hold his bulk and strong enough to anchor the bonds. His head, drooped to his chest, barely moved, his breathing shallow. An open flame design brand around his left nipple puckered out in its newness—raw, weeping, angry.

"We found him standing over the bodies, holding a knife dripping blood," Gal Fritz said. "His shirt was slit open and the branding looked worse than it does now. When we examined the bodies, the brand over the prisoner's chest faded as we watched until it completely vanished. We checked the others and their brands had disappeared."

"How did you get him here?" Lenzel asked.

"He didn't seem to know his name, but he followed commands. He didn't struggle when we placed him in chains. Shortly afterwards, he fell into the stupor you see now. All this must have started at first light."

"Userron was sent to the healer. Was any prognosis given last night?"

"Only that he wanted him to rest. He gave him a potion to help him sleep. It was found next to his cot. He didn't take it. I think..."

Userron let out a mighty scream, muscles tensing, veins pulsing outward, lifting the chair, bent double by its structure. His shirtsleeves ripped by straining muscles, a link in the chain whipped through the air, the rest giving way as the chair splintered. Blood dripped from his eyes, nose, and the right corner of his mouth. Free from restraints, his back arched and he gave another howling scream.

Lenzel grasped his Channel Stone, sending calming powers to Userron. They seemed to have no effect. A pebble of guardsmen had entered the tent and surrounded the man. He gave no protest, his eyes rolling back into his head. He fell forward, face first to the floor. Two of the guardsmen turned him over on his back. The brand faded from view within a few heartbeats. His body jerked, convulsing, eyes coming back, head twisting side to side in panic until he slumped back, unconscious, breathing becoming normal.

Lenzel motioned to the pebble's skimmer. "Get a stretcher and move him to a tent large enough for guards. Keep a close watch on him and let me know when he wakes or dies. I don't think he'll attack, but he's a big and strong man. Make sure your men can handle him."

Sumtom had come in and after answering the skimmer's salute, Lenzel sat at the command table, motioning the gals to join him. Concentrating on his Channel Stone he could barely sense Zack in the distance. He added all the power he held and sent, *"I'm in the encampment on the road. Come."* Then, he faced the gals. "Report on the condition of your men."

Fritz answered first: "Apex, between Sumtom's men and mine, we have three hundred and twenty-three tents set up. Most are four-men tents. We made incursions into the forest to set those up and to build the cook pits, latrines, picket lines, etcetera. The men's tents are placed three deep from the road. The whole bivouac runs approximately half a mile north of the east-west road and the same to the south on east and west sides of the road. The horses have been grazing, but that won't last long; we'll soon have to start using hay from our supplies and that will give us two more days before resupplies will be sent."

Sumtom looked around the tent before asking, "Do you know when *he'll* get here?"

A good question, Lenzel thought. He sent to the Zenith, "*Highest One, do you know when you'll arrive? We've had strange happenings here.*"

"*I should arrive by mid-day tomorrow. Is it a large dark cloud that worries you?*"

"*Yes, Highest One.*"

"*It's dissipating. I should know more by tomorrow.*"

"*Highest One, how many men are with you? Should I release the two small boulders here when you arrive?*

"*I have a boulder and support men and wagons with me. You may have the men there ready to return to their posts when I begin to arrive.*"

After the shock of the Zenith knowing of the cloud settling, Lenzel said, "Your men should look sharp by mid-day tomorrow. It's important that the road be finished by then, even if it means working through the night with torches. Send for the engineers."

Sumtom went to the tent and passed on the order. He returned, looking doubtful. "Can a road be cleared in that time?"

"We'll soon find out," Lenzel answered. "Is there something to eat and some water?" Using his Channel Stone always made him want food and water, but the craving became more insistent this time.

Fritz went to a chest, opened it, and returned with bread, cheese, and a skin of water. Lenzel ate several mouthfuls before slowing down for water. He looked up to questioning faces and chuckled. "I used my Channel Stone to contact the Zenith Lord; it always makes me hungry."

"You are able to do that," Fritz asked. "Obviously, you are. Forgive the question."

"That is one of many things you might hear or see in

the next few days you'll need *not* to discuss with anyone," Lenzel replied between more leisurely bites.

The engineers arrived as Lenzel completed his small meal. He motioned them to seats at the table. "What's to keep you from completing the road by sundown tomorrow?"

Both men sputtered.

"You have over a thousand men to use. The road doesn't always have to be wide enough for two wagons. The extra width is for guardsmen on horseback and foot. As I see it, scout the way and mark any trees that must fall and any boulders in the way that cannot be gotten around in a more benign way. Get that work started at once. The gals will give you their strongest men for sawing and axing the trees. As soon as the way is clear, other men will follow behind clearing the underbrush. I would suggest a pebble working abreast in an arrowhead formation. Immediately following them will be men to pile the dirt down. I suspect a pebble wide and three ranks deep would accomplish it. I don't expect rain, so rock won't be needed for the surface. Using men in rotation will speed things up. You have horses to pull the felled trees and stumps out of the way. I didn't see boulders, but we'll address that problem if it arises. Using these steps as a guideline, will it work?"

The taller of the two engineers looked hard into Lenzel's eyes. "Apex, we'll make it work." He looked at his cohort. "There's much to do; let's get started."

Lenzel addressed the gals. "The Zenith Lord will arrive tomorrow around midday. You and your men will return to normal duty when he arrives. The men not working on the road should get everything ready for your departure."

"What if the road is not finished?" Fritz asked.

"I want the two of you to assist the engineers in finding the most efficient ways to complete the work. Let them tell you what is needed for manpower and supplies, and you see that they get it. You know your men best. Task your resources for the greatest results." Lenzel could sense the heaviness of command falling on the gals and it reflected in their faces. *Don't worry, my friends; I'm well aware what unfamiliar duties feel like.*

When Lenzel left for the mountain camp, the area resembled a disturbed anthill. He felt the gals and engineers attacked the problems with a natural endurance coming from years of command. Perhaps a man being called *iron-producing ore,* had been well chosen.

On the way to the mountain camp, one of the engineers marked trees to take down, while other men took measurements. He left Challenger with Andress and crossed the river, noticing some of the meat eating fish had returned from up stream. Still, the rapids remained clear of the carnivorous devils and he crossed without difficulty. Looking up at the mountain where the cave should be, he noticed a golden glow emanating from the cave's ridge.

He asked the maidens if they noticed anything different on the tor. They did not. He called Zack and Currat to him and asked them the same, requesting them to use their Channel Stones. They turned back to Lenzel at the same time.

"There is something there," Zack said. "I'm not sure what it is, but I feel it pulling me to it."

Currat nodded in agreement.

Lenzel thought of climbing to the cave, but then discarded the notion to wait on the Highest One. The afternoon and night, filled with activity, kept the men alert. He found falling trees not advantageous to sleep. The trees falling didn't make much noise, but horses, chains, and men did. The morning sun brought new activity of men forming the boundaries of the road and others using heavy plates of iron to pound the ground.

He assumed another team had started from the opposite end.

He again called Zack and Currat to his side, asking the two of them to concentrate on the cave with him. The glow showed brighter to Lenzel. He settled his mind in concert with the other Channel Stones. Brilliant spears of golden light flared from the mountaintop.

Currat's mouth opened and closed before he said, "I certainly saw that!"

"What happened?" Zack asked.

"Something very interesting," Lenzel said. "It seems we can join the power of our Stones at times. I joined my mind with the effort you used to see the mountain. It seems to have worked!"

"Do you think we should climb up to the cave?" Currat asked.

"I thought of that earlier. I think it best we wait for the Highest One. He may have more knowledge concerning how to continue. I wouldn't be surprised if he wanted to make the ascent alone."

Zack looked unsure. "Do you think that would be wise?"

Lenzel smiled. "He has mastered many talents. I don't know them all."

* * *

LENZEL rose at daybreak. The last thing he remembered before sleep took him was a torch being installed every ten feet along the newly made road. Early morning light, filtering through the forest's canopy, allowed the road to stand out in the gloom.

Lenzel heard a voice he'd become familiar with in his head. *"What progress has been made?"*

"Highest One, I'm about to travel the road from the river camp to the north-south road. From what I can see, I suspect it is, or nearly is, complete and able to carry heavy wagons."

"Have any last concerns met by midday. Inform the gals to have

their men on the east-west road to return to their duty stations when they hear my fanfare. They'll need to clear the north-south road before I arrive. I travel with a full boulder and support teams. Have them stand by until my convoy is in sight. I'll speak with them briefly before they leave. Contact me if you encounter problems."

"It will be as you command, Highest One."

Lenzel felt Jarod withdraw from his mind and counted it a loss.

31

LENZEL, impressed by the condition of the road accomplished in a short time, found the gals at their firstmeal. He motioned them to stay seated and joined them at their table. A guardsman approached, asking if the Apex wanted a firstmeal. Lenzel answered in the affirmative and settled in between Sumtom and Fritz.

"Gentlemen, I'm impressed with the road progress," he said.

"The men worked most of the night," Sumtom answered. "The engineers used your suggestions and added to them a bit. Any place they found work that could be duplicated, they added men and had the same work going on in several areas. I heard one of them say they would use the techniques on future assignments."

"I think you'll have a busy morning, too. The Zenith Lord will arrive at midday. He requests you have your men repositioned on the east-west road and ready to move out when he arrives. He'll speak to you before you leave."

"Is he fully protected?" Fritz asked.

"I believe so," Lenzel answered. "He travels with a full boulder and support wagons. I'm concerned about the gray cloud phenomenon, but he is not disturbed by it at this time. Be ready when you hear his fanfare."

The rest of the firstmeal centered on the types of conversations tired men have after successfully completing a long and arduous task. Shortly, the engineers arrived and offered to show Lenzel the road in detail. He agreed.

After the tour, he was even more impressed and used

the rest of the morning inspecting troops from a distance and appraising their overall attitude. He heard more than one comment of excitement on the arrival of the Zenith Lord. The food preparers began passing out travel rations and then closing down the food wagons. The gals took charge of their units and began the repositioning activities. As the last wagons moved out onto the east-west road, the faint bugle call of the Zenith's fanfare sounded in the distance. Lenzel marveled at the timing.

The two small boulders lined the north-south road, pushing their horses completely off the road, and stood at position. The officers gathered at the intersection of the east-west road. The fanfare sounded once more, much closer. Lenzel, mounted on Challenger, sat at the intersection.

He watched the vanguard's officer stop upon reaching the first guardsmen, one on each side of the road. The van pulled together in close formation, halting the column behind them and riding forward. Lenzel returned the officer's salute. In a precise movement, they did a turn about and faced south. The gals and their officers mounted and formed on the west road. The bugler with the van sounded a call.

The guardsmen along the road mounted their horses. As the Zenith Lord approached, each guardsman saluted and rode forward at a canter, clearing the way for the full boulder behind Jarod. The Zenith Lord stopped at the intersection. Lenzel saluted from atop Challenger and rode to Jarod's right side. The men on the road north started the same procedure of saluting and riding toward their outposts. Then, the officers saluted and rode toward their units until finally, the gals gave their salute and turned to follow their men to the front of their boulders.

Highest One, would you like to go directly to the mountain? Lenzel sent out.

Yes, came the answer.

Lenzel started north as the Zenith's boulder started setting up their encampments. The road seemed to impress the Zenith Lord. When they reached the river camp, Andress had his men in formation and at position. They saluted as one and Jarod nodded to them. They dismounted and guardsmen came to take Blackwind and Challenger for grooming, water and food. Lenzel led Jarod across the rapids where Zack, Currat, and the maidens awaited them. Jarod greeted each in turn, barely able to take his eyes off the mountain peak. Finally, he said, "I can feel the power."

"Can you see the glow?" Lenzel asked.

"To me, it's rather bright."

"Those of us with Channel Stones see only a glow. When would you like to ascend?"

"I'm tired. It has been a long, quick ride. I think it best to start at first light after firstmeal. The Stones have waited this long for me; another night won't make a difference. Members of the van stopped on the other side of the river. Lenzel showed them where to cross. The guardsmen dismounted and started taking supplies across and setting up the Zenith Lord's tent. They finished in record time and crossed back to await orders.

Lenzel joined the Highest One in the tent that would double as a command post and his sleeping area. The large cushions eased Lenzel's physical stress from the last few days and he relaxed.

"Highest One, the gray cloud?"

"I heard about it from Segquo. His watchers reported Shadure creating the cloud in those areas he could not see in to. Shadure couldn't see through the mists, but explained to Wathdure that men coming under the influence of it would kill guardsmen, including me. When your men killed the men who attacked you, it caused Shadure much pain. He went in a long discussion with Wathdure about him attempting to do the same to see if he could accomplish the desired results. Wathdure controls flesh and men. He could not make the cloud appear and when Shadure created one, he was not able to control the men they found. They gave up after a while with Shadure commenting he would continue to work on solving the problem."

Zack stuck his head in and Jarod motioned him in; Currat followed him. Jarod spoke to the spies for a few moments and then, they left.

Syrill stuck her head in at the tent's entrance. "Highest One, I have fowl and venison if you're hungry."

"Thank you, Syrill; the fowl sounds good."

"I'll start at once, Highest One." She ducked back out and closed the flap.

"You're in for a treat," Lenzel said. "Ever sense she heard you would arrive, she has been going through supplies and the area finding herbs and spices.

Lenzel marveled at the feast Syrill managed to prepare. Sated and relaxed, he slept the best in a long while.

* * *

LENZEL woke in predawn greyness, dressed and made ready for the day, looking from time to time at the glow that seemed to call to him evermore. Still full from the previous night's dinner, he ate some flatbread with a thin slice of cheese while staring at the highest mountain's peak.

What lies in store? What treasures of strength and power will it provide? How will it help defeat the Dark One?

He felt a tug of his heart and sent a message to Ellrill. *"Good morning, my love. How are things there?"*

She replied at once: *"Oh, Lenzel, I'm so happy. I'm being given my own patients to help even in some of the more difficult cases. The High Healer is pleased and he still teaches me. How are you?"*

"Good. We've found what we seek and the Highest One arrived yesterday. Our discoveries will come today. I see a lamp in his tent; I

must go. Be well, my love. I miss you."

"*Oh, I miss you so much!*"

Soon, Zack, Currat, Jarod, and the maidens joined Lenzel by the fire he had built up. Syrill made a light firstmeal and hot tea seasoned with fresh mint she'd found the day before. Static excitement stirred the air like lightning flashing, unpredictable and discerning. Jarod signaled for the lieutenant of the van to cross over.

When the guardsman arrived, he gave brief orders: "Bring over the van to guard this side of the river. Send a message to guard the length of the road here and its entrance. No one is to enter. Have a lookout watch for signals signifying intruders from my scouts."

As the lieutenant saluted, Lenzel wondered at the added security. Jarod turned and must have seen the questioning look on Lenzel's face. "It's the report you gave of the smaller box," he said.

He motioned Zack and Currat to him. "Scout the areas around the mountain. If you see anyone, signal the Guard with arrows like we discussed." The two spies nodded and hurried off in opposite directions.

Lenzel pointed out various features of the mountain to Jarod and they made ready to climb. Jarod handed Lenzel a pack for his back and strapped on one, too, next to a crossbow. He wondered about the contents, but didn't question Jarod. He started out, on a slightly different path than before to take advantage of gains he'd noticed on his previous descent.

They made excellent time. At stretches, he thought his hands and feet barely touched the mountain's surface, feeling great power drawing him from above. He didn't slip once and from what he noticed, neither did the Highest One. By midday, they stood on the ledge in front of the cave. When Jarod's Stone had come even with the ledge, the light from the cave intensified tenfold to his eyes. He watched Jarod shield his eyes from the brightness he felt until his eyes must have become accustomed to the brilliance.

They entered the cave and the light, thankfully, mellowed into a soft glow with a vibration surrounding them, which, surprisingly, eased their tension. The chest lids fell back on their own, displaying gold and gems, weapons and scrolls, except for the small box sitting alone on its pedestal. Only the light from the large Stone on its top lid continued to emit near blinding light. Lenzel watched as Jarod barely noticed the chests while walking to the pulsating Stone.

Jarod pulled his shirt over his head. The effect came instantly; the light concentrated into a blinding, narrow beam focused on the Sire's Stone embedded in Jarod's chest. He floated toward the cave's high ceiling, the beam never losing contact. Slowly, the light began to fade and he began a gradual descent. The Sire's Stone, nearly covered in gold, palpitated with his heart, matching the throbbing vein in his neck, then began to lessen until it disappeared. A golden glow emitting from Jarod's body lighted the cave and Lenzel felt at peace. The Stone on the boxes' lid, a brilliant diamond, sparkled, catching the light from Jarod and the natural light in the cave from outside. Jarod turned toward Lenzel, looking as if waking from a deep trance until his eyes became clear and his body alert.

Lenzel stood awestruck as Jarod walked to the cave's ledge. In natural light, the glow dissipated to nothingness. The Highest One removed a shaft from his pack with bright blue ribbons flowing from it. He loaded the crossbow and sent the dart flying in a huge arc over the north road. From their vantage point, Lenzel saw wagons at the ready start up the road to the river. He judged a hundred guardsmen followed on horseback.

When the last of the mounts gained the river road, another arrow streaked across the sky, aimed to land where Jarod's had done. It bore red ribbons at the top and one black ribbon behind them. The calming peace on Jarod's face evaporated; his eyes focused on the remaining guardsmen from the boulder on the North road where a tress immediately rode north at a gallop. Jarod motioned Lenzel upward. They climbed to the mountain's wide crest and ran to the far side, Jarod taking his pack and crossbow.

Looking down the side of the mountain, Lenzel couldn't see anyone scaling the rock. He heard Jarod let out a sigh. They scanned the countryside; he pointed to a clearing where about fifty men gathered a half-mile away. Jarod nodded as he found the clearing. The men grouped together on foot. Jarod nudged Lenzel and nodded farther along the North road where horses stood tethered, waiting alongside one man. He grabbed his Channel Stone and concentrated on the clearing. It came in sharp focus, showing men indicating the path of the arrows to the others with the look of bandits.

Lenzel watched as Jarod took three arrows with yellow ribbons from the pack. He loaded the crossbow, his muscles bulged with the effort. Lenzel wondered at the strength of the bow, with it requiring such power to arm it. The shaft flew, arced high, landing in the center of the clearing, bringing down one man. The other two bolts flew with barely a couple of heartbeats apart. Two more men fell as the rest scattered into the forest. Jarod took another arrow with green ribbons and fired it at the horses, coming down at the man's feet.

The question showed plainly on Lenzel's face. Jarod smiled. "The red ribbon signified danger, yellow indicated fifteen men for each shaft fired, and the green meant horses. The Guard's response will be to take the location of the horses and ambush the men when they emerge from the forest. If they try to climb the mountain, we can handle them as they come up with just the stones from around here. A pebble thrown with the strength of our Stones behind it will go through a man. After one or two men fall with holes in them, I suspect they'll give up the effort. Besides, it would take an experienced climber to scale this mountain. If they circle toward Currat, he'll let loose a red bolt. I don't think we'll be surprised. Also, as you know, the Stones are able to protect themselves. Nonetheless, we need to get them to camp.

Back in the cave, Lenzel assessed the three larger chests about half the size of the chests he found in Deepwells. Without emptying them, they seemed to have much less gold and more Stones. He thought that would bode well in the fight against the Dark. He watched as Jarod put on his shirt and took the small box from its resting place where it had sat for two millennia and carefully placed it in his pack, strapping it tightly against him. Jarod turned back with a look of deep satisfaction.

The pack Lenzel had carried and not opened lay at his feet. He found coils of rope and additional shafts inside. With Jarod helping, they lashed the three chests one on top of the other. The height of them came only to Jarod's waist. They looped rope into handholds, securing the whole well past what would normally be needed.

"Before we leave," Jarod said, "let's see what our bandits are doing."

It didn't take long to reach the top ledge and go to the far side. No one could be seen moving about, but they frowned when they saw black signal smoke coming from a small clearing midway between the first larger clearing and the North road. *Of course, the Guard will see it, too,* Lenzel thought.

He heard Zack's voice in his head and the look on the Highest One's face said he'd heard it, too. *"Between three hundred fifty and four hundred men, more or less. Some keep moving around; it's hard to get an accurate count."*

Climbing down to the cave's ledge, Lenzel watched the

north road. What looked like a scree moved north. *Two hundred and seventy men may not be enough!* Next, he sensed Jarod's projection to the gal in command and the thrower leading the Scree of *danger.*

Within moments, another Scree joined the first and the remaining two hundred and sixty men converged on the river road, some on horseback while others led their horses into the forest, establishing a picket line where possible and forming into pebbles, fanning out to the north. The support team stayed with the wagons with swords drawn. The van must have sensed Jarod's warning.

Lenzel watched as they moved across the river and set up defensive positions. *That's as much as can be done. But then, I don't know the extent of the Highest One's power or what the diamond on the small box added to his abilities.*

Jarod made no effort to move the chests out of the cave. "We'll leave the chests here. The cave's protections will keep them safe." Jarod took hold of Lenzel's arm. He looked at the Highest One, guessing what to expect. They walked to the ledge's edge; Lenzel clasped his hand on the Highest One's forearm. They stepped out into nothingness, pushing away from the mountain. On their relative slow descent, they kept kicking away from the rock and stopped two feet from the ground. Jarod nodded to Lenzel; they released their hold on each other at the same time and fell to the grass. The van's lieutenant looked at them in awe.

Jarod addressed him—"Start a round of danger bugle calls. We might as well let our enemies know we're here."

The lieutenant called a guardsman forward and issued the command. The bugle sounded, crisp, clear and loud, projecting slightly northeast. Within a few heartbeats, another call sounded from the river road, one more came from the second scree, and finally, one from the first scree.

"That should at least set them on edge," Lenzel said.

Jarod smiled. "The buglers will keep us informed."

Moments later, the call of engagement sounded small over the van, followed at once by another signaling the same. Then, a new call followed by four chirps. Lenzel looked at Jarod's concerned face. The enemy numbered four hundred or thereabouts.

Jarod addressed the bugler directly. "Send a hundred to the screes." The bugler drew in a long breath and a different call blasted out over the trees, picked up by another cry Lenzel knew would send the designated men up the north road. He wished they were back on the high ledge watching the action. The thought barely left his mind when Jarod again took his forearm. Lenzel followed suit and they began to climb. Not so much climbing as racing upward, their hands and feet hardly touching the rock as they pushed skyward. Passing the cave's ledge, they landed on the mountain's top shelf and hurried to the farthest advantage point.

"That's new," Lenzel said.

Jarod's face formed a wide grin then peered northeast, his hand positioned next to his Sires' Stone. Lenzel followed his action, grasping his Channel Stone. His vision cleared. Guardsmen now held the midway clearing facing back toward the road and began walking their horses into the forest. At the road, swords flashed in the sunlight, slicing, stabbing, and countering attackers. The enemy didn't fight like bandits. Their training showed as they tried to keep a formation. The Guard stopped that from happening, engaging men, separating them from the group and cutting them down. More assailants fell than guardsmen, but not a lot more. The fighting continued— bloody, fierce, and determined. As the fighters appeared from the midway clearing, the battle took on a different bearing. The guardsmen now clearly outnumbered their enemies. More bodies fell as the guardsmen began to work in pairs, singling out a man and making short work of killing him.

The men the Guard fought didn't give up and fought to the death. From his vantage point, Lenzel saw the four hundred lying on the ground, not moving or unable to stand. Scowling, he estimated nearly three hundred guardsmen had fallen. These were not ordinary bandits, if indeed they *were* brigands. He had his doubts. Their descent to the mountain base took less time than before.

A new thought entered their minds with Currat's unique signature. *"Zack and I captured two men. We are at the midway clearing and have them tied to horses. We're going to the north road."*

Jarod considered for a moment before turning to Lenzel's side. "Have them brought to the river road but no farther. I won't leave the mountain until the chests are safely stored on wagons and adequately guarded. Interrogate them; if you can manage it, look into their minds to see if they tell the truth and any other information you can gain." He motioned the van's lieutenant to him. "You have birds for the East and West Outposts. Send a message to each for a small boulder of guardsmen to meet us back here. I want them here rapidly, but not so tired they can't fight. Make that plain."

Answering the lieutenant's salute, Jarod retired to his tent, leaving orders for any new information to be brought to him immediately.

Lenzel crossed the river and found Challenger waiting. He mounted and rode toward the north road, noticing the condition of the guardsmen and their deployment on the way. Overall, he was pleased. He found the boulder's gal in his tent. The man rose and saluted.

He answered the officer's honorific and sat near him at his table. "Zack Stand and Currat Duval have captured two of the attackers at the midway clearing and are heading for the north road. Send a couple of men to escort them. The attackers fought to the death. We need all the information we can pry out of them. I don't want them killing themselves on the way here."

The gal rushed to the tent's entrance and gave the orders. He returned to the table. "We haven't met. I'm Gal Thursman Crinner."

The two men grasped forearms and Lenzel motioned for him to sit.

"Have any of the wounded attackers made it here that can talk?"

"We have two with hamstring cuts. We stopped them from killing each other. They had swords at each other's throats ready to lunge when guardsmen pulled them apart. They've said little; their accent is strange and scarcely discernable. The majority of the rest have heavier wounds; most are near death."

"Take me to them."

Crinner led Lenzel out of the tent to a larger healer's tent. The two prisoners stood out amongst the guardsmen. Others of their kind lay on the ground; the healer doing what he could. Several men of both groups had covered faces and guardsmen took their fellows out, leaving the attackers for last.

Lenzel walked to the two men. They glared up at him. He probed them first for any sign of the Dark and found none as he expected. He or the Highest One would have noticed the Dark's influence from the start. Projecting first calm and then guilt at the men, he noted minor changes around their eyes and they relaxed, but not enough. Delving deeper, he discovered something not known before. It took a while before realizing what hampered them, an imperative planted deep in their consciousness to meet their objective or die trying. He wrestled with the command, pulling at it from different approaches. After several tries, he found a thread of memory and pulled on it with his mind. The domineering control weakened and began to dissolve. The man looked startled and his face seemed to collapse in thought. It took only a moment to achieve the same result with the other fighter.

Doing what he could, Lenzel searched the men's memories, finding military drills and weaponry at the forefront. One was married, but that memory lay buried. It became clear the men had been pressed into this action by mental duress. Other memories of sandy beaches, calm seas, and beautiful women lying in the sun, nearly naked, surprised him. The Seven Realms had sandy beaches, but women didn't dress, or in this case, not dress as the man projected.

Well, they don't surpass Ellrill's beauty, but they come close.

The healer came over and, after a signal from Lenzel, began to undress the man. His tied hands lay still. Guardsmen stood ready to subdue him if he tried to kick when the healer untied his feet. The patient seemed to only slightly notice. He did pull his head up and look when the healer pulled his boots and trousers off, but soon lay back looking resigned. The healer examined the cut hamstring and shook his head. "I can repair some of the damage, but it'll take a High Healer to put the tendons to rights."

He moved on the other man and soon said the same about him.

Lenzel continued to gently probe the man's memories until he found one of a sergeant calling him by name—Qurist Darst. It was not a name from the Seven Realms. He looked again at his ruddy complexion, not similar to that of any of the men he had ever seen. While the High Desert People had a reddish undertone to their skin, this man's had a purplish quality. The healer undid the prisoner's privatecloth displaying an even deeper purplish color on his genitals.

Catching the healer's attention, he asked him, "Have

you seen this coloration before?"

"No Apex, but I've heard of it. I suspect the man comes from the lands of the Eastern Kingdoms across the sea. There was a shipwreck some years ago during a fierce storm. The dead and much of the ship washed up on the beach. The ship was known to be from there. All the men aboard had this color. None had blue or green eyes; only black and dark brown like these here. Some had a darker brown skin, but none were black."

Nodding his understanding, Lenzel thanked the healer and waited until he moved on to the next man before asking the one lying before him, "Qurist, how long have you been here?"

Qurist started, looking bewildered. "How do you know my name?"

Lenzel could only make out the man's meaning by listening intently and conjecturing some of the words before answering. "We know who comes to our shores. Do you think you weren't discovered? We wanted to know what your objective would be. How did you come to that particular mountain?"

Looking wide eyed, the answer came in subdued words, making him even harder to comprehend. "We were given two places to go. One is your Deepwells and the other here with preference to this one. We were to locate anything unusual about the area and especially the mountains."

"Were you given specific mountains to find?"

"No, they told us there would be something different and we were to find out what made them that way. It sounded pretty strange when we got our orders."

"How are you to return?"

"A ship will come in up the coast from Stonefire in four moons."

The other man piped up, "I don't think we're supposed to tell them anything, but I don't really care.

They're holding my family and I don't think they'll live if I get back or not."

"Who would do that to your family?"

Both men sneered and said in unison, "The Dynast!"

*　*　*

LENZEL thought of the name on his way back to the mountain camp. He had sent *"Dynast."* to the Highest One and he answered almost straight away, *"Understood."*

Upon hearing the name in passing, he had never sought out its ramifications. *It seems I should have.*

He found the Highest One in his tent and was motioned in and to a chair.

"What else did you find?" Jarod asked.

"Their memory had been altered and a strong imperative put in to look for mountains here and in Deepwells. There will be a ship to take them back in four moons up the coast. Once I loosen the memory bonds, they seemed to be ordinary seamen who were pressed into this action by threats to their families. They seemed reconciled to finding them dead when they returned, no matter what they found or reported, and I think that is why they are cooperative."

"You did well. The Dynast is a problem for another time. I'll see that the ship is captured. Now, we both need rest and I understand Syrill is outdoing herself with tonight's lastmeal. I suggest we see if that is correct.

The lastmeal proved to be as promised and Lenzel fell asleep with his deathcat cuddled next to him.

32

THE deathcat stirred, waking Lenzel and putting him on edge. He looked around and found the mountain camp quiet. Guardsmen stood at strategic points while others patrolled across the river. The beginning of false dawn lightened the sky. He went to the fresh water of the rapids and performed his morning routine, washing and changing into fresh clothing. His second uniform had been cleaned and pressed while still damp, leaving proper creases when dry; he suspected by an officer's guardsman.

On the way back, he saw Syrill starting the cooking fire and a lamp on in Jarod's tent. He announced himself at the flap.

The Highest One said, "Enter."

Jarod stood by a table looking at a map, barefoot and wearing no shirt. The Sire's Stone, pulsing with the beat of his heart beneath wide bands of gold, drew his attention and, as he walked to the table, he continued to stare.

"Impressive, isn't it?"

"I apologize, Highest One. It certainly draws the eye. May I ask about the Dynast?"

"Yes. He calls himself, 'Supreme Dynast' of his possessions. His kingdom, Sis'on, was landlocked so he conquered the two kingdoms to his north and on the coast. We have two informants in one of the smaller kingdoms. They report he is ruthless and sadistic, and his expansion is expected to continue. There were eleven kingdoms, now nine. The other kings are disorganized and often fight among each other. None of them are banding together to stop any further invasions. I found it strange that he would send men here looking for mountains until I remembered Segquo telling me there are certain places Shadure cannot peer into from the Gray Plane. The Stones fog his view. I have to wonder if he's figured that out, or, he only wanted reconnaissance on the areas he can't perceive. Either way, it's certain he's in the Eastern Kingdoms and that doesn't bode well. If he's influencing the Dynast like he did Mountglen, there's more trouble ahead."

"Are we able to send spies?"

"We have none that speak their dialect. It's a strange one, as you heard. I'm reluctant to send anyone who doesn't speak the language fluently. They probably wouldn't make it back. It seems all the kings are so nervous about their neighbors, strangers don't live long. I've alerted Segquo to the danger. I don't think any of his watchers have travelled that far. It may be beyond his scope and too far away from his physical body. I'm eager to capture more men from their ship when it arrives."

"It's clear the men we have hate the *Supreme Dynast*. Do you think they can be turned to spy for us?"

"I'll give it some thought. It's a possibility. Perhaps Zack and Currat can talk to them."

"The chests?"

"We'll move them today. The extra men from the outposts will be here by midday. I also sent a bird to Stonefire ordering a boulder of guardsmen to start north. They'll relieve the outpost's men to return to their normal duty."

"Highest One, may I ask about the small box?"

"I'm not sure of its total properties. The gold it lost to the Sire's Stone seems to bind me closer to the Stone's magic. I'll have to do some research and try to find its full purpose."

Pounding sounded from the river. Jarod and Lenzel rushed to the tent's entrance and threw back the flap. A guardsman saluted.

"What is that noise?" Jarod asked.

The guardsman ran toward the sounds.

Syrill arrived with two full trenchers of eggs, venison, and toasted flatbread. The Zenith Lord and the highest-ranking Apex followed her to where she put the food on a table. They both thanked her and pulled chairs over to start their firstmeal. Several moments passed before the guardsman returned, reporting engineers had built the parts of a bridge, the space of three men abreast, to go over the rapids and were now putting it together and the wagons were due to arrive shortly.

Jarod returned his salute and dismissed the guardsman to duty.

"That solves one problem," Lenzel said.

Jarod nodded and began to eat. Lenzel followed suit.

* * *

LENZEL followed the Highest One's gaze up the mountain to the cave's ledge. It still glowed, but not as bright.

"Shall we?" Jarod asked.

Lenzel answered by starting to climb as they did before, hands and feet hardly touching the rock at breakneck speed. Their Stones seemed to attract them to the mountain. They reached the ledge in the amount of time a running man would cover the same distance on level ground, only slightly out of breath. The chests and box, still strapped together as they'd left them, sat in regal splendor, golden light streaming from them. The diamond's strength had returned.

Without words, they lifted the load and moved to the ledge's edge. Jarod looked at Lenzel and nodded. They stepped off the outcrop and descended slower than before, holding tightly to the rope handles and nudging outward from the rock face as they came close. The Van's personnel watched; dumbfounded expressions and open mouths prevailed. When they reached the ground, they lightly set the load down.

Jarod looked at the van's lieutenant who managed to close his mouth after gaping at him for the longest time.

"I want a guard placed around these chests where they cannot be seen from the other side of the river. Touching them will be considered high treason. The lieutenant saluted, his mouth open once more.

Lenzel raised an eyebrow.

"I'm a little paranoid about the Stones and gold, more so the Stones," Jarod said.

Zack and Currat approached the river at a gallop, dismounted, and crossed the bridge at a run, skidding to a stop before Jarod and Lenzel.

"Bandits! A lot of them two miles down the north-south road."

"Perhaps paranoid is best," Lenzel concurred.

Jarod seemed he couldn't help but smile. "Did they show any signs of moving northward?" he asked.

"No sir," Zack responded. "They have clearings several yards off the road."

"Do you know their numbers?" Lenzel questioned.

Currat shook his head. "The way they scattered about, we couldn't get an accurate count, but there's several hundred, at least. If I had to guess, I'd say five hundred. They had cold camps. We saw some eating cold cheese and bread. Zack and I climbed trees and couldn't see smoke or anything else to give them away."

"Their horses," Zack offered, "are picketed farther back. If a mounted patrol heard them, they might think the sound came from their own column. There was little talk; most men lazed about, obviously waiting for an occurrence."

Lenzel shook his head. "How could they have known about us? I dare say we're the most guarded secret in the Seven Realms."

"If more than one person knows, it's not a secret any longer," Jarod said. "You're right, though. Not many people know what we're doing here besides the participants."

"Then how?" Lenzel asked.

Jarod started and then frowned. "Wathdure!"

Deep concentration showed on Jarod's face and Lenzel assumed he had contacted Segquo.

After several moments, Jarod said, "Segquo states Wathdure has been away from the Gray Plane several times in the past weeks. He certainly has the power to implant directives in men's minds. He must know we can detect the Dark in a man or woman. This way, there would be nothing to give them away except by discovery.

"Zack, you and Currat circle around them and contact the boulder coming north. Have the guardsmen get behind them and squeeze them onto the road. Our men will be ready for them, whatever is left when they reach us."

The two spies nodded, again crossing the river, Zack mounting Spellbinder and Currat mounting Snowflake. The two large warhorses moved quietly into the woods. Within a few moments, they couldn't be seen.

Jarod, Lenzel, and Gal Grinner sat mounted in front of the van.

"The wagons must be protected and that's the highest priority," Jarod said. "Position half your men in wedge formation toward the south and the other half in block formation ahead of the Van. Post scouts on the north and east-west road to detect other *visitors*. Pass the word for quiet. The men can dismount and stand beside their horses, but be ready to mount at an instant's notice. Altogether we should outnumber them nearly four to one once the boulder arrives. Still, we're dealing with the Dark's influence; be ready for anything."

An hour passed before shouts floated on the wind.

Men entered the road seeing the wedge to the north and half a boulder to the south. A few dropped their swords and fell to the ground, covering their heads. Most of the bandits raised swords and screamed, running toward the closest guardsmen.

Lenzel started to move south and Jarod stopped him with a raised hand. "The men have their orders. I need you here."

From Lenzel's viewpoint, the attackers fell in numbers, being grossly overmatched in fighting skills and ability. Most fought until death overtook them. It was a slaughter, the ground soaked in blood, the deceased with determined masks covering their features. Only a few of the Guard sustained injuries and none fell to the madness of the enemy.

A lieutenant approached the van and saluted. "I believe they're all dead. They fought like little children. They came at us with mad stares and screaming, but it was like they'd never been trained for any kind of fighting. The carnage became sickening after a while."

The gal thanked him for his report and returned him to his men to start burial details. The healer rode south to tend to the injured. Jarod started and wheeled Blackwind around before it reared high in the air.

"*Lenzel!*" he screamed.

PART III

33

LENZEL fought to control Challenger, when something slammed into his back on his right side. He looked right; his eyes widened at the sight of an arrow protruding from his chest. *Strange, it doesn't hurt.* He started sliding off Challenger's back to the ground. Landing on his back, he pushed the arrow farther through his chest. Jarod kneeled beside him in a few heartbeats. The gal yelled for the healer who returned at a gallop.

Jarod took Lenzel's hand and placed it on his Channel Stone. He examined the wound, wincing at the amount of blood. The healer knelt on the other side of Lenzel's still body. "We must pull the shaft through. The shaft is probably holding back some of the blood, but that won't last long and riding in a wagon would not be wise. Be ready to place these bandages against the wound with pressure."

The wood and feathers came through Lenzel's chest. He screamed. Shock settled over him once more. The healer saw the amount of blood issuing from the wound and shook his head. Jarod kept pressure on the hole. He jerked when he heard the anguish in his mind. He recognized Ellrill's sending.

"My love, what's wrong? Are you hurt?"

"Ellrill, Lenzel has taken an arrow through his chest," Jarod answered. Ellrill gasped. Jarod continued, *"Can you and High Healer Sternwood work through me to stop the bleeding?"*

"He's here. I'll ask." A precious moment lapsed. *"We might be able to use your strength. Put your hand on Lenzel's Channel Stone and touch your Sire's Stone."*

Jarod did as requested. *"Yes, that's good,"* Ellrill sent. *"I can see the wound. A major vessel is open. Let me see if I can affect it.*"

More moments went by during which Lenzel's pulsing of blood slowed from the wound. Then, *"Yes!"* The sending nearly caused Jarod to jerk back. Ellrill continued, *"I'm closing the vessel. The High Healer is helping to guide me. Highest One, you're giving me so much strength. I couldn't do it without you. There, almost done."*

High Healer Sternwood's signature sending came through. *"My Zenith, his wound is closed, but he's lost much blood. He still might not survive. Keep him warm with his head slightly elevated. Get as much venison or other meat broth down him as you can. Fowl will benefit him, too. We, mostly Ellrill, blocked his pain. He should rest well, but each time he stirs, try to get fluids in him. No wine or ale; water is best. Try rigging a sling with rope and a wood bottom. Pad the wood and lay him on it. Mount the sling on a wagon where it will swing freely above the bottom and without touching the sides if the road swings him that far. That should keep him from being jarred by the road. Cover him with his furs and make sure he stays warm. Dress the wound with clean bandages every day. Have someone with him at all times and contact me if he starts to bleed. That's all we can do at this time. The water and broth are very important."*

"Thank you, Highest One." Ellrill's trembling came through with her thought.

It took most of the remaining day to bury the dead. The men from the east-west outposts returned to their assignments and the boulder formed up. Jarod spoke with Gal Grinner. "It's too late to start," he said. "We'll move north, above the east-west road. There are latrines, banked fireplaces and picket lines established. We'll start at first light. Have your firstmeals done by then."

Jarod had the engineers working on the sling for Lenzel. When gently laid on the padded wood, he barely stirred. A guardsman softly placed Lenzel's furs over him and put the rest of his belongings in the wagon out of the way. He swayed slightly as the wagon moved up the road. His sling was set down into the wagon with enough clearance to not strike the wagon's sides from swinging side to side as the High Healer wanted.

At Jarod's pleased smile, the guardsman grinned. "I'll watch over him, my Zenith."

* * *

LENZEL'S dream showed Ellwill nervously sitting in front of the three High Healers of the Seven Realms. Their questioning on many healing subjects had drained her. Now, they spoke in whispers; Ellrill caught a few words here and there. Finally, High Healer Sternwood spoke as the others sat quietly beside him.

"Ellrill, of the Clan of the Cat, you will be known throughout the Seven Realms as High Healer Ellrill. Birds will fly with the news to all the High Lord's keeps and wherever the Guard gathers. Likewise, your portrait will be drawn and sent by courier. You are welcomed and needed in our numbers. Do you accept the responsibilities of High Healer?"

Ellrill stood. Her breath shortened, she uttered, "Yes."

* * *

SLEEPING fitfully, Jarod woke several times during the night and walked to Lenzel's wagon. The guardsmen, awake, spooned sips of broth between Lenzel's lips. It took a while, but finally, the liquid went down.

"He's not taken much, but I try when he partially wakes. He hasn't come fully awake all night," the guardsman said.

"Did you know the Apex?" Jarod asked.

"Yes. Before he became an Apex, he helped me a lot in sparring matches when we trained with the sword and Silver Stars. I could never master the Stars, only bandaged a lot of cuts. He was good to me. I'll do whatever I can to help him now. I heard the gal say he's very important in the fight against the Dark. If I hear or see anything at all out of the ordinary, I'll call out."

Jarod placed his hand over Lenzel's Channel Stone and willed any positive thing he could think of into his senior Apex. Lenzel's eyes fluttered open for a few heartbeats before closing—his heartbeat regular, his breathing deeper, and the anxious look smoother.

I'll have to do that more often.

The guardsman looked at his Zenith Lord with a bit of awe showing in his expression.

* * *

JAROD woke at the sound of movement in the camp. Washed and dressed in record time, he went to Lenzel and repeated his actions from his last visit with the same results. The guardsman stated he took more broth afterwards, and indeed, he began spooning sips of the liquid into Lenzel's mouth when Jarod had finished. He felt pleased and returned to his tent for firstmeal as predawn grey settled over the area.

Syrill served him an excellent firstmeal of bread, fowl basted in herbs and spices, root vegetables, and ale. "I think it's much better than the cooks' wagon fare," she said.

Jarod chuckled around a mouthful of bread and nodded.

Sounds increased as guardsmen made ready to depart, horses fed and watered, the cook wagons dishing out the morning's offering, tents being stored, and then, horse sounds of tact being settled in place. Jarod relinquished his tent as guardsmen from the van packed his belongings and took down the tent. He went straight to the wagon holding the cave's treasure. Two pebbles stood, facing outward around the wagon with weapons at the ready. Their two-hour posting was coming to an end and their relief showed as they filed in to change the guard, which took place with precision.

I wonder if they are that good when their Zenith Lord is not standing by.

Still, he was impressed and returned salutes with a smile and nod. The small box of Stones stored in a pack and strapped to his back felt reassuring.

As the Guard formed up for marching, Jarod received a sending from Segquo. *"Highest One, can you join me on the Grey Plane? It's important?"*

Jarod motioned for the lieutenant of the Van. When he arrived at his side, he said, "Have the van guard me. Tell the gal we'll catch up." From the trees, three deathcats surrounded him as he sat cross-legged on the ground. Jarod concentrated.

His gossamer appearance materialized beside the Desert People's leader inside his shield.

"Highest One, we cannot sense Shadure on the Grey Plane," Seqguo said. "Wathdure is alone and seems to influence men. They stop what they are doing and move toward the areas he cannot see from the Plane."

That explains a lot, Jarod thought. He watched Wathdure from a hundred feet away. "Segquo, position us behind him." In a heartbeat, the shield's occupants looked at Wathdure's back. "Drop the shield. If you sense Shadure, we must leave the Plane at once." Segquo nodded.

Jarod felt the shield drop. He poured ever increasing killing power into Wathdure. The creature screamed. His façade of epitome male beauty began to drip away, exposing the hideous creature in its true form, his face distorted and deformed in inhuman manifestation. Its uneven eyes went wide, bulbous pulsating sores oozed vile secretions from its cheeks, and mismatched limbs jutted from its malformed body; the monster screamed again as Jarod pushed more power into it. He wanted desperately to kill the beast. It didn't happen.

The shield went back up. Segquo said one word:

"Shadure!"

And they disappeared from the Gray Plane.

* * *

SHADURE raced to the side of his second in command, who still screamed in agony. Shadure searched the Grey Plane around them. Becoming satisfied, he focused on his creature before him, forcing black lightning bolts into its body. Slowly, very slowly, the screams faded into moans of pain.

The creature began to rebuild its body. The hideousness slid away under its glamour of male exquisiteness.

Wathdure rose, stretching his limbs with a smile centering on Shadure. He bowed low to his master. Rising, he said, "Thank you for saving me. As always, I'm your true servant."

"What happened?" Shadure asked.

"I worked on creating more men to go into the areas we cannot see, planting the imperative to kill the highest ranking guardsmen they found. Pain erupted throughout my body in every pore. I lost control of everything. I could feel no other presence here to cause my destruction and if you hadn't arrived, I believe I would be no more. I fear what I'll find in Ozlid and I must go there to assess the damage."

"Go now!"

Wathdure disappeared.

Shadure turned in a circle, sending out his formidable senses for anything existing on the Grey Plane that shouldn't be there. He found nothing and cursed.

Could Wathdure's work cause his near obliteration? We must discover what attacked him. Perhaps so much work on the spirit Grey Plane eroded his capabilities. This is my domain and if something is affecting it, I need to destroy whatever it is. I'll stop his physical work here. I loathe not being to go below except in spirit form. He is my Physical Master and I need him.

* * *

JAROD pushed beneficial power into Lenzel's body at regular intervals throughout the day from inside the wagon while holding him steady over the rutted road. His efforts seemed to comfort the patient, for that was what he considered him—no longer an Apex, but a true friend. One day out of Stonefire, Lenzel gained full consciousness. He even managed to feed himself broth and drink water from a small cup. Jarod watched while he fell asleep soon afterwards. He looked forward to the comfort of the Spires, but more so, the research on the contents of the small box in the secret library deep in the building's foundation.

At midday the next afternoon, he heard his fanfare blown from the top of the Spires carried on cool breezes. The sun gleamed bright and warm. When he removed the furs from Lenzel, the man smiled for the first time, but only mumbled, "Thank you," before closing his eyes and settling back into his pillows on his right side, his breath and pulse regular and strong.

I hope my efforts helped.

The van had formed in front of the boulder, its usual place with the Zenith's banners stirring in the wind. His fanfare sounded once more as he entered the Spire's outer gates. Seven days on the road, slowed by an easier pace for Lenzel's comfort, had worried him. He yearned for the reports from across the Seven Realms almost as much as the research he craved.

The inner gates opened. He wasn't surprised to find High Healer Sternwood and the now High Healer Ellrill waiting. The healers took charge of Lenzel's wagon and led the horse to the side, toward the healing facility inside the Spires.

Ellrill looked surprised, and then, turning back, she mouthed, "Thank you," to Jarod.

Emerging from the lift onto the twelfth floor, Jarod's

face showed his own surprise at seeing the Pinnacle, his second in command of the Seven Realms, High Lord Geoffrey Lockley was waiting for him. They hugged warmly before Jarod asked, "Trouble?"

Geoffrey nearly snarled his answer: "Yes."

"I need to bathe, eat, and clear my head. Meet me in the small study with whomever you deem necessary in an hour."

The Pinnacle nodded and moved away, motioning for a guardsman to follow him. Rolo left at a fast pace to make ready all the Zenith Lord would need. Jarod moved to his exercise room and started the water flow from the rainmaker to allow the colder water to escape the bottom of the rain tank on the roof. He stripped nude and stepped into the warmer water, lathering the soap from head to toe, completely and quickly over his body. His knife scraped across his face, leaving smoothness behind.

Rinsing clean, he toweled dry with soft cotton strips of cloth before cleaning his teeth and putting on a fresh privatecloth and uniform. Feeling rejuvenated, he rushed to his small study to enjoy his midmeal Rolo would have ready for him. Pouring a goblet of wine, Rolo quickly finished and departed to await his orders.

He had finished eating and Rolo had cleared the table when he sensed Geoffrey's presence. He swung the door open with his mind and motioned the Pinnacle to a plush chair. Feeling another familiar mind, he left the door open. Gaz closed it before joining the other two leaders at the table.

The Pinnacle nodded to Gaz for him to start. "My Zenith, I have reports from across the Seven Realms of bands of bandits forming, but doing little. They seem to be waiting for some occurrence to happen. I've mapped the group's positions. Many don't make sense. They are in areas of mountains with nothing around them but trees."

Jarod's heart skipped a beat. He pulled the cord next

to his chair and Rolo stuck his head around the door. "Send for Zack and Currat."

"At once, my Zenith."

Jarod went on to explain the Grey Plane, not allowing Shadure or Wathdure to see where caches of Stones resided or where persons with major Stones dwelled or traveled. Discovering the bandits may lead us to the Stones' caves in other realms. Gaz, have you had reports of bandits in Deepwells or Stonefire?"

"Stonefire, yes. Deepwells, no"

"Well," Jarod said, "we wiped out the ones in Stonefire. They fought poorly to the last man, all four hundred of them. I believe they operated under the influence of Wathdure's imperatives. We had no casualties and only three injuries, none of them life threatening with the exception of Lenzel. An archer hidden high in a tree shot him in the back. Ellrill has reached High Healer status. She and Sternwood are working on him."

"If this *is* the case, the positioning of the bandits may lead us to the Stones in the remaining realms. It would be ironic if Wathdure led us to the means of his destruction."

Jarod again opened the door to allow Zack and Currat to enter.

The spies nodded to him, the Pinnacle, and then to Gaz. Jarod motioned them to plush chairs, explaining the earlier discourse. "This could be what we need to speed up our discoveries of Stones. I'll send the Guard out to find the bandits and take or kill them, reporting the location. With Lenzel's injury, the two of you will find the mountains near the bandits and see if a cave is there. When you find one, contact me with your Channel Stones."

* * *

JAROD used the power of the Sire's Stone to open the

secret locks on the door leading to his secret library deep below the ground floor of the Spires while his four guards in the small anteroom faced away. He entered and lit the torch beside the door, disabling the traps, as he walked the long hall, hardly aware of his actions. Reaching the door, it, too, opened with his mind's power. Torches sprang to life around the room.

He took the small box from its canvas container strapped to his back. The large diamond on top of the lid sparkled with the same brilliance as the first time he'd seen it. Opening the container, he looked down on the ancient scroll at its bottom. Carefully lifting the vellum, he unrolled it, placing small weights at its corners. He remembered seeing the fiery characters blazing across the animal skin in a similar prewar scroll. Not having a reason to translate the writing, he had put the scroll away. The daunting task of finding it and the more pressing work of locating something to provide a translation, nagged at his consciousness. He felt lost.

Above, birds flew in five different directions to Guard outposts closest to the bandits' locations Segquo had provided.

* * *

LENZEL rode Challenger to the wide expanse where the first battle with Wathdure's necromantic army had taken place. He wanted to satisfy his curiosity about the stories he'd heard and figured it also made a good place to run through. He'd finished a ten-mile run two days before and hardly broke a sweat.

Looking at the edge of the plateau, he saw where the ramp had touched down, allowing the army to materialize from the Grey Plane and march on the Highest One's forces. The trench where oil had flamed against the necromantic dead stood out in stark contrast to the new grass covering the huge area.

I wonder what it must have looked like to see over a hundred deathcats emerge from the trees.

He dismounted to start his run when, as if on cue, Dark-killer sprinted to him from the trees, butting its head on his chest, knocking him down and lastly, licking his face. Lenzel laughed with pleasure and managed to get up between more head butting and licking. The great feline stayed with him as he resumed his run. He wore his High Desert leathers and soft moccasins, a short sword, and his ever-present Silver Stars.

This is great for running! I wonder if I can do more miles today. It doesn't seem that long ago that I ran with the clan all day. I know I wouldn't have recovered so quickly without the Highest One's power surging through me, which means I have the Light's Source to thank, also.

It's been wonderful to have my breathtaking Ellrill beside me in bed and not just feeling her through our Channel Stones. I'd nearly forgotten how spectacular her kisses are, tender and sweet, passionate and demanding, covering my body. With her kindness and her true love for me, I can't possibly imagine loving someone more.

He reached the ten-mile mark and his pace hadn't suffered. Turning, he headed back toward Challenger, which he had left standing close to the indentation of Wathdure's ramp. The deathcat loped beside him, bulging but sleek muscles moving in silky patterns beneath his fur.

Later, judging himself to be at the nine-mile mark, nineteen miles in all, he saw Challenger race toward him. The deathcat stopped, reared up on its hind legs, resembling the patch on Lenzel's uniform, and roared. Within a few heartbeats, another male deathcat came from the trees and padded up to the other side of him. Now escorted by two deathcats, one on each side, he wondered what had spooked them. Challenger still galloped to him, his long mane flowing upward, fanning out with his stride, his tail flowing even with the ground, the heavier hairs dipping and rising as he moved.

He continued running, stopping when horse and man met. Challenger reared, facing the way he came, hooves pawing the air. Both deathcats stopped and thundered the call of war once more. Looking at the end of the grassy plane, he spotted black smoke swirling upward in a vortex, menacing and wild; its stench reaching him a mile away. His breath caught, nearly choking him.

He touched his Channel Stone to sharpen his vision. The smoke split apart into five man-structured beings—all black, no longer smoke. Their faces radiated hate. They seemed to start taking notice of where they stood, looking around until they focused on Lenzel.

They started to run, awkward at first, and nearly falling several times, but then, with a steadier gait, they closed the gap to him.

He sent to the Highest One, his thoughts urgent— *"Highest One, five beings have formed on the plateau. Their stench is nearly overpowering. Challenger and two deathcats are with me and they are in fighting stances. The monsters are coming at me!"*

Jarod sent an instant reply, *"I'll order the Guard out. Fight as best you can until they arrive."*

Lenzel drew his short sword and readied three Silver Stars. The beasts came to a hundred yards away and stopped, sniffing the air, sounding a guttural growl. The felines roared anew. Challenger reared, his sharp hooves again striking through the air. The monsters settled on him and they ran.

Lenzel threw a Silver Star channeled through his Stone, hitting a creature in the throat. It stopped, grabbing at the weapon, cutting its three finger-like appendages and forcing a muffled croak, the only sound coming from it. Within three heartbeats of the first Silver Star, another lodged beside the first, cutting substances. Its head fell to one side by something resembling a tendon. Lenzel thought it a rope at first. It tried to continue forward but, disoriented, it stumbled, and finally dropped to the ground, no longer moving.

The same didn't prove true of the other four monsters. They slowed a little after seeing one of its numbers fall. They tried to encircle Lenzel and the animals. The deathcats attacked two of the creatures, tearing out throats, biting until the head rolled away. The remaining two closed on him, stopping a few feet away, merging into one gigantic being eleven feet tall. His Silver Stars cut less than an inch into the thick covering, which roughly approximated skin.

The huge beast lunged for him. He stooped under it, cutting its leg as he passed. Stopping, it looking at the cut from which black liquescent substance oozed onto the ground. The smell alone nearly brought him to his knees. Dark-killer jumped, landing on what would have been a shoulder on a man; its razor sharp claws raking down its back, sinking deep into the bulk, spilling more obnoxious slime. But, the beast shook free and took a wild swing with its appendage catching the feline at the shoulder as the other male deathcat copied the first, cutting deeper into the trenches the first attack made. This time, the creature howled, raging up in blind fury.

Lenzel saw his chance and lunged its midsection, stabbing his sword deep inside it. Whirling around, it struck him on the hip, sending him rolling several yards away. He stopped on his back, his vision blurred, pain reverberating through his senses. He finally swallowed air, partially clearing his head. Looking up, he found it looming over him, its leg raised to slam down at his crotch.

Two deathcats knocked it on its side, landing face up. Challenger's hooves crashed on its head. The black substance, resembling a man, groaned and fought to stand. Lenzel drove his sword downward into its right eye. Using all his strength, he jerked the blade free and brought it down into the left eye.

It struggled, limbs waving, half snarls forcing through its head, until it collapsed completely. Again, it took all of Lenzel's muscle to pull the sword free.

When the creature didn't move for a few heartbeats, he ran to the deathcat, which limped with its injuries where the monster attacked. Stopping the cat and remembering how the Highest One had sent healing forces into him, he held his Channel Stone and gently pressed against Dark-killer's shoulder. The feline started but then relaxed as Lenzel continued to lightly massage the tissue. After ten minutes, he got a generous tongue licking across his face. The deathcat stretched, its limbs extending forward and back, pushing its size to one and a half times its length. It still favored its right side a little, but soon, as it went back toward the trees, it started to walk normally.

The other deathcat brushed its full length against Lenzel's side and followed the first into the woods. Mounting Challenger, he rode toward the Spires, wondering at the extent of his strength.

The Guard met him half way. Ellrill waited at the Spires.

* * *

IN the eastern kingdoms, Shadure silently stirred above the Dynast's castle, pain ripping through his body in ever increasing waves. He cursed, and then settled, vowing to destroy the Seven Realms and all those therein.

GLOSSARY OF TERMS

MILITARY

Pebble: Ten men led by a Skimmer.

Rock: Thirty men led by a Rocker, first level officer.

Tress: Ninety men led by a Lieutenant.

Scree: Two hundred and seventy men led by a Thrower.

Small Boulder: Six hundred men led by a Gal (iron bearing rock).

Boulder: Eight hundred men plus forty support personnel led by a Gal.

Tor: Twenty-five hundred men plus fifty support personnel led by a Looker.

Mount: Fifty-one hundred men plus one hundred Support led by an Apex.

MAGIC

Stones: Stones of power created by Light's Source and Dark's Source.

Graystones: Minor stone helps healers, allows a priest to send messages by controlling birds, enhances warrior skills and aids in farseeing.

Channel Stones: More powerful and allows kinetic and telepathic abilities.

Major Stones: Physically joins with the owner, provides great powers.

Dark Stone: Evil stone of great power created by Dark's Source.

Grey Plane: A plane of existence where the minions of the Dark One can reside and where The High Desert People can visit.

ACKNOWLEDGEMENTS

I once wondered why an author acknowledged so many people. Now, I know! I'll start with my writer's group founded by Sam Barone who brought a talented group together, although to my dismay, the group is disbanded: Sharon Anderson, Deborah J. Ledford and Thelma Rea. Deborah, an award-winning suspense thriller author, has gone on to be a good influence and excellent in her many talents: formatting my novels for one. These folks gave of their talent, friendship and time. Besides that, they are nice.

And then there are the editors. One thinks they have written a masterpiece until an editor gets their head wrapped around a manuscript. Nonetheless, they found the writing, character and plot flaws I never thought of while writing my first novel. Even with college training, this craft has a huge learning curve. I had a fine editor on this novel: Natalie Owens.

Beta-readers are important and Nichole Galbreath fills that role with intelligence and bravery.

Fellow authors have given support, time and friendship. Chief among these is L. E. Modesitt, Jr. He has become a friend and good advisor of authorship over the years. Paul Genesse has been supportive and become another friend.

Other friends in the industry have always been helpful and thoughtful in their counsel: Krista Wallace is one of these. For several years I've attended the World Fantasy Conventions held in a different city each year. Nearly all of the authors, editors and other industry professionals are approachable and helpful.

I have been fortunate to know and learn from all these fine people. I wish them all the best in life and careers. Of course, the minute this manuscript goes to press, so to say, I'll remember someone who should have been included!

AUTHOR BIOGRAPHY

Mr. Cox grew up in Atlanta, Georgia before joining the United States Air Force, and served in Texas, France and Germany. He worked with large mainframe computers, and became a real estate broker before he obtained a nursing degree and practiced as a Registered Nurse. He then began to write and stated he found it more satisfying than his previous endeavors. He lives in Phoenix, Arizona with a large Great Dane that thinks he's a lap dog!

Also From The Zenith Series
by DAMEON COX

Now Available in Print and for Kindle:

THE ZENITH'S SPY

ZACK Stand, the Zenith Lord's spy has faced murderers, bandits, torture, the intrigues of the High Lords and worse. Now, an ancient evil the first Zenith Lord defeated two millennia ago grows once more. Reports of a malevolent power emanating from a subcontinent far from the Seven Realms causes concern. Zack is sent to discover the truth. What he finds is unimaginable horror.

THE ZENITH LORD

JAROD Greatstone, the Zenith Lord of the Seven Realms, must face the Dark's Source in battle as the minions of the Dark gain power. Their existence confirmed by the Zenith's Spy as the same evil the first Zenith Lord defeated two millennia ago.

Through the use of the Major Stones, Jarod starts to build his army: Apex Kyle Byrne, Captain of the Guard; The Holy One; Segquo, Leader of the High Desert People; The Protector, The Lords and Angels of Death and Deathcats to name a few. Jarod explores the Gray Plane while dealing with murder, treason and personal loss. Be ready for a great adventure in *The Zenith Lord!*

FORTHCOMING in 2015

THE SPIES QUANDARIES

ZACK Stand, Currat Duval and Ursel, the Zenith's Spies return to Hamptor to form a resistance to Ozlid's domination of Hamptor and Arestead. Reuniting with old friends, they learn of Men-in-Black from Ozlid, directed by Wathdure, creating havoc, robbery and murder throughout Hamptor. Hamptorians, bribed or coerced into helping these new threats, work unnoticed and must be found along with new ways to block Wathdure's efforts. Ursel, a Hamptorian, trained in the Seven Realms, sets up the opposition to the Men-in-Black with Zack and Currat's assistance.

URSEL uses his new skills with a natural, growing maturity to coalesce the men and their talents into an effective counteraction against evil.